MW01233248

THE AWAKENING
OF
LA MUSE

THE AWAKENING OF
OF
LA MUSE

A Novel

S. R. Strickland

© 2018 S. R. Strickland
All rights reserved.

ISBN: 1977664075
ISBN 13: 9781977664075
Library of Congress Control Number: 2018900895
CreateSpace Independent Publishing Platform
North Charleston, South Carolina

Thanks, Mom
Thanks, Dad

AN UNLAWFUL EDUCATION

Der Brunnen Plantation
Southern Virginia, March 1844

The chimes of the old grandfather clock struck six. Low, rhythmic tones resonated throughout the house. Muse was in the woodshed, riffling through piles of firewood that looked like shadows in the predawn light. She smiled when she heard the tones; it meant she was on schedule. But she also liked to think it chimed in new celebration for every year she had lived on the earth. She finished filling her basket with logs, then scurried to the rear veranda, where she put the basket on a tea table. Knowing no one was allowed to go barefoot in the big house, she slipped into her shoes. She laced them up as taught but fumbled with the limp strings. Awkward attempts to orchestrate the loops and folds forced her to tie them several times before they looked presentable. Once satisfied, she picked up her load and opened the back door. She hurried through the kitchen, down the hallway, and up the stairs. Her thin, wiry arms struggled to balance the basket of firewood, and she prayed none slipped to the floor.

She knocked lightly on Mistress Cassandra's door. Her mistress, only one year older than she, would still be asleep, so she did not wait for permission to enter. She tiptoed into the dark room to the fireplace and what was left of the dying flames. She took a poker and rekindled the embers before piling on the fresh wood.

"Muse, is that you?"

"Yes, Miss Cassandra."

"What time is it?"

"Six o'clock."

"I don't feel well. My face, is it swollen?"

Muse rushed to the window and pulled back the heavy brocade curtains. A hint of daylight poured in. Cassandra sat up, rubbing her face. Strands of dark, long locks escaped from the knots of rag strips used to twist her hair into vibrant curls, and her face was red and inflamed.

Muse gasped.

"What's wrong, Muse?"

"Oh, Miss Cassandra . . . yo' face."

"Run and get Mama. Hurry!"

⟞⟝⟞⟝

Panic-stricken at the sight of her daughter's face, Mrs. Hallisburg yelled out for Muse to go find Perche, the plantation's wood-carver.

"Tell him to take the carriage and fetch Dr. Jamison. Be quick about it!"

"Yes, ma'am."

Muse ran.

By the time Dr. Jamison arrived, the hives on Cassandra's face had transformed into rouge spots like tiny rose petals.

"Oh! Dr. Jamison, what's wrong with my baby?"

Dr. Jamison told the slave Mary, Muse's mother, to close the curtains, let in no sunlight. He cautioned everyone to leave the room while he examined Cassandra.

Mrs. Hallisburg paced the corridor with Mary by her side.

"Oh my God . . . my beautiful baby!"

"Mrs. Hallisburg, don't worry; everythang's gon' be all right," Mary said. "God ain't gon' let nothing happen to little Miss Cassandra."

At that same moment, Jonathan, Cassandra's older brother, ran up the stairs; he, too, complained.

"Mama, Mama!"

"Shh, chile," Mary said.

"Mama . . . Mary . . . what's wrong with me? My face itches."

Mrs. Hallisburg took one look at her son's face and screamed again. The doctor ran out of Cassandra's room.

"What is it, Mrs. Hallisburg?"

"My son!"

The doctor knelt before Jonathan, examined his face, and told Mary to take him to his room at once.

By late afternoon, Mrs. Hallisburg, Mary, and Muse sat in the hallway, waiting for Dr. Jamison to tell them something. Then Muse started to squirm and perspire.

"Be still, Muse," her mother admonished.

Muse trembled, rubbing her eyes and her face.

"Stop it!" Mrs. Hallisburg warned. "Stop it right now!"

"I can't, ma'am."

Mary looked at her daughter.

"Oh my God!"

Again, Dr. Jamison ran into the passageway.

"Now what?"

"Doctor, Doctor . . ." Mary cried.

Dr. Jamison looked at Muse.

"She's got it too. Well, there's nothing I can do for the little *negra* . . . just get her out of the house and quarantined somewhere. The rash is contagious."

"What is it, Doctor?" Mrs. Hallisburg demanded.

"I don't know. Make sure your children stay in their rooms, and keep them out of the schoolhouse. Don't let the little *negra* near the other slaves, Mrs. Hallisburg, or you will have an epidemic on your hands. You understand me?"

"Yes."

The doctor turned to Mary.

"You understand me?"

"Yes, suh, Dr. Jamison."

They removed Muse from the big house to a shed attached to the old storage room. Most doctors in the state refused to tend to the health concerns of the slave population, a common practice. And some who serviced the slave communities did so in a crude and covert manner. Although Dr. Jamison refused to treat Muse, he allowed Mary to aid him in nursing Jonathan and Cassandra. She followed his every instruction and directive as applied to the Hallisburg children. In the evening when she returned to her own daughter, she repeated the treatments using the medicine Dr. Jamison had spared for her.

Once the rash swelled into tiny droplets, and the boils burst and crusted over Muse's face, Mary took matters into her own hands. She extracted the oil from an aloe plant and mixed it with dried chamomile and comfrey leaves. With the mixture, she concocted a salve. Besides the remedies offered by Dr. Jamison, she lubricated Muse's face every morning and every night. She presented the homemade ointment to Mrs. Hallisburg, but she refused it.

"Dr. Jamison is an excellent doctor . . . he needs no help from you."

The children's recovery took weeks. During that time, Muse remained isolated in the shed. At first, she protested, pleaded to be let back into the big house where she felt safe.

"It's scary in here, Mama," she said.

But the answer was still no. Mary gave her a candle and told her not to fret.

"There is no other way," her mother said. "You have to make do."

After a while, Muse grew accustomed to the isolation. Mostly, she enjoyed the silence and took advantage of her secret thoughts and an imagination that held no boundaries. For the most part, she remained quiet, allowing her recovery to take its natural course. But sometimes, she struggled to suppress the pent-up energy rumbling within her. She found it difficult to yield to stillness and to resist the desire to sprint down to the cool, calm lake for a swim. Even the old birch tree in the slave quarters beckoned; she longed to climb its narrow limbs to the top to view the countryside or watch the birds wing by.

Boredom soon took hold. She wrestled the blanket off the cot. The shed was warming, no doubt from the afternoon's sun overhead. Her eyes combed her new surroundings; save for the cot she lay in, a side table with water and medicines, and a window, the shed was bone bare.

She scrambled out of bed, her toes imprinting the surface of the dirt floor. She paced the length of the wall that separated her from the room on the other side. The wall was built of inferior wood panels—panels with gaps between them, slits wide enough for her to see through. A storage room! Skimming the wall again, she noticed a misaligned panel at the corner end. Her small hands gripped both sides of the wood plank. She pushed and pulled until the panel shifted, creating an opening large enough for her to slip through.

Once in, she met with stacks of boxes obstructing her way. The room had two tiny windows, but it was vast and chockablock with junk. She maneuvered through a forest of cobwebs, dust, discarded furniture, old paintings, and books. One book, opened facedown on the ground, tripped her up, and she fell over it. Its hardback cover was torn and soiled. When she turned it over, the pages revealed pictures of flowers and plants so vivid in color, it made her heart sing. She sat cross-legged on the ground, turning the pages carefully so as not to do it more damage. Each page divulged a new wonder. *What beauty in nature,* she thought.

She continued to explore. From an old barrel, she pulled out a hurricane lamp with a cracked glass shade. In her eyes, it was still pretty. In the big house, she was not allowed to touch anything without permission, but in the storage room, she handled freely everything that took her fancy.

Before long, another wall confronted her—stronger, better built, yet she could still see between the gaps of the panels. The schoolroom. Often, curiosity led her to trump up an excuse to walk past the school. With heed, she would lean up against the structure and give ear to the chatter and laughter of the young, white, privileged children as they studied. At the end of the wall, she sighted a door that no doubt led into the school. She touched the handle, wanting so much to unlatch it, but she dared not. The school was a forbidden place for all slaves. She returned to peering through the openings in the wall, recording in her mind what she saw: a blackboard, several small desks with chairs attached to them. On the teacher's desk sat a pile of papers and pencils in a cup. She once again looked at the door but restrained herself. Then she heard the rattle of the school's front door. Before the door opened, she scuttled back through the storage room and jumped into bed, faking sleep.

The next afternoon, after her mother left, she heard the school bell ring. She leaped out of bed, scampered through the storage debris, and found a place on the ground, wedged between several boxes. She could see the goings-on in the schoolhouse.

The Hallisburgs were still out sick, and she learned that two other white children in the community had been stricken by the same illness. Only a few muffled voices floated from the schoolroom that day. Cassandra had taught her how to count to ten. She held up one finger for each child sitting at a desk. Two fingers for the girls, and three fingers for the boys.

"Five," she whispered.

Most of the pupils she recognized as the daughters or sons of local plantation owners or from playdates with Cassandra and Jonathan. She envied the girls and their colorful cotton dresses and the shiny silk ribbons in their hair, but none of them, she decided, was as pretty as her mistress.

She eavesdropped on the lectures, watched the alphabet drawings on the blackboard, and mimicked the sounds the teacher voiced. In whispered tones, she practiced with her classmates when instructed to repeat a phrase or recite a sentence with correct grammar.

Little by little, she started to identify the letters on the blackboard and studied pronunciation, imitating the accents of the teacher and the other students.

"*G* as in *goat* . . . *H* as in *hat* . . . *I* as in *ice* . . . *J* as in *jump*."

With a stick, she drew the alphabet on the dirt floor, making meticulous and careful letters until she thought she had spelled her name. She put her hand over her mouth to stifle her glee.

"*M-u-z*," she whispered.

One night, Mary came into the shack, hauling a large washbasin. Perche followed with several buckets of warm water laced on a pole straddling his back.

"Where you want dis water, Miss Mary?"

"Set it down over dare. I'll po' it in. Thank ya, Perche."

"You welcome."

Perche turned toward Muse.

"And how you, Miss Muse?"

"I'm just fine."

"Yo' face looks so much better."

Muse smiled.

"Thank you."

Mary poured in the first bucket of water.

"The doctor say you have to stay clean," Mary said.

"Is that all you need, Miss Mary?"

Mary nodded.

"Well, I'll be gon'. Evening, all!"

Perche smiled at Muse and then left.

"Thanks again," Mary said.

"I like Perche, Mama."

"So do I . . . now, let's get you cleaned up."

Mary scrubbed and brushed Muse until her ebony skin almost squeaked clean. Then she combed, brushed, and braided her hair.

"Ouch!"

"Shush!"

Each braid had its own artful square section, a pattern that looked like the squares on a checkerboard but with sprouts. She then oiled her daughter's face with the homemade aloe lubricant until it shone like a polished button.

"Muse, yo' face looks good. But little Miss Cassandra ain't doing so good as you."

"Why, Mama?"

"Her face still got dem marks on it."

"Oh, Mama! She is so pretty."

"Yeah, but she ain't looking so good as before. But she'll be fine."

Mary paused before she continued.

"Baby, it might be a good idea for you to stay in this shack awhile longer."

"Why, Mama?"

"Because yo' face is clearing up . . . you healing faster than Miss Cassandra. It's gonna be difficult for her to see you back to normal when she ain't. The Hallisburgs are concerned that if she don't heal right, and her beauty's gone, she may not find the right husband."

"All right, Mama."

"You just be patient."

Mary slipped Muse into a clean nightgown and tucked her into bed.

"You get some sleep. I'll see you in the mornin'."

Just as she was about to blow out the candle, Muse protested.

"Don't blow out the candle, Mama. I'm afraid."

"All right, I'll leave it lit."

She lay in bed, eyes wide open. An orchestra of crickets chirping in the fields made her smile. She got up and went to the window. The plantation slept. The coast was clear. She grabbed the burning candle, searched for the vulnerable spot in the wall, and slipped through. Hidden from view was the damaged hurricane lamp. She retrieved it and installed the burning candle. Again, she battled through the storage room until she stood before the door leading to the school. She took a deep breath and reached for the handle. It twisted with a soft, crying screech and unlatched the door.

A mysterious, well-ordered room, musty and odorous, greeted her. She prowled through the schoolhouse, knowing every step was on forbidden soil. At a desk, she sat, posture erect, playacting as if a student. She raised her hand and proclaimed: "I know the answer, mister suh. I know."

Pinned on the wall were various detailed geographical maps. She stared at them, baffled. Row after row of softbound books lined three enormous bookshelves. Did the books hold tales and great secrets about the world beyond the plantation? She opened a few, ran her fingers across the crisp pages, and admired more pictures. The blackboard was wiped clean; nevertheless, with a piece of chalk, she wrote out the letters *Muz*, then erased them. She found a discarded half-worn pencil on the floor and a crumbled-up workbook in the trash, pages still blank. She took them and hurried back through the storage room and through the wall.

The trespassing continued for more than a week when one night she heard an unexpected noise. It sounded like a book dropping. Someone else was in the schoolroom. Before she could flee, a huge hand snatched her up by her wiry braids.

"Ouch! Let me go!"

"Who the hell are you?"

She fought loose from his grip but stumbled over a box and sprawled to the ground.

"I said, who are you?"

"I'm Muse, suh."

"What are you doing in my schoolhouse?" he demanded.

He was tall and lean, with thin, sand-colored hair but thick, wide sideburns; his complexion was so pale that even up close he looked ghostly. She recognized him at once; he was the schoolhouse master. She hastened up from the ground. In doing so, the workbook dropped from her hands. He picked up the book and fingered through the pages, looking at her rambling letters.

"What do you think you're doing?"

"Nothin', suh, I was just playing. You gon' tell Mrs. Hallisburg?" she cried.

"Sit," he said.

She turned the box she tripped over right-side up and sat down, still trembling.

"Are you learning how to read and write?"

She looked at him and shrugged.

"You know it's against the law for Negroes to read and write?"

She shrugged again.

"People go to jail and are severely punished for breaking that law."

"I knowed that, suh," she said. "I knowed someone who was whipped fifty times for opening a book . . . but, I was just playing. I won't do it again. I promise."

"And do you know why that is?"

"Why what is?"

"Why there is a law forbidding your race from an education?"

"'Cause we slaves ain't good enough?

"No!"

"Miss Cassandra . . . everybody say so."

"No! It's because education, reading and writing, are powerful tools. It's like a bullet in a gun. Many people of my race believe if Negroes possessed such a weapon as knowledge, you would become dangerous and upset the order of things."

"The order of things?"

"Yes," he replied. "The playing field would be leveled . . . a threat to the so-called prosperous Southern livelihood would come to an end."

She looked at him and blinked.

"Do you understand what I'm saying?"

"No, suh. They just say we ain't 'telligent enough to learn."

"Well, little Muse, can you keep a secret?"

"Yes, suh."

"You are as intelligent as anyone . . . even me."

"But you a teacher."

"Yes, I am," he said. He looked around. "How did you get in here?"

She pointed to the open door.

"Where do you live?"

"Behind the storage room."

"Why?"

"I been sick."

She looked at him again.

"I'm gonna get in big trouble, huh?"

"No . . . not if you can keep a secret. Can you?"

"I can keep a secret," she said.

"I can teach you," he said, "to read and write and more. But if we are caught, you will be punished, and I will go to jail. Do you understand?"

"I understand." She stared at him with wide, curious eyes.

"I knew someone like you before," he said, "when I lived in New Orleans . . . he was older than you, but he was smart, inquisitive, just like you. But he could not keep his secret, and it cost him."

"What did they do to him?"

"They blinded him . . . hot coals on his eyes. They made damn sure he never read or wrote again."

"What did they do to you?"

"I had already moved on. But I heard he never told who educated him."

The tutor softened after he told the story, and she relaxed.

"What's yo name?" Muse asked.

"My name is Wilfred Müller."

"You from New York?"

"No. Bavaria."

"Bavaria! Where's dat?"

"Come over to the map, and I'll show you."

Framed on the wall was a gigantic map of the world. She stood spellbound.

"Is that the world?"

"Yes, it is." He picked up a wooden pointer. "This is America. This is Virginia, where you live. This is Europe, and this Bavaria, where I was born.

He looked into Muse's eyes.

"Muse, listen to me carefully. Education is a task you must take seriously, and for you, it is fraught with danger. Do you want to learn how to read and write?"

"Yes, suh."

"Do you want to be tied to a tree, whipped fifty times or more?

"No, suh."

"Do you want to be blinded and never see again?"

"No, suh."

"Then I ask one more time. Can you keep a secret? Will you keep counsel of what you are taught? Swear not to tell anyone, not even your mother, until you are a free human being."

"I will tell no one, suh. I swear. Not until I'm a free human being."

CAUGHT

April 1845

It was an unusual spring morning. Der Brunnen pulsated differently—a slower, peaceful rhythm shared by all who lived on the plantation, the slaves and the overseers alike. The Hallisburgs were visiting relatives in Louisiana.

Muse also took advantage of their absence.

The secret between her and Mr. Müller continued. Their routine rarely wavered. They met twice a week: Sunday mornings when the Hallisburgs went to church and Wednesday evening when they traveled to Bible studies. Mr. Müller created a space for her in the storage room. The small desk and chair were camouflaged in a way that if anyone came upon it, they would be none the wiser of its purpose when confronted with the other discarded furniture and items surrounding it.

Mr. Müller was also on spring break. But he left Muse with a learning project to complete before his return if possible.

That morning she escaped the eagle eyes of her mother. The overseers and the field slaves worked at the other end of the property.

She found a secluded area for her purpose. Near the birch trees, not far from the pond, was where she moored. From the pockets of her apron, she pulled out a small book on wildlife and a sketch pad. The assignment Mr. Müller left was to observe the animals on the plantation and to draw and document what she surveyed.

⋙⊹⊹⊱

"But I don't know how to draw, Mr. Müller."

"Of course you do. Writing is drawing. And your lettering is good."

"But . . ."

"No," Mr. Müller said, wagging his forefinger in the air. "Draw a circle."

Muse turned to a clean page in her notebook and drew.

"What do you see?"

"A circle," she said, her eyes looking confused.

"You know what I imagine it is? A ball."

She looked up at him and smiled.

"So do I."

"Draw a small squiggly line on the top of the circle. What do you see?"

"An apple?"

"Exactly. You've drawn an apple. Never be afraid of your imagination. Let it take you far."

⋙⊹⊹⊱

She was excited about the assignment because she loved to watch wildlife roaming in their natural habitat. To date, she had drawn and labeled a bluebird, a squirrel, a red fox, and a raccoon.

Yesterday, while gathering sweet potatoes for her mother, a bald eagle had appeared, circling in the sky. She found its exact image in the book. She hoped to see it again.

Crouched down, trampling through a field of tall grass, she scoured the skies, waiting. Then it showed itself, flying overhead. She dropped to all fours, crawling through the grass, scrutinizing it until it landed on a tree branch. She scribbled as fast as she could. Black feathered wings that spread like a fan, burnt-orange tail, slick white head, and a yellow beak. She stood gazing up at it as it soared. So beautiful, she thought. So free!

The sound of a voice startled her—someone had called out her name. She dropped to the ground, hiding in the tall blades of grass.

"Muse!"

It was Perche. She could see his wild gray hair, bushed out like a bird's nest.

"Muse, I see you. What you doing in dere? Who you hiding from?"

Before she could get up, he was standing before her . . . tall, thin, glistening with perspiration.

"You getting yo'self all dirty."

In his efforts to help her up and brush her off, the wildlife book fell from her pocket.

His eyes widened, and he backed away, a look of horror on his face.

"What you doing wit' dat book, chile?"

Muse did not know what to do, what to say.

"Dey'll whip you, if not kill you, if dey see you wit' that thang."

"It's not what you think," she said. "I was just looking at the pictures."

"I don't care—dey'll kill you. Give it to me . . . I'll bury it. No one will ever know."

"No, Perche. I'll take it back myself."

"If dey catch you—"

"They won't catch me. I promise."

"For God's sake, girl!"

16

"I promise!"
She put the book back into her pocket.
"Please, don't tell."
"I never would. You know dat."
Shivering, she started to walk away, then stopped.
"What did you want with me?"
He sighed as if he had been holding his breath all that time.
"I thought it was a good day for a swimming lesson."

THE ASSAULT

Der Brunnen
Southern Virginia, November 1854

Muse was exhausted. Master Jonathan returned from university in New York without notice—suspended for smoking, not regular tobacco but exotic smokes he and his cronies encountered at a saloon in Chinatown. For several days, she traipsed back and forth between Mistress Cassandra and her demanding brother. She scurried around, trying to satisfy his relentless requests, all the while aware of him watching her with an intense glare that made her uncomfortable; nevertheless, she pressed on. The chill in the morning air pierced her to the bone. Her lower back ached, and her muscles tightened. Sixteen years old and she felt ancient. How she looked forward to the evening and the quiet space of the old shack where she still spent much of her time, the solemn hovel that afforded her the solitude she craved and where she read and practiced writing.

That night when she returned to the shack, fatigued, she forewent her clandestine pastime. For the past week, she had been rereading a document Mr. Müller had urged her to learn by heart before he had left the plantation two years ago.

She remembered when he first read the passage to her: *We hold these truths to be self-evident, that all men are created equal, that they are endowed by their Creator with certain unalienable Rights—that among these are Life, Liberty and the pursuit of Happiness.*

"What does it mean?" he asked.

Muse recalled that she had hesitated to answer, fearful of her interpretation.

"Go on. Don't be afraid to own your thoughts," Mr. Müller urged.

"Does it mean," she began tentatively, "that everyone is born the same, made the same, and should live the same . . . as free people?"

"What happened to that philosophy? How did it go so wrong?"

But she could not answer.

Muse eyed the wood panel in the wall that separated her from the now-abandoned schoolhouse, storage room, and her books. Mr. Müller had loosened one of the wood panels to make it easier for her to slip through as she grew. Although she was inspired to unhinge the panel again that night, she was too tired. She undressed, slipped on her white cotton nightshirt, and flung herself on the cot. As soon as she extinguished the candle, she fell asleep, but then she was jolted awake. She discerned a presence in the room . . . a low, heavy breathing. How long had she slept—minutes, hours? She spotted the faint glow of a candle moving about the room. She sat up.

"Mama?"

At the sound of her voice, the movement ceased.

"Mama, is that you?"

The light from the candle gradually brought into view the face of Master Jonathan.

"Master Jonathan!"

"Shh!" he said.

"Master Jonathan, is something wrong? Is Miss Cassandra all right?"

"Quiet!" he said, putting his finger up to his mouth.

Jonathan approached the bed.

She saw him clearly now. He was half-dressed in a robe loosely tied at the waist, his bare chest exposed.

She recoiled.

"What is it, Master Jonathan?"

He drew closer. She pulled the thin coverlet up to her chin. Her eyes widened.

"Remember . . ." he said. "Remember when we were kids, you and I, and Cassandra . . . remember when we'd go skinny-dipping in the pond?"

"Yes, Master Jonathan. I remember. We were very young then."

By now, she whiffed the stench of liquor on his breath.

"Master Jonathan, you've been drinking."

"Shh! I just want to talk to you . . . like we used to . . . when we were kids."

"It's late. I have to get up early."

"Be still!" he ordered.

"Master Jonathan, you have to go now."

"No," he said. "I don't."

His hand reached out to stroke her face.

"No . . . stop!" She pushed his hand away.

"Come on, Muse! I've always been fond of you. Out of all the *negras* on the plantation, you've always been my favorite."

"I beg you, Master Jonathan, please go. If you don't, I'll scream."

"Go ahead."

"What's wrong with you, sir? What have I done? Why are you behaving like this?"

"You've done nothing."

He touched her again.

"Your skin is so black . . . silky. So different from that scrawny, ashy little girl you used to be. You've grown up nicely."

"Please, don't . . ."

But before she could finish the sentence, Jonathan leaped forward and, in an instant, pinned her arms above her head. With his full weight, he pressed himself on top of her. She was half his size, but she fought, kicked, and scratched with the fervor of a trapped wild animal. Jonathan stripped off her gown, but she, scrappy, continued her self-defense and slammed her knee into his groin. He yelled. She tried to get up, but he grabbed her by her braids and wrestled her to the dirt floor, slapped her again and again, and soon overtook her. She let out a blood-curdling shriek that brought Perche and Bailey, the overseer, racing to the hut.

Perche got there first.

"Master Jonathan, stop! I beg you . . . get off her! Master Jonathan, please!

Even as Muse screamed and fought, her peripheral vision discerned an outraged Perche, conflicted, tormented, wanting to help her but knowing he could not lay a hand on Master Jonathan. But then Perche grabbed Jonathan by the hair and flung him across the room.

Bailey came stumbling in just as Perche took hold of Jonathan. Muse lay on the ground, naked, twisted, bruised, and bleeding.

"Perche, cover her!"

Bailey turned to Jonathan and helped him up.

"Mr. Jonathan, are you all right, sir?"

The look in his eyes was wild, unsettled, as if he didn't know where he was. He tightened his robe and brushed himself off. He leered at Muse and then at Perche.

"You'll pay for this! I swear . . . both of you . . . you'll pay!"

"Come, Mr. Jonathan," Bailey said. "Let's get you back to your room."

Moments later, Mary rushed in. She howled at the sight of Muse on the ground in the fetal position, hands covering her face, wailing.

"My baby, my po' baby . . . what did he do to you?"

—<del>—</del>—

Later that night, Muse was summoned to the big house. She sat outside the parlor door, simmering in fear. The main house was well built—walls thick and solid except for the wall separating the parlor from the hallway where she waited. The area had been recently expanded, and the new wall was paper-thin. She heard everything the Hallisburgs were saying.

—<del>—</del>—

"She's lying, I tell you," Jonathan said. "Muse lured me into her hut. It was consensual . . . I swear, Mother, Father! I swear!"

"I don't believe it," Cassandra retorted.

"But, Jonathan, why would she do such a thing?"

"I don't know, Father. She said I was working her too hard. Anyway, she is always flirting with me."

"That's ridiculous!" Cassandra countered.

"But why invite you to her hut?"

"She thought if she was nice to me, I would let up on the chores that needed to be done."

"Why haven't you mentioned this before? We've never had trouble with her . . . never! She's been obedient . . . does as she's told."

"That's true," Cassandra said. "And she is my servant, not yours, Jon. Mama, I've told you he needs a slave of his own. But you just won't listen."

"What does it all matter? The black whore tore my shirt, scratched and bit me."

"Watch your language!" Mrs. Hallisburg said.

"Mother, Father, look at my face. She hit me. You must get rid of her. Enough! She's young; you'll get a decent price. Slaves are a dime a dozen these days."

"Oh, shut up, Jon! You're still drunk! Anyway, a few minutes ago, you said it was Perche that beat you . . . which one was it?"

"Honey, I don't know," Mr. Hallisburg said to his wife. "What do you think?"

"I don't know either, my dear."

"No, Mama . . . no. Muse is mine. You gave her to me. You can't just take her away. I need her."

"Well, she can no longer work in the house after this fiasco. Maybe the fields."

"No, Mama. Nobody does my hair like Muse. And she fits my dresses so well. You've said so yourself. I've trained her the way I want her. Please! Don't take her away. I don't want to replace her. Anyway, it would kill Mary."

"Well, what are we supposed to do? If Jonathan is right, and she's trying to . . . to . . . well, what are we to do?"

"Papa, don't believe a word Jonathan says; he's a liar. Muse would never think of such a thing. I know her. Why, she blushes when I read romantic poetry. For heaven's sake, Mama! I'm sure Muse is innocent of these charges."

"All right, all right . . . we'll think of something," Mr. Hallisburg said. "Jonathan, you're back at university in two weeks. In the meantime, you stay away from Muse. Do you understand?"

"Well, who's going to take care of me?"

"We'll get Sarah to help."

"Not Sarah! She's too old."

"It's Sarah or no one at all . . . you choose. And, young man, we need to have a serious talk, right now! Let's go."

"But what about Perche? He beat me . . . I want him whipped."

"I thought it was Muse who beat you," Cassandra countered with a smirk.

Muse could hear Mr. Hallisburg and Jonathan leave the room by the garden door, which gave forth a creaking groan when opened and closed.

"We must let Muse explain," Cassandra insisted.

"What is there to explain?"

"Mama, let her speak."

"Cassandra, Muse has no rights in this house . . . she is a slave . . . and must conduct herself as such. What could she possibly have to say? And do you think I'd take the word of an inferior over my own son? Perhaps it was Perche; the savages will attack each other."

"Mother, please, she belongs to me . . . I want to know her side of the story."

"All right."

⚔

The lack of air circulating in the passageway intensified the warmth. Muse remained seated, perspiring but listening. At last, the door opened. Mistress Cassandra, who was still in her night clothes, told Muse to come in. She stood up, trying to find balance; she had twisted her ankle during the altercation. When she passed her mistress, their eyes met, and Cassandra gave her an encouraging smile, as if to say, "Don't worry—all will be well."

She hobbled into the room, trembling, eyes downcast, hands clasping each other. Her body had gone stiff from sitting so long, her face was swollen, and her head throbbed. Yet, the moment she set foot in the parlor, it seemed the space itself offered sanctuary. Two of its narrow side windows were open, and the evening breeze floated through. At last, she could breathe. She stood before Mrs. Hallisburg, quiet, erect, waiting for her mistress to speak.

"Muse this is very serious. Do you understand?"

Muse nodded.

"Speak; do not nod."

"Yes, Mrs. Hallisburg."

"What happened?"

Muse adjusted her weight to the stronger leg.

"I don't know, Mrs. Hallisburg . . . I swear I don't know."

"Do not swear in my house. Just speak plainly."

"Ma'am, I was asleep, and when I awoke, Master Jonathan was standing there, in my room. At first, I thought it was Mama, and then I saw it was he . . . I froze. I didn't know what to do. I don't know why he was there, why it happened. I did nothing!"

"I believe her, Mother," Cassandra said. "Muse knows nothing about this sort of thing, men and such. She is an innocent. Do you honestly think that if Muse was involved with any type of lured indiscretion, especially with Jonathan, I would not have noticed? Please, Mama. Give me some credit."

"You are right, darling . . . nothing gets past you," Mrs. Hallisburg said, smiling inwardly.

"Muse, my son said you lured him into your hut. Is that true?"

"No, ma'am."

"Have you ever flirted with my son?"

"Absolutely not, ma'am."

"Mama, it's not Muse's fault—it's Jonathan . . . something's wrong him."

"I don't want to discuss your brother now. This is about Muse."

She turned to Muse.

"Has he ever"—Mrs. Hallisburg could barely form the words—"touched you before?"

Muse stalled, hesitating, not sure what to say, how to explain, or if she should. For she had been warned never to accuse her masters or to criticize; it was not her place. However, she had noticed a change in Master Jonathan's manner some time ago. His demeanor had altered drastically; he seemed discombobu- lated, out of sorts all the time, and just plain mean for no reason. He touched her inappropriately, brushing up against her breast, pinching her buttocks, or running his hand down the back of her neck—abuses he had never committed before, not even when they were children. One night, he had cornered her in the laun- dry room and tried to force a kiss, but she broke free. Without mentioning these mistreatments to anyone, she became adept at staying clear of Jonathan unless tasked with serving him. So many other young female slaves were less fortunate . . . rumors circulated throughout the slave community. She had been clever, shrewd, and triumphant in escaping his advances, until tonight.

"Has he?" Mrs. Hallisburg continued. "Has he ever attacked you before?"

"No, Mrs. Hallisburg."

Mrs. Hallisburg paused.

"Muse, I tend to agree with Cassandra and her observations that my son might have instigated this fiasco. But that does not relieve you of some responsibility."

Again Mrs. Hallisburg paused—a silence so deafening Muse trembled. Then Mrs. Hallisburg sighed.

"I tell you this, Muse, and I won't tell you again. It is your job to stay away from Jonathan, whatever the circumstance. Sarah will take care of him from now on; therefore, you have no reason to be in his company. Do you understand me?'

"Yes, ma'am, I understand."

"I don't know what happened, but if you are ever caught in a compromising position with my son again, you will be sold . . . no discussion.

"Yes, Mrs. Hallisburg."

"Were you hurt?" Mrs. Hallisburg asked.

Muse dared not respond in truth. Instead, she offered, "I'm fine, ma'am."

"All right, you may go."

Muse turned to Cassandra.

"Do you need anything tonight, Miss Cassandra?"

"No. Sleep in my room. I'm staying up a little longer with Mama."

"Yes, mistress. Good night."

AN EDUCATION FOR CASSANDRA

Muse lay on the cot up against the wall in Cassandra's bedroom. She could not sleep. The curtains were ajar just enough for her to gaze up at the stars—sparkling, twinkling, so joyful in their dancing. Normally, she would smile, show her delight, but every time she moved or turned, pain pierced through some part of her body. The horrific deed of that night played over and over in her mind . . . she felt every blow, every pull and twist of her flesh.

When Cassandra entered the room, she was fumbling with the candle. Muse tried to get up to help.

"No. Stay in bed. I'll manage."

She lit another candle, then placed the candleholder she held on a table. The room lit up.

"How do you feel?"

"I'm fine."

"You always say that, Muse."

Cassandra paused.

"Did he hurt you . . . you know what I mean?"

Muse nodded.

"I'm so sorry."

Cassandra untied the ribbon around her neck and slipped out of her robe; she fluffed up her pillows and crawled into bed. She did not ask Muse to roll her hair; instead, she pulled it back into a ponytail and sank into the covers.

"Muse, I think Father is going to have Perche whipped for wrestling with Jonathan."

"No!" Muse groaned, putting her hands over her eyes.

"I'll see what I can do."

"Oh, please."

"Something else . . . Mama told me tonight it is time I prepare myself for a husband. She wants me at my best to snare someone of means."

Muse turned to look at her mistress.

"But who will want me with such a foul complexion?"

"Miss Cassandra . . . you're still pretty."

"It's curious, don't you think," Cassandra said, "that we had the same illness at the same time, and your skin is flawless."

"I'm sorry."

Cassandra sighed.

"Well, at least I have money . . . that's something. The good news, however, is that we're going to Paris for my social education and training."

"What do you mean, we?"

"I mean Father, Mother, me, and you."

Muse's eyes grew wide.

"Why must I go?"

"Because you are my slave and will be educated as a lady's maid."

"But . . ." She searched for an excuse. "I can't read or write."

"Doesn't matter . . . you will learn how to take care of me, *à la française.*"

"*À la* what?"

"The French way."

Lord! Muse thought.

THE JOURNEY

New York Harbor, 1855

By midmorning, the veil of gray clouds had waffled away. The sky opened to a cluster of soft, warm sun rays revealing a pristine day, typical of spring in New York. The docks that lined the city's harbor overflowed with people, many of whom waited to board an international steamship bound for France.

Amid the chaos, Muse hovered around a mountain of expensive baggage and trunks belonging to her masters. Her skin shimmered from the now-warming temperature. She wore a proper uniform: a drab, brown dress made of coarse wool. The cumbersome, full-skirted garment draped in such a way as to sweep or tangle up against the worn-out wood planks of the old docks. The formfitting bodice squeezed her small waist and ample breasts; long sleeves swallowed her arms, tapering tight at the wrist; a starched white collar smothered her neck, and an off-white rag of a scarf twined around her hair. One hand rested on the curve of her hip; the other held a handkerchief she used to sponge moisture from her brow.

She lifted her large brown eyes to the sky and watched the clouds floating farther into the distance. *What must it feel like to soar through the sky, light, breezy, and as free as you please?* The squeal and laughter of children running rampant along the docks startled her from her fantasy. Alone, she waited for the ship's porters to arrive. She stood near the enormous vessel she would soon board, drinking in the unfamiliar sights of a major port. The hurried pace of the public excited her, yet unsettled her. Everyone seemed to sprint like wild horses scrambling every which way. People shoved her and barked at her to get out of the way, but she held fast, guarding the luggage cases as if they were children.

At the end of the dock, a few paces away, she observed a chain of stalls cluttering parts of the waterfront. Merchants selling a variety of produce and products: food, drink, personal travel items, and souvenirs such as miniature versions of the American flag. One vendor at a newsstand shouted in a high, cadenced pitch: "Paper, paper, get your morning paper!"

She turned toward the *New York Daily Times* poster and scanned the latest headlines: "Border Ruffians Key to Pro-Slavery Territorial Legislature." It was about pro-slavery supporters who crossed into Kansas and affected the outcomes of key elections by claiming to be settlers and intimidating valid voters—she knew this because she had read a disturbing article about it in the same paper yesterday. Another successful fraud of an election to keep slavery alive. Her curiosity stirred, and she wondered what else the newspaper reported. She squinted, trying to read the smaller print on the poster, then stopped dead and averted her eyes back to their normal state: the downcast gaze she practiced her whole life, the fixed, set eyes of a submissive. With her peripheral vision, she canvassed the immediate surroundings, hoping no one had seen her reading the poster and speculated about her literacy, especially her owners. But she smiled, confident her long-kept secret remained intact.

A rancid odor oozed around the harbor. She overheard a passerby say it was the sulfurous fumes from the ship's funnel, or the vapors rising from a polluted river, or the city's natural fetid air, or perhaps all three. The sharp scent brought her to long for the sweet fragrance of honeysuckle and jasmine that spiced the breezes on the plantation where she lived. They had been traveling only a few days, yet she already missed home. She wanted again to envision the fresh, wide-open spaces of Virginia, to know the familiar routine of her life, no matter how restrictive or repressive. The unknown was daunting.

⇌

Soon, two tall, burly Negro men approached, dragging behind them a four-wheeled baggage cart.

"Are you the baggage porters?" she asked.

"Yes'm," they replied in unison.

She gazed up at them. *Free black men,* she thought, *free!* Yet they seemed unfazed about their liberty . . . took it for granted, no doubt.

She smiled, and they smiled back.

"These two huge trunks," she said, "and those five leather pieces are for Stateroom 12. The third trunk and the rest of the pieces go to Cabin 11."

"Yes'm," they replied.

Among the various pricey pieces, one, a large fabric bag frayed at the seams, appeared out of place. Muse grabbed it by its crude wooden handles.

"This one is mine."

She remained until every piece of luggage was secured in the baggage cart. One of the men gave her a series of claim tickets. Satisfied, she put them in her pocket and again peered up at the sky to check the sun's position; it was nearing noon. Boarding would soon begin. Clutching her bag, she wended her way through the crowd in search of the Hallisburgs.

⭤

Within minutes, Muse spotted them lounging at a dockside café set up to accommodate first-class travelers. Mr. Hallisburg, Mrs. Hallisburg, and Mistress Cassandra sat at a small table, sipping tea. They looked every bit like wealthy Americans traveling abroad. She pushed through the mob to reach the thick, gold ropes that framed the outdoor café and guarded its entrance. Mistress Cassandra acknowledged her presence with a wave, motioning for her to wait there. She nodded. But her eyes lingered on her mistress and the iris-blue traveling dress she wore. With pride, she followed the contours and folds of the heavy, cotton-and-silk mix, a simple fabric for a simple ensemble. Muse had not only made the gown but had copied it from a picture in a fashion magazine. It was the color of the fabric, not its quality, that lured Cassandra—a singular tint that brought out the azure shades of her eyes. The dress had a fitted bodice with a soft, jewel neckline, a pointed V at the waist, and long bell sleeves. The cut of the style veiled her figure, giving the illusion of a much thinner waist. She wore a yellow shawl and a pale straw bonnet, held secure by a blue silk ribbon. Miss Cassandra owned many dresses, and Muse was thrilled that she had chosen the one she crafted.

Mrs. Hallisburg had told her that one of the chief reasons she was accompanying them to Paris was because of her potential to create a wardrobe.

"Cassandra will learn how to behave like a Parisian lady," Mrs. Hallisburg said, "and you will learn how to keep her looking like one."

34

Muse loitered near and around the café, her bag pressed close to her person. While watching an endless stream of people traipse by, she spied a building on the other side of the river. It was a good distance away, but she recognized it. Atypical in shape, circular like a fort; she knew it from pictures in the newspaper. Castle Garden: the official site for processing immigrants seeking residence or asylum in America. A huge gathering of people assembled about the building. She wasn't close enough to see faces, but in her mind, she imagined people from all parts of the world, all nationalities, seeking refuge and freedom in America . . . something she would never know. She sighed. Her thoughts turned to her mother, whom she would not reunite with again for a year. At that moment, she wanted to kiss her bright but aging eyes. The other house slaves told her she was lucky to journey from the plantation and experience something of the world. Maybe she was lucky, she thought, but then, maybe not.

"Muse, where are you!"

She recognized the raspy voice of Mr. Hallisburg and, with speed, pushed her way back through the crowd to the ropes of the café. Of medium height, he sported an average build, save for the small, balloonlike gut that encircled his middle.

"There you are," he said.

Despite his fifty years, he owned the harsh face of a man much older: dull gray eyes; tight, bony lips; thinning, flaxen hair; heavy sideburns; ears protruding out like a woman's small hand fan. The ears always held a sense of amusement for her, ever since she could remember. Try as he might, she decided, Mr. Hallisburg never could pull off the air of a distinguished gentleman, even when smartly dressed; it was always the ears.

"Is everything all right with the luggage?" he asked.

"Yes, sir."

She put down her bag and reached into her dress pocket to retrieve the claim tickets.

"Good girl!"

He patted her on the head, a gesture she despised but learned to tolerate long ago.

"Now, you wait here. We'll be boarding in half an hour," he explained. "Oh! And keep an eye out for Jonathan. He's got permission from the university to see us off. You stay clear of him!"

She cringed inside but said, "Yes, sir."

When the master turned away, she frowned. Jonathan! The last person on earth she wanted to see. But no sooner had she thought it than she spied him walking toward her.

Jonathan Hallisburg: tall, attractive, shoving through the crowd in his usual lofty way. Clean-shaven, he wore a new tailored frock coat, and much of his curly brown hair was concealed under a low topper made of straw and tipped slightly to the side. He looked so different from when she last laid eyes on him. *At least he's sober,* she thought. Within seconds, he stood before her, a sardonic smirk on his face and his eyes a piercing, icy gray. His steely glare locked on her with intensity, and he leaned in.

"How are you, Muse?" he whispered in her ear.

She shrank and tried to pass him.

"Ah! Let's be friends again."

She held her tongue, careful not to meet his eyes.

He brushed his fingers across her face as if stroking a cat. A single braid escaped from beneath her headwrap. He twisted it around his finger and yanked.

"Ouch!" she cried. "Stop it!"

"Shush!"

She stared out into the roving crowd; she felt invisible to the world. A master abusing his slave? So what—it was no concern of theirs. Her eyes froze as she tolerated his subtle torments.

Then the shrill voice of a female protested. Jonathan flinched and stepped away from her. He put his hands in the air as though surrendering.

"Leave her alone, or I'll tell Mother!"

Muse turned to see her seventeen-year-old mistress standing on the other side of the café's ropes, hands on hips, blue eyes blazing.

"Leave her alone, I tell you," Cassandra repeated.

Jonathan smiled. A spark flickered in his eyes. He beamed.

"How are you, my dear sister?"

"I'm fine."

Muse watched the convoluted interaction between brother and sister in silence. She had observed their ongoing bickering and banter for years. He made a smart-aleck comment about Cassandra's auburn hair straining under the bonnet she wore. Already, locks of hair sprang from under the hat. Muse had spent half the night trying to put her mistress's thick strands of hair into order, all for naught. But he complimented her on the way she wore the iris-blue traveling dress. Muse thought her mistress attractive despite her complexion, the unforgiving blemishes that tracked her milky-white skin, and the baby fat that never melted away. To her, Mistress Cassandra was still pretty and, for the most part, good-natured. But as she overheard Mrs. Hallisburg say, more than once, "It doesn't account for much these days if one is to make a superior match."

"Well, you look wonderful," Jonathan said to his sister. "Those Parisian women will have fierce competition from you this year."

Cassandra gave her brother a half smile, intimating she bought none of his compliments today.

"Father and Mother are waiting for you; you're late!"

He shrugged and then breezed into the café. Cassandra turned to Muse and mouthed, "Are you all right?"

Muse nodded and faced back toward the river.

Sometimes when she closed her eyes, the savagery of that night crashed back in on her. The sight of Jonathan towering over her, lunacy burning in his eyes, the stink of his breath panting against her face, and the horrible days that followed. He tried to convince his parents to put her on the block, blaming her for seducing him. And because of his lies, Perche suffered miserably for disrespecting his superiors. It was, however, only ten lashes instead of the twenty-five as prescribed by plantation policy. Thank God for Mistress Cassandra!

"Muse!" Mrs. Hallisburg cried. "Don't you hear me calling to you?"

"What? I mean, yes, ma'am!"

"It's time to board."

Muse shook off the disturbing images of Jonathan.

"Sorry, ma'am. I'm ready."

She lingered in the background while the Hallisburgs made their farewells. At last, the ship's horn blurted out two long, thunderous roars. The deck officer unfastened the chains that blocked off the on-ramp, and the boarding of the Atlantic steamer began. Cassandra let out a shriek.

"Shh, darling," her mother reprimanded. "Young ladies don't scream."

As a multitude of people embarked, Muse felt a nudge at the small of her back. Jonathan was standing behind her.

"Enjoy yourself," he whispered. "I'll be looking forward to your return."

She moved closer to the on-ramp. Just a few steps more, then up the plank she ran, trailing her owners. She never looked back. Save for her mother, she would not miss Der Brunnen that much after all.

AT SEA

As soon as the Hallisburgs settled into their cabins, Muse was ushered to different accommodations in the belly of the ship, three decks below. She would have taken her now-and-again place, sleeping on the floor at the foot of Miss Cassandra's bed, but the cabin was too small. For the next three weeks or more, she would reside in the steerage quarters.

Mr. Hallisburg tipped a porter to escort Muse down to her berth and to see her situated.

"She's illiterate," Mr. Hallisburg said.

Muse followed the porter down a series of stairs, struggling to keep pace as he sliced through and dodged passed throngs of passengers. The entire ship looked to be in a state of chaos. A lofty buzz of discourse emanated from swarms of passengers who rummaged around, looking for reserved cabins and misplaced baggage, and who exuded an excess of emotion from saying final goodbyes.

Within minutes, the porter delivered Muse to the steerage hall, shoved the ticket in her hand, and disappeared, leaving her to fend for herself. She read the ticket and then peered into the room; her stomach tightened.

The room was like a barn. Hundreds of people—men, women, children, old, young—milling about like cattle, vying for space. She hesitated, took a deep breath, and pressed forth across the room. Holding firm to her bag, she penetrated through the flock of passengers, never once making eye contact.

Rows of wooden berths, two tiers high, lined the back of the room. She immediately deciphered the layout: one side of accommodations for single women, the other side for single men, and the center reserved for families. Berths were limited, which left the majority to find a spot on the open floor or nestled up against the sidewalls. The travelers would eat, sleep, and congregate in the restricted area.

Having an assigned bed, Muse compared the numbers stamped on the bedposts with the ticket she held. Ah! A top bed. She threw her bag up first, gathered the tail of her dress, and then, using the small stepladder attached at the bottom of the bedpost, ascended, hoping for improved air circulation at the slightly higher altitude. But the ventilation remained the same: stifling and rank. She scanned the confined area, her eyes studying the people who fought or negotiated for space. It was mayhem. So many people of different origins and races speaking foreign languages or English so broken she understood not a word. Most of the travelers were white and poorly clothed, but soon she focused in on a small minority of people so different from anyone she had ever seen. Foreigners. Some with yellow-toned faces and slanted, exotic eyes; dark-skinned men, much darker than she, draped in long, white silk robes and wearing turbans, sitting on small rugs, smoking what looked like wooden pipes; a group of women with golden-brown complexions covered in bright-tinted veils revealing only anxious eyes and a curious reddish-brown tattoo, a small spot, planted square in the middle of their fore-heads. *What is it symbolic of?* she pondered.

Her stomach rumbled. The ship had yet to leave the dock, and already she feared herself unwell. In her satchel, she packed fresh fruit, bread, and two canteens of water. She pulled out a canteen and drank. Soon her stomach quieted down, as did she.

Shortly afterward, a tall, slim female figure, wearing a tat-tered brown cape with a huge hood covering most of her face, entered the quarters. She moved easily through the assemblage, confident and regal-like. She stopped short in front of Muse's row, checked her ticket, and then tossed her valise onto the lower bed. She unwrapped the cape and pulled the hood from her head. Tresses of long red hair fell around her shoulders. As she scooped her trailing locks and twisted them into a secured bun, she glanced up at Muse, released a half smile, and bounced onto the bed. Rummaging through her bag, she retrieved a book. Muse strained to read its title, but she couldn't make it out. She watched the young woman open the book and fling herself into its pages, oblivious to the pandemonium of her surroundings.

Then another woman of color entered: middle-aged, big-boned, her hair hidden beneath a white cloth, much like Muse's. The woman looked weary and out of breath as she made her way through the chaos, using her large straw bag almost as a weapon to nudge people out of the way. She stopped in front of the berths, panting, but gathered herself to ask for help.

The redhead approached her and said something. She read the woman's ticket and pointed to the top berth next to Muse. The woman frowned, as if to say that she could not take anoth-er step, let alone climb to a top berth. They continued to talk, but Muse could not hear them. The redhead pointed to both berths in a gesture that indicated they should switch. The wom-an smiled in agreement. The redhead grabbed her belongings and climbed up to the berth next to Muse. She looked at Muse again and nodded, but Muse averted her eyes.

━◁┼┼▷━

The first night at sea pacified Muse unexpectedly. She, who had never been on a ship, found the rocking rhythm of the waves soothing, as though bundled up in the arms of a comforting soul. Even within the dubious environment of the steerage quarters, among the whimpers and ills of passengers disrupted by the ship's motion, she closed her eyes and slept.

It seemed as though she had been walking for miles. The gravel road twisted and turned. The enticing bouquet of honeysuckle permeated the air. She stood in front of her small living quarters, opened the door, and stepped in. She felt the familiar raw earth beneath her feet; nothing had changed. The wooden cot with its mattress stuffed with horsehair hugged up against the wall in its rightful place. The one square-shaped window showcased its normal view overlooking the tobacco fields. The south wall and its loose wooden planks remained intact and secure as she left them. How many times had she disengaged the wood panels to sneak into the storage room? The small, three-tiered wooden dresser, with its cracked mirror and wobbly legs, stood in peace. She stared at the mirror and the diagonal fracture that sprawled from top to bottom. She was the only slave on the plantation with a mirror, thanks to Mistress Cassandra. She roamed around her room, touching her few possessions. Then suddenly she felt threatened. The shed trembled and shook; it took on an altered look of hardwood floors instead of raw earth, a huge bookcase lined with leather volumes appeared, blocking the wall and any way to steal into the storage room. The window, now protected with a sturdy, translucent glass pane, showed a vista much different from before. Instead of acres of tobacco fields, she witnessed a raging river, an ocean rushing through the old plantation, sweeping away everything in its path.

"Hey, wake up!"

Muse startled from her sleep.

"Hey. If you don't hurry, you'll miss breakfast."

Muse opened her eyes and then yawned. It took a second to focus; she rubbed her eyes and thought, *Where am I?* The face of the young woman with the red hair leaned over her.

"What's wrong?" Muse asked.

"Coffee!" the girl said.

Muse sat up and looked across the room. In the middle of it, spread around a huge wood beam that went straight up to the ceiling, pots of hot coffee and loaves of freshly baked bread awaited, compliments of the ship.

"Don't worry," the girl said. "I'll get you a cup."

The young woman climbed back down and returned with a chunk of fresh bread and a tin mug of coffee.

"Thank you," Muse said.

"You're welcome. There was no milk left."

"That's all right. I like it black."

Muse grew conscious of her curious gaze.

"Are you a slave?" she asked.

Muse reddened.

"Yes," she said. "I belong to the Hallisburgs."

"I'm a slave too."

"You are?"

Muse met the potent green eyes of the young woman, amazed, but then relinquished her gaze.

"I'm a domestic . . . a nanny. It's the same thing."

Muse smiled inwardly.

"No, it's not the same thing."

"Well, perhaps not. My name is Claire Price."

Muse hesitated. She was not used to talking to or making eye contact with white people other than the Hallisburgs. "Muse, look at me when I'm talking to you!" was all she ever heard from Cassandra and her mother and father. But with a little effort, she met Claire's eyes again and smiled.

"Hello. I'm called Muse."

"Muse! Is that your real name?"

Again disconcerted by the girl's bluntness, Muse paused . . . what was her real name? Had she forgotten it? She looked at Claire, embarrassed, as she racked her brain. Then she recalled it.

"My real name is Aggrey."

"Oh! That's pretty. Is it French?"

"No. My mother says it's an African name."

"What does it mean?"

"'Ancient bead,' I think."

"That's beautiful!

Muse took a sip of the coffee.

"Thank you. It's the name my mother gave me when I was born . . . but even she now calls me Muse."

"Why?"

"Because Muse is the name the Hallisburgs chose for me."

"Oh. How old are you?" Claire asked.

"Sixteen. And you?"

"Nineteen."

They smiled at each other.

"Muse is not a bad nickname, mind you," Claire said. "It actually means a source of inspiration, but it sounds so trite, don't you think? Aggrey, on the other hand, sounds regal. If you don't mind, I will call you Aggrey."

"All right."

Possessing no experience in making polite conversation with strangers, Muse summoned to mind Cassandra's skills when talking to unfamiliar people.

"Do you enjoy working as a nanny?"

"For heaven's sake, no! I do it because there's not much else I can do. I'm poor, no family, no husband. I got this job because I speak French. Do you speak French?"

Muse shook her head.

"No. But my mistress does. She's taught me some phrases."

"Like what?"

"*Bonjeur, madam e mesieur.* And . . . *mersey bou coupe.*"

"No. No. Your accent is horrible! Do not learn French from your mistress. Learn from someone of the native tongue. My mother was French."

"And your father?"

"Irish."

"Where are they now?"

"My mother died five years ago on the ship that brought us to New York. My father, well, he placed me in an orphanage and went out West in search of gold. I never heard from him again. He's probably dead too. So I've been on my own for a while."

"I never knew my father," Muse said.

"Was he also a slave?"

"Yes."

"Sorry."

"I'm sorry too."

"You speak well for a slave. How come?"

"I work in the main house. It's different than living in the slave quarters and working the fields."

"Oh! Well, you are lucky."

"Am I?" Muse asked.

"Yes, because you're going to a country where slavery is outlawed."

"I've heard people speak of it . . . is it true?"

"Absolutely! You could run. Emancipate yourself."

"I would never do that."

"Why not?"

"I just wouldn't, that's all."

———

After a few days at sea, Muse crept out of her shell. She and Claire struck up an amicable relationship, luring Muse to open up to companionship. Muse even found the courage to speak with the older woman on the bottom bunk.

"Hello, my name is Muse, uh, Aggrey . . . I mean Muse."

The woman frowned.

"Which is it?" she asked.

Muse laughed.

"My real name is Aggrey, but I'm called Muse."

"My name is Martinique."

"Nice to meet you."

"Who do you belong to?" Martinique asked.

"The Hallisburgs."

"Are they fair people?"

"I suppose. And you?" Muse asked. "Who do you belong to?"

"I don't belong to anyone . . . not anymore, thank God. I'm free. I've got my papers to prove it." She patted her breast, indicating the proof was safe and sound, lodged in the deep folds of her underbodice.

Muse's eyes widened.

"How did you do it?"

"I bought my freedom. It took years, but I did it. I worked off my price. I'm exhausted, but I did it."

"Really! And where are you going now?"

"Home."

"Where is that?"

"Haiti."

Muse looked perplexed.

"Then why are you going to France?"

"Because I no longer have family or friends in Haiti. But I have a friend in France. I've just enough money to get there. He will help me find work. I'll save money and then go back to Haiti. When I get there, I'll buy a small parcel of land and build a shack. I'm going to learn to read and write, and I intend to live out the rest of my days free and in peace, staring out at the sea."

The ship's steward lit the lanterns in the steerage quarters. A chain of lamps fixed on the walls came to light, one by one. The room, once murky and dim, illuminated. And all knew it was closer to dinnertime.

"What kind of work will you do in France?"

"Servant, maid . . . I don't care what it is. I speak French even though I have a dialect. But I can improve it. Whatever it takes to get me home."

"Why didn't you wait until you had enough money so you could go home without detour?" Muse asked.

"Because in New Orleans, where I lived, people with legal free papers are being recaptured and forced back onto the slave market. I know this to be true. I've seen it done." She paused. "I hate this country!"

Muse watched the rage seethe in Martinique's eyes.

"I spit on everyone who condones slavery. I wish a pox on them all. Who are they to treat people like cattle? I will never go back to being owned . . . never!"

Martinique's loathing and determination frightened Muse, yet her deep personal indignation was forcing her to think about her own existence differently. Why did she not sense that kind of fury?

They sat on the bottom bunk, chatting. How long had it been since she talked about her private feelings and opinions? Not since Mr. Müller, but now, even if only for a little while, there was Claire and Martinique—both women who lived and knew independent lives and had different perspectives about life. She unyoked her emotions more in the brief time aboard the ship than since Mr. Müller had left the plantation.

"Aggrey, what do you want to do with yourself?"

Muse shrugged.

"I'd like to buy myself and my mother free someday. But . . ."

"But what?"

"I don't know how to do it, or if I really want to do it. My mother doesn't . . . she's afraid. Even if we bought ourselves free or escaped, how would we manage? How would we live? We're completely dependent on the Hallisburgs."

"How would you live?" Martinique said. "You would work. You've a wealth of working skills you haven't yet realized. For God's sake, you're slave labor."

But Muse only half heard Martinique's response. Her eyes drifted elsewhere. A similar conversation with her mother had taken place only a few weeks before the journey.

—◁+▷—

The sweet potatoes had boiled for fifteen minutes. Muse remembered draining them carefully so as not to be scalded by the hot water. She removed the skins, chopped them, then mashed them until they were smooth.

"Is this all right, Mama?"

"Yeah, baby, that's good," Mary said.

In a bowl, Mary sifted together flour, baking powder, and nutmeg. To the bowl of sweet potatoes, Muse added eggs, milk, and butter. Mary blended both bowls together in a larger bowl to form the batter.

Mary dropped a large spoonful of the batter mixture onto the hot grill. Muse remembered the sound of sizzling batter and the fragrance of sweet potato and nutmeg pancakes penetrating throughout the kitchen.

"Mama."

"What?"

"Have you ever thought of running away?"

"Oh, hush! Don't even say such a thing."

"But, Mama, have you?"

Mary looked at her daughter with sadness in her eyes:

"One time . . . the time they took yo' father . . . sold him. I thought about it. I was so outta my mind with grief that I couldn't think straight. I wanted to run so bad. But shortly after dey took him, I was sold to the Hallisburgs. Thank God I didn't run because I found out you were growing in my belly."

"But what about now?"

"It would be foolish. I'm too old . . . and where would we go? Who would take care of us?"

"We would take care of ourselves," Muse said.

"No, baby . . . no! It's too late for me. We belong to the Hallisburgs—body, mind, and soul. That's the way it is. Anyway, what dey do to runaway slaves deese days, if dey is caught, it's horrible. I knowed a runaway once . . . a woman. The overseer caught her, stripped her naked, and bullwhipped her till she passed out. I knowed her. Her name was Baethsheba. Some months later I saw her in town . . . we spoke. She told me she tried to run and what dey did to her after she was caught. She say her back was cut up bad. She looked at me so peculiar-like. 'Mary,' she say. 'Why didn't God just let me die? Does he hate us so much that we gotta live like this . . . like animals? It ain't right. Why didn't he just let me die?'"

Muse looked at her mother in dismay.

"I know you is afraid of that Jonathan boy, but if we was on the run, you would be much more afraid . . . looking over yo' shoulders every two minutes. Believe me, the consequences is too high."

"Mama, why can't we buy ourselves free?"

Mary rolled her eyes at her daughter.

"What's gotten into you? Where you get deese ideas? To buy us free, we would have to get permission from the Hallisburgs . . . and you know what dey gon' say. But even if dey did say yes, den we would have to find paying work outside the plantation. Now, baby, as much as I love you, I can't hardly take care of the Hallisburgs, you, and some other *burgs* . . . I don't have the energy. It would just kill me. You understand?"

"Yes, Mama. But suppose if one of us has the opportunity to buy us both free?"

Mary dropped the last spoonful of batter onto the grill. She sighed as she flipped over each pancake.

"Muse, if you get the opportunity to go, then run. But I can't come wit' you."

"Why, Mama? Can't you imagine being a free person . . . to do what you want, when you want?"

"No, I can't. I know it ain't right, but I can't see other than what is. The next place I want to travel to is the heavens. I'm tired, baby. I'm old now, and there ain't no freedom for the old, no matter where you go."

Muse's attention stumbled back to what Martinique was saying.

"The Hallisburgs aren't so bad," Muse said. "They treat me and my mother well enough. We have our own rooms."

Muse caught the look of pity Martinique shot toward her.

"I was enraged every moment of every day I was owned by another person. Maybe it's different for you. I mean . . . you were born into captivity; you know nothing else. I was not. I was forced into it. Maybe that's the difference. But still, it ain't right you should seem so content. You were born to be free. It is God's gift to you. It was taken from you." She paused. "Take it back!"

Martinique's alarming words chilled Muse.

"I hear you," Muse said. "But, I don't know how to . . . I mean . . . in my head, I can only see freedom as an unreachable dream, like trying to hold on to mist."

"It's reachable! But, Aggrey, you'll never know or understand liberty until you've tasted it, even if it's for a moment. If you ever drink from that well, you will never rest again. To be your own person, to be who you really are . . . it takes courage, the kind of courage many people are prepared to die for."

"Die for!" echoed Muse.

"My dear Aggrey, don't you realize that living as someone's property, you have—with all due respect—no life at all; you're dead already. If you get the chance, take it!"

"Yes, I understand."

A bell pealed, long, loud tones alerting the wealthy passengers up top that it was dinnertime.

"Oh! I've got to go and see to the Hallisburgs. I should have been up there a while ago. I'll talk with you later."

Muse climbed up onto her bed, grabbed her satchel, and ran out of steerage, her mind in turmoil from talking with Martinique.

＝≼┼┼≽＝

Each morning, Muse reported to the Hallisburgs to carry out daily chores, as did most of the servants traveling with their employers. Because the first-class passengers had access to cabin stewards and a few staff valets, her duties were minimal. She continued, however, to keep the small cabins tidy, set out clothes for the day and eveningwear, dress and coiffure the Hallisburg women, and perform various personal errands as directed. After taking her afternoon meals alone in the cabin, she did laundry. A small corner of the ship provided space for that task. Servants and slaves alike assembled at the spot almost daily. Muse often met Claire there. They chatted as they washed the delicate apparel of their superiors and, for Claire, the undergarments of her two young wards.

"What I wouldn't give for a hot bath," Claire said.

"Me too," Muse replied as she wrung out her mistress's soft white bloomers. "Or just a warm bucket of water to douse over me."

"Yes. That would be nice."

Even for the wealthy on board, hot baths rarely happened. The most common option was a basin and a pitcher of warm seawater. A discouraging rumor circulated—discouraging for the women, that is. It reported that men had an option to take showers.

"But how?" Muse asked.

"Well," Claire said, "I heard when the cleaning crew comes to wash down the deck, male passengers show up wearing nothing but robes, tipping the crew to spray them down with a water hose."

"Ha! Really?"

The uncharacteristic outburst of hearing her own genuine laughter startled her. She put her hand over her mouth to stifle the cackling. But from her peripheral vision, she saw odious looks flung toward her from nearby passengers. She heard murmurs: "The little *negra*—too loud!"

She froze, reclaimed her composure, her humility . . . her place.

"Ignore them, Aggrey," Claire said.

Muse smiled half-heartedly but continued washing in silence.

⊷⊢⊷

One night, just before dawn, Claire shook Muse from her sleep.

"What . . . what is it?" Muse mumbled.

"I can't stand it anymore. I'm itching; I'm scratching. I smell like an animal . . . I have to wash."

"But how?" Muse asked.

"Come with me," Claire directed.

Muse rose, wiping the sleep from her eyes.

"Where are we going?"

"Come," Claire urged.

Everyone in steerage appeared to be asleep. The two girls climbed down from their bunks, stepped cautiously over the people lying on the floor, and crept out of the lodgings.

"I've been searching all over the ship, looking for that hose and barrel of water. I found it."

"Oh! Claire, we shouldn't."

"Don't be afraid. This time of night, the captain and most of the crew are asleep. The others are down in the boiler room, and there's a few on the bridge. I've checked."

Claire grabbed Muse's hand.

"Shh!"

They crept along the deck to a small storage compartment at the extreme end of the ship. Claire twisted the knob of the door.

"If we get caught . . ." Muse said.

"Well, at least we'll be clean," Claire replied.

"Ha!"

"Shh!"

Claire opened the door and showed Muse the huge barrel of seawater with a hose attached. Buckets, rags, and mops leaned against the wall. She unraveled the hose. Brown eyes gazed wickedly at green eyes; they laughed.

Muse unfastened the top two buttons of her dress, then stalled. What was she doing? She looked at Claire.

"Don't be afraid," Claire said.

But Muse had trepidation. She was on the deck of a ship in the dead of night with a white girl she didn't even know, stripping down to her essence to bathe. Never had she taken such liberties. So deep in forbidden territory, her behavior so out of character, she hardly recognized herself.

But she had taken chances before—those times when her spirit could no longer remain repressed or when her body longed for stimulation. More than once, guided by the full moon's light, did she sneak down to the old creek-fed pond when the plantation was dark and all asleep and, without a second thought, remove her clothing and jump unabashedly into the pool for a swim, unhampered and unnoticed. This time the fear was different, deeper. It was not about the Hallisburgs or the punishment that would follow if caught, something she could not yet break free of. In her mind's eye, she again recounted the horror of Jonathan's attack.

"Are you sure no men are around?" she asked Claire.

"I'm sure."

Muse took a deep breath.

"Then I'm not afraid."

Each girl glanced about and then stripped, dropping their stale dresses onto the damp deck. They removed petticoats and bloomers and various other undergarments, helping each other to unlace or unfasten.

Two nudes, front to front, shivered in the chilly air: one, a shapely figure as smooth and bright as a summer's day; the other, equally cast with alluring contours, fresh and supple, as raven as a winter's eve.

"Hurry, Claire," Muse said, shivering. Her one arm wrapped around her bare breasts, the other covering her modesty. "Unleash the water."

Claire stared at Aggrey's body.

"What?"

"Nothing. I've never seen a dark-skinned person naked."

"C'mon, Claire, it's cold!"

"Wait!" Claire said. "I almost forgot."

She reached into the pocket of her crumpled dress and pulled out a small cloth pouch.

"What is it?"

"Perfumed soap," Claire offered. "And look what I pinched from a stateroom."

"You stole it?"

"Shush! No one will miss it."

Claire hid a clean, fluffy towel in the storage room.

"A towel," Muse said.

Muse looked at Claire.

"I've never met a white person like you," she said. "You're different."

"Am I?"

"You treat me as if I was just another person . . . as if my skin color makes no difference to you at all. Why is that?"

"I don't know . . . I just don't think that way. Anyway, there is no law that says a white person can't befriend a colored person, is there?"

"There is in Virginia."

Claire shrugged.

"I'm not from Virginia."

Claire continued to unravel the hose.

Are you ready?" Claire asked.

"Yes. I'm ready."

Claire turned on the hose. A vigorous stream of seawater flushed forth, drenching their bodies. They tried to smother the screams and giggles brought on by the cool moisture. Soon the temperature of the brisk flow stabilized, seeming lukewarm compared to the chill of the night. They lathered up between gales of whispered laughter while the scent of lavender floated around them.

⟩⟨⟩

Muse overslept. She mounted the stairs, taking two steps at a time until she reached the hallway that led to the first-class cabins. She was anxious that morning not only because she was late but because of her mistress's emotional state.

Cassandra had suffered a humiliating experience at dinner and spent the rest of evening in tears while Muse comforted her. She explained, as she wept, how she had overheard two young men commenting about and debating over the attractiveness of the young women on board. She sat with her parents at a table near the bar. From her seat, she only saw the men from the back and admired their dashing figures. Her parents were busy giving their meal orders to the garçon. Amused by the young men as they chatted, she listened.

Then one of them said, "The Hallisburg filly could be promising if she'd lose weight and clear up that awful complexion of hers. Even with her money, she wouldn't tempt me."

Cassandra was devastated.

Muse paused long enough to straighten out her apron and readjust her headwrap. She walked along the hallway, dodging a handful of passengers scurrying around early in the morning. By the time she approached Mistress Cassandra's cabin, her walk had diminished to a slow tiptoe. She stood in front of the door for a moment and pressed her ear against it. All seemed silent. She turned the handle of the door and pushed it open. The room was still dark, save for a stream of morning light that poured through the two portholes. She eased inside. There was a tiny flicker of light coming from burning coal in the small iron stove. She heard her mistress breathing, a low, rhythmic, guttural sound.

Then she stopped short. Cassandra's cabin was in a state of disarray. Dresses, petticoats, hats, and shoes were scattered around the room, as if she had been trying to decide what to wear but could not settle. Muse sighed, looking at the mess left for her to put back in order. What happened? When she left her mistress last night, Cassandra had cried herself to sleep and at last was silent. She shook her head. Mrs. Hallisburg explicitly told Mistress Cassandra she could wear only two dresses during the trip. The other ensembles were to remain packed and untouched until they arrived in France. Muse set about picking up the discarded clothes one by one and putting them back into their rightful places. A few dresses she hung on the hooks jutting from the wall. Other pieces she folded and placed back into the trunks. She worked, unaware of an inner voice tugging at her spirit: "I don't want to live like this anymore!"

As she worked, she thought of last night and how good it felt to rinse the grime and odor from her body. She reminisced about letting go of her inhibition and, for a few minutes, experiencing the thrill of abandonment to her own free will.

"Good morning, Muse."

Muse startled at the sound of Cassandra's voice. She turned toward her mistress.

"Good morning, Miss Cassandra."

Cassandra was sitting up in bed. Dangling locks veiled most of her face. Her arms elongated as if reaching for the sky, her mouth wide open as she let out a woeful yawn. A musty, perfumed order emanated from across the room.

"I am so sick of waking up at sea. Will this journey ever end?"

"Yes, Miss Cassandra. Two weeks more," offered Muse as she moved about the room, arranging and rearranging clothes.

"Two weeks more is a lifetime."

"Do you want me to have breakfast sent?"

"No. I'm eating with Mommy and Daddy in the saloon this morning."

Muse nodded.

"What happened in here?" Muse asked as she gestured to the garments on the floor.

"I couldn't sleep. I was pretending to dress for a summer's ball in Paris."

"Oh!"

"I can't wait to go shopping in Paris!"

Muse smiled despite a tinge of envy.

"Did you want to wear the burgundy day dress this morning?"

"Yes."

Muse was reaching for the burgundy one when she sensed her mistress's glare.

"Is there something wrong, Miss Cassandra?"

"Have you been in my perfume?"

"Of course not, ma'am!"

"Then why do you reek of scent?"

"Oh! I can explain . . ."

She was dressed in a fresh uniform with a spotless headpiece, and her skin glowed, the aftermath of a good scrub. Cassandra jumped out of bed and stumbled on the hem of her long nightgown.

Muse instinctively reached out to stabilize her mistress.

"Don't touch me," she yelled, pushing Muse's hand away. "Have you bathed?"

"No, Miss Cassandra."

"You smell clean . . . of lavender."

"No. I mean yes . . . I had a washup. You see, my bunkmate lent me a bar of soap, and—" She stopped cold. The anger was building in Cassandra's eyes. She had said too much. And before she could brace herself, Cassandra struck her across the face. Muse staggered backward, her hand smothering the pain of an inflamed jaw.

"Bunkmate? Soap? What are you talking about?"

Cassandra paused as if to catch her breath.

"Since when does the steerage quarter have more amenities than the staterooms?"

"No, Miss Cassandra. It's not that way at all."

"Well, we'll just see."

Muse knew Cassandra was still in agony over what happened at dinner. But also, she had been suffering since setting sail, on edge and claustrophobic. Within the first few days out at sea, she grew ill. The rolling motion of the ship did not sit well with her, and the stench of the sea air kept her queasy. She had nothing close to the pampering privileges she experienced on dry land. And no matter how much she sponge-bathed and drenched herself in perfume . . .

"I still stink!" she yelled.

Muse stood facing her mistress, wiping tears from her eyes. What was she thinking? She pranced into work as fresh as a new spring morning while her mistress smelled like a goat! Did she expect no consequence?

"How dare you! Slim-figured and perfect complexion. I hate you! You should be the one who is fat and made ugly by scars on your face. You are of no importance. You will never have to find a husband or even have a life . . . what a waste. God is so unfair. Get out!" Cassandra shouted. "And don't show your face for the rest of the day."

Muse ran out, down the stairs to the steerage quarters. She climbed to the top of her bunk and wept silently. Her suppressed sobs, however, did not go unnoticed.

"Child, come down," Martinique said. "Do you want to talk?"

Muse shook her head.

"Well, come down anyway. You could use a hug."

⟩⟨⟩⟨⟩

The first thing the next morning, Muse received word from Mrs. Hallisburg to gather her belongings and move into Cassandra's cabin. She would spend the rest of the voyage sleeping on the floor at the foot of her mistress's bed.

⟩⟨⟩⟨⟩

The closeness of the cabin space strangled Muse, no different than if someone was pressing their fingers around her throat. She struggled to breathe—so much so that whenever she found the chance, she stole away. She walked aimlessly around the deck. Anything to get away from the constant prattle of her mistress, the annoying bird-pitched tone of her voice, the complaints, the criticisms, all day and most of the night.

During the last days of the journey, most passengers had grown weary of the sea, the cold, and ventured less frequently from the coziness of their cabins. The decks remained virtually empty. When Muse managed an escape, she slipped across the deck toward a secluded area near an arched entryway. She sat, nestled in the folds of a tatty old shawl, and stared out at sea. The fresh air and the rolling sounds of the waves crashing against the ship mesmerized her.

Muse turned the mini-escapes from Cassandra into an art form as her friendship with Claire and Martinique blossomed. The excursions lasted only half an hour, and no matter what time of the day the Hallisburgs returned to their rooms, she was puttering about, looking busy. During her crafty jaunts, she would slip into steerage for a quick word with Martinique; other times, she and Claire caught up while they did laundry. But on the last day of laundry, Claire was a no-show. Muse considered one last trip back to the steerage room to bid them both farewell but thought better of it. The Hallisburgs had changed their routine now that the trip was ending. So little time to herself. She would not chance it, as she was in enough trouble already.

The next morning, Muse and Cassandra awoke to the sound of a man's voice yelling at the top of his lungs, "Land ahoy!"

FRANCE

Disembarking proved more chaotic than embarking. Even Mr. Hallisburg, the only one in the family skilled enough in French to manage the business of customs, soon grew frustrated with his own endeavors. He had to repeat himself twice to be understood, and he was constantly asking whoever was speaking to speak slower, "*S'il vous plaît.*" While Mr. Hallisburg struggled with language, sorting out papers and the lot, Mrs. Hallisburg, Cassandra, and Muse stood on the platform before a pile of family luggage. The intentions of traveling light had failed. The sorting, counting, and recounting of dozens of bags proved nerve-racking. Pieces went missing, and damage occurred on one of the larger trunks. While they labored to retrieve boxes and valises and complain to officials of baggage mutilations, Muse kept a peeled eye out for Claire and Martinique, but neither materialized. Her heart saddened.

At first glance, the port of Le Havre appeared bleak—cold, damp, and fog so thick it looked as if covered by a garish, smoky veil. Muse discerned none of the vibrant colors and warmth that coated the canvas of Virginia, and she felt once more the pang of wanting to go home. Would she hate this strange land called France?

It was the month of May, yet the climate felt the same as March in Virginia. Under her dress, she wore one of Cassandra's cast-off petticoats, and over her uniform, a thick, hooded woolen cloak of indigo blue. The expensive-looking garment was not intended as adornment; its sole purpose to ward off the cold for Muse until the entourage reached Paris. The indigo was designed for Cassandra in hopes the exotic color would offset her deep-blue eyes. But to her mother's dismay, the cape served only to whey-face her daughter's complexion and make more noticeable the pockmarks. So the wrap was handed down to Muse, who gratefully nestled deep within the folds of the quality wool. The rich-colored cape complemented the dark hues of her skin tone as much as it failed to for Cassandra. Muse raised the hood of the cloak over her usual cloth headgear; the garment framed her face in such a way as to accentuate her gazelle-like features. More than one man on the French docks caught sight of the brown-skinned girl busying herself with baggage. Some stared at her with curious, lingering gazes; others watched her with a twinkle in their eyes and indulged in lurid fantasies. But Muse labored on, absorbed in her task and oblivious to the heads she had turned.

<hr />

A hired coach awaited the Hallisburgs. The family wearily piled into the vehicle. Muse climbed atop to ride with the coachman and guard the luggage secured on the coach's roof. The journey to Paris would consume a few days. The carriage moved at a swift pace, but the layout of the great country road was primitive, making for a coarse, unsteady ride. The family tossed and joggled inside the cab, as did Muse up top, holding steadfast to the roof's safety handles. But after little more than a mile of travel, Mr. Hallisburg ordered Muse to come down from the roof and into the carriage for fear she would topple off.

As required, the travelers made regulated stops at designated inns. At some taverns, they stopped only to eat and refresh the horses; at others, they dined and slept. The first overnight evening at an inn, the Hallisburgs ordered hot baths, and after revitalizing themselves, they dined ravenously on the local food. Muse bathed also, but as was the custom, she washed in what was left of Cassandra's bath. She grimaced at the murky, lukewarm water and thought of the French word Claire pronounced for "dirty": *sale.*

After her bath, she heard a timid knock at the door. She dressed in a hurry and answered. In the hallway stood a sallow-skinned, marshmallow-eyed child, ten or eleven years old, with two dreary brown braids drooping from both sides of her head. She held a tray of food. The child looked petrified as she stood before Muse. The tray rattled.

"*Bonsoir,*" Muse said.

"*Vous-est noire!*" the terrified girl mumbled.

Muse noticed her alarm and rescued the tray.

"*Oui.*"

"*Excusez-moi,* mademoiselle," the child said, then curtsied and ran off.

I've frightened her! Muse thought. *She's never seen a colored person before.*

Muse closed the door, put the tray on a side table, and sat. Upset by the child's disparaging behavior, her appetite vanished. She wondered if everyone in the country would react to her in the same way. At home, she was hated because of the color of her skin; now, would she be feared because of it? She pushed the tray away. But in doing so, the white serviette covering the food slipped to the floor. The aroma enticed her: *poulet roti*, steamed seasoned vegetables, pureed potatoes and a small decanter of red wine. A whiff of the herb-scented chicken restored Muse's hunger almost at once. Unquestionably, she thought her mother the best cook in the world, but nothing prepared her for the savory taste of the supposedly ordinary local fare. She was somewhat familiar with red wine, having occasionally pirated leftover decanters after a Hallisburg formal dinner, and the regional blend at hand tasted intense, yet smooth and refreshing. It sent a glow throughout her beleaguered body. She sliced through the chicken, marveling at how easily the meat separated from the bone. She ate heartily until nothing was left except one last sip of wine.

The clock in the hallway struck six; it was still light. Muse surmised the Hallisburgs would retire no earlier than nine o'clock. From the window, the view of a dense but grassy forest beckoned. She put on the cloak and, without a sound, slunk out the back entrance of the inn.

With every brisk step, her land legs returned. She rambled along a narrow pathway all but hidden by a myriad of ancient trees; she peeled off pieces of bark and inhaled their musky, sweet perfume. Flowers bloomed everywhere—in colors of yellow, violet, and red, so vivid and alive. She kicked rocks, jumped over logs, and skipped along the rough, twisting path as if still a child.

After a while, she heard the rippling song of water. She pushed through the thicket and stopped short, in awe of a flowing brook. A large tree had fallen across the stream. She fancied striding athwart the narrow trunk to the other side . . . to liberty, she pretended—but liberty from what, and to what? She gradually felt pensive about her mother and how she fared, wondered if Claire and Martinique made it safely to their final destinations. Especially Martinique . . . Martinique, who planted a seed in her brain, an unnerving germ that caused her to think about the meaning of freedom in a way she dared not think of it before.

Lifting her skirt, she stepped onto the log, one foot in front of the other, her arms spread wide out like wings. She strode carefully but made it only a few feet before teetering. She jumped back onto solid ground. *What does it feel like to be a free human being?* That was the question.

The landscape was vastly different from that of Virginia's, and it had changed for the better since leaving the port, decided Muse—lush, more appealing than first imagined. Not wanting to seem disloyal to her homeland, she mindfully considered the French countryside beautiful in its own right, no better and no worse, just a different kind of charm. As she gazed around the woods, she intuitively experienced a stronger sense of self emerging, as if a decidedly different being was trying to push forth, one with new depths of thought and observation. Was it the wine? She snickered and then froze. Ears alert, her eyes canvassed the landscape. A stir in the brush, the sound of sheep bleating, then before her stood a small boy.

Mousy brown hair and a colorless freckled face peeked out from under a shabby cloth cap. His trousers and jacket hung loosely on his frame, tattered and sullied down to his worn-out wooden clogs. He held on to a long wooden staff, curved at the top like a question mark. The boy stared at Muse in much the same awful way as did the servant girl at the inn. She faced him, letting her hood fall back. Having forgotten her headpiece, her braids, now longer, dangled to the nape of her neck. She offered him a smile.

"*Bonsoir,*" she said.

The boy took off his cap and responded hesitantly, "*Bonsoir,* mademoiselle."

An ill-at-ease silence passed between them as they stared at each other. In the distance, the sheep came into view. The boy said something in French. Muse did not understand. She searched to remember another phrase Claire taught her.

"*Je ne parle pas Français*," she said.

"Ah!" acknowledged the boy. Silence fell again. And then, pointing to her, the boy said, "*Africaine?*"

Muse almost answered yes, but then shook her head.

"No. *Americaine*," she said.

He pointed to his chest.

"Jean-Luc."

Muse mimicked the same gesture and said, "Aggrey."

They smiled at each other.

PARIS

The Hallisburg entourage had dozed off, but all knew the moment they crossed into the city limits of Paris. The sound of hooves altered from rhythmic thuds to high-pitched clip-clops, caused by the obdurate strength of the cobblestone streets. Muse peered out of the carriage window, trying to digest the many sights and sounds offered by the foreign town. They drove along avenues and boulevards for another hour, and then the coach stopped. It parked on a narrow street in front of a huge wooden arched door. Muse gaped up at the massive entryway and the enormous figure carved above it. A large horse with vast wings and piercing eyes looked down upon them. Two lanterns, beaming with full light, hung on each side of the equine, and at its feet lay a sheathed sword with the words *La Lumière* written across it. Muse looked up at the form with starry-eyed wonder, thinking, *A horse that can fly!*

LA LUMIÈRE

La Lumière situated itself on boulevard de Longchamp, a
pleasant street near a small wood. The Hallisburgs entered
through the massive arched doors, guarded by the winged
horse and his lanterns. They met with an attractive brick-paved
courtyard, which led to the entrance of the home. A discreet,
two-story, seventeenth-century classical manor, as noted by Mr.
Hallisburg, fixed neatly between a sizable, well-manicured garden, welcomed its guests.

The Hallisburgs followed a footman up to their private quarters. Although the rooms were not large by plantation standards,
the chambers were well furnished. The Hallisburgs scanned the
room.

"My dear," Mrs. Hallisburg said to her husband, "we will do
very well here, I believe."

"Yes, dear, I think you're right."

If the interior and fittings of the chambers impressed the
elder Hallisburgs, Cassandra was beside herself. Set up in a

chamber scattered with antiques, artwork, and a lush tapestry, she raved.

"Oh! Everything is so beautiful."

"Yes, Miss Cassandra, everything is so beautiful."

"Muse," she said. "You go to bed. There is nothing for you to do tonight. Monsieur Furet has arranged for servants to help us undress and acclimate ourselves. There is dinner waiting for you in your room. We'll unpack in the morning. Wake us early, so we can dress and organize ourselves."

"Yes, Miss Cassandra."

Muse followed a maid, who maneuvered her through long, handsome corridors lined with paintings and portraits framed in gold. Her eyes widened at the sumptuousness of the hallways. The furniture appeared so polished and elegant, displaying the most delicate of bric-a-brac that she found herself conserving her stride so as not to bump into anything. They exited the house and ventured across the garden and upstairs to the servant's quarters, located atop the carriage house at the rear of the property. The maid, a tight-lipped, cold-mannered person, led her to a room: a small but quaint space with a large window overlooking the roses. In awe of her new surroundings, she turned to the maid and said, "*Merci.*"

But the maid made no response. She stared at Muse, smirked, and then left without a word.

Muse closed the door and turned to observe the room. It had solid wood floors, a small rug, and an armoire with a full-length mirror on its door, a mirror with no cracks or scratches. A covered tray of food rested on a small table by the window, its aroma stirring her appetite. Was she to spend the next year in such a pleasant room?

After eating, she unpacked, took off her traveling clothes, and set them aside to be washed. At the pottery washbasin, filled with fresh water, she sponged down her face and her torso. She put on a nightshirt, slid into bed, and sank into a mattress of soft feathers. White cotton sheets and a thick duvet covered her . . . a far cry from the floor at the foot of Cassandra's bed.

At the prime of morning, Muse awoke to the twitter of birds coming from the garden. She gazed out the window. Framed by the morning sunlight, La Lumière appeared even more splendid. On the other side of the stone walls that enclosed the property, she heard the traffic noise of horse carriages trotting up and down the boulevard.

"Paris," she whispered.

Muse washed, put on a clean uniform, and left the room. Along the corridor she walked, hoping for the chance to greet the other servants, but there was no one about. She made her way down the stairs and across the garden, where she stopped to gaze at a bed of roses. The garden: neatly shaped topiaries and patterned hedges gave the garden path a mazelike effect. She lowered over a cluster of blooms to take in their sweet fragrance. But her peripheral vision caught sight of someone watching her through a curtain from an upstairs window. She looked up just as the curtain closed. *This is not Der Brunnen,* she reminded herself, and she hurried into the house through the servant's entrance. In the kitchen, she found Monsieur and Madame Laurent.

Muse learned that Madame Laurent, along with her husband, Serge, supervised the running of La Lumière. She was introduced to Madame Brisac, a nurse who aided the ailing Monsieur Furet, the owner of La Lumière, and Agnès Dumontet, the head maid who escorted her to her room.

"*Bonjour,*" Muse said.

"*Bonjour,* mademoiselle," they replied.

No one spoke English. Madame Laurent motioned for her to sit—a first, for she never sat in the company of whites, let alone dined with them. Once she relaxed, she tried to communicate. In slow, broken French, she asked the proper name for each item on the table: plate, *une assiette*; napkin, *une serviette*; coffee, *un café* . . .

"Oh! Mademoiselle Muse," Madame Laurent said. "*Vous apprenez vite.*"

Muse only understood the word *vite*, meaning "fast," and responded with a confident "*Merci.*"

MADAME NÉVILLE

On the second morning, Muse woke fully rested, bursting with energy and optimism. Today she would meet with the infamous Madame Néville, the tutor hired to transform Cassandra from a pockmarked plantation girl into a debutante of grace, charm, and international sensibilities. She would train Muse as her lady's maid. Muse accompanied the Hallisburgs abroad to prepare as servant *à la mode Français* to support Cassandra. The more Muse considered what opportunities might await her with such finely honed skills, the more she wanted to learn. The new discipline could lead her and her mother out of bondage.

She quickened to the kitchen, took one sip of coffee, and made her way up the servant's stairwell to the Hallisburgs' chambers. She knocked and waited for permission to enter.

"*Entrée,*" Mrs. Hallisburg said.

When Muse entered the room, everyone fell silent. She curtsied and acknowledged Mrs. Hallisburg and Cassandra, who were seated on a canapé near the fireplace. Mr. Hallisburg stood near the window, sipping coffee from a small cup, *demitasse*. On one of the upholstered fauteuils sat an elegant woman, audacious and intense. She wore a stylish two-piece outfit of lightweight linen, navy. The fitted jacket was finely designed and did well in controlling the vacillating figure of a woman of advanced age. Her matching hoop skirt, while less extravagant than those of Cassandra and Mrs. Hallisburg, was far better tailored. But Muse's fascination was with the headwear she wore, a turban made of the same fabric as the ensemble but with an added accessory: a feather pinned on with a brooch. Muse smiled inwardly. The word that came to mind was *chic*, an expression she learned from Claire. Muse curtsied to the madame.

"This is Muse," Mrs. Hallisburg said.

"*Bonjour*, Madame," Muse said.

"*Bonjour*, mademoiselle."

"Do you think you can do anything with her, Madame?" Mrs. Hallisburg asked.

Muse stood silent. She felt the eyes of the Madame Néville appraising her from top to bottom. She looked to Cassandra for instructions, but none came. The silence grew awkward.

"Mademoiselle Muse, will you please walk back and forth across the room," Madame Néville said in French.

Madame's rapid French threw Muse off; she conveyed a vacant look toward Mr. Hallisburg, prompting him to repeat the instructions in English. Muse moved back and forth across the room as she was told.

"Would you please take off your headwrap?" Madame Néville asked in English.

Muse obliged. When she removed the cloth from her head, half a dozen ill-managed braids fell to the nape of her neck.

Madame Néville let out an exasperated sigh.

"The problem is grave, Mrs. Hallisburg," Madame Néville said. "I don't know how I can be of service."

"Excuse me, Madame?" Mrs. Hallisburg responded.

"Might mademoiselle sit with us as we discuss the challenges?"

"She's fine standing."

"Very well. Mrs. Hallisburg, the fact is this . . . many times, a lady's maid is trained to be better poised, better informed, and better educated than her own mistress. She needs to know what is going on in society, how her mistress is to be presented, to be cared for, long before the mistress knows herself. I ask you, how is that to be done if the person in question cannot even read or write? I mean . . . what can we do? It's really impossible."

"Madame, please, we need your help," Mr. Hallisburg said.

"Well," Madame Néville said, "her figure is svelte, a nice face, but her posture is awful. She walks like she is plowing through an open field.

How absurd! thought Muse. *I trample through fields every day of the week; how else would I walk?*

"She would need deportment lessons befitting her station. Her hair is simply outrageous . . . she must be groomed, mani-cured, and polished. Is she efficient at following instructions?"

"Very much so," Cassandra said.

"A diligent worker?"

"Absolutely!"

Madame paused.

"*Oui,* I can do something with her."

Muse stood silent, controlling the anger she felt revving up inside her. The way they spoke of her, as if an object, an invisible, a nonperson. She should be used to it by now, she thought, yet it still tore at her. If she could but rise and declare her literacy, affirm how intelligent she was. But instead, she lowered her eyes, pursed her lips, and tried to tune out the malignant thoughts pounding in her head. In her efforts to suppress her emotions, she sneezed, but she quickly covered her mouth.

"Are you all right? Mrs. Hallisburg snapped. "You're not com-ing down with anything, are you?"

"No, Mrs. . . . I mean . . . Madame Hallisburg."

"Well, don't. We've only just gotten here. We've got a lot of work to do."

"Mama, she's fine," Cassandra said. "She's adjusting to the climate change, that's all."

"The problem is this, Madame Néville," Mr. Hallisburg interrupted. "You understand our culture, the American South, has strict and inflexible rules on educating slaves. It goes against the very membrane of our institution. It cannot be otherwise."

"*Oui*, monsieur. It is your way of life . . . your culture . . . I understand, but still . . ."

"Our prime concern is to improve our daughter's abilities so that she may make a suitable match among refined society. Muse was brought up to serve our daughter, and she will continue to do so as long as she is owned by our family. If Cassandra were to have an educated maid, it would greatly reduce her standing in refined society once we return to Virginia. And it would certainly go against the laws of our state. You are the best tutor in Europe for this sort of thing, your credentials are impeccable, and we are sure there is some way to work around this minor impediment."

"Madame Néville," Cassandra said. "It is true—Muse is ignorant in many ways—but she is talented in others."

"How so?"

"She learns extremely fast; she is thorough, dedicated, loyal, and obedient."

Like a trained pet, Muse reflected.

"We've never had trouble with her . . ."

The elder Hallisburgs' eyes met briefly, both reminded of their son's misconduct.

"She has talents—"

"Ah!" interrupted Madame Néville, turning to Muse. "What talents are these?"

Muse went blank. She couldn't think of anything to say on her behalf; finally, she said, "I have a good hand for embroidering, sewing . . ."

Madame Néville, unimpressed by the remark, shrugged her shoulders.

"Everybody can sew, *ma petite.*"

"Yes," Cassandra said, "but Muse can replicate a dress just by looking at a picture of it. She made me a gorgeous blue dress copied from an image in a fashion magazine . . . I loved it so much I wore it on the ship over."

Madame Néville shrugged again.

Mrs. Hallisburg's eyes narrowed in on her daughter's as if to say, "Close your mouth, sweetheart." Cassandra blushed slightly and went quiet.

"What else?"

"Cooking," Cassandra ventured timidly. "Her mother is our chief cook."

"Ah," Madame Néville said. "But these are not talents. She is a slave; these are duties—and unremarkable ones, I might add."

"What we would like," Mrs. Hallisburg began in a conciliatory tone, "is that with your help, Muse might be able to perfect and Europeanize her domestic organizational skills and bring them back to America."

"Well, yes, yes. I can have her exposed to a few people who might help her to advance in those areas *à la mode Française.* But it will take more than that to groom her for a lady's maid."

"Madame," Cassandra interjected, "if Muse has been able to accomplish what she has already achieved, like speaking English well, keeping me ordered and properly groomed, and cooking, sewing, and so forth without the aid of a proper education, what would prevent her from doing the same thing when learning the finer points of the European style? I mean, as I learn and develop, so will she."

Muse moved from the center of the room closer to the coffee service, where she poured out fresh cups for all present. She floated the tray around the room until all were refreshed, then returned the tray and remained beside the coffee service and listened while the Hallisburgs and Madame Néville mapped out her future.

"There are some concerns," Madame said. "For example, how would Mademoiselle Muse handle your mail, your invitations?

"We do expect to employ, at a later date, a social secretary," Mrs. Hallisburg said. "In time, we will have organized a system that works, not to worry . . . but first things first."

Then Muse noticed Mr. Hallisburg tapping his foot while he sipped his coffee, a sure sign he was getting bored with the conversation.

"Madame Néville," he said, "will you accept the position or not?"

Madame paused again.

"*Oui*, Monsieur and Madame Hallisburg, I will accept the task."

"Ah! Thank you," Mr. Hallisburg said.

"At last!" Mrs. Hallisburg joined in.

Madame smiled and rose.

"May I speak with the young ladies alone?"

"*Oui*, of course," Mrs. Hallisburg said.

"Send your papers for the contract around as soon as possible, *s'il vous plaît*. I will sign them, and then we'll get started," Mr. Hallisburg said. "We will leave you to it, Madame."

Muse watched the Hallisburgs bustle out of the room in a flurry. Her eyes smiled as they combed over the general splendor of the sitting room; then they moved toward Cassandra, lounging at ease on the canapé, and finally, her eyes rested on Madame Néville. *Now what?* she thought.

TRAINING

Two weeks passed. The training grew vigorous. Both girls
moaned, complaining of exhaustion, especially Cassandra,
who whimpered about the impossibility of remembering so many
details at once. Muse nodded in agreement. By day's end, mistress and servant fell dead to the world as soon as their heads hit
their respective pillows. A great deal of information belabored
their minds—intense tutorials on the art of social conversation,
graceful walking, entrances, exits, correct dining practices, how
to dress effectively. The proper relationship between mistress
and servant was at the forefront, with lengthy sermons stressing
professional demeanor at all times. A French language profes-
sor arrived to instruct Cassandra daily and to coach Muse when
warranted. In fact, Madame Néville had informed Muse that if
she proposed to emulate anyone on the premises, it would be
Mademoiselle Dumontet, the head maid.

Madame explained: "Mademoiselle Dumontet has the natural ability to shadow; she is almost invisible. Note that when she
comes into a room, she is not noticed. She remains silent in the

background, performing duties before they are required and as requested. She has a sixth sense about service. Watch how she refills a glass or teacup. It was the first thing I spotted. If a napkin falls, she is there to pick it up, immediately. Also," Madame Néville continued, "her command of the French language is excellent. I believe she is from Lyon, an interesting place, which sports an excellent accent. Listen and learn from her."

That evening, Muse lay in bed, recalling Madame's directives. Did she really need lessons on how to be invisible . . . how not to exist?

"Surely, I am an expert by now," she mumbled to herself.

What had she gotten herself into? Once advised as to what her new duties required, she shuddered. Is it possible the new training would oblige her to become more of a slave to Cassandra than ever before? What time would she have to herself?

Just the thought of her new obligations made Muse lightheaded. Madame Néville had recited to both ladies a synopsis of morning and afternoon duties mastered by a well-trained lady's maid: "Mademoiselle Muse, you will wake up no later than six o'clock. You will wash and eat breakfast. Before Mademoiselle Cassandra rises, you should have put away any clothing from the evening before and have laid out what she is to wear that morning. At eight o'clock, you must wake your mistress and bring her coffee, *le petit déjeuner,* and her correspondence. But since you cannot read, you will have to work out a system between you."

Cassandra attempted to interpose, but Madame Néville continued: "Mademoiselle Muse, you will then run your mistress's bath, do her hair, and help her to dress for the day. And then you will be free to assist Madame Hallisburg if it is required, though I understand she will be hiring a temporary maid and valet. You have no obligation to attend morning prayers with your mistress if your culture does not permit."

Both Muse and Cassandra stifled yawns.

"Please! It is most undignified to yawn in public."

"*Pardon*, Madame," Muse said.

"Let us continue. By nine o'clock, the family should be at breakfast, while you, Mademoiselle Muse, are left to tidy up Mademoiselle Cassandra's personal effects and arrange her outdoor costumes should she choose to go riding or take a long promenade."

"Madame, I don't ride."

"Tsh! What do you mean you don't ride? You must learn. Every self-respecting young lady rides. I have never heard of such a thing—you don't ride, and you live on a plantation? *C'est ridicule!*"

Muse lowered her head, half smothering a snicker, for she knew Cassandra feared every living creature on the plantation. She spent most of her time lounging on the veranda, dreading an encounter with a stray critter.

"*S'il vous plaît*, Mademoiselle Muse," Madame Néville snapped. "Pay attention!"

"*Excusez-moi*, Madame."

Madame had then resumed summarizing the tasks and behavior required of Muse in her new capacity. The duties, many of which Muse had performed before, now necessitated exact precision and timing.

As she lay curled up on the bed, she heaved a heavy, sleepy sigh. Her body ached much the same as during the harvest season when everyone worked double shifts, and the number of chores tripled. She folded the pillow over her head and tried to force sleep, but it would not come. She sat up, flung the pillow across the room, and watched it bounce off the armoire. *I don't want to be a shadow!*

The window was open. She got up and pulled a chair against it. With both elbows pressing on the windowsill, she stared out into the misty night. Two lit torches in iron baskets highlighted the grounds. She could barely make out the garden. Murky silhouettes of the rose beds danced against the rough stone wall like gloaming figures: a magical sight. But even in its splendor, La Lumière seemed to be closing in on her, like an elegant but small jeweled box with no opening, no window, and no air. The sounds of a vivacious city sang out to her, the tunes of a town still unseen. She heard hooves cantering along the cobblestones, the bark of a dog, then its whimper, as if lost, maybe hungry. She perceived the murmur of subdued voices or bursts of laughter escaping from people walking past the estate. So much life beyond the walls, so much to see, so much to do; her imagination soared.

LE SALON

A visit to an exclusive fashion house was under way. Measurements for the Hallisburgs and for Muse's uniforms had been sent earlier. Mother and daughter prepared to pick up their first Paris originals and choose fabrics for more elaborate eveningwear. The excursion excluded Muse until Madame Néville sent a personal note requesting her presence.

Muse quaked with joy.

⚒

The coach drove through broad, bending avenues. Muse, sitting in the cab with her back to the driver, drank up the sights of the magnificent city. She felt her eyes straining as she lionized buildings, arches, and bridges.

"Be still, Muse!" Mrs. Hallisburg said. "Stop fidgeting!"

"*Oui*, Madame."

"Mother, we shouldn't have brought her. She doesn't know how to behave."

"Dear, Madame Néville insisted."

"Yes, but still . . ."

Muse ignored the remarks, her concentration directed toward the Seine, her first glimpse of the celebrated river.

The cabriolet soon pulled up in front of a fine-looking building on a corner of a street swollen with well-dressed men and women. The Hallisburg entourage waited for the cab door to open. In remembering Madame Néville's strict instructions, the entourage descended and moved with poise toward the entrance just as its large, carved wooden door opened. A tall Nubian man, muscular in build, greeted them, and in flawless French, he bade them to enter.

Muse hesitated. Was there a mistake? Shouldn't she wait outside as normal? But the footman, dressed in a red waistcoat and tight-fitting white breeches and wearing a white *peruke*, settled his detached, vacant eyes upon her and repeated, "*Entrée*, mademoiselle."

Intimidated by the whole setting and unsure of how to respond, Muse curtsied to the footman. When he gave her a queer expression, she knew she had committed a faux pas. She smiled remorsefully, apologized, and hurried in.

The salon accommodated dozens of women—different shapes, sizes, and ages, albeit cut from the same cloth of the well-to-do. The Hallisburgs set forth toward the back of the establishment to a second room, where Madame Néville waited. Muse trailed behind, her eyes darting back and forth, absorbing the lush surroundings: long mirrors in gilded frames, satin-covered sofas and chairs, and tall potted ferns and palms standing on pedestals. Once the Hallisburgs had anchored in, Muse, who remained standing, was offered a chair, where she nervously flopped. This time the faux pas caught the eye of Madame Néville, who frowned.

Aware of Madame Néville's stark gaze, she shuffled through her memory to recap every lesson drummed into her head in the past few weeks. She looked at Madame again; had the woman been giving her the evil eye? Muse took a deep breath and regained her composure. She sat up straight, smoothed out the creases in her skirt, folded her hands on her lap, and crossed her legs at the ankles. Madame nodded in approval and then looked elsewhere.

The footman fascinated Muse. Her eyes gravitated toward him and lingered. He reminded her of Perche, who helped rescue her from the assault of Master Jonathan. The footman was the first dark face she had seen since coming to Paris. He spoke well and owned a handsome physique despite the *drôle* costume he wore. *A white wig on a colored man*—ridicule! she thought. Still, to behold another person of color . . . She smiled at him once more, but again he ignored her gesture and only gazed at her with blank eyes.

Her attention moved back to her surroundings. A tasteful room: walls made of well-varnished walnut, matching floors covered with a thick, rich, varicolored carpet. Large, arch-shaped windows welcomed in the light of a bright morning. A fragrance penetrated the room, the scent no doubt coming from the huge white urns overflowing with recently cut flowers. Porcelain, she heard Mrs. Hallisburg say. Scores of assorted fabrics well placed for viewing. Yards of silk draping across tabletops, rolls of linen and cotton cascading down from shelves. Colors, prints, textures, all added to her amazement. Many of the bolts exhibited labels of description: walnut sheer wool, china blue lawn, autumn green taffeta. She felt dizzy by the splendor.

An attractive woman walked through the salon wearing a beautiful evening gown of yellow silk with a cloud of tulle draped around the waist like a peplum. She held a framed sketch of the gown she wore, showing customers and explaining its details.

"Oh, Mama. *C'est magnifique!*" Cassandra whispered.

Cassandra's behavior took on a childlike quality, as if she were in a toy shop. Every *robe*—which Muse quickly learned meant "dress"—or yard of fabric brought forth a gasp or a sound of delight. All to the annoyance of Madame Néville.

Une demoiselle de magasin brought several bolts of material to show to the Hallisburgs. Cassandra's eyes fixed on a satin floral print draping on a statuelike mannequin.

"Oh, Mama! This is also beautiful."

"A lady's maid must have an eye for color and fashion. If her mistress is not perfectly turned out, it reflects poorly on them both. What do you think of the fabric, Mademoiselle Muse?" Madame Néville asked.

Muse regarded Madame, Mrs. Hallisburg, and Cassandra. She hesitated but then moved toward the display of fabric and brushed her hand across the nap of a raw silk the color of pale sunflowers. Then the shimmer of a soft, pure, woven taffeta, baby blue, caught her eye. She gazed at the gown on another mannequin. It was a subtle, deep pink, simple in cut, with a low boatneck trimmed with Chantilly lace. She lifted the hem to note the stitching. *How was it possible to suture stitches so tiny and so straight?*

"This one," Muse said.

"Oh, no!" Cassandra cried. "It's so plain."

"Muse, why did you choose that design and color?" Madame asked.

"Well," Muse said, "I think . . ." She hesitated again. "Somehow, the pink enhances Mademoiselle Cassandra's natural complexion. You don't notice the marks on her face as much."

Mother and daughter flinched and glared at Muse; no one in the Hallisburg household ever spoke of Cassandra's disfigurement.

"The pale yellow also seems complementary."

"And . . . ?" Madame encouraged.

"The simplicity of the style gives Mademoiselle Cassandra a younger appearance and flatters her figure. The cut of the other dresses, especially the satin floral, would make her appear older, frumpy . . . the floral print is too busy," Muse offered.

"*Excusez-moi*, Madame," Mrs. Hallisburg said. "Muse doesn't know what she's talking about."

"Maybe not, but that's why she's here," Madame countered. "You said so yourself: she has talent in sewing and an eye for fashion. One must have an objective and informed opinion if one is to offer options for Mademoiselle Cassandra. If a time came where the mademoiselle might find herself unsure of a decision, she would need the help of an impartial voice. And Mademoiselle Muse has one that is relative."

Moved by the laudable encouragement for her opinion, Muse's cheeks flushed.

"That may well be, Madame. But my daughter and I are both attracted to the floral."

"As you wish, Madame Hallisburg," Madame Néville responded. "In the end, it is always your decision. I am here merely to recommend and make suggestions. And my advice is that Mademoiselle Cassandra, for the moment, should concentrate on simplicity, as Mademoiselle Muse mentioned . . . colors that will best diminish her facial imperfections and minimize her figure. But, I repeat, it is up to you."

A silent standoff between Mrs. Hallisburg and Madame fell across the room.

"Well, dear," Mrs. Hallisburg said, speaking to her daughter, "let us think more about it before we decide."

Cassandra, brow puckered, responded, "*Oui*, Mama."

"Madame Hallisburg, I wish to borrow Muse for the rest of the afternoon if that is possible. I have instructions for her. I trust you can continue shopping without me. Here is the itinerary of shops to visit. The driver knows where to go."

Mrs. Hallisburg and Cassandra looked at each other.

"Of course," Mrs. Hallisburg replied. "But where are you taking her?"

"Muse requires help with her personal appearance. She has a rather provincial look. I am acquainted with someone who can help cultivate her form."

A GLIMPSE OF PARIS

Muse sat next to Madame Néville in a cabriolet. The bubble-shaped vehicle teased her imagination and made her smile. They moved briskly through the broad, tree-lined streets in silence. Madame jotted down notes in a small black notebook. Muse sat quiet, erect, but her eyes darted back and forth, trying to drink in more of the city. Soon the cab slowed to a languid pace, no longer able to maneuver through the streets. It stalled, then started up again, then stopped. Hordes of people overtook the streets, jostling against and impeding cabs and omnibuses, causing a horrific traffic jam.

"What's happened?" Muse asked.

"Nothing," replied Madame Néville, never looking up from her little book. "We are on the Champs-Élysées, near L'Exposition Universelle."

"The World's Fair!" Muse said.

"*Oui.*"

She strained to see the imposing main building where the fair was being staged. An outrageous structure made of iron and glass—and what else, she knew not—dominated the street.

"Oh-o-o!" she purred. "The fair is one of the key events my masters have come to see."

"Will you go with them?" Madame asked.

"Non."

"Pity. If you get an opportunity, you must go. It is a remarkable effort by the French to bring the world together and create a marriage of industry and of art."

"Have you attended?" Muse asked.

"Of course."

"What's it like?"

"Like traveling around the world in only a few hours. You see so many international wonders."

Muse smiled again, her fertile mind spinning.

"What was your favorite exhibit?"

"The display of crystal glass from all over the world—Paris, Vienna, Moscow—it is something to behold."

The cab forced its way through the mob and trotted forth.

"Oh!" blurted out Muse, pointing across the avenue.

She was looking at a fountain. Water jutted from the mouth of a golden fish held by a copper-skinned woman . . . a mermaid.

"What is it?"

"La Place de la Concorde," Madame said.

"How beautiful!"

Muse put her hand to her breast in rapture. She then asked, "Where are we going?"

"I am taking you to meet someone who will help you to refine your physical appearance."

"My appearance?"

"Your hair . . . to be exact. It will not do. It's too wild and distracts from my labors to polish your presentation."

My hair! thought Muse, who started fiddling with her head-wrap, tucking in loose strands.

Later, her eyes caught sight of a blighted stretch of landmass and debris where it looked as if a block of buildings had been torn down.

"So much of the city seems under construction. What's happening?"

"*Oh! Oui,*" Madame Néville responded. "Hundreds of houses destroyed. Whole neighborhoods wiped out by right of eminent domain. The area is to be cleared to broaden roads and construct modern apartments. This is the dawn of a new Paris."

"What do you mean?"

"It's a pity you can't read," Madame stated. "For then you would know of the ambitions advocated for a modern, cosmopolitan Paris."

Muse's eyes lit up.

"What's going to happen?"

"It's the project of Napoleon III . . . you know who he is?"

"The emperor?"

"*Oui.* He has hired an architect by the name of Georges Eugene Haussmann, a baron. Together they scheme to revitalize Paris. A massive team of demolitionists and builders has taken on the work. In a few years, this city will be a great wonder of the world."

"Really?"

"*Oui.*"

"What do the people think?"

"Some are in support of the evolution of Paris; others not so much. Many embrace change, while most fear it. It's human nature."

"And you, Madame, do you welcome change?"

"I will miss the old Paris, to be sure. Its medieval ambiance, its narrow, serpent-style roads. In its way, it was a very romantic city."

Madame's eyes gazed out along the road as if remembering something fondly.

"The city is disappearing before my very eyes. But in my business, I could not survive without change. Clients come and clients go. It's a good thing. Life is about transformation, and many times, it turns out different from what you've planned. One must be prepared, *en garde*, as they say. One should move with the tide or risk being left behind. It's that simple."

"I never liked change," Muse said. "I was afraid of it . . . but less so now. I understand it differently."

"How do you mean?"

"On the plantation, change was a threat. It meant someone had been sold, killed, or died . . . someone punished or attacked. When there was no change, no tragedy, you felt safe for a while."

"Ah."

"But now . . . everything's different, so strange, so new. It's exciting, in a way. The only other time I've ever felt excited in a good way was when Mr. Mül—" But Muse stopped short. She forgot herself, almost said too much.

"Go on."

"Oh, it's nothing," Muse replied.

THE TRANSFORMATION

The cabriolet made a left turn off the main avenue. Within minutes, the streets of Paris altered. They plodded down a narrow, dingy road lined with ill-kept buildings. Even the odor of the streets mutated. Smells of sewage and garbage cut through the quarter. The locals also appeared different: diverse in look, ragged in dress, rough in manner. A glut of impoverished people absorbed in a sordid slum.

Muse tensed up, her hand covering her nose.

"Don't be unnerved, my dear. You'll be all right."

The coach stopped in front of a decaying apartment building. A thin, ebony-skinned woman in a drab gray dress approached the cab. She wore a weathered straw hat that attempted to cover a mass of long silver-gray braids. The woman possessed coal-black eyes and furrowed skin, but when she spoke, her voice sang with the pitch and vitality of a young girl. She greeted Madame with a smile, and the glint in her eyes suggested a decades-old friendship. Madame made no effort to descend but spoke to the woman in a dialect unknown to Muse.

"Muse, I will leave you with Madame Rolin. She will take diligent care of you. I will inform you that she is the best *coiffeur* in the city. She will do wonders with your hair. The caretaker from La Lumière will fetch you in a few hours. Have no fear."

"*Oui*, Madame."

—⊰┼⊱—

Madame Rolin's adroit talent attended to styling, sculpting, and managing the most difficult, mangled, damaged hair in the city. Her expertise: braiding, a specialized technique of grooming hair worn by women in Africa and the West Indies. With her mature but still nimble fingers, she shaped strands of uncultivated hair into elegant and fashionable styles.

A modest two-room apartment awaited them. It was cozy, equipped with essentials; the only luxury was a floor-length mirror. When Muse understood the purpose of Madame Rolin's role in her makeover, she relaxed. Her hair was washed, dried, and oiled. The woman sat on a well-worn sofa and urged Muse to sit on the floor between her legs with her back up against the sofa. And then, the laborious job of braiding human hair began.

Muse and Madame Rolin made efforts to talk, but communication floundered, as neither commanded a solid grasp of the French language. She deciphered from Madame Rolin's wavering French dialect and broken English that she came to France from a small village near Cap-Haitien years ago. She married twice, losing both husbands to illness: one during a plague, the other from cholera. She and Madame Néville did each other favors from time to time.

"You must have good friends to survive in France. *C'est très important!*"

Muse listened as best she could to the slow drone of Madame Rolin as she manipulated the crinkled strands of her hair. But soon her eyes grew heavy, and she drifted off. When she awoke, the job was done. Muse stood up and approached the mirror; she was left speechless by the transformation. Long, thin braids, as neat and orderly as a regiment of well-trained soldiers, fell to her shoulders. Madame Rolin showed her numerous ways to style them: up, down, pulled back into a chignon, to which she added, "Your eyes, cheekbones. *Mon Dieu, ma petite, tu es belle!*"

"Am I?"

"*Oui*, but maybe we make mistake."

"Why?"

"Paris is not kind to young *belle* women, *spécialement* if poor, foreign, and unprotected. Less difficult as a slave . . . your owners will guard you. But if you choose freedom, *attention!* The city will devour you if you no learn its rhythm, its pulse. Survival depends upon street knowledge and invisibility if you want to lead a clean life. Be very careful, *ma petite.*"

Muse only half heard the advice of Madame Rolin, so gripping was her own new image.

"I want to wear it pulled back," Muse said.

Madame Rolin produced a blue ribbon. She gathered up Muse's many braids from the nape and secured the hair with the strip of silk, leaving a few strands to cascade around her face.

"It's as if I'm a different person."

THE ACCIDENT

Serge Laurent waited outside on the streets. The caretaker from La Lumière sat atop a rundown four-wheeled cart attached to a weary old mule. He had just come from the markets of Les Halles. The quarter where he marked time owned an unsavory reputation. It was no place to be after dark with a cartload of fresh produce. He could see the time from a large clock hanging above the counter of a café across the road. Half past five. He wanted to leave, but his orders were clear. Wait for the mademoiselle. Soon Muse appeared on the narrow roadway. He stood up at once, waving his black woolen beret high over his head.

Until now, Muse had paid no attention to Serge, a middle-aged man, moderate in height. His form was thick-set, with heavy jaws and glassy brown eyes. And he discharged a pungent body odor that seemed to linger long after he left, as if he spent his nights sleeping in a horse's stall instead of with his wife. Muse stayed clear of him. But that evening, alone on a foreign street, she met his eyes with gratitude as she ran toward the cart.

The driver's seat was narrow and unstable looking, which meant she would have to squash up against him as they journeyed home. For that reason alone, she sat in the back of the cart with the produce. It took two attempts to crawl into the back as she battled with an expanded skirt and wrestled with an all-too-large petticoat belonging to Cassandra. Then she struggled to find room among the fruit, the vegetables, the raw fish, and the cage of cackling chicken. At last, she came to rest, exasperated.

They had been on the road only a quarter of an hour when a sudden, harsh thump vibrated the vehicle, followed by the crackling sound of wood shattering. The cart gyrated, then collapsed, sending fresh cargo and a panic-stricken Muse tumbling to the ground. She screamed.

Serge pulled to an immediate halt.

"Ah, *mon Dieu . . . mon Dieu,*" he cried.

He jumped from his driving bench and ran to aid the disabled Muse, who was sitting on the ground.

"*Vous-est bien? Va bien?*"

Muse, although dazed, assured him of her well-being. He helped her to her feet.

"*Ah, non*! What a mess! My cart, my goods. Oh! My wife will have my hide."

"What are we going to do?" Muse asked.

"*Je ne sais pas.*" It took a few moments for him to reclaim his calm; he had to think.

"I must repair the axle or find another wheel. A blacksmith lives not half a mile away. You stay here and watch the cart. I won't be long. Make sure no one steals my food."

"*Oui*, Serge."

"It is still light, so you will be safe. If someone tries to take anything, stop them. I will leave my crop. Whip them if you have to."

"*Ah, non,*" Muse responded. "I couldn't do that."

"You must. Here, take the crop. There is water for you and the mule. Eat fruit."

It was bad enough to be left alone in the streets with a mule and an overturned cart, she thought, but ordered to ward off people with a crop . . .

Serge unbridled the mule, tied it to a lamppost, and hurried off, leaving Muse standing on the side of the road beside the ruptured cart. She stared at the crop in her hand as if it were a thirty-inch sword. A cluster of folk routing by pointed and chuckled at the amusing scene. Two young men approached and asked if she needed help.

"*Non, merci.* Help is on the way."

Another man strolling by tipped his hat and said, "*La belle.*"

Muse's eyes widened, and she released a timid smile. But when she realized what she was doing, she snatched it back and lowered her eyes. Then she remembered her new hairstyle and that she had left her headwrap at Madame Rolin's. Her hair was bare. She patted down the tussled braids, rearranging the strays back to order and making sure the blue ribbon was intact. She took a deep breath, silently urging Serge to make haste.

Carriages continued to drive by, maneuvering around the mishap as best they could. Pedestrians whisked past, frowning, shaking their heads, annoyed by the snarl-up blocking their passage.

Half an hour passed, and still no Serge. It was growing dark. Her fears escalated. Why hadn't she worn the indigo cape? It would have warmed her as well as concealed her.

Hurry, Serge!

With want of something to do, she reorganized the produce in the cart. A tighter fit, which better obliged the cart's lopsided posture. The chickens seemed pacified, and the mule was absorbed in its own world. What else could she do? She climbed up onto the driver's bench, odd angle and all, and sat and waited. A spectacle of people strolled the streets. She was as much curious about them as they were of her. The only difference was that they had lives. While absorbing the melodic rhythm of the city and its inhabitants, she heard a faint call, a whisper from afar: "Aggrey. Aggrey. *C'est toi?*"

The voice sounded muffled, but it called out again.

"Aggrey!"

At first Muse thought, Mon Dieu, *someone else has the same name as me!* She turned to look. On the other side of the road, wearing the same old, brown, bedraggled cape, strands of red hair escaping from its oversize hood, stood Claire, her former shipmate, waving.

THE REUNION

If the Hallisburgs possessed a keen eye for observation, they would have noticed—albeit subtle in essence—a difference in Muse, a variation in her spirit, her movement, her speech. She felt a change but could not explain what it was. That morning when she accompanied the Hallisburgs on the shopping spree, her mind, body, and soul belonged to them. But upon her return, she no longer evoked a subjugated young woman; something had shifted. As if an expansion occurred. Still of the same body but not of the same mind. At the moment of her meeting with Claire, a portal opened, one that would never close again.

As soon as Muse entered her room, she noticed it. A parcel, wrapped in newspaper, secured by a single white string, rested in the center of the bed. She opened it. Three new uniforms, folded neatly: one black, one gray, and the other white. Each came with a matching cloth cap with a thick flounce around its edge. She looked in the mirror, untied the blue ribbon that held her newly styled braids, and let them fall about her shoulders. She placed one of the caps on her head and stuffed her hair into the drab piece.

With regret, she watched the uniqueness of her fresh, new style dissipate as, once again, she became a person of no distinction.

She unfolded the garments and studied the stitching, impressive handiwork even for mundane uniforms. She hung the outfits in the armoire and placed the caps and ribbon in the bottom drawer. As she organized her new belongings, she thought of Claire and the in-depth conversation that took place earlier in the gathering dark.

Claire possessed something Muse admired: a quiet, no-nonsense demeanor of strength, confidence, and a daring sense of *joie de vivre*. Claire spoke with such candor that Muse, unhampered, responded in kind, as if to a trusted friend.

They sat on a nearby bench. Muse kept a vigilant eye on the wrecked cart, the produce, and the old mule. While they waited for Serge to return, they chatted.

"How are you enjoying Paris?" Claire asked.

"I've not seen much of it. This is the first time out of the house. But what I've seen is . . . I don't know the right word . . . thrilling?"

Light and polite conversation ensued, but it soon evolved into intimate details about their personal lives.

"How did you get this job?" Muse asked.

"Once I became of age, the institution where I lived found me a job as a *femme de chambre*. I was so excited to be on my own and independent. But months after I took service, the master of the house assaulted me. I ran away and found myself on the streets."

"You're brave," Muse said.

"Not really. I had no choice."

"And then what happened?"

"I got a job in a saloon waiting tables, serving drinks. Saved every penny I made until I could afford a decent set of clothes so I could apply for a proper job. I speak fluent French, and the orphanage gave me a reference. *Voila*! And here I am."

"*Mon Dieu*," Muse said.

Claire smiled.

"Your French is much improved."

Muse shared with Claire as well, telling of the attack she sustained by her owner's son, the hardship and humiliation of being owned. And before she realized it, she let slip her ability to read and write and that she knew math.

"I knew it! There was something about you . . . you seemed far too intelligent to be illiterate."

Muse stared at her new friend.

"No one must know," she said.

"What does it matter? You're in Paris!"

"Not for long. And it matters . . . it matters a lot. For me, it could be severe punishment, even death."

"Oh! Southern laws prohibit education of slaves, yes . . . but would they go that far?"

"It's happened."

"How did you . . . I mean how—"

"How was I educated?"

"Yes. The Hallisburgs?"

"No. Never! They don't have a clue. I had a tutor."

"A tutor!"

Muse looked about the dark streets, the city still energetic. The clock at the café across the way read seven.

"It's all because I got sick," Muse said. "If not for that, I would have never met him. His name was Mr. Müller."

"How old were you?"

"Six. I've been reading and writing in secret ever since."

"What a tale!" Claire said. "I promise, your secret is safe with me. I swear."

Muse once again looked across the street at the clock.

"We have to stay in touch," Claire said.

"But how?"

"I don't know."

Claire got up and moved toward the cart. She examined the wooden casing of the lopsided vehicle, her hand moving along the rough interior of its frame.

"Aggrey, come look."

Muse jumped from the bench and came up alongside Claire.

"Look!" Claire said.

Attached to the inside beam of the cart was a leather pouch. The hide, brittle and cracked, was tubular in shape, with an opening secured by a worn cap that unfastened. It lay against the interior of the wooden board, undetected.

"What is it?" Muse asked.

"It's a pouch."

"So?"

"Do you know what it's used for?"

"No."

"In olden times, when merchants journeyed across country to sell their wares, they were often robbed. After a while, the traders originated a process to attach a leather apparatus, like this one, underneath the wagon to hide their coins and valuable papers. If attacked, the hidden pouch usually went unnoticed by thieves."

"How do you know this?"

"My father was a tradesman in Ireland. He adopted this scheme. I have an idea! Today is my day off—every Wednesday. I assume that Serge goes to Les Halles every week."

"I guess so."

"Well, I spend much of my day off at Les Halles because there is often much to see and do. What if I could insert a letter in the pouch while Serge is busy ordering his weekly goods? Les Halles is huge, but I'm sure I can find him."

"I know for a fact he takes his morning coffee at Café la Chapelle; I heard Madame Laurent speak of it."

"*Bon.* Then you, on the other end, will wait for the right moment to retrieve the letter and continue the correspondence by placing your communiqué into the pouch just before Serge leaves for the market the following week, and so on. What do you think?"

"I suppose we can try it."

"What have we to lose? If the letter is intercepted, it will be addressed to Aggrey, not Muse, and they'd never think you would ever receive a letter."

"OK. Let's do it."

⊷⊱⊰⊶

Muse swept and dusted her room after tidying away the new uniforms. Many thoughts ruminated while she worked. How early to wake the Hallisburgs? What clothes to set out for their trip to L'Exposition? But also, she agonized over the plan she and Claire concocted—the scheme to communicate with each other. She had deceived the Hallisburgs before, but this time, the degree of risk was heightened.

She was about to throw away the newspaper that packaged the new uniforms when a light tap sounded at the door. It was Agnès, the head maid, carrying a tray with a glass of fresh milk. A faint smile graced her face.

"I wanted to make sure you got your package."

"*Oui, merci,*" Muse replied.

"This is for you. It might help you sleep better after such an ordeal. Are you all right?"

"*Oui. Merci beaucoup.*"

Mademoiselle entered the room and placed the tray on the side table. She looked around the room as if taking mental notes.

She smiled at Muse. "You have a good rest. *Bonne nuit,*" she said and left.

Returning to the business of the room, she again picked up the old newspaper, crumpled it, and threw it in the trash basket. As soon as it dropped in, her eyes alighted upon it. A newspaper! She retrieved the journal, smoothed out its creases, and read the date; the paper was but one day old.

The armoire balanced on four well-carved cabriole legs, which lifted the bold piece about six inches from the floor. In the gap of the dark space is where Muse hid the only book she brought from Virginia, a book she studied from time to time entitled, *Teach Yourself to Read French*.

She folded the newspaper and placed it deep within the dark space under the armoire, along with the book.

THE NEXT DAY

M use awoke. She sat straight up and gasped. Her breathing was heavy. Where was she? She looked around the room. *Paris,* she reminded herself. Her breathing calmed. But something felt wrong. She studied the room, glancing at her hiding place beneath the armoire; all seemed in order. Still, she felt disturbed. Had someone been in her room? A faint fragrance of rosewater circulated. She scanned the chamber again; nothing seemed out of place. Wait! The tray and the empty glass of milk—gone.

Threads of light streamed through the closed curtains, too brightly for five o'clock in the morning. Muse hurried out of bed, but the moment her feet hit the floor, her head spun; she sat back down. After a moment to settle herself, she shook it off and rose again. When she drew back the curtains, rays of bright sunshine poured in. It could not be! Below, she saw Andre, the gardener, removing weeds as he often did—but he never arrived to work until noon. *L'Exposition Universelle!* she screamed in her mind. "*Mon Dieu!*"

She rushed to the water basin, splashed water on her face, and dressed. By the time she reached the Hallisburgs' door, she could barely breathe. She knocked once, then—no reply. She opened the door and entered. Before her was the usual chaotic aftermath, the residue left behind after the masters had break-fasted, dressed, and departed to a social outing. But where were they . . . and Cassandra?

A young maid in the adjacent room was cleaning out the bathtub.

"*Bonjour*, mademoiselle," Muse said. "May I ask where the Hallisburgs are?"

"L'Exposition Universelle," she replied.

"Did the madame and mademoiselle dress themselves?"

"*Non.* Agnès."

Muse found Agnès.

"*Bonjour*, Agnès."

"*Bonjour*, Muse."

"Did the Hallisburgs get off all right?"

"*Oui. Pas de problème.*"

"Why didn't you wake me?"

"I tried to, but you wouldn't budge. I assumed the accident was too much. So I volunteered my services. Do you feel better?"

Muse considered her eyes: sly, icy blue. She was lying.

A CHANCE ENCOUNTER AT
THE FAIR

"Your parents are angry with me?" Muse asked Cassandra.

"Not so much angry as annoyed."

"I'm sorry I overslept."

"Don't worry. Agnès took diligent care of us. It was wonderful to be waited on by someone experienced. I'll be so glad when you are fully trained."

"Me too," Muse lied.

"Miss Cassandra, tell me about L'Exposition Universelle. What did you see?"

"Well, to tell you the truth, it was a tiresome day! It was dull; it was . . . what's the French word for 'boring'?"

"*Ennui,*" Muse said.

Cassandra was sitting in front of her dressing table, staring at her reflection in the large oval mirror. The table dripped a white lace cloth cluttered with accessories designed to beautify. Perfume bottles, elaborate brushes and combs, assorted makeup and powders—lip color and ointments guaranteed to fade scars and skin discolorations visible on the complexion.

"I don't understand," Muse said. "What happened? Didn't you enjoy the fair?"

Muse stood behind Cassandra, arranging her banana curls to resemble a picture in one of the French journals.

"First," Cassandra said, "no one bothered to tell us there were several locations for the exposition. You know how adamant Father was about seeing the agricultural exhibits, but that exhibition was held at Trappes, outside Versailles. Father insisted we drive there to take a look-see, and it took forever. Oh . . . oh, try these yellow ribbons."

Muse threaded the thin strips of ribbon through the curls sitting on top of Cassandra's head. The ribbons dangled like a waterfall.

"Then what?" Muse asked.

"When we got to the site, hundreds of people of all classes were in attendance. Pushing, shoving . . . all kinds of people. Even darkies like you . . . but not like you . . . I mean, not slaves. A group of Arabs attracted such attention, much whispering and oohing and awing. They looked distinguished, yet like caricatures. They wore ornate robes and headwear . . . expensive fabric and jewels . . . you could tell."

"Arabs!" Muse echoed.

"The entire exhibition revolved around the future of farming and the farmer. Father was ecstatic. The representatives talked of soil rejuvenation, climate, water, irrigation, that kind of rhetoric. I hated it! Mother and I wanted to see fine art and the household revelations of the future."

"Well, surely Mr. Hallisburg will allow you to return."

"Yes, yes, he promised to . . . but still. No, no . . . take the ribbons out. I don't like it. Where is that magazine, *Le Follet*? There is another hairstyle in it I like."

Muse approached the desk, where a pile of magazines lay. She riffled through several of the fashion journals: *Courrier des Salons, Journal des Modes*, then *Le Follet*. She handed it to Cassandra.

"It was on page twenty-three," Cassandra said as she flipped the pages.

Then she stopped. She looked at the magazine cover and then at Muse.

"Out of all the magazines I have, how did you know this one was *Le Follet*?"

Muse's heart quivered. Her breathing stalled.

"Because," she said, "it's the cover that has the pink jacket with the fur trim you admired so much."

"Ah! Of course."

Muse reached for the comb and continued experimenting with Cassandra's hair. She chastised herself for being careless. Studying the picture in *Le Follet*, Muse gathered up the dangling ringlets, twisted them up, and secured them with a large decorative hair clasp.

"*Voila!*" Muse said. "What do you think?"

Cassandra took one of her handheld mirrors.

"Yes, it's nice." She patted the bundle of curls. "It'll do."

She placed the mirror down and continued: "The day was, however, not lost. Father ran into an old acquaintance from university in New York. His name is Monsieur Saint Aubin. He's French and has a small estate on the outskirts of Paris. Get ready to be excited!" she announced to Muse. "He is having a small soirée and has invited us to attend. He said he has a daughter my age whom he wants me to meet. Just imagine . . . our first real invitation. I can't wait to tell Madame Néville."

She took Muse's hands.

"Do you think I'm ready?"

"Of course you are."

"I'm so happy! My first soirée," she sang. "What shall I wear?"

The wardrobe was filling up with new and lavish outfits.

"Muse, we must clear out some of these old things. *Trop passé.*"

The first garment Cassandra pulled out was the iris-blue dress Muse made for her. Her heart sank.

"Get rid of this old thing, and these two . . . give them to the poor or something. I don't care what you do with them."

During the laborious discarding of dresses and accessories, the rare ting-a-ling of the front-gate bell resounded.

"What's that?" Cassandra asked.

Muse peered out the window. A man on horseback entered the courtyard. Two large leather bags hung from both sides of his saddle.

"Mail!" Muse said.

MAIL

That evening, the Hallisburgs gathered around to read aloud portions of the various communiqués they received. Muse poured coffee.

Cassandra recited two letters received from friends in Virginia. Mrs. Hallisburg entertained with a lengthy correspondence from her sister who, along with her family, was visiting Der Brunnen. But it was Mr. Hallisburg's correspondence that acknowledged disheartening news.

"Muse, I especially want you to be privy to the letter I am about to read."

"Oh! Mr. Hallisburg, is something wrong with Mama?"

"No. Mary's fine. She sends you her love."

Muse smiled with relief.

"There is disturbing information in this letter."

Mr. Hallisburg cleared his throat and continued: "First, Bailey reports of an outbreak of yellow fever near the docks. Some Norfolk townspeople have taken ill. But so far, it remains near the harbor. The countryside is, for the moment, unaffected.

"Secondly, I'm sorry to say, Bailey writes that Perche attempted an escape."

"Oh God!" Muse exclaimed.

"Which one is Perche?" Mrs. Hallisburg asked. "I forget; they all look alike."

"He's the wood-carver, Mother."

"Oh."

"He was caught three days later and brought back to Der Brunnen. Bailey said he had no choice but to discipline him. Perche was severely whipped, allowed a couple of days to recover, and then sent out to the fields."

"Why the fields?" Cassandra asked. "He was the wood-carver."

"I don't know."

Mr. Hallisburg looked at Muse and then at his family.

"That's not the worst of it. A few days later, according to Bailey, Perche, after finishing a day's labor, returned to his cabin and fell ill, complications from his wounds. Perche is dead."

As Mr. Hallisburg spoke, Muse stared at the hand-painted figures on the porcelain coffeepot she held: a blue couple riding in a blue carriage led by blue horses through a blue countryside. When Mr. Hallisburg said Perche was dead, she went numb. The room swirled. A quaking motion rattled in the pit of her stomach; her hands quivered. Before she could regain composure, her grip on the coffeepot weakened, and the pot fell to the floor and shattered. Tears drizzled down her cheeks. She glared at the Hallisburgs as if seeing them for the first time. She released a whimper and ran from the room.

REFLECTION

Muse remained in her room for the rest of the evening. She ate nothing. She lay in bed reading and rereading news about the Crimean War in the now-dated French journal. By midnight, she was pacing; pent-up energy rumbled. She could not stop thinking about Perche.

Perche is dead . . . all because he wanted to be a free man. It was wrong. The tugging sensation in her stomach tightened, and the room grew airless. She opened the window. The coolness of the night air and the fragrance from the garden brought relief. Perche taught her how to swim almost before she could walk. He dragged Jonathan off her that horrible night. He was a sweet man.

What did Martinique say? What did she believe?

It takes courage to be free, the kind of courage you must be prepared to die for, she remembered.

Perche had courage, she thought.

She picked up the iris-blue dress, cast off by Cassandra, and ripped it at a side seam in frustration, but then she put the fabric up against her skin. The blue flattered her complexion. She gathered up another dress and tore off the lace that trimmed it. Among the *robes* to be discarded, she reimagined an outfit as chic as those in the fashion house, one that complemented her own figure. Muse sorted through the various gowns, mixing and matching fabric and alternative accessories, when she remembered what day it was: Wednesday.

"Serge goes to Les Halles this morning," she said to herself.

———

The thought of hearing from Claire made her appetite return. She threw the indigo cloak over her nightgown and went down to the kitchen to feed on whatever leftover food she could find. Would Claire's idea work? After eating, she crept out to the carriage house to Serge's cart. She ran her fingers alongside its bottom and felt the leather thingamajig underneath; it might work.

Back in the room, she folded the dress pieces and put them away. She would tend to them later. Cushioned against the bed, she knelt to pray for Perche, hoping he found peace.

———

The night was warm and balmy. Muse walked along the dirt road that led from her old shack to the lake. She inhaled the scent of honeysuckle rose. In the distance, the glint of a clouded figure walked toward her. It was Perche: tall, sparse, bushy hair sprouting out like a bird's nest. His chest uncovered and his feet bare, he wore his usual ragged cotton trousers rolled up to the knee. He was smiling.

"Are you going to the lake?" he asked.

"Yes."

"Well, hurry up! You'll be free to swim if you wish. Free to do whatever you want. But do it now while you're young. Don't wait!"

"You all right?" she asked.

"Yes," he responded. But he seemed distracted. He gazed out into the hills and pointed up toward the sky. "I see light. I have to go now."

"Goodbye, Perche," she said.

"Goodbye, Muse."

DISTRACTED

Her mind scattered like puzzle pieces trying to come together as one unit but unable to find a match . . . or make sense of it all. She thought about Perche all morning. Madame Néville droned on about etiquette, and Cassandra just prattled about nothing. And she no longer cared about the mission or the lessons.

"Is there something wrong, Mademoiselle Muse? You seem distracted."

"*Non*, Madame."

"Why do you keep looking out the window?"

"No reason, Madame."

But there *was* a reason. Serge was due back from Les Halles today.

"Mademoiselles," Madame announced, "fortune may have smiled upon you, Mademoiselle Cassandra. I have done some investigating, and I believe the afternoon event you're invited to might well be more of an opportunity than imagined."

Cassandra shrieked.

Madame spoke about the Saint Aubin family at length and discussed their relationship to *haute société*.

"It has been brought to my attention," Madame continued, "that the guests who will attend this event might be very well situated. It is an excellent chance, Mademoiselle Cassandra, for an unofficial debut."

"Oh, Madame!"

"Mademoiselle, if you devote the next two weeks to your studies and exercises, especially dancing, for your waltz needs work, you will do well. What do you think, Mademoiselle Muse?"

But Muse did not answer. She was peering out the window, watching Serge drive the carriage into the courtyard.

THE FIRST COMMUNIQUÉ

As soon as the house fell dark, Muse stole down to the carriage house, aided only by the light of a single candle. She approached the vehicle and crouched to where her hand could paw under its side panel; she fingered the grainy leather pouch.

The candle brought it to light so that she could see better; she untied the drawstring and pulled out a folded letter. It worked! She grabbed the candle and rushed back to her room. She had secured a pen, paper, and a small container of ink and would return them before Cassandra missed them. During the quiet, cool hours of the evening, she read and reread Claire's letter. In the latter part of the night, sitting on the chair, hunched over a side table, she scribbled her reply in English with spurts of French.

EXPECTED GUESTS

O n the day Mr. Hallisburg announced the death of Perche, another note came to him from Monsieur Furet. The owner of La Lumière informed him that his youngest son, Olivier, a naval officer stationed near the Black Sea, was returning home on leave. A former comrade of his would also join him. The friend, Monsieur Jean-Paul Chevreau, had been wounded in battle. Although forced to give up his combat career, he would need no special assistance.

Therefore, wrote Mr. Furet, *you will understand I am opening additional rooms for my son and his visitor. It should cause you little inconvenience. I also will host a small dinner in my son's honor and hope you and your family will join us.*

"Officers!" Cassandra cried.

Muse was also told about the special occasion and that she would take part in its preparation.

"Incidentally," Mr. Hallisburg said to Muse, "Monsieur Furet has decided that because of his son's visit and the added pressure of reorganizing the household, he will give his servants the day

120

off in two weeks. He himself will be on an overnight excursion with Madame Brisac. Unfortunately, the timing coincides with the day of our invitation to the Saint Aubins. This means, Muse, you will be alone in the house."

ALONE IN THE *MAISON*

Two weeks later, La Lumière stood vacant, save for Muse. She finished her chores early so as to roam the halls of the estate unrestricted, particularly the private quarters of Monsieur Furet. She pushed open the solid oak doors to his room; the smell of sickness rushed forth, although the chamber was tidy. Madame had rigorously coached them on identifying the quality and craftsmanship of fine European furniture. "It is vital you are able to differentiate," she said.

Muse recognized elaborate walnut furniture: a bed, armoire, commode, chairs—too thick in design to be French; more Italian, she guessed. The paintings on the walls were imposing. Artwork bordered in expansive gilded frames depicted the same theme: landscapes in soft pastels. The adjacent room lured her in like a charismatic set of friends. Shelves lined with volumes of exquisitely bound books.

She picked up one, then another and another. All with French titles, which she could read. But one book, thick in content, lay on a table of its own. When she opened it, it fell to an etching of a bearded, half-naked man chained to a prison wall. She flipped through the pages and then turned to the cover: *L'Comte de Monte Cristo.* Enticed by the images in the book, she ran to Mr. Hallisburg's desk and returned with his dictionary. She sat down, turned to the first chapter, and read.

She had been laboring over the novel all morning when the tinkling sound of the courtyard bell pealed. As if caught red-handed in the most forbidden place in the house, performing an illegal act, she jumped, nearly knocking over a vase.

"Oh God!"

Muse slammed the book closed and scanned the room, making sure nothing looked disturbed. She ran back to Mr. Hallisburg's room to return the dictionary and then stopped dead to listen.

The bell rang again.

"Perhaps it's the mail."

She took a deep breath, straightened her apron, and rushed down the stairs and across the courtyard. When she opened the massive door, to her surprise, there stood a lovely young woman. She wore a smart cotton dress, off-white, with subtle burgundy-colored stripes. Red banana curls dangled from under a neat straw bonnet, and she carried a pale silk parasol.

"*Oui*," Muse said.

"Well, aren't you going to invite me in?"

Muse's eyes widened.

"Claire! What on earth?"

"I'm here to take you out."

"Have you lost your mind?"

"Probably. You wrote you would be alone all day."

Muse nodded.

"Well, it's a perfect time for you to see Paris. How many chances will you get?"

Claire entered the courtyard.

"You live here? My God! I wish I were a slave," she said, admiring the garden.

Muse gave Claire a sharp look.

"I live in a wooden shack, built on a dirt floor, on a fenced-in plantation."

"I was just kidding. But it is beautiful here. Show me your room."

Up the stairs of the carriage house they trotted, giggling like schoolgirls. She showed Claire her living quarters, her sewing projects, and her hidden reading material and shared just about every other secret.

"Turn around—let me see your dress," Muse said.

Claire spun.

"It's lovely."

"It's new," she announced.

Muse lifted the hem of the skirt to observe the needlework.

"The seams are generous, and the stitching so small. How do they do it?"

"Now," Claire said, "show me the dress you are making."

Secured in a bottom drawer, Muse singled out the iris-blue dress redesigned for her fit.

"This is gorgeous. Perfect for a dance!" Claire said.

"A dance?"

"You never know. By the way, I brought you something to read . . . written by a woman, Harriet Beecher Stowe. It's interesting and very controversial!"

"What's it about?"

"It's about you."

"Me?"

"I mean slavery."

Muse accepted the gift and slid it under her pillow.

"Thank you."

"Well, let's go," Claire said.

"Go where?"

"I've got money. Let's take a carriage to the Champs-Élysées and go to L'Exposition Universelle. The tickets are only a franc. It's a beautiful day! I promise to have you back before the house returns."

"But . . ."

"No buts! Come! But wait—you can't wear that old thing. What else to do you have?"

Muse pulled the white uniform from the armoire and slipped into it. Claire helped her to lace up. Having no bonnet, Muse tied her braids up with the blue ribbon.

"You look pretty, Aggrey."

"Thank you."

"At what time do they return?"

"About six."

"We've got plenty of time. Let's go."

L'EXPOSITION UNIVERSELLE

The cab meandered along a winding route through the city as Claire pointed out various sights of interest. As they neared the Champs-Élysées, she motioned for the driver to stop.

They descended into mass pandemonium. Endless queues of visitors waited to enter the public event. Hordes of people going to or coming from the exhibition impinged upon groups of loiterers, spectators, and vendors, blocking the walkways. More people were gathered on the site than either could have imagined. Claire took Muse by the hand, and together they pushed forth.

While waiting to buy tickets along with scores of others, they stood in awe of the edifice constructed for the occasion—a huge, long, tubular-shaped structure built of iron and stone and glass. They entered the exhibition arm in arm, craned necks looking up at the shafts of light pouring through the glass roof, which was secured by magnificent columns and beams of iron. The first thing they grew conscious of was the heat and stagnant air. Claire bought two inexpensive oriental handheld fans and gave one to Muse.

"This part of the fair focuses on the sciences," Claire said.

A multitude of booths devoted to mechanical engineering, shipbuilding, railroads, and industrial machines used in fabric weaving were on display. Muse's keen eye absorbed it all, then narrowed in on a little machine. It caught her full attention.

"Look, Claire!"

Unaware of her boldness, she approached its vendor.

"What is it?" Muse asked.

"Ah, mademoiselle, this is the future. It's called a *machine à coudre*, invented by an American."

"What does it do? How does it work?"

The machine was set for demonstrations. It looked like a small iron horse attached to a table, Muse thought. The demonstrator sat down on a stool in front of the odd-looking mechanism. He inserted two pieces of fabric between a threaded needle and the flat surface of the appliance. He placed his feet on a treadle and pressed it up and down at a rhythmic pace. The needle shifted up and down, piercing through the fabric, intertwining the thread with the material and attaching the two pieces together. Muse squealed at the result. She turned to Claire.

"Can you imagine the time saved on making clothes?"

"*Oui*, mademoiselle," the man said. "*Exactement!*"

They moved on, observing everything—not only the displays but also the attendees, who were equally fascinating. A mixture of social classes and diverse cultures mingled, talked, and interacted openly, with an equal sense of expression and representation, a melting pot of human existence.

Claire led Muse to a section exhibiting the future manufacturing of mineral products: glassmaking, ceramics, and jewelry. Like moths lured to light, they followed the swarm of spectators to a podium. Displayed in a case of thick, framed glass was a huge diamond known as the Star of the South. It glittered with shimmering lights of pinkish and brownish colors. Like the others, Muse and Claire murmured in delight. Next to it, a stall gleamed with splendid specimens of glass manufactured all over Europe—England, Bavaria, France. Two large green-and-white candelabras hovered over the finest illustrations of crystal objet d'art ever shown. Also epitomized were bits and pieces of bric-a-brac showing the delicacy and finery required in the art of glass-blowing. Opposite, another centerpiece illuminated the marvels. Spun from glass, it depicted a serpent coiled about the body of a huge lion.

"This is unreal," Claire said.

"Oh!" Muse said. "It looks like an ice palace."

The allure of textile manufacturing clutched Muse's attention; the machines used to create cotton, wool, and even lace captivated her, as did the quality of the fabric itself. She moved nearer.

Claire found a display of modern furniture and home decorations of the future, and she drifted the opposite way.

Soon, the sound of music penetrated a section of the showroom, and Muse moved toward it. The latest evolution of the piano dominated a center platform: a grand piano. A young man, in dress tails, sat before the instrument, playing a passionate piece that attracted a large crowd.

"What's he playing?" Muse asked.

"Hungarian Rhapsody Number Two, Franz Liszt," responded a male voice.

Startled by the voice, she gasped. She was speaking to a stranger and not to Claire. Terrified, she rushed through the various salons in search of her. In her zeal, she knocked up against a man observing a display of ancient maps of Paris. The collision caused him to lose balance and drop his walking stick.

"*Pardon*, monsieur."

She curtsied but recognized that the young man was disabled and that his cane was not an accessory. She picked it up and handed it to him. He was tall and well dressed in a light-gray suit, and he wore a low-topper straw hat. A white bandage covered the right side of his face. She tried not to stare. He bowed, tipped his hat, and thanked her for retrieving the cane. His eyes held hers longer than was proper.

"Are you all right, mademoiselle?" he asked. "You look distressed."

"No, I'm fine. I was looking for my friend. *Excusez-moi,*" she said and hurried away.

A few more anxious minutes passed before she beheld the familiar straw bonnet, only a short distance away.

"Oh, there you are!" Claire said. "I was getting worried. Here, take this."

"What is it?"

"Two francs. If we lose each other . . . take a cab home. You know your address?"

"Yes."

Muse examined the two coins, shrugged, and put them in her pocket.

Then Claire, hands pressed against her breast, twirled around.

"This exposition is the most exciting event I've ever seen!"

"It is!"

"Well," Claire said, "it's time for lunch. And then we'll visit the fine arts section."

⋈⊹⊹⊱

Muse quaked with exhilaration. She reveled in the moment and would remember it always: a café, a table under a bright red awning, a Parisian afternoon sitting opposite a friend like she was a normal person.

The waiter gave them both *une carte.* Muse accepted it. She glanced at the menu and then at Claire, asking her to translate. But when the waiter returned to take their order, Muse only looked at him.

"Shall I order for the both of us?"

"Please do."

They dined on quiche Lorraine, fresh tomato salad, and brioche.

"How will I ever repay you?"

"Don't be silly!"

"But this must be expensive."

"Don't worry about it," Claire said, giving Muse a guarded look. It was an odd look that baffled her.

"Is something wrong?"

"No!" Claire said. "Well, to be honest . . . luck has smiled down on me."

"What happened?"

Claire explained how she had come into a considerable sum of money. Her employers, she said, approved of her work ethic and ability to manage the children, especially during the difficult journey of crossing the Atlantic.

"So to express their gratitude, they gave me a monetary bonus and authorized me to buy two dresses on their account."

"Claire, that's wonderful! I'm so happy for you."

"Thank you."

Again, Muse heard curtness in her tone and didn't know how to reply.

"You're lucky to have such a wonderful job!"

"I'm quitting!"

"But why? If your employers are so generous—"

"I want to work for myself. I can find a better way to make a living in Paris . . . and now that I have a little money, I can take time to find a proper venture to invest in."

"Invest? What does that mean?"

"To buy a business or partner with someone in a business."

Muse's eye widened.

"How much money did they give you?"

"A lot," she said in a dry tone. "But I don't want to talk about money anymore. Let's drink up and go back to the fair."

Claire picked up her glass.

"Let's toast to the future and whatever it brings."

Muse looked intently at Claire. Only then did she notice the change. Something was amiss in those Irish-green eyes; the gleam had dimmed, a hint of hardness had set in, and they no longer held the fresh, keen eyes of youth. For one so lucky, Muse saw anger and sadness in her eyes. Nonetheless, she lifted her glass.

"To your future," Muse said.

"And to yours," Claire replied.

The rims of the glasses clinked as they touched.

"*Salut.*"

⟩⟨

They held the fine arts exhibits at a different location, at l'avenue Montaigne off the Champs-Élysées. It was a congenial site that offered a more intimate arena to view the art. Even though it attracted many viewers, the temperature was less intense, making the experience much more pleasurable.

Although Muse and Claire made earnest efforts to stay together, they eventually drifted apart, both in pursuit of their own experience with paintings and sculptures. Muse knew little of what she witnessed, reacting only from an emotional base. An English painting absorbed her gaze; it portrayed a woman in a dress shop choosing a wedding gown. Muse thought it so authentic-looking, she flushed with embarrassment as if intruding on a private moment. Then an oil portrait of an African male wearing a colorful red toga wrapped around his torso. His black skin glistening like silk; his hair uncombed, tussled, reminding her of Perche. The intensity in his eyes was disturbing. A look of desperation, so often seen on the plantation. She wanted to reach out and touch him, befriend him.

Claire found the art exhibits less inspiring.

"It's predictable," she said to a male observer standing next to her.

"Too much on the safe side," he said.

Rousseau was well represented: his landscapes and studies of nature were impressive, but merely the rehashing of the old school. She wanted to see the work of the new attitudes of contemporary artists . . . what they called *realism*, but none of it was on view at the exhibition. Still, she walked through, highly contented with the display.

At a prearranged time and place, they met up again, full of smiles and gaiety.

"How I wish the day would never end," Muse said.

They exited into the bustling avenues. Claire looked up at the setting sun.

"Aggrey, it's late. We have to go."

Claire hailed a cab. And while she negotiated the two separate stops, Muse's eyes fell on a young man with a cane exiting the exhibitions—the same man she ran into earlier. He was having trouble getting into a cab: he fumbled with his injured leg; the walking cane and the straw hat kept rearing into the top frame of the cab's door. She wanted to help him, but he managed and maneuvered himself into the cabriolet, and it drove off. She wondered who he was and what happened to him. Even with a bandaged face, there was something about him, she thought.

ONCE AGAIN A SLAVE

The sun was setting when Muse entered La Lumière after L'Exposition Universelle. Except for the clock striking six, she heard not a sound. They would soon be home. She hurried to her room, stopping only to retrieve candles. She undressed and checked the uniform for signs of wear and tear; a small stain of red wine blemished the skirt. With cold water, she dabbed and scrubbed the white fabric until it appeared fresh.

Having shown Claire her different sewing projects, followed by the chaos and excitement of rushing off to the fair, Muse returned to an untidy room. But as she picked up and replaced her things, the events of the day swirled in her head. What would she remember the most? The sewing machine—what an invention! If she owned one, she would make glorious clothes. But no, the most exhilarating was to lunch at a café, served and waited upon like a normal person. Then she recalled the vivid oil portrait of the African male, his eyes intense and angry . . . Perche. But Perche was dead now, all because he wanted freedom.

Her smile soon faded. Sudden despair triggered a mélange of sensations, as if something inside of her died. She asked herself how she was to continue in this way . . . as a captive.

From under her pillow, she pulled out the dog-eared book Claire gave her: *Uncle Tom's Cabin.* She skimmed through the pages, and just short of absorbing the first paragraph, a light tap sounded at the door. She flinched, dropped the book, and kicked it under the bed without thought.

"Qui est-ce?"

"C'est moi, Agnès."

She stood paralyzed for a moment and then opened the door.

"You've returned," Muse said.

"I got back over an hour ago. I knocked at your door, but there was no answer. Were you out?"

"Non."

Agnès looked past Muse as if inspecting the room. Muse's eyes followed hers, then shifted to the floor where she saw the tip of the book's binding under the bed. With a faint smile, she narrowed the door another inch, obstructing Agnès's view.

"Are you sure?" Agnès asked.

"Am I sure what?"

"That you haven't been away. Off the property, perhaps?"

"Quite sure."

"I looked all over for you. Where were you?"

Muse thought fast.

"In the basement."

"The basement! What were you doing there?"

"Madame Laurent gave me permission to use any of the sewing accessories I found down there. I was looking for a certain shade of thread."

"Oh. I didn't know. Well, then, *bonne nuit.*

"Bonne nuit."

Muse closed the door and breathed a long sigh of relief.

She retrieved the book from under the bed and glanced around the room. Had Agnès been snooping while she was away? If so, could she have seen anything suspicious? The room was in disarray . . . but nothing more than scattered cuts of cloth and old dresses strewn about the floor. Her reading material was in its hiding place, but the iris-blue dress was on the chair. Did it matter? Cassandra gave it to her to do what she wished. *Still, beware!* she thought. Agnès was on the prowl.

CLAIRE'S LIE

Other than assuring Muse of her devoted friendship, every-thing else Claire told her at the café was a lie. She wilt-ed under the weight of an inflamed misdeed. Since arriving in France, her hopes of building a new life had remained optimis-tic, but providence stepped in and tempted her at a moment of weakness, and she committed a grievous offense. But would it catch up with her as in the past?

The exhibition had been the only excursion she experienced since coming to Paris. Those few hours spent with Muse were as invigorating and medicinal as if she sipped a potent elixir that, for a fleeting time, soothed the misery of her days. The story she told Muse was convincing; in fact, Claire almost believed it herself. *She had come into a large sum of money.* Muse seemed to ac-cept the story without suspicion. But several weeks later, Claire's actions still haunted her; she wished she had never laid eyes on the man.

The Grossmonts of New York, the people who hired her, had claimed to be an ambitious couple in business who were moving to France. They needed a nanny for their two children. Claire was deemed qualified not only because of her natural sensibilities toward the little ones but also because of her excellent French.

Claire thought it the perfect opportunity to get as far away from New York as possible. Maybe she could even find some of her mother's people, although she had little to go on. The Grossmonts proposed room, board, and good wages. With the steady income, she planned to save and prepare for a more lucrative situation in Paris and to make her home there. But despite the experience gleaned from having lived on the streets, Claire had been conned. She soon discovered the true character of the Grossmonts.

As soon as the Grossmonts set sail, Claire's salary stopped. They told her the monies they expected had been delayed but assured her that once the family settled in Paris, all would be well. But weeks after their arrival, still no wages. When Claire left America, she possessed but a few dollars, which she pinched from on her days off. She approached the Grossmonts and insisted on her pay. They apologized but said that at that point in time, they could not pay her. Be patient, they said!

"Do you expect me to work for free?" she appealed.

"Of course not," Mr. Grossmont said. "You may leave anytime you want. We will not prevent you. Do what you think is best."

The Grossmonts understood, as did she, that there was no place else for her to go. And even if she quit, they would hire a French national at half the salary, if not less. The alternative to quitting was not an option—she had neither the strength nor the wherewithal to tackle life on the streets in Paris.

After she crossed paths with Muse, a surge of new energy and hopefulness emerged. It was comforting to have someone to talk to. The following week, Claire appeared at Les Halles, with great anticipation, to wait for Serge. But when she arrived at the café, he was already there, drinking coffee *avec des amis*. She stood off to the side for a few minutes. Then, without hesitation, she approached the cart and slipped a letter into the leather pouch beneath the vehicle. Her execution in implementing her street-smart skills proved first-rate. So, pleased with the endeavor, she treated herself to a coffee. Her favorite café was just off the rue Rambuteau. She sat reading, quiet and content. Occasionally, a man would try to engage her in conversation, but she gracefully refused his company.

"*Merci, mais non!*" she replied.

But that morning, an undistinguished man spoke to her. A sullen being, of medium height, dressed in an expensive pair of striped yellow trousers and a blue waistcoat of raw silk, he held in his hand a somewhat oversize top hat. At first glance, his clothes were well tailored, but too tight-fitting for his figure, as if the garments belonged to someone else, she surmised. His smile was crafty, his speech peasantlike, and he reeked of cheap cologne. And the more she ignored him, the more he edged closer, trying to coerce conversation. At one point, he reached into his breast pocket and pulled out a bulging, blue silk purse, obviously filled with coins and bills—a large amount of money for anyone to carry on the streets in broad daylight.

"I have many francs in this little bag, *ma chérie*. We could have a gay old time together if you're willing."

He jingled the blue silk in front of her face like bait. She turned away and muttered, "*Quel homme!*"

Her snub enraged him. He hurled an array of abusive remarks. The proprietor rushed to her rescue and apologized for the disturbance.

"Monsieur, get out of my café!"

The man in the yellow trousers smirked at the owner but retreated.

"And do not come back!"

He turned to Claire.

"*S'il vous plaît,* mademoiselle. Finish your coffee and take lunch, compliments of the house."

Claire accepted gratefully. This was what she loved most about the French. She patronized the café once a week and spent only the cost of coffee and perhaps *un petit pain*, yet they treated her as if she came daily with an entourage.

As she ate, still burning with scorn, she stared out at the crowded marketplace. Transfixed, she never took her eyes off the striped yellow trousers. She watched as he harassed unattached women walking by, her mind all the time machinating.

By early afternoon, she watched Serge leave Les Halles and observed the occupancy in the marketplace dwindling; only a few people buzzed around the square. She exited the café, keeping the yellow trousers in clear view. He loitered near a booth of fresh vegetables. There he approached two young, shabby-looking women making purchases. He greeted them, tipping his hat. They responded with smiles. As they conversed, she noticed another group of shoppers heading for the same booth. She inched closer. Suddenly, a human traffic jam occurred, a small herd of people vying for the same space, the same stall, and the same fresh produce. Claire slithered into the midst of the teeming interchange. With the tip of her boot, she nudged the wheel of the vegetable stall; the booth jerked sideways, triggering the front end to collapse. The produce fell all over the ground, and the customers, including yellow trousers, in an effort to thwart the mishap, collided and bumped into each other, sprawling down in a heap. They apologized to the owner and to one another as they helped each other up; some laughed at their folly and clumsiness, while others seemed exasperated by the calamity. By the time the human confusion ordered itself, Claire had left the grounds unnoticed, concealing something heavy within the folds of her skirt.

As soon as Claire dropped Muse off in front of La Lumière, she instructed the cab to take her home. She asked the driver to let her out a few blocks from her living quarters. In a nearby shrub, she hunted for an old bag where she stowed away her shabby brown cloak. The garment served as camouflage to conceal the smart new dress she wore. It got her out of the house and would get her back in without suspicion. She secured the drab garment over the new dress and secreted all accessories. She entered the apartment.

"*Bonjour*, Madame, Monsieur Grossmont," she said.

"*Bonjour*, Claire."

She smiled and curtsied.

"Are the children well?"

"*Oui*, mademoiselle. Quite well."

"If you don't mind, I will go to my room; I am exhausted."

"*Bonne nuit.*"

She mounted the stairs to the attic where she slept.

It was a rank, odious room with one window. She undressed and put away her new things. Several stray coins rattled at the bottom of the straw bag she had salvaged. She unlocked the lower drawer of her dresser and slid her hand beneath a layer of expensive new female undergarments. She pulled out a blue silk purse, the same silk purse belonging to the man wearing the yellow trousers, the prize she picked from his pocket as he tumbled to the ground at the marketplace, the moneybag he by now missed. Never did she imagine it held so much money. So much that she could rent a nice apartment, hire carriages, or portray herself as a woman of means and perhaps snare a lucrative marriage.

At first, she was overjoyed with the fantasy of what she could do. She was in her mother's homeland with an unexpected windfall. The possibilities were endless. Then she grew frightened, so scared that if she could have taken her prize back, she would've. She consoled herself by deciding the loot itself was probably stolen, for she sized up yellow trousers the moment he spoke. However, it did little to ease the pang of guilt she felt. In New York, they accused her of theft, but that was different; she stole to survive. This time, she stole out of spite—or was it desperation? Despite her best efforts, she once again needed to resort to primitive measures to keep afloat. She sighed, unfastened the pouch, dropped in the coins, rerolled the many loose bills, and placed the purse back beneath her lingerie.

GUESTS ARRIVE

La Lumière was washed down, straightened up, primped, and fluffed like an old petticoat still in good condition. An heir had come home. The return of Olivier seemed to restore Monsieur Furet back to health. He even discarded his wheelchair in favor of a walking cane with a gilded eagle for a handle. When his son walked in to greet him, he embraced him so tight Olivier could scarcely breathe.

"*Mon père*, you are still as strong as an ox."

"But you, *mon fils* . . . Oh! how you've altered. Don't they feed you on board?"

"We eat when we can; you know that."

Three days later, Olivier's friend Jean-Paul Chevreau arrived. Agnès was the first to greet the new guest and show him to his rooms. But before the young man could unpack, Olivier was knocking at his door. The two comrades fell into each other's arms. And for the following twenty-four hours, no one heard hide nor hair of the former comrades-in-arms.

They stood next to the open fireplace, staring at the blaze, each with a brandy in hand.

"*Mon père*," Oliver said, "he says I look older and frailer than even he. He asked if they fed us on the ship."

Jean-Paul grimaced.

"I hope you told him about the slop they feed us. No wonder you're thin."

"*Oui.*"

"At least you were never wounded," Jean-Paul said.

"I am wounded . . . mentally."

"Nonsense! You need rest. You have much to look forward to."

"As do you, my friend. How is your leg?"

"It is better . . . wobbly. I no longer need a walking cane. But my face is a different matter. The scar is hideous. Where women once gazed into my eyes with smiles and flirtation, they now seem only to stare at the wound."

"You're fine. When did they take off the bandages?"

"Last week."

"Let me see. Looks like an arrow. Tell them it's a tattoo. You'll be all right."

"Let's hope so."

"What are your plans, now?" Olivier asked.

"I was offered an opportunity to work with Baron Haussmann."

"Baron Haussmann! Doing what?"

"You remember, before I was seduced by the navy, I finished my studies in architectural engineering. I'm credentialed."

"*Mon Dieu!* You couldn't be in better hands—Baron Haussmann is the head architect of this city; he practically owns Paris."

"I know. It's a perfect opportunity."

Olivier smiled.

"I can't imagine you behind a desk all day, in a suit. *C'est drôle.*"

"Neither could I at first. But according to my doctors, my body is done with hard battle . . . and to be honest, so am I."

"Well, I for one can't wait to get back aboard ship. My land legs, I fear, are gone forever. And I hate this city."

"You hate Paris—why? What could you possibly hate?"

"Her intensity . . . her decadence. A relentless display of artistic fervor that overwhelms me, and most of all, I despise her bourgeoisie and nouveau riche who seep around every corner like fumes."

"Ah!" Jean-Paul replied. "It is precisely those elements that draw me to Paris like a fragrant wonder drug."

LA SOIRÉE

Although Muse met neither the heir nor his guest, she was actively involved in the planning of the grand dinner. On loan to Monsieur Furet, she took direction from Madame Laurent and Agnès. Once the Hallisburgs were dressed and ready to appear, she donned the white uniform, put on its matching cap, and reported to the kitchen.

The guest list included, besides the Hallisburgs, an old family friend, his wife, and an age-appropriate daughter: Monsieur and Madame Philippe Moret and Mademoiselle Janine. Two other business associates arrived with their wives, and several neighbors whom Olivier had known all his life soon followed. Most of the young men who schooled with Olivier and Jean-Paul still battled in the Crimean conflict, so they were the only two men under the age of thirty present at the dinner.

To comfortably contain his guests, Monsieur Furet opened the dining room, an elaborate and impressive space normally kept dark. It was a sumptuous room, adorned with a hanging chandelier supporting dozens of lit candles, a grand fireplace, large gilded mirrors, and walls festooned with silk coverings *à la chinoise.*

Olivier's father had hired a pianist, and Chopin's music filled the room. The guests, in formal attire, mingled. Cassandra and Janine bonded, both being of similar age and circumstance. Janine, taller and leaner than Cassandra, flaunted bright brown eyes and a flawless complexion, but she possessed none of Cassandra's sparkling personality and vivacious spirit, leaving Cassandra to attract most of the attention.

After introductions to Olivier and Jean-Paul, Cassandra and Janine soon fell under the spell of the two dashing young men. The fantasy of amour with an architect and a naval officer spun in their minds. They paraded their natural feminine guile in its most polished manner. Both showed skill in polite conversation, although Janine excelled in her own native tongue. Their sense of light humor and unadulterated charm easily captivated both men. But it was Cassandra who surpassed in dance. All her re-hearsals and practice of proper form paid off; Chopin and the dance floor became her stage. Janine remained on the sidelines, content to chat with Jean-Paul.

Madame Laurent was short one footman, so the extra responsi-bility fell to Muse. She entered the dining room, balancing a tray of widemouthed crystal glasses, half filled with champagne. She walked tentatively, her eyes staring at the tray, fearful of spilling even a drop.

"Just amble to each guest and let him or her take a glass, and then move on. You need not say a word," Agnès had said.

As she moved across the dining room, Cassandra waltzed by in the arms of Olivier. Glancing over at her mistress, she smiled, noticing how well she glided. She continued around the room, now with confidence, head held high, and holding a steady tray. She approached Mr. and Mrs. Hallisburg, who took drinks. They nodded their approval. She ventured over to Monsieur Moret, then toward his daughter, who was still talking to Jean-Paul. He retrieved a glass from Muse's tray and offered it to Janine and took one for himself. He was about to thank Muse when his eyes steadied on hers. A flash of recognition caused him to cling to her glance. Their eyes held each other for only a split second—a split second too long. Muse lowered her eyes and moved away.

It couldn't be, could it? Oh, mon Dieu!

Muse scampered to the kitchen, put down the tray, and exited through the back of the house, unseen. Once outside, she tipped around a side window so that she could get a closer look at the young man who accepted the champagne from her. He was without the cane and seemed to walk with less of a limp, yet she was sure it was the man she had almost knocked over at the exhibition. Even devoid of face bandages and the low-top straw hat, Muse recognized his darker complexion; his lean body; his wavy, ebony hair; and his almost-black, soulful eyes.

Ah! What if he remembers me? What if he tells someone he saw me at the fair? her brain screamed.

She paced across the garden path, one hand on her hip and the other fanning her face as if the temperature outside was rising. It took a few minutes to compose herself. After all, he made no sign of acknowledgment—or had he? She reminded herself that she wore a uniform cap that covered much of her face, although she was wearing the same white dress.

"Mademoiselle Muse, what are you doing out there?" Madame Laurent snapped. "We need you!"

"*Oui*, Madame," she said. And she hurried back into the house.

The evening wore out. As the pianist played the last of an impromptu medley, the guests gradually departed. The Hallisburgs extended thanks and appreciation for a most enjoyable evening and disappeared into their private chambers. Monsieur Furet excused himself, complaining of fatigue. But the two young men, left alone to their leisure, repositioned themselves in Monsieur Furet's master study, where he kept the brandy.

"Nice room," Jean-Paul said.

It was a warm, spacious area, filled with shelves of books and a massive mahogany desk smothered by papers and files. Two brown leather armchairs hovered close to a well-lit fireplace. A small table was positioned between them. The room would have been stark and masculine save for the lime-green curtains of thick silk draped in such a way as to frame the large French windows that overlooked the garden. Despite the newly cut roses placed hither and there, the room reeked of disuse.

"Yes, this room used to be my father's sanctuary. But nowadays, he rarely leaves his bedroom, I'm told."

Olivier poured a glass of brandy for Jean-Paul and then for himself. They raised their glasses.

"*Salut.*"

"What did you think of the evening?" Olivier asked.

"It was good."

"And the two young ladies?"

"Ah!" Jean-Paul responded. "Since I haven't been near a woman in ages, I doubt if I can complain . . . they seemed charming enough."

Olivier laughed.

"I agree. It's been so long since I've embraced a woman, let alone danced. I, as well, cannot complain."

Jean-Paul sat down. Olivier followed.

"How is it going between you and your father these days?" Olivier asked.

"Ah! The feud continues. However, he has conceded somewhat."

"In what way?"

"He still will not recognize me as a legitimate son, but he has included me in his will . . . I am to receive something of an inheritance when he expires."

"And your mother?"

"She returned to Algeria ages ago. She is married and has started a legitimate family. I have two more new half brothers. And she has returned to the traditional Muslim values of her own culture, which excludes me and my bastardly state. So I am quite alone. My father's family is uncomfortable with my existence, as is my mother's family. I'm half French, half Algerian, yet I belong nowhere."

"You nearly lost your life for the sake of France. That should account for something, at least in the eyes of this country," Olivier said.

"Perhaps, but many times, I still feel like an interloper, although it has helped to improve my relationship with my father. What about you—you've committed your life, again and again, to battle . . . is it truly all for love of country?"

"If I am to be honest with you, the answer would be . . . I don't know. It's just that if I didn't fight battles, wars, skirmishes, what have you, I wouldn't know what to do with myself. Unlike you, my friend, I have no real profession."

Silence fell between them. They contemplated their discussion while sipping brandy and savoring a contented moment among friends.

"*La femme noire*, who is she?" Jean-Paul asked.

"Who?"

"*La femme noire.*"

"Oh, I don't know. She belongs to the Hallisburgs."

"How do you mean . . . in service?"

"No, not in service . . . *enslavement.*"

"A slave?"

"Oui."

"*Criminel*," Jean-Paul said. "One rarely sees women of color in Paris, but I swear I've seen her before."

"No chance. She's never been off the property."

"Really?"

"Well, not unless she's with the Hallisburgs."

"*Oh, la!* Well, I guess I haven't seen her before; I'd never forget such a clan."

"A common lot."

"I agree, but the girl looks so familiar," Jean-Paul said.

THE ATTRACTION

Muse stopped in front of the mirror to check herself. Dressed in full uniform, her headpiece not only covered her hair but obscured her face. She had chores to do but was uncertain about leaving the room. *He* would stay for a month at least. How to avoid him? If they met, what would she say? Would he remember? If he recognized her, she would deny it—it was not her; she was not there. But something else preyed on her, a fleeting feeling, a disquieting impression. The sensation of meeting his eyes. A rare moment of delight, warmth that brought forth a lost memory.

At the age of ten, she encountered an innocent brush with love. It was a steamy day in August. Der Brunnen was celebrating the fiftieth birthday of its owner. To commemorate the milestone, the family went all-out. Several neighboring plantations received invitations to a feast, and in an unprecedented gesture, the slaves of local communities were permitted to fraternize at a separate festivity on the grounds.

His name was Joseph; he was twelve or thirteen years old . . .
he didn't know for sure. She remembered a scraggly youth with
a shaved head, a victim of lice. He introduced himself to her by
pulling her braids. She hit him. He retreated but later returned
to apologize. Muse accepted his regrets, and they fast became
friends. The two slinked away from the festivities to the peaceful
atmosphere of the lake.

"You know how to swim?" he asked.

"Uh-huh. Perche taught me."

"Can you dive?"

"No."

"I'll show you. Watch me."

Joseph stood at the edge of the pond. In one motion, his knees
bent, his body curved, his arms rose above his head to make an
arch, and on tiptoes, he pushed off into the pond headfirst.

Muse laughed with delight. When Joseph came up for air, she
asked, "Who showed you how to do that?"

"Our overseer—he don't want no drowned *niggras*."

"Teach me."

"Sure."

They practiced diving and swimming across the pond until
their limbs grew weary. She remembered it as a special day—
a sensation like a bird being let out of its cage. After the sun
fell, the guests, along with their human property, made their way
back home. It was then, just at the point of saying goodbye, that
Joseph kissed her softly on the mouth. Muse's first instinct was to
hit him . . . again! But she didn't. Days afterward, Muse, pretending to be on an errand, hiked out to the border of the property,
hoping to get a glimpse of him, but she only saw cows. The next
evening, she did something much out of character. She crept off
the estate and onto the neighboring plantation Joseph called
home and searched for him. But she never saw him again. A few
weeks later, she learned he had been sold.

Joseph touched her in a gentle way. She recalled the sacred moment, like responding to a melody. How she wished she had not struck him and cursed her reflexes! She wanted to apologize, but even more, she wanted to taste again his sweet lips on hers. In her sadness, she began to decipher the world and its befogged messages: first, her father taken, then Joseph, Perche . . . now she was separated from her mother. Muse questioned even more. Was it a mistake to feel deeply in a world that permitted her no choice of expression or personal fulfillment?

A seed, a kernel, germinated in her mind to guard against further manipulation of her heart. It had done its job; she remained detached. There was no future for her to fantasize about this man or any other man in France. She would control her useless impulses; nothing good could come of them, and one day soon, she would be back at Der Brunnen—where the future of her life was as a bondage woman.

She tried to be firm in this belief, but night after night, Muse struggled to resist thoughts of Jean-Paul. Something about him called to her; she felt certain he was an outsider just as she was. But soon, she surrendered to the knowing that a man from another culture, another race, pulled a chord in her heart, and taboo as it was, it was unsealed. She smiled, thinking of his shining dark eyes, and wondered, for the first time, what it might be like to be with him.

SNUBBED

Only three months into the project, the Hallisburgs were overextended; they would have to withdraw more funds. It wasn't so much the money but Cassandra's sluggish pace of cultivation. And now she was moon-eyed over Monsieur Furet's son.

"I won't have it," Mr. Hallisburg announced.

A breakthrough should have occurred by now, a coveted invitation to mingle in higher circles, affording Cassandra exposure to the social experience she needed to perfect her style, her manner, and her overall polish. The family paid Madame Néville a fortune, yet nothing was happening.

After the event at Pierre Saint Aubin's, the Hallisburgs believed the opportunity they sought was imminent. The day appeared to have been successful, having included an introduction to a high-profile guest, the honorable Alicia de Minion, daughter of Baron de Minon, who seemed excited to meet the Americans and to practice her English. So much so, she promised to invite them to her annual summer ball, one of the most prestigious events of the year. But the invitation never came.

The Hallisburgs questioned Madame Néville about the snub.

"It would be one thing if the honorable Alicia de Minon had not made the gesture," Mrs. Hallisburg said.

"And," Cassandra added, "it was sincere. Something must have happened."

The ball was an exclusive event, comparable to the affairs held at court. Madame, even with her solid connections, conceded that she could not have managed such a high-profile invitation. Why had the Hallisburgs not received the invitation?

Days later, seated at an informal dinner in the private suites of the Hallisburgs, Madame Néville shared her findings with her clients.

Muse poured coffee.

Madame Néville began, "Monsieur, madame, I have found out why the invitation to the de Minon summer ball has not arrived."

"Well!" Mr. Hallisburg said. "Out with it!"

"The de Minons are from an ancient family, but they are a very enlightened clan."

Madame paused.

"Yes, go on!"

Muse positioned herself against the wall near the serving trolley. Erect posture, arms folded in front of her, eyes straight ahead, she seemed to pay no attention to the conversation, but she took in every word.

"It seems Monsieur le Baron and Lady de Minon have learned of your philosophical views and active behavior of condoning and supporting the enslavement of human beings."

"Oh, for heaven's sake!"

"Monsieur," Madame continued, "because they are a free-thinking family, they prefer to embrace the mind-set of 'to each his own.' The problem is this: The event in question is a grand four-day affair. Guests are required to bring their valets, their maids, etcetera. Nonetheless, any servant working under their roof, living in human bondage, would, to the outside world, appear as if the de Minon family condoned such a less progressive attitude toward humanity—an association they cannot abide. That is my understanding."

Muse smiled to herself.

"But what if we don't bring Muse?" Cassandra asked.

"Who would support you? You certainly could not attend the event without help."

"Madame Néville, we have, in the last month or so, asked on occasion for the assistance of Mademoiselle Agnès. Her services have been impeccable. In addition, Father now has a personal valet. We would have the proper entourage."

"That is true," Mrs. Hallisburg added. "We all hope Muse will one day mirror the precision and expertise of Mademoiselle Agnès. But Agnès will do splendidly on her own."

Muse noted Madame's subtle facial expression, which seemed to say, "*Mon Dieu*, these Americans!"

"*C'est dommage!* We have put so much effort into training Mademoiselle Muse. But I understand your point."

"Is there a way," Mr. Hallisburg interjected, "for you to propose this change of circumstance, of staff, to the Baron and Lady de Minon?"

Madame Néville raised an eyebrow.

"The better course of action would be for you first to contact the Saint Aubins. Communicate to them the modification within your staff, and ask if they would be willing to articulate the change to the de Minons. If that fails, I'll see what I can do."

"Muse," Mr. Hallisburg said. "May we have more coffee?"

"*Bien sur.*"

Within a week's time, the Hallisburgs received the invitation. Cassandra set off posthaste to the dress salons, with only Agnès in attendance.

THE RECOGNITION

With Monsieur Furet's approval, the Hallisburgs hired a temporary maid to replace Agnès. After Muse had been assured that the changes in her responsibilities were short term, she dutifully accepted her new assignments without question. She answered to Madame Laurent and to Agnès, who now took orders directly from the Hallisburgs.

And to Muse's annoyance, Madame Laurent's first request was, "Take breakfast up to Monsieur Jean-Paul's room, *s'il vous plaît.*"

She knocked. It felt as though hundreds of butterflies swarmed in her stomach.

"*Entrée!*"

When she entered, Jean-Paul was sitting on the settee, dressed in a morning coat, his face buried in a journal.

"*Bonjour*, monsieur. Where would you like your tray?" she asked, keeping her eyes lowered.

"*Là-bas*," he said, pointing to a small oval table near him.

She put the tray on the table.

"You speak French well," he said.

"*Merci.*"

She curtsied and then moved toward the door.

"*Excusez-moi,* mademoiselle. Have we met?"

"*Non,* monsieur," she replied and left the room.

Jean-Paul endured a testy night. It was his leg. Now and then, late in the evening, it throbbed. The doctors warned him of such side effects—poor circulation, aggravated by the slow healing process, all normal. They prescribed various pain remedies, but Jean-Paul took none of them; instead, he walked it off.

Another warm evening tempted him to embrace the open air. His friend resided in a lovely home, and he was envious of how well Olivier got on with his father. Jean-Paul was grateful to be roosting with his *ami* instead of in his family's nest, the great, drafty château in Marseilles they called home. He loved Paris. New energy was revamping the city, and he was on track to be a part of it. No one knew of his lineage, only his professional achievements. His first assignment broke ground last week: a small apartment building adjacent the rue de Rivoli. A project approved by the baron himself.

He walked along the garden path, taking in its scent. The torches in iron baskets gave just enough light for him to amble without incident. He took a deep breath. Every few steps, he stopped, bent and flexed his legs, and stretched his torso, then his arms. As he wandered around the grounds, he observed the exterior of the estate with interest, the stone wall that protected the property, sixteenth century, he imagined. The sculpted-granite water fountain depicted two horses raised on hind legs in battle.

"Good chiseling!"

Then he heard a strange noise coming from the carriage house garage. He stopped. Curious, he went to explore.

"*Bonsoir?*"

No answer.

"Is anyone there?"

Again, silence.

He entered the carriage house and looked around—nothing but carriages and wagons. As he turned to leave, his peripheral vision caught sight of a figure huddling behind a cart.

"Who's there?"

"*C'est moi*, monsieur," Muse said. Having discreetly slipped an envelope into her pocket, she rose and revealed herself.

"What are you doing in here?"

Muse, dressed in a nightgown concealed by the indigo cape, came forth. She brushed herself off.

"I could not sleep," she lied.

"Neither could I. But why are you hiding in the carriage house?"

"I wasn't hiding . . . my mistress . . . lost a bracelet. I thought she might have dropped it somewhere near the carriages," she lied again.

"Oh . . . Well, do you want to take a turn with me?"

"*Non*, monsieur, I must go."

"Ah, *s'il vous plaît*. What harm will it do? Everyone's asleep. Come, let's walk near the roses. The fragrance is sweet, even at night."

Having no idea how to deal with a polite but persistent man, Muse gave in.

"Just one turn," she said.

"As you wish."

Jean-Paul introduced himself and asked her name. They exchanged small pleasantries as they strolled. When they reached the fountain, a stillness fell between them.

"Is it true you are in bondage to the Hallisburgs?"

She turned her face away, loathing the question.

"It's true," she said.

"I can't imagine what your life is like."

She gave no response.

They walked around the fountain. The light from a torch fell on her face. Jean-Paul asked her to remove her hood.

"*Pourquoi?*"

"I want to see your face."

She obliged. As she pulled back the indigo hood, rambunctious braids fell around her neck.

"L'Exposition Universelle," he exclaimed. "That's where I've seen you."

She stiffened.

"Monsieur, I beg you . . . please, tell no one."

"*Pourquoi pas?*"

"If they knew, I would be in grave trouble."

"I don't understand."

"I am prohibited from leaving the property. That day . . . I escaped for a few hours . . . to see a little of Paris."

"You unfortunate thing. How old are you?"

"Seventeen . . . next week."

"You unfortunate thing," he repeated.

"Stop saying that!"

"*Pardon.* I didn't mean to . . . I mean . . . I know what it's like."

"What, to be a slave?"

"No," he said, choosing his words carefully. "I know what it is like to be an outcast, to be shunned and treated like a pet rather than an equal. I promise," he continued, "I will never utter a word."

"*Merci*, monsieur."

They walked farther along the path.

He was watching her. She reminded him of his mother. Her complexion was darker, but it glistened in the same way as when his mother moistened her face with scented Algerian oil. She had a similar long, lean neck; clear, dark, intuitive eyes; and even the braids were so alike, except his mother's braids were always laced with beads.

"Your face is healing nicely," she said.

"I will always have a scar, but less noticeable, I hope."

"I know of a salve that will help you heal faster. I'll make you some."

He smiled at her. She blushed.

"You were wounded in the war?" she asked.

"*Oui*. But let's not talk about the war. Tell me what you thought of L'Exposition?"

"Oh!"

They talked about various aspects of the fair. He mentioned his passion for ancient maps of the old city and neighborhoods. She listened. When he asked what she loved most, she said, "The sewing machine."

"Is it . . . was it . . ." he began, faltering, not knowing how to phrase his question. "Was it less enjoyable for you not knowing how to read?"

Muse reflected before answering.

"Does one need to know how to read or write to enjoy music, or admire the theme and colors of a painting, or even swoon over beautiful jewels?"

"No. You're right. Very well put."

"I've encountered nothing like it," she said. "And probably never will again. But I'm grateful for the experience. Had I been caught, disciplined . . . it would have been worth it."

"Are you disciplined often?"

"Enough," she answered.

"Do they beat you?"

Again, Muse said nothing.

He saw it in her eyes. His questions made her uncomfortable.

"Right. None of my business. But may I ask one more question? One you do not have to answer . . . but I am curious."

"What is it?"

"Why did you escape for only a few hours . . . and not permanently?"

She backed away from him as if assaulted.

"I have to go. *Bonne nuit*," she said and ran off.

UNSETTLED

Back in her room, Muse's head was spinning. She stared at the pieces of cloth scattered everywhere, a half-finished gown she would never wear, embroidered handkerchiefs and table serviettes, pastime activities to help relieve the days' tension. Why bother? She wished he had not asked that question. Why a temporary escape? A farrago of emotions washed through her. Why did she return? Mantled in strength, her confidence surged to where she could barely contain its energy, fighting an urge to burst from her shackles and run free. But as soon as she entertained thoughts of liberation, she sank back into the abyss of her servitude. A constant battle raged within her. She grappled with Jean-Paul's presence; a fraction of her wanted something from him—something real, a touch, an embrace—despite everything.

"Get a hold of yourself," she whispered.

Still, she sensed that there was more to him than the charming young architect he presented to the world. He understood what it meant to stand on the outside looking in. *He said so!* As she pondered these thoughts, Muse grew conscious of a deep hunger, an unyielding thirst to love. She was no different from any other woman, same needs and desires. A maze of feelings awakened her to the verity of her loneliness.

So distraught by the episode in the garden, she never opened Claire's letter, which she had rescued just before Jean-Paul's interruption. Instead, she slid it under her pillow to read the next day.

A squeak from a door gently opening and closing diverted her thoughts. She listened. It was Agnès's door. The wood-planked floor in the hallway creaked as if someone was tiptoeing down the corridor. Why was Agnès up so late? Then she smiled. "Why are you up so late?" she asked herself. Curiosity forced her to the window. Jean-Paul was still walking along the garden path. She recalled how tanned his skin was, much darker than most Frenchmen. His hair so black and wavy, and he was so tall . . . she had to look up at him. He must be of mixed blood, she thought. Could that explain the loneliness she felt from him?

She lingered only a moment when, out of the darkness, crept Agnès, dressed in her night robe, sneaking up behind him and playfully covering his eyes with her hands. He startled, then turned in surprise. Agnès laughed.

"May I walk with you?" Muse heard her say.

"*Oui.*"

Muse closed the window curtain with such force the curtain rod derailed. A tiny tear on the drape was visible. She would have to mend it, but not tonight.

DALLIANCE

At the first sign of daylight, Jean-Paul watched as Agnès hastily retrieved her clothes and dressed. Their eyes remained linked as she buttoned and laced up. She smiled at him and, with her index finger, blew a kiss. He returned the smile as she departed. A refreshed man lay in bed, alive again. It seemed a long time since he had lain with a woman, and Agnès was a delightful creature. He appreciated her candor and lack of inhibitions; she came to him knowing exactly what she wanted. He wondered idly if she would have been so eager if she knew the truth of his parentage and dubious position in society. *I bet she thinks I'm the heir to some property or other,* he thought. He sighed, stretched, and turned over on his side. Within minutes, he was asleep.

CLEVER CLAIRE

Claire maintained a low profile, never flaunting her new financial status. She bode her time and kept to her daily routine, doing nothing out of the ordinary and concealing her new purchases. It was in her best interest to stay on as nanny because it gave her a mundane image—plus full room and board, although still no salary. The Grossmonts, she deduced, were having little success infiltrating the world of business and society in France and would probably soon relocate. If they planned to move, she thought, they'd likely even give her a reference if she timed it right. Claire maintained patience and caution as to what to do next. Several possibilities vacillated in her mind, from teaching in a private school to taking on another position with a high-ranking family. Her self-debates wore on, but nothing fit. The money wouldn't last forever. She must put it to work soon and stop spending. Her father was self-employed— why couldn't she follow his ambitious nature? There must be something she could do, somewhere to put the money . . . she always heard money made money. Paris was beginning anew, and she knew this was her chance to make a good life for herself. Opportunities for a woman with cold, hard cash must exist somewhere. But where?

MADAME NÉVILLE'S ADVICE

A day drifted by before Muse found time to read Claire's letter. Her new responsibilities assisting Madame Laurent kept her busy, leaving little time for personal pursuits. But when she read the letter, she sensed Claire's despondency. She rambled on about her frustrations at wanting to be her own person, to do something worthwhile. She was bright and intelligent; there must be some suitable occupation. Muse agreed with her. She wondered what she would do if free and financially sound. *I would teach*, she thought. *Open a school for freed children of slavery.*

With the many changes taking place in the house, Muse was no longer tutored by Madame Néville and rarely encountered her former mentor. But late one afternoon, as Madame Néville was leaving the Hallisburgs, Muse ran into her in the courtyard.

"How are you getting on, Mademoiselle Muse?"

"*Je vais bien*," Muse replied.

"I'm sorry you cannot continue your tutoring; you were a good student."

"*Merci.*"

"Well, I'm in a hurry . . . must go. You take care of yourself. *A bientôt!*"

Muse paused for a moment.

"*Attendez* . . . wait, *s'il vous plaît.* Madame, I have a question . . . hypothetical."

"Hypothetical? That's a very sophisticated word."

Muse hesitated again.

"What if a young girl, alone in Paris, came into money . . . what should she do with it? I mean if she wanted to go into business . . . or something."

"Muse, what are you up to?"

"*Rien.* It's just a question."

"What type of girl is she, and why is she alone?"

"Both her parents are dead," Muse replied. "She works as a nanny but wants to do something more."

"What type of girl is she?" Madame repeated.

"She is beautiful, honest, educated . . . an American who speaks French fluently."

"Are you sure this is a hypothetical question?"

"*Oui.*"

"Well, if she is as you say, she should open a shop . . . a ladies' boutique. Style and beauty will dominate this city. Trust me! L'Empresse Eugénie and her court are obsessed with fashion and *coquetterie*; their tastes and style are mesmerizing the nation and all of Europe. *La mode* is becoming an addiction with the middle class. Your friend should get on board, now."

"Selling what?"

"Accessories, clothes, perfume, that sort of thing. Listen, *ma petite*, I must go. We'll talk again. *Au revoir.*"

"*Au revoir*, Madame."

Muse stood aside as Madame got into the cabriolet. She waved goodbye.

This time it was Muse who devised the plot. She ran to her room and wrote to Claire.

UN CADEAU D'ANNIVERSAIRE

Thinking her infatuation with Jean-Paul was in decline, Muse no longer avoided him. During the day, they inevitably ran into each other. He bowed, she curtsied; he wanted to linger, but she moved on. She regained control of her sentimentality and romantic notions. But one morning she awoke to find a sheet of paper pushed underneath her door, facedown. It was a watercolor. A sketch of an enchanting blackbird, wings stretched long, soaring high in the sky over the azure waters of the Seine. Fields of green trees, wild lawn, and flowers abloom defined the landscape. There was no inscription or lettering, but she understood its symbolism and who it was from . . . it was nearing her birthday. He remembered, and she melted.

⊱⊰

It was Agnès who slipped the watercolor under Muse's door at Jean-Paul's request.

"*Pourquoi* are you doing this?" she said in a tone of irritation. "She can't read!"

"I know . . . there's no verse, only a picture," Jean-Paul said.

"*Pourquoi?*"

"I feel sorry for her."

"Well, I don't think it's wise to fraternize with inferiors."

Jean-Paul shot her a dark look.

"What do you mean inferiors?"

"You know what I mean."

"She is a slave . . . true," Jean-Paul said, "but a human being, the same as you and me.

"*Non*," Agnès said.

His eyes swelled with anger.

"I'm not fraternizing. It's her *anniversaire*, for God's sake."

A NIGHT OF FREEDOM

"A re you sure you're all right?" Madame Laurent asked.

"I have a headache," Muse responded.

"Well, go up to your room and lie down. I don't want Monsieur and Madame Hallisburg to think I've overworked you because they are away."

"*Merci*, Madame."

"I'll have dinner sent up to you."

"No, don't bother. If I'm hungry, I'll fix something myself."

"As you wish."

Muse returned to her room and took a deep breath. Her adrenaline surged. Insubordination again! But this time, by her own hand. The Hallisburgs and Agnès left for the grand summer event yesterday. She was alone. Earlier, she saw Messieurs Jean-Paul and Olivier leave for the evening. Monsieur Furet was indisposed, and Madame Laurent and Serge would soon disappear into the privacy of their own rooms.

Night fell. It was time. Muse stepped into one of Cassandra's crinolines, slipped on a petticoat, and poured her mistress's discarded iris-blue dress over her head. Redesigned and transformed, it draped down the contours of Muse's slim body until it kissed the floor. For several weeks, she had worked to re-create the gown—an exercise for the sheer love of sewing, but never did she expect an opportunity to wear it.

She emulated the petite, staccato-like needlework of the French by copying the stitches from one of Cassandra's new outfits. Cotton-silk mix was not a modish fabric, yet it inspired her to add a flounce of salvaged lace at the waist, giving the gown a mosaic appeal and a dramatic flair. She restyled the fitted bodice from a modest V shape to a low-cut, crescent curve that settled just off the shoulder. With no appliqués to work with, she instead adorned the deep neckline of the bodice with a bouquet of fresh roses picked from the garden. Muse separated the braids of her hair down the middle of her head to where they crowned her face. The back was scooped up and gathered with strings of cut lace. She even created an accessory: a matching bag of the same fabric but contoured like a teardrop. She stood in front of the mirror, soaking up her reflection.

The dresser Cassandra gave her at Der Brunnen came to mind. Portions of the looking-glass were in shards, but she could still make out her form. Sometimes at night, by the light of a burning candle, she'd gazed at her reflection, especially while developing into a young woman. The ballooning of her breasts, the shrinkage of her waist, and the curving of her hips—it seemed to have happened overnight. Muse remembered hiding her development by strapping down her breast or wearing aprons loosely tied. But despite her cautionary devices, the male population on the plantation looked at her differently, a gleam in their eyes whenever she passed. "Bring no attention to yo'self," her mother had urged. "You will only attract trouble, trouble a female slave is to be wary of." But the struggle to control her body grew tiring, and soon she gave up and let nature take its course.

And now, standing before the mirror at La Lumière, an attractive young woman stared back, altered in so many ways. She thought back to Jonathan, but the fear of him had lessened. True, the plantation was so full of menace and abuse. But as Muse smiled at her new image, she told herself, *I'm not on the plantation now.*

At the rear of the property was a door: a wooden structure in the stone wall secured by a huge metal bolt. It seemed never in use. Muse questioned Serge.

"It leads to an alleyway. No one uses it. For emergencies, I suspect."

That was how Muse left the estate that night. Wrapped in the indigo cape, she tiptoed off the grounds and walked down the dark alley. At the corner near the *bois*, a carriage waited. She waved at Claire, who waved back.

AN EVENING CAPER

"Lights!" Muse said.

"Gaslights," Claire corrected. "See, they're all along the boulevards."

"I've never been out at night before. It's beyond words."

The carriage moved through to the center of the illuminated city. Absorbed by companionship and the intoxicating city streets, Muse grew silent in the wonder of it all.

"Your dress is lovely. You sew beautifully!"

"Thank you."

"The gaslights are the vision of Baron Haussmann."

"Haussmann?" Muse said. "I know that name. Monsieur Chevreau works for him."

"Who is Monsieur Chevreau?"

"A guest at La Lumière. An architect."

"An architect?"

"Yes. And he's nice."

"Oh, really?"

They dined at a popular brasserie off the grand boulevards. When they entered the restaurant, the dinner set stirred. The men marveled, curious as they watched Muse and Claire being led to a table.

"Do they think we're courtesans?" Muse asked.

"Probably. But it can't be helped. Beautiful women, whores or not, must eat as well."

Muse laughed.

"But this is Paris. No one cares unless they're certain. We're a mystery, and Paris loves a mystery."

During dinner, they talked nonstop about the news of the day both in France and in America. They gossiped about the scandals at court and the latest fashion of L'Empresse Eugénie and her ladies-in-waiting.

Then Claire asked, "This Monsieur Chevreau, is he a real architect?"

"Yes."

Muse looked at Claire, hesitant.

"What?" Claire asked.

"Something odd happened."

"What?"

Muse confided to Claire of her meeting Jean-Paul in the garden and the conversation that transpired. She confessed of her tangled feelings . . . one minute romantic thoughts, the next minute none.

"Aggrey. This is all normal. You're just lonely, as am I. There are times I could surrender to the paperboy . . . just for someone to talk to . . . to touch."

"But he is not of my race."

"People do have relationships outside of their race; we're having one."

"Yes, but—"

"But what?" interjected Claire. "You think a Frenchman could never love a woman of color?"

"I don't know what I think."

"That is so . . . Southern. Right now, in this city, a very famous poet is in love with a woman from the islands. He flaunts her, cherishes her, and takes care of her well. It's a tumultuous relationship . . . but still. It's in all the gossips columns."

"Who is he?"

"His name is Baudelaire."

"Are they married?"

"I doubt it. Is that it? Are you wishing to marry, Aggrey?"

"No, absolutely not. Not as I am. If I were to marry . . . even *mate*, all I would do is bring another slave into the world. Why would I do that to an innocent? If I can help it, I will never do it. I was lucky I did not conceive from Jonathan's attack."

She paused.

"What I want most is to make my own way."

Muse sighed.

"We should have more wine," Claire offered. She caught the garçon's eye.

"Yes, let's do."

"Aggrey, you've got to break the cycle . . . run—no, walk—away!"

Muse waved Claire away as if to say, "This conversation is madness."

"He gave me a watercolor for my birthday."

"Who?"

"The architect. Jean-Paul Chevreau. And he painted it himself. It is beautiful."

Muse described the blackbird flying over the Seine and the colors of the Paris riverbanks when suddenly she remembered Madame Néville's advice.

"Oh! There is something I must tell you. I didn't put it in my letter, but it's the reason I wanted to see you in person. It's about what to do with your money."

The garçon brought the wine, opened it, and replenished the glasses.

"Will you be having dessert?" he asked.

"*Oui*," Claire said.

"I spoke with Madame Néville."

"The tutor."

"Yes, and she made suggestions."

Muse iterated the conversation with Madame. Claire listened, her mind processing.

"A shop . . . a ladies' shop. Hmm . . ."

"It's a good idea," Muse said.

"What kind of merchandise?" Claire asked.

"Ladies garments and accessories—scarves, handkerchiefs, that type of thing."

"Yes. I see," Claire said. "We could go into business together."

"No, Claire. It's impossible for me . . . with you or anyone else."

"I don't understand you, Aggrey. You can just walk away from them . . . away from the lunacy of Southern culture. France will give you opportunity. True, it will be difficult, especially for a woman alone, but at least you would have options . . . a life!"

"You forget that if I ran, I would never see my mother again. I would have no family at all."

"Bah! After we make money, you can buy her freedom and send for her."

"She wouldn't come, and the Hallisburgs might not sell her to me. Would you have left America if you thought your father was still alive?"

"No! But . . ."

Claire tried again.

"If we managed a shop, you would have a venue for creating your wonderful clothing and accessories. I know something of business. I mean, I know how to negotiate. I was on the streets long enough. Think about it Aggrey . . . starting a new life, bringing ourselves up in the world together."

Muse *did* think about it. Once she envisioned only a captive's life, but of late, a faint new image emerged, where she imagined leading a different existence. She straightened the bouquet of roses that graced her bodice and pushed away a wayward tress of hair that dangled across her face.

"Remember, you won't be alone. We'll do it together: partners!"

⚊⫞⫟⊐⚊

Both women were silent as the dessert was served, and then Claire cleared her throat.

"Now for my surprise . . . we're going to a masked ball."

"A ball!"

"*Oui.* It's an annual gathering given by the artist community—musicians, painters, sculptors, the lot, maybe even fashion designers."

"*Mon Dieu!* What about masks?"

"*Voila,*" Claire said, reaching into her bag and producing two black, catlike visors, one with red feathers and the other with blue. "The blue one is for you."

"Claire, I'm sorry I can't pay for anything."

"I know—one day you will. But understand, Aggrey, I'm not doing you any favors; this is not charity. I need this evening just as much as you. Do you believe me?"

"I do."

LE BAL MASQUÉ

-

The masked ball took place in an abandoned warehouse near the village of Plaisance, outside Paris. Claire and Muse arrived by carriage, as did many others. Most of the frolickers reached the destination by horseback, in carts, or on foot. The fête attracted an eccentric collection of people hiding behind masks. Camouflages ranged from a mere piece of cloth wrapped across the eyes like a bandage, with poorly cut slits barely revealing eyes, to flamboyant concealments amazing to behold. One shape copied the skull of a wolf, and another imitated a dragon's head, while the majority replicated clowns or court jesters. The rustic gathering was a gay asylum of artists, poets, and musicians who dwelled in the shadows of the city and away from the shimmering gaslights.

The warehouse looked like a barn swelling with revelers, thought Muse. Its vast, smoke-filled space was lit by a multitude of candles. Blankets of sawdust covered the wooden floorboards. A makeshift stage rested at the rear of the building, leaving ample room for dancing. Tables and chairs assembled at designated spots favored a dancehall café, albeit rough in décor.

"There's a table," Claire shouted. "Grab it!"

Muse scuttled over to the empty table, seizing both chairs. They sat.

"Isn't this exciting?"

"Oh, yes," Muse replied.

Several paintings hung on the walls: oils, watercolors, sketches—works by the locals. A gamut of representation greeted the viewers. Muse and Claire were transfixed by the abundance of creative energy running rampant in the city. The music coming from the orchestra was vibrant, lively, a force that seduced dozens of dancers to take to the floor.

"What dance is that?"

"Mazurka. A Polish dance."

Muse put her hands to her mouth as if suppressing her gaiety. With delight, she ruminated that Cassandra was at a ball in Paris, and so was she. For a moment, Muse wished the folks down on the plantation could see her now, dressed up and looking lovely . . . her mother would be overjoyed. Claire ordered drinks; they sampled hors d'oeuvres and soon settled back to enjoy the pulsating scene of dancers and spectators alike.

The clothes worn by the revelers fascinated Muse. She sat engrossed, studying how fabrics swayed and draped over the body, how shapes of dresses flattered a figure or not, and how colors and patterns coordinated in harmony or disharmony, like music.

A man in a full mask approached Claire. He whispered a few words. She smiled. Moments later, they moved toward the dance floor. The music changed to a waltz. Claire allowed the concealed man to put his hand around her waist, and they twirled in unison across the floor. *What a handsome couple they make!* Muse decided, but before she could linger on that notion, she, too, was approached. She froze, not knowing what to do. Claire gestured from across the room to get up and dance. She rose.

Muse knew how to waltz but had only done so with Cassandra. She, along with her partner, stumbled at first. But soon she relaxed, and together they spun around the room in rhythm with the music. Her dress flowed as if in a breeze. The whirling invigorated her. How different it was to dance with a man, in the firm, muscled grip of his arms.

The evening continued: music, dance, food, drink, and laughter, along with a whirlwind of introductions to strangers—some who complimented, with manners kind and considerate, whereas others proved roguish even scandalous, but Muse took it all in. She realized for the first time her power to accept or decline an invitation. She felt the puissance of liberty and her own free will. More than ever, she desired a life, a life with choices and options. Sovereignty to think on her own accord, to voice an opinion, be it informed or ill-informed . . . to make her own mistakes, to be a part of the world.

Unlike Claire, who exposed her face to several gentlemen, Muse revealed her face to only one person. He was a middle-aged man of slight stature and rustic complexion. His clear black eyes looked tired but focused. Hair, gray and receding, tumbled in full locks to the nape of his neck; he sported a silver goatee. He asked Muse to dance.

"You are an attractive-looking woman," he said with an accent she could not place.

"How can you be sure?" she responded. "I'm masked."

He took her hand and kissed it.

"I'm sure."

He looked steadily into her eyes as they danced.

"One does not see many women of color. You are from the French colonies?"

"*Non.*"

"Would you show me your face?"

She lifted her mask.

"I was right," he said. "You are beautiful."

She blushed.

"Will you let me paint you?"

"You're not serious."

"I am. I pay well."

"Really?"

"I do. My work is my life. Here, take my card."

She took it.

"One of my paintings is on the wall nearby, number fifty-two. Before you leave, look at it."

"I will."

Muse thanked him for the dance and excused herself, putting the card into her bag.

⚔

At the onset of dawn, the ball ended. The scene of rabble-rousers trying to beat the sun home looked like burlesque in slow motion. When Claire and Muse got a cab, they collapsed into the back of the vehicle in fits of laughter . . . about what, they knew not.

THE MORNING AFTER

I t is said the luminosity of the sun is paradoxical in its ability to disperse an illusion. As on the night of a full moon, when sinister reflections gyrate against a stone wall and are mistaken for a malevolent force in search of prey, but by morning, now painted in a filter of light, the terrifying image is nothing more than a silhouette of gnarled tree branches separated from its base. Muse, upon rising, faced a discouraging ambiguousness of her evening caprice. The venture of last night filled her with such tenacity—valor she never knew she possessed, a stimulated will, robust and alive. But as she lay under the covers in the full light of a late morning, the hard reality of her existence tempered her will, and the girl of last night was put back into perspective. Her body turned away from the sunlit window, her head pounded, and she ached all over . . . yet, she smiled.

The faces and the masks of the partygoers all melded into one. She still heard rhythmic cadences, voices articulating various thoughts and points of view in a wide variety of accents, dialects, and languages. The difficulty in understanding words spoken too swiftly or interrupted by roars of mirth, discussions, debates, engaged chatter about art, music, politics, the war, Napoleon III, the Empress—all while the wine flowed and as the orchestra played. Lulled into the confines of her bed, she punched the pillow, curled it around her head . . . would the room ever stop spinning?

A tap at the door.

"Mademoiselle Muse, are you up?"

"*Qui-est-ce?*"

"*C'est moi*, Madame Laurent. I've brought you breakfast. It is very late. Are you still unwell?"

"I am . . . a little."

The door handle rattled, but she jumped out of bed and held the door closed. No one could see the state of the room.

"*S'il vous plaît*, Madame Laurent, leave the tray at the door. I will eat something later."

"Are you sure?"

"*Oui.*"

"I don't want Madame and Monsieur Hallisburg to think I have overextended your services."

"Not at all," Muse responded. "I am feeling better. I will be down shortly."

"You take your time."

"*Oui*, madame."

The iris-blue dress, stained and smelling of tobacco, lay crumpled in the middle the floor just where she peeled it off. Petticoats straddled over the back of the chair. Speckles of sawdust covered the tips of Cassandra's gold satin slippers. Muse flopped back down on the bed. With a heavy head, she slipped back into the folds of the pillow and closed her eyes.

By late evening, the satin slippers had been cleaned and returned to Cassandra's wardrobe. In their absence, the Hallisburgs'

rooms conveyed a sense of peace, yet wanted for their daily dusting and straightening up, in particular, Mr. Hallisburg's desk. Amid the disarray, a pile of letters tied with a leather string protruded from an open drawer. Most of the letters had postmarks from America—not especially intriguing, but as there was nothing else to do, she set about sorting them when she came across the letter telling of Perche's death. She read it twice and lamented. Oh, how she missed him. Then she noticed two new letters, which Mr. Hallisburg did not share.

The first correspondence addressed to Mr. Hallisburg was from Mrs. Hallisburg's sister and brother-in-law who lived in Shreveport. The gist of the letter focused on concerns over Jonathan, who was staying with them until university reconvened. Because he was bored, they gave him permission to go to New Orleans for diversion. The proposed visit was only for a week's stay, but Jonathan did not return. Mrs. Hallisburg's brother-in-law traveled to the city to fetch him, but Jonathan refused to come back. The brother-in-law decided to set Jonathan up in a friend's apartment who was traveling abroad. Had they done wrong?

Muse shook her head.

"Silly."

The next letter came from Bailey, the overseer. It revealed two more runaway slaves: Moses and Debra. Muse knew them both; they were about the same age. This time neither one was found. The overseer expressed deep concern over the fact that several other slaves across the county had escaped successfully—how were they doing it? He also spoke of the change in attitude and motivation among the captives under his command. He said he needed more help in controlling the slave community, adding:

It's not just the slaves themselves who are becoming restless and willful; it's the talk, debates coming from the East seeping down into our

local communities and disturbing the minds of everyone—they're
talking as if there could be a war over the matter of slavery. It's very
disconcerting. Please advise me of your direction. I need more help!

The letter from Bailey continued in the same vein until the last
page:

I'm sorry the undertaking to France is not progressing as fast as
you would like, but you still have time. Also, I've analyzed the
slave inventory as you requested. Despite the friction that has
arisen over the slave markets here in Virginia, if you want to
proceed, I've listed the slaves that would fetch the highest price if
placed on the market.

As Muse read the list, horror ripped through her like a blunt
dagger. She dropped the letter and backed away as if bitten. For
a time, she stared at it and then into space. Hoping she misread,
she scanned the pages again, but she had not. The third name of
the list: *Muse.* Her thoughts swarmed like debris in a hurricane.

"They're going to sell me. Oh, God! They're going to sell me.
But why?"

Rage swelled. When she calmed down, her senses grew astute
like a solved mystery. She put the pages back into the envelope,
gathered up all the other communiqués, rebundled them, and
placed them back in the desk drawer. From another drawer, she
took a fresh sheet of paper from Mr. Hallisburg's private stock
and scribbled a note to Claire:

Dear Claire, I'm ready!

⊱⊰

Walking through the gardens along the winding path of roses,
Muse no longer saw the beauty of the grounds or noticed the

sweet scent of the flowers. She moved as if running from a shroud of despair as thick and dark as a high fog. Everything around her seemed to move in slow motion. Even the water spurting from the fountain seemed sluggish. Adrift, almost like sleepwalking, one foot in front of the other, frightened thoughts hammering away: *I am to be sold!* Toward the carriage house she walked, tears tracking her face, and just as she mounted the first step, a firm hand grasped her arm. She gasped and pulled away.

The imposing figure of Jean-Paul stood before her.

"*Bonsoir*, Mademoiselle Muse."

She glared hard at him as though she did not know him.

"*C'est moi*, Jean-Paul. You are all right?"

"No. I mean . . . *oui. Je vais bien.*"

"You don't look well. Come have a seat."

"No . . . go away. I don't want to talk you . . . to anyone."

He was stunned by the severity of her voice.

"Nonsense! We haven't talked for a while. What's wrong? Have I offended you?"

"Just go away!" she yelled. "Go away!"

She grabbed the tail of her skirt and ran up the stairs, sensing his eyes hard upon her. When she reached the room, she slammed the door behind her and sank to the floor and wept.

"Why?" she cried. "I've done everything you've asked me to do."

UNE SORTIE

W eeks ago, Jean-Paul had received notice that his own apartment was ready for habitation. Yet, he continued to accept Olivier's hospitality. Other than wanting to remain with him until he returned to the Black Sea, there was another motive for not leaving, one he was not conscious of—his fascination with Muse. He thought about her often. The misery of her plight wrenched his soul. He never mentioned his disquietude to Olivier. How could he explain feelings he didn't understand?

He was slow to realize that whenever she entered the room, served a meal, or just walked near him, he was on alert as if her very scent made him dizzy. His growing attraction to Muse vibrated at a much higher level than his dalliance with Agnès. But after their recent encounter in the garden, her face was etched in his mind: a look of complete despair. *What could have happened? What plagues her so? Oh, the loneliness she must possess.* Her distress and almost violent repulsion to his touch were obvious. Was he in denial? Was her behavior a sign of a woman who wanted nothing to do with him, not even as a friend? But the saddest thing of all was that when he looked deep into her troubled, angry eyes, it broke his spirit, and he realized his hope of ever knowing her would come to naught. And he condemned his own idealism. Even if she were free, their class and status could never mix, not in the old world nor the new.

"What a hypocrite you are," he said to himself, "to think such a thing. If it wasn't for the generosity of Father, your life would not be that much different from hers."

The following morning, he moved to his new home. Before departing, he painted another small watercolor and slipped it under her door himself. The image depicted his likeness boarding a horse-drawn caliche, his hat tipped in adieu toward a beautiful blackbird perched upon a windowsill.

THE ALTERCATION

La Lumière again functioned in full force. The Hallisburgs returned, exhausted, from their four-day affair. As Muse restored order back into the lives of the weary travelers, she ruminated over Jean-Paul and the watercolor he left. She stared at the work for a long time. Her fingers brushed along the lines of his face. How striking the drawing, the colors, the blackbird. She wished she could have at least said goodbye. Her heart felt heavy. She would never see him again.

━┥┝━

By day's end, all inhabitants had been fed, bathed, and tucked into bed, making for an early night.

The clock chimed midnight when an abrupt bang on the door stirred Muse awake. It sounded like a sturdy blow in anger. Perplexed, she got up and started for the door, but before she reached it, it flew open. Agnès stood before her, fists clenched.

"Where is he?" she yelled.

"Where is who?"

"Don't play with me. I've come from his room. It's empty. All his clothes . . . everything. He's gone."

"Oui."

"What happened?"

"I don't know. He just left."

She showed Agnès the watercolor.

"Did he give it to you?"

"No, not personally. It was under the door."

"You've been seeing him, haven't you?"

"I have not."

"You lie."

"I beg your pardon, Agnès, but I'm not the one who's dallying with him. Didn't he leave you a note?"

Agnès grew angrier. She snatched the watercolor and threw it on the floor.

"You nigger whore," she yelled in English.

"What is wrong with you?" Muse asked in French.

"You know what's wrong," Agnès countered, her eyes wet.

She advanced into the room. Muse moved back. Eye to eye, neither blinked.

"Get out of my room!"

Agnès shouted obscenities in rapid French. Her hands poised like claws. She rushed Muse. But Muse sidestepped her. Agnès turned, seething, and grabbed her by the hair. They tussled. She slapped Muse, but Muse, not missing a beat, slapped her back, a solid, flat blow to the face. Agnès staggered backward, lost balance, and fell through the open door onto the hallway floor just as Madame Laurent and Serge hurried forth.

"What's going on?" Madame Laurent demanded.

IN SEARCH OF A NEW LIFE

C laire sat in the café at Les Halles, waiting for Serge to arrive. He was late. The large gilded clock struck nine. Where was he? Normally, she would not have minded the delay, but she agreed to a rendezvous later that evening and wanted to prepare. At last, she saw Serge poking along the road in the old cart. He stopped in front of the vegetable section and descended from the wagon. *Can he move any slower?* she thought.

As soon as he started his rounds, she walked up to the cart and casually slipped her hand beneath the vehicle. She removed the latest correspondence from Muse and replaced the pouch with her own news of the week. Then she moved away.

The news Claire shared with Muse was of a romantic encounter. A man she met at an outdoor concert.

He is like someone you dream about meeting but never expect to, she wrote.

His name was Gerard, tall, blond, and from Dijon. Claire penned several pages about him: how interesting he was, how stimulating, how articulate. She composed her message as if writing in a trance. Muse never heard her express herself so fancifully, so poetically. She told of the impending invitation to a concert, a late supper, and perhaps more.

Oh, Aggrey, I am undone!

Claire was so zealous in readying for the evening ahead that she had no time to read Muse's letter until late the following day. She read it twice to make sure she understood.

"I'm ready" was all it said.

The moment Claire read Muse's letter, she sprang into action. By midday, she had walked blocks, crisscrossing avenues and boulevards near the center of Paris. Her feet ached from traipsing in and out of commercial shops displaying "To Let" signs. Nothing was affordable. Blisters formed on the back of her heels, yet she kept walking, only one thought in her mind: an opportunity to do something with her life had appeared, and nothing would stop her from taking advantage of it. Claire would be her own woman and never again dependent on another person or on crime. She, too, was ready.

An hour or two later, she stepped foot on the fashionable rue de la Paix: a grand boulevard with elegant shops and extravagant window displays. She walked passed them, drifting into fantasy; one day she would be one of those women who frequented such expensive salons.

She reached the end of the boulevard, but having lost all sense of direction, inadvertently turned off into a wide cobblestone passageway; it led to a cul-de-sac. The modest little square was off the footway but near enough to the elegant boulevard to lure in foot traffic if the signage was adequate. Three small shops faced each other on the secluded street: a candlemaker, a wicker furniture maker, and a third one, vacant. A "To Let" sign hung from inside the window. Claire knocked, but there was no answer. She opened the door and entered.

A PLAN

At times, Muse thought she would go mad. During the many nights spent cocooned in her room, idle sewing kept her sane.

To Muse, stitching was like a mantra, like the sound of soothing chimes that rang at the flurry of a breeze. What happy silent hours! The recycled fabric from Cassandra's discarded wardrobe took on many new shapes and forms: pillows, festive pincushions, small tablecloths, and serviettes. Cassandra's soft, off-white linen dress, now too plain for Paris, was cut into squares the size of a lady's handkerchief. On each piece, she hemmed and then embroidered an elaborate design from an array of multicolored threads: fleurettes, tiny animals, and other colorful images. Her favorite illustration was the black swallowtail butterfly. She remembered one that somehow flew into the shack. It soared around for hours, frantic to get out. She recalled how it must have felt. It was pure black with what looked like white brush strokes on its wings and, at the tail, a single dramatic spot of orange. How vividly it came back to her. The image made such an artful contrast against the white linen.

Muse had created and stockpiled dozens of pieces over the last months and hid them under the bed. It never occurred to her that one day the whatnots might be useful.

In the basement, she found two ragged old burlap sacks. In preparation, Muse filled them with the various pieces she created, and in no time, the bags bulged to capacity. She and Claire planned that on a certain evening, if safe, she would drag the bags through the exit door of the garden and leave them hidden beneath a bramble bush.

The next evening, she checked to see if Claire had claimed the bags. She had. Muse felt a thrill, as it brought her one step closer to freedom.

GERARD

Claire had lain with Gerard after their second meeting. She couldn't remember who seduced whom . . . she didn't care. All she knew was that being with him was living again. What was it about him? She couldn't tell you. Was it because he was an attractive man, suave, well bred, and attentive? No! It was something more. She smiled when she thought of him, placing her hand over her heart as if to calm it down. His eyes, his smile . . . what was it that captivated her so? When in his embrace, a new vibration soared through her, a recalling of peace and security. She searched far back in memory to recall the sensation, further into her childhood for thoughts of protection and of belongingness—back to when her mother and father were alive. She drummed up those forgotten memories and buried herself within them, but now there was Gerard.

TENSION

The tension between the Hallisburgs and Muse grew each day, a strained anxiety as each held on to a life-changing secret. Mr. and Mrs. Hallisburgs treated Muse with a casual kindness and respect, an altered benevolent attitude portrayed just before a planned injustice occurred.

"Oh no, Muse. You've had such a strenuous day. You are excused. Go to bed early," or "No, no, Muse, let Agnès do it."

Agnès now managed the Hallisburgs entirely. Muse functioned more or less as Agnès's servant. They worked side by side in cutting silence. Neither Muse nor Agnès told the Hallisburgs of the altercation. Madame Laurent warned Agnès that if she spoke a word of what transpired, she would be terminated at once. She swore not to speak of it only because the Hallisburgs had yet to make her an offer of employment. As for the bruises on her face, she explained: "I tripped up the stairs . . . my face hit the banister. I'm all right. *Merci*, Mademoiselle Hallisburg."

While Muse continued to harbor a fondness for Cassandra, she ceased caring about the Hallisburgs' needs and wants, about what they might or might not think, or what they might or might not do. The services of Madame Néville ended. With the help of Agnès, younger, more energetic, and in a better position to fine-tune their daughter in language and manners daily, hopes for Cassandra's accomplishments still flickered. But Cassandra wished for more invitations that would allow her to observe, to experience, and to take part of the European social world at an elevated level. Weeks passed, but no major invitations arrived.

A REVELATION

M r. and Mrs. Hallisburg were dining alone.
"I hope she is enjoying the opera, darling," Mrs. Hallisburg
said as she motioned for Muse to refill her glass of sherry.

"What did they go to see?"

"Verdi."

The clock struck eight.

"Darling," Mr. Hallisburg said. "It's time to go back to
Virginia."

"What do you mean?"

Muse startled and looked straight at them. *What perfect timing!*
she thought.

"This was a mistake . . . the whole venture. I can't get the
four-day event out of my head. We were laughingstocks. Fools,
American novelties invited to a grand *fête* for the amusement of
the aristocrats and wealthy bourgeoisie. What were we thinking?"

"We want the best for our daughter . . . to prepare her to
marry well, to live a life of security and status."

"She's done very well, and I'm proud of her . . . but enough! There is no more that can be done."

"How do you know? We have a few months left. She still has a lot to learn."

"No, it's time."

"More sherry?" Muse asked.

"Yes, thank you," Mrs. Hallisburg said.

Muse refilled both glasses and returned to her place next to the service table and listened in silence.

"I suffered a very disturbing conversation with a man at the *fête*," Mr. Hallisburg said. "The fact that our fortune depends on forced labor invited intercourse and exchange that I found alarming. Especially when asked to share my point of view . . . my philosophy on the institution of slavery and the lack of moral consciousness that seems to prevail in the American South."

Moral consciousness, thought Muse, *they don't know what the term means.*

"Go on, dear," urged Mrs. Hallisburg as she sipped her sherry.

"A gentleman, Monsieur Albert Gitane, expressed curiosity as to how I planned to protect my status, my lofty state of affluence, in the inevitable near future.

"'What do you mean?' I asked.

"'How will you sustain your prosperous lifestyle should change—that is to say, political amendments—transpire in your country?' he replied."

Muse's eyes turned toward Mr. Hallisburg.

"'Amendments!' I said. 'What kind of amendments? I don't understand you, monsieur.'

"'Your livelihood is based on a formula of a coerced subservient community, explicitly free labor remaining the status quo, *n'est-ce pas*?' he replied.

"Darling, he was so irritating. And he would not stop talking."

Muse smiled.

"'It is impossible!' Monsieur Gitane continued.

"'What is impossible?' I said.

"'That forced labor will remain the norm in the South.'

"'Of course, it will,' I countered.

"Then he said: 'My dear monsieur, you are a guest in a country that is a model for the development of the human soul at any cost. A cradle, so to speak, of human rights. It is what the revolution was about.'

"'But monsieur,' I said, 'France is not America, and the Negro slave cannot be compared to the lowest of your classes, not even the peasantry of the French . . . it's simply apples and oranges.'"

Muse raised an eyebrow in contempt.

"He said, 'Then, monsieur, you believe there is no human insight within the Negro and that they will continue to allow themselves to be treated as nonhumans?'

"'They have no choice. Unquestionably, they depend on us, on their owners. If nothing else, for their very livelihood, their very survival.'

"'And this you are sure of?' he asked.

"'*Bien sur*,' I said. But then, darling, my mind rushed back to the letter we received from Bailey of the unrest among our community of slaves and the comments relating to the runaways."

Muse's eyes looked straight ahead as she remembered reading the letter.

"Monsieur Gitane continued, 'Monsieur, I read a lot of foreign newspapers, especially from America. I ask you this: What if your countrymen who are, shall we say, more attuned to the measure of human realization than you and your Southern patriots, what if . . . I'm trying to say . . . could it be imagined that your comrades in the North would take on the fight . . . the debate . . . whatever it is called, to come to the rescue of the downtrodden, those who are enslaved. If nothing else but from a purely economic standpoint, namely, the abolishment of chattel labor. It would foil the entire institution and therefore your fortune. How would you cope? How would you reinvent yourself?'"

Muse's eyes widened.

"'That will never happen,' I said.

"'For your sake, Monsieur Hallisburg, I hope not,' he replied.

"That man left me with a bad taste in my mouth."

"Honey, you are upset."

"Very much so. The damned nouveau riche. They are almost all in industry, not . . ."

Mr. Hallisburg went quiet.

"Honey," he said. "He's right. If we suddenly didn't have access to the institution of slavery, what would we do? It's time to go home. And take care of our own business there."

Through the letters carried back and forth between Muse and Claire, they devised an escape plan: a plot that required no confrontation. The samples and merchandise Muse created were systematically removed from the house. Once a week, she left bags in the alleyway, and Claire retrieved them with the help of her new beau. The flight would take place at midweek, by the light of the next full moon. On the designated night, the Hallisburgs were scheduled to dine out. Monsieur Olivier Furet had returned to sea, leaving his father once again bedridden and requiring constant attention from his nurse. The Laurents retired at the same time every evening, and Agnès, for reasons not known, retreated to the privacy of her room earlier and earlier, not stirring until morning.

CLAIRE IN LOVE

The man mesmerized Claire. For weeks on end, she existed only for him. At last, the gods smiled on her behalf. For so long, she fought to survive, but now it seemed she would get a chance to live. It was happening so fast: the start of a new business and a new love. Gerard Diderot was a man of means, although no profession to speak of. He always behaved with an air of affluence and genuinely appeared to adore her. Within weeks of meeting him, she quit the Grossmonts and moved into his apartment. Inseparable: theater, concerts, art galleries, long, slow walks through the *bois*. And they made love so completely.

She never actually knew where his money came from, but he always carried plenty of it. The assumption was his family fueled his finances.

The new business adventure she was embarking on intrigued Gerard. He also seemed legitimately compassionate for her partner, who was on the verge of emancipation. He wanted to help, not only financially, but in other ways. It was he who suggested to Claire that Muse smuggle out her merchandise little by little before the escape, leaving her without a heavy load to carry. He also offered to supply furniture and to invest in required necessities—fabric, accessories, and employees.

But soon, even looking through her rose-colored glasses, Claire detected inconsistencies in Gerard's character. A pendulum of behavior exhibiting drastic mood swings. At times, he grew anxious, nervous, as if adrenaline surged through his veins one minute and ceased the next, only to again rush forth, then return to normal. He suffered from sleep deprivation and fits of paranoia.

"*Mon chérie*, you must see a doctor."

"No! There is nothing wrong with me."

On the night of Muse's planned escape, Claire and Gerard attended the opera. Patronizing the opera afforded an opportunity to mingle with belle society. For many, it was the main reason for going. Not so for Claire. Engrossed in the moment, she relished the genre's grand spectacle, the unity of drama, music, and voice.

During intermission, Claire noticed Gerard's mood swing—again sudden, but not unexpected.

"Are you all right?"

"I'm fine."

"You look pale. Are you concerned about our helping Aggrey to escape tonight?"

"No, I want to help."

"Then what is it?"

"Nothing! I look forward to meeting her."

Then he excused himself, leaving Claire marooned in the foyer. He was gone for a long time. As the opera reconvened, Claire was forced to return to their box alone. Vexed, her eyes scoured the theater. No sign of him. He returned just as the third act finished, flustered. Apologetic, he pecked her softly on the nape of the neck. While distracting her, he slipped a small pouch into her evening bag.

The opera ended in a thunder of applause. Leading soprano and star tenor both took numerous bows, as did the baritone. The audience appreciated the new production by Verdi and lingered on with a standing ovation.

"Come, sweetheart," Claire said. "It's time. Aggrey will be waiting. Hurry, or we'll be late."

"*Oui*, let's go," he said.

Hand in hand, they cut their way through the theater mob, bidding goodbye to friends and acquaintances. But just as they reached the exit, two uniformed gendarmes stopped Gerard and asked him to step aside.

THE FUGITIVE

Muse sat idle on the floor, the circumference of her full skirt gathered around her. She stared at her luggage. The same cloth bag she brought from Virginia. She packed the iris-blue dress and the uniforms; she was wearing the black one for camouflage. Claire had cautioned: "At the appointed time just leave—no word." But Muse found it difficult to do; something tore at her. A slim line separated love from hate, and she realized the Hallisburgs, in a strange way, were extended family, at times, more so than her own mother. Her first sense of consciousness was her mother's presence and then theirs. Inexplicably, she already missed them. And what about her mother? If she succeeded, she might never see her again. She could not just walk out.

Of her own accord, she penned a lengthy letter confessing all. She told of her ability to read and write from a very early age, under the mentorship of . . . no, she would not reveal his name. Thoughts of emancipation surfaced almost at once after Jonathan's attack. And then she scripted the final jolt—that she knew she was to be sold once they returned to Virginia . . . how could they?

The city of Paris awakened her in a most profound way; she could never go back to the life of a subservient bound on a plantation. She would sooner perish like Perche. Also, she believed she owned skills strong enough to make her own way. Her final request: "Do not pursue me or take revenge out on my mother; she knows nothing about it." After a few carefully selected lines of openness and self-determination, she bade the Hallisburgs goodbye, then added the final line: "And please tell Mama I love her."

A full moon stood high; its brightness lit the way. Luggage in hand, she passed through the back exit and eased along the alleyway and into the *bois* to wait for Claire and Gerard. The night bore out unusually cool. She shivered under the indigo cloak. Winter was approaching. Alone in the woods, she kept guard. It was oh so quiet! Tinges of anxiety rose within her. It seemed like everything happened so fast; the past several months spun by in a foray of images, flashing like currents of a storm. She forced her mind to dwell on positive thoughts. What she could look forward to, simple everyday occurrences most people took for granted: reading openly, eating out, coming and going as she pleased. But most of all, the ability to exert her own free will and no longer walk in the shadow of another.

An hour or more passed. No Claire. Surely the opera was over by now. The moon glowed; it must be midnight, at least. She settled down on the soft, moist ground, her knees drawn up to her chin. At last, she heard the clip-clop of horse hooves and the trundle of iron wheels. She jumped up and ran out toward the road, but the cab cruised past. Inside, a well-dressed elderly couple sat at their leisure. She retreated into the woods.

Tangled in a web of panic, Muse stared into the darkness. Had she mistaken the day . . . the time . . . the place? Soon it would be light. In a few hours, she would be missed. Only two choices: go back into servitude or get to the city, get lost in the crowd, and then think of what to do next.

She held tight to her bag as she marched along the deserted road; she hoped she was going the right way. Her mind squirmed back and forth like a trout caught on a hook. Had she been tricked? Had Claire been lying to her? But why? She owned nothing in the world . . . nothing but the samples, which Claire took. She thought, *Was there ever really a shop? Was she after the samples after all? No, that makes no sense . . . Claire has money.*

She moved down the road, her silhouette drifting alongside her like a phantom. Besides the mist and the deadness of the night, a chill nipped at her nose. Emptiness gripped her, and she felt as hollow and as eerie as the dark companion that followed her. But oddly, almost at the same time, a sense of lightness crept in; a sense of elation embraced her. Her pace quickened, and suddenly she was running.

At a crossroad, Muse caught her breath. The moon still lit the way, a cold but clear night. And then she heard the lazy, rolling sound of a mule and wagon trotting up behind her. She stepped aside and waved for the driver to stop. He pulled up. He was hauling a wagon loaded with fresh vegetables heading for Les Halles, she imagined. When she saw suspicion in his eyes, she flung the hood from her face and smiled.

"*Excusez-moi*, monsieur. I want to go to the center of town, am I going in the right way?"

"What street?"

"Rue de la Paix," she said.

"I can drop you off within a few blocks."

But Muse hesitated.

"You getting in or not?"

"*Merci.*"

The driver extended his hand and pulled her up into the cart.

"*Merci,*" she repeated.

⇥⇤

The driver stopped a few yards from the rue de la Paix, the street Claire mentioned in her last letter. She was now convinced of a mix-up; Claire was not capable of such duplicity. Something must have happened. Muse had to find the shop; she was sure it existed. The only description: a small boutique with a large window facing two other shops; one sold furniture, and the other sold candles. Muse roamed up and down the damp, soundless street, looking for shops that resembled Claire's description. Nothing. But as she searched, she reflected, *This can't be right.* The salons along the rue de la Paix were the most fashionable in Paris. It was where the Hallisburgs of the world shopped. *This can't be the right street.*

Day broke; bit by bit, the streets came alive. Cafés opened, as did newsstands and other street vendors. Soon pedestrians poured down the boulevard like a rushing stream. Muse dodged them left and right, taking refuge against the wall of a building. Her feet ached, and her stomach growled. A bench in the public square sat vacant. Muse ran to it. In her satchel, she brought food and water, but what she wanted most was something hot: coffee or chocolate, anything to warm her freezing body. Across the square was a crowded café, boisterous and animated with laborers and domestics, but she could only observe. She had no money. The café's clock showed half past six. Another hour or two before her absence was discovered.

Again, she skirted the streets, looking for the shop; by noon, she had exhausted all possibilities and returned to the public bench. The rest of the day she spent watching people walk by. *What a show!* Muse thought. But when the amusement of Parisians on parade wore off, she worried; what was she going to do?

Nightfall. In her wanderings, she noted a small, dark space concealed under a staircase on the side of an old stone building; it was a dank, sordid cavity of a hole, but it was secluded and not visible to the mainstream passersby. She remembered reading that the Préfecture de Police were cracking down on *délit de vagabondage*, the homeless. *God,* Muse reflected, *what if I get arrested?* That night, her first evening as a liberated woman, she claimed the isolated spot under the staircase. Using her meager luggage as a pillow, she lay down, bundled up in the indigo cape, and drifted. She lay there, eyes half opened toward the flickering gaslights that brightened the night. She listened to the quick steps of people darting through the noisy avenues. A huge city rat scuttled across the way, dodging traffic; her eyes widened. But then she closed them again—rats fielded the plantation all the time. After some time, the streets grew quiet, and her spirit exhaled; safe for the moment. She slept curled up on the ground and dreamed of running but then jolted awake. A flash of information prodded her memory: a cul-de-sac. The shop was in a cul-de-sac.

At daylight, she gathered her things and went down to the Seine River to wash her face. She nibbled on bread and cheese. Once refreshed, she hit the streets again, unaware of the half smile that painted her face or the determination in her eyes. She was not conscious of the joyful feeling of roaming the streets on her own, reporting to no one.

She trudged on, exploring every possible opening, every nook and cranny in the general area of the rue de la Paix. But soon Muse gave up in frustration and dropped her bag where she stood. A small tobacco kiosk across the street caught her attention. The vendor looked friendly enough; he would know the neighborhood. She greeted him. In slow, careful French she said, *"Pardon, monsieur. Je cherche mon amie. Elle habite dans une voisine du cul-de-sac. "*

He responded in rapid French; she understood only a few words. But his animation, his arms flailing, pointing, urged her to continue down the rue de la Paix. She followed his instructions and walked about twenty minutes until the street tapered off. She came upon a wide, cobblestone entrance almost hidden by the frame of a whitewashed stone archway; it led to a quaint dead-end street.

She entered the large open square. No pedestrians and only three small shops: two still closed, one unoccupied. She dropped her things in front of the empty shop and peeked through its windows. The door was locked. At the rear of the building, she made the same efforts. She cupped her hands around her eyes, pressing her nose against the windowpane. With great relief, she saw her burlap sacks leaning up against the wall in a huge empty room.

There must be a way in. She scrutinized the façade of the building; a small window on the second floor, ajar, came into view. With the help of a large overturned flowerpot and the iron rail of an adjacent gate, she clambered up, scaling the wall to the second floor. She pulled open the window and attempted to climb through the aperture, but she got tangled up in skirt and petticoats. Once again, she tried, but this time she rucked up her dress and undergarments and tied them between her legs like a loincloth and then slid through the casement. She fell to the other side. Down the stairs she ran, then unlatched the front door and dragged in her bag. She secured the door, sank to the floor in a heap, and drew in a deep breath.

A loud knock at the front door tore Muse from her sleep.

"Claire!" she shrieked.

Scrambling from a makeshift bed, she threw an old blanket over her nightgown and ran downstairs. A short, bulbous man stood out front. Dressed in dark, frayed clothes, he held his top hat in his hand. Muse opened the door.

"*Oui*, monsieur," she said.

"Is Mademoiselle Price in?"

"Price?"

"Claire Price."

Until then, Muse had forgotten Claire's surname.

"*Non.*"

"Who are you?"

"My name is Muse . . . uh, Aggrey . . ."

"Good morning, Mademoiselle Aggrey, I am Jacque Metier, the owner of the building."

"*Oui.*"

"Do you work with Mademoiselle Price?"

"*Oui.*"

"Well, I'm here to make sure you have moved in without incident. And to confirm the lease has been paid in advance up to six months. After that time, you may pay in advance again or at the beginning of each month thereafter."

"*Oui, bien sûr,*" Muse replied.

Monsieur Metier handed her the lease and a second set of keys to give to Mademoiselle Price.

"*Merci,*" Muse said.

She returned to her room and read the lease. Claire had put both their names on the contract. Whatever happened, they had six months to make the shop work.

LE BOUTIQUE

The building claimed three floors, but only two were at their disposal. In the front of the shop, a large bay window overlooked the courtyard and the two neighboring shops. A wooden counter with a smooth surface prevailed over the room, allowing for ample shelving behind it. Muse ran her index finger along the countertop, the dust so thick it left a trail. She wrote: *Claire and Muse's Dress Shop,* then erased it with her palm. The oak flooring was sturdy but creaked in certain areas. A crude wooden chair with a tattered cushioned seat and curved legs leaned up against a corner wall. A musty, damp odor existed. She recalled the wonderful fragrance exuding from the finer salons in Paris. But the morning light spiraling through the window gave the shop an enchanting appearance. In the back room, a huge, rectangle-shaped table stood in the middle of the floor like an island. Muse found in the cupboards a box of candles, matches, discarded mugs and plates, and two tins of sardines. A cast-iron, coal-burning box stove rested in the corner. It was enough for now, she thought.

Where to begin? She poked around the cold, empty space, envisioning how the shop might look once transformed. But then she stalled, trembled as if lost. Uncertainties crept back into her mind. The blazing joy of freedom dimmed to a low flicker when she thought, *How am I going to survive on my own?*

But as she perused the ceiling, the stairs, her mind pivoted from fear toward her natural instincts of esthetics and the details of managing a shop. She reflected on the many times she accompanied Cassandra to local shops in Virginia County and in Paris. What had she noticed all those hours of waiting for Cassandra to make up her mind? What did she remember? How did it work?

She rummaged through the burlap sacks. At the bottom of one sac, two more of Cassandra's unwanted dresses: green velvet and pink linen. What could she make from them? What would sell?

CLAIRE'S INTERROGATION

"I don't know," Claire said.

"You must know. They were found in your evening bag," the chief inspector said.

The room was dingy, stifling. There was no window. Claire sat on a hard wooden chair before a table, where she rested her hands, fingers laced together. The inspector, in full uniform, paced before her.

"Mademoiselle, this is very serious. Theft is a criminal offense here in France."

"It is also in America," she replied. "I swear to you, I've never seen those jewels. I did not steal them."

"And to make matters worse," he said, "you have no papers."

Claire explained she was employed by the Grossmonts until only a few weeks ago.

"I didn't have time to get new papers. The Grossmonts will vouch for me."

"We will speak with them; fear not."

"And," Claire said, "my mother was French. Her family name was Hébert."

"You have no papers—how will you prove it? Do you know how many Héberts live in this country? If you found them, would they know you? Would they vouch for you? *Non!*"

Claire hung her head.

"Let's get back to the jewels, *s'il vous plaît.*"

He placed the jewels in front of her: an emerald brooch, a man's gold farthing watch and chain, a diamond pin, and matching bracelet.

"Well, you've got good taste."

"I did not take them."

"If not you, then who?"

Claire pursed her lips.

"Mademoiselle, you are stupid. You would risk going to jail for something you did not do? Yes, we have discerned you could not have taken them."

"Then why am I here?"

"Because you are the one in possession of stolen goods!"

She looked down at her hands. They glistened from perspiration; her forehead grew warm.

"We have a witness. Next to the opera is a well-established hotel. Are you familiar with it?"

"*Oui.*"

"The witness, a patron of the opera, was outside having a smoke. He saw a man come from the back of the hotel. He was in formal dress. While he did not see his face, he noted the man's blond hair and his disheveled appearance. He held a handful of bright objects that caught the light from the lamppost across the street . . . the items shone like jewels. It made no sense to the witness at the time. But he thought it odd the man stuffed the sparkling objects in his pockets."

"Well, you see, it was not me."

"It was not you, but your companion has blond hair. We detained every blond male in attendance and their companions— which led to you."

"It was not him. He never left my side during the entire performance," Claire blurted out.

"He says the same thing, and he has also never seen those jewels. But I'm afraid, mademoiselle, the consequences of the robbery will be yours alone."

She swallowed but held her ground.

Gerard told her it was a misunderstanding . . . to say not a word, to sit tight. His family was on the way. They would be out in no time.

"Mademoiselle Price, please talk to us. For your own good."

"I did not steal these jewels," she repeated, "and neither did Monsieur Diderot. I have nothing more to say."

THE SEARCH FOR A RUNAWAY

Mr. Hallisburg was livid. His heart palpitated. His breathing shorted to staccato-like gasps; he could barely speak. He sat down and then got up again. Around the room he paced, waving Muse's letter in the air like the flag of betrayal. Mrs. Hallisburg, fearing he would injure himself, told Agnès to send for the doctor.

"This is your doing, Cassandra!"

"No, Father. I swear I knew nothing about it."

"But you were with her day and night. Did you notice nothing? This has been going on for years, she says. Educated! How is it possible? It's against the law!"

"I swear, Father—I did not know."

He read and reread excerpts from the letter out loud like a stage actor in the final throes of a soliloquy. Then he stopped, cut a look at his daughter, and said, "She writes better than you."

"Oh, Father!"

"We have to find her; we have to get her back. That's all there is to it!"

"But how can we, sweetheart?" Mrs. Hallisburg interjected. "Have you forgotten this is France? They have abolished all laws upholding slavery."

"I don't care!" Mr. Hallisburg screamed. "We are not leaving here without her. She is our property. She belongs to us."

The doctor arrived and gave Mr. Hallisburg a sedative to calm him. He slept. Mrs. Hallisburg hovered around him until the late evening and then went down to dinner with Cassandra.

"Have you ever seen Muse reading?" Mrs. Hallisburg asked quietly.

"Mother, I've seen her looking at fashion magazines, but I assumed that's what she was doing—looking at the pictures."

Cassandra stared at her mother.

"Was Daddy really going to sell her?"

"Hush, Cassandra, and eat."

⇒‖⇐

At sunrise, the Hallisburgs, including Agnès, scoured the neighborhood and *bois*, looking for Muse.

"How did she get away? Where could she have gone? Surely she doesn't think she can survive on foreign streets alone?" Mrs. Hallisburg rambled.

"She must have hated us to run off like this," Cassandra said. "Did we treat her that badly?"

"Shut up, Cassandra," Mr. Hallisburg said.

"Father, were you going to sell her?"

"I said shut up!"

When the search party returned to La Lumière, Agnès put forth a suggestion.

"Why not ask Monsieur Furet for help? He is still connected, knows people. Perhaps he can give you advice."

"Clever idea, Agnès," Mr. Hallisburg replied.

—≺‖≻—

Monsieur Furet had no interest in recapturing a runaway slave. But Mr. Hallisburg pleaded his case with vigor.

"She is young, naïve, helpless, not to mention penniless. There is no way she can survive the streets alone. She must be found if only for her own safety."

Monsieur could not, in all consciousness, debate the verity that a young, impoverished female would likely meet her demise without protection. With reluctance, Furet penned down the name of a viable solicitor.

THE SOLICITOR

It was half past ten when Mr. and Mrs. Hallisburg reached the legal offices of Monsieur Hibou. Another few minutes passed before he met with them. Despite his less-than-average height and his slight stature, he, a man well into his forties, originated an elegant air offset by his curt manner. He gave off the effect of a resourceful and powerful man.

"So," he started, "you are guests of Monsieur Furet, *n'est-ce pas?*"

"*Oui*, monsieur."

"How is his health?" Monsieur Hibou asked. "He is a dear friend of my father, which is why I have cleared my morning appointments to speak with you. How can I be of service?"

The Hallisburgs told Monsieur Hibou of their dilemma and how imperative it was they find their runaway before departing for Virginia next month.

"Well," responded Monsieur Hibou, "I see your difficulties. But I am afraid, we, that is to say, my firm, cannot help you.

Slavery is illegal in this great sovereign country of ours. We believe the person in question has the right to choose freedom."

"We know, but there must be something we can do. She is very valuable to us."

"Let me ask you this: Has the young woman stolen anything from you or destroyed private property like furniture or artwork?"

"No. She literally left with the clothes on her back," Mr. Hallisburg said.

"I can't do anything for you."

"Oh, please, Monsieur Hibou. Muse has been with us since the day she was born," Mrs. Hallisburg said, speaking with unusual passion.

"Her mother is waiting for her in Virginia. We simply cannot walk away and leave her vulnerable on the streets of Paris. Surely that is far more immoral than slavery."

"I'm sorry, madame. My hands are tied. Except . . . maybe . . ."

"What?" Mr. Hallisburg asked. "We'll do anything."

"There might be a way, but it would have to be strictly under the table, so to speak."

"What?"

"My firm could not by any means be connected to the contact I am thinking of."

"What contact?"

Monsieur Hibou opened his desk and pulled out an address book. He fingered through several pages.

"I have the name of an individual who, in his earlier years, along with his father, owned a slave-trading business. They lived in Africa for many years. If anyone can find your lost property, he can. His name is Peltier, Louis Peltier. This is his address."

That afternoon, Mr. Hallisburg sent a messenger to track down Peltier. The messenger, a bushy-haired, gaunt adolescent, plodded the pavement of a seedy neighborhood cramped with sewerless apartment buildings. He searched for boulevard de l'Hôpital. Eventually, it came into view. The boulevard snaked through a block of poorly constructed one-room residences. He located the address and climbed four flights to apartment number 45. He knocked twice. No answer. He put his ear to the door. Silence. From the pocket of his jacket, he withdrew a sealed envelope addressed to Louis Peltier and slid it under the door.

A BREATH OF AIR

For two days, Muse dared not leave the shop. She feared missing Claire if she turned up, and she was certain the Hallisburgs were searching for her. The solitude tore at her. At one point, she thought she would go mad if not for the concentration and focus needed to do the delicate embroidery required for the handkerchiefs. In the back room, she sat bent over a piece, plying her needle meticulously. She was humming a solitary tune: a soothing, slow melody her mother used to sing. It helped subdue her mind from wild speculation. Suppose Claire never showed up. What then? What if the Hallisburgs found her and forced her to return? The food was almost gone save for a can of sardines someone left behind. A sardonic smile spread across Muse's face; had she come this far to die of hunger? Filled with dread and the walls closing in, she went upstairs to change. She would take a chance and go for a walk.

Having no furniture, she never unpacked until she spotted two hooks nailed into the wall. From her bag, she pulled out the iris-blue dress and then the uniforms. When she hung up the white uniform, two coins fell from its pocket and rolled across the floor. At first, she stared at them, baffled, and then picked them up. She didn't know what they were. They were the color of faded copper. One side showed an engraved profile of Napoleon III, bare head with a goatee, the other side read, *un franc*.

"Ah!" she said.

The money Claire gave her at the fair, to take a taxi in case they got separated. That was months ago. Other than the visit to the exhibition, she wore the white uniform one other time, the time she served drinks at Olivier Furet's dinner, the night she recognized Jean-Paul. She grew pensive; how was he? Where was he?

She put on the black uniform and took to the boulevards. Enticed by the marvels of the city, she made her way to various architectural sites and gardens and watched with interest the reconstruction going on in many parts of the city. But most of all, she studied the behavior of the Parisians in their daily habitat, especially those well dressed. Curious about how the elegant salons on the *rue* operated, she fostered up courage enough to enter one of the establishments, a small boutique she came across. Uncertain if she would be admitted, she paused, took a deep breath, and walked in. After receiving a courteous *bonjour* from the salesgirl, the rapid beating of her heart settled. She browsed. The knowledge Muse searched for was a basis to set a price for her simple odds and ends. If a boutique such as this one charged such-and-such for a simply embroidered handkerchief, then she could charge so-and-so. She was also curious as to what sort of merchandise this boutique offered and its arrangement.

At a nearby café, she drank coffee, ate a croissant, and lingered. Life was changing, resonating at a higher beat; a transformation was in progress, and she could feel the difference.

On the way back to the cul-de-sac, she bought fresh food: *une baguette, du jambon, du fromage, et du lai.* Just as she was about to cross the street adjacent the cul-de-sac, she noticed a young girl holding a basket of flowers. The girl strolled the boulevard, chanting, "Roses . . . violets . . . roses . . . violets."

A few customers buzzed up to her. Two men bought tiny bouquets for their lady friends. Muse monitored how the girl conducted herself—the way she strode, how she carried her basket. Her eye contact, although limited, was a carefully orchestrated glance as she moved down the boulevards. She attracted potential customers with hardly a word.

By the time Muse got back to the cul-de-sac, the wicker store across the way was closing. She rushed over, introduced herself, and begged the owner for one more minute. For a few *centimes*, she bought a sturdy, used wicker basket.

First thing the next morning, she assembled her many novel pieces. She folded the custom-made handkerchiefs and scarves in an eye-catching way and placed them in the wicker basket on top of a bed of wild fern and vine leaves she picked from a nearby field. She tied a scarf, a long strip of pale green linen, around the neck of her gray uniform and carted the festive basket about the streets. Although she was concerned about being spotted by the Hallisburgs, she took the risk. She walked the rue de la Paix and other adjacent streets, mimicking the flower girl.

"*Les mouchoirs . . .*" she chanted. "*Les écharpes . . .*"

That night she calculated her first-ever earned income.

THE BOUNTY HUNTER

Louis Peltier lay passed out on the bed, the repercussion from an all-night binge at a local café. When he came to, he was knotted up in a fetid blanket with only an empty whisky bottle at his side. The woman he hired to sleep with him left. How he hated waking up alone. The sun was setting when he forced himself up, his head swimming. Hunger and thirst caused his stomach to burn. He grabbed the bottle, turned it upside down, and stretched out his slithering tongue; a few drops of the hard liquor dripped into his mouth. Frustrated, he threw the empty bottle on the floor. It shattered.

—⚔—

He was half-dressed, ready to go out carousing again, when he saw the envelope on the floor.

He tore it open without preamble. The instructions were detailed; he read and reread them closely and understood the assignment as secretive and time sensitive. Peltier went to his armoire to examine his clothes. He owned but two decent suits: daywear and eveningwear, both well tailored but frayed along the jacket cuffs and trouser legs. He stood before the small oval-shaped mirror hanging on the wall—unrecognizable. His once-appealing looks had vanished; his nose curved, now deformed because he'd left it to heal on its own after a barroom brawl a year ago. Black, cold eyes that no longer gazed out into the world but leered at it, a stark stare that, if turned on you, was disconcerting. Even he thought he looked ragged, wastrel. He dragged a hairbrush through his long, greasy hair, black with streaks of muddy gray; it would be washed, cut, and put in order, and the wiry-looking beard that streamed down to his neck would have to go. He needed this job.

The following afternoon, Peltier stood in front of La Lumière: clean-shaven, washed, scrubbed, and suited. He rang the bell.

By evening, Peltier was back in his room. An open bottle and a small half-full glass befriended him as he pored over the notes he wrote in his journal—detailed information on and description of the slave called Muse. The notes factored her height, her weight, her hair, her teeth, how she walked, how she talked, the possibility she might be wearing an indigo cape, and that she had no notable scars. He grinned as he read his scribbled handwriting; if anyone could find a runaway slave, it was he.

A wad of francs lay on the desk. A liberal retainer, but it was the promise of the bonus on completion of the task that truly motivated him.

He fingered the bills. It would get him through the next few months, thank God! From his breast pocket, he pulled out a small city map. The quarters he circled were where he would begin his search, environs that housed the ethnic cultures of Paris. He was certain he would find her there.

A LIFE BEGINS

Muse created a budget. Living necessities and the tools of her trade were the order of the day. She allowed herself three luxuries: *Le Figaro*, pen, and paper. After keeping a low profile for weeks and still no word from Claire, she decided to contact the only person who could help her find her friend. But she hesitated. Could she trust the woman? If she knew where she was hiding, would she inform the Hallisburgs? But from dealing with her in the past, she seemed decent and fair, Muse thought. Almost instinctually, she resolved to take the chance. She remembered the return address on a correspondence written to Mrs. Hallisburg months ago. With some angst, Muse penned a letter to Madame Néville.

⤙⫸

Muse continued to wander along the avenues with her basket of oddments, but as customers learned of the cul-de-sac, she kept the shop open at least twice a week. The iris-blue dress was on display, but as yet, none of the new clientele sought a dressmaker. Therefore, Muse carried on making the novelties and extended her merchandise to aprons and small decorative pillows. The rest of the week she spent cutting fabric, sewing, and embroidering.

Aside from the distress over Claire's disappearance, Muse longed for her mother, Mary. Knowing she could not communicate to her save through Bailey, the overseer, she explored another possibility. She salvaged a scrap of fabric spared from the iris-blue dress. Remembering the curtains that draped her mother's window were made from leftovers of the same fabric, she cut the material in the shape of a heart and stuffed it with fragments of soft material. She parceled it and addressed the package to her mother at Der Brunnen in Virginia. Even if Bailey heard of her escape, he would assume the package was from the Hallisburgs. Hopefully, Mary would interpret the gift as a sign her daughter was safe.

AN UNEXPECTED VISITOR

It was early. Muse began her morning working on a drawstring evening bag of green velvet, to which she attached tiny white faux pearls. The pearls she rescued from a tattered old scarf dumped in the city trash. There came a light tap at the front door. She perceived the time as not yet eight, and the shop never opened before ten. *Claire,* she hoped and ran to the door. To her surprise, there stood Madame Néville.

"*Bonjour,* Madame. Please, come in."

When Madame entered, Muse curtsied.

"*Bonjour,* Mademoiselle Muse."

Madame looked around the salon with no expression whatsoever.

Muse stood flustered.

"*Excuez-moi,*" Muse said. "Please, have a seat."

Muse gestured at the only chair in the shop.

"No, no," Madame said, eyeing the chair suspiciously. "Show me around."

"*Bien sûr,*" Muse said.

She led Madame through the various rooms and the upstairs. Madame fingered the green velvet bag.

"Pretty," she said.

"*Merci.*"

"Your hair has gone wild again," she said. "You have not visited Madame Rolin in a while. It's time."

Muse smiled as she smoothed down unruly strands of hair.

"*Oui*, Madame."

Try as she might, Madame could not refrain from smiling.

"I can't afford Madame Rolin just yet."

"Don't worry about the cost. Just go. Appearance is everything."

"*Oui.*"

"I received your letter," Madame said. "Very surprising. Who wrote it?"

"I did."

"I was led to believe you were illiterate."

"Please, *do* be seated. I can explain."

Madame sat down. The chair wobbled. She stiffened as if expecting it to collapse, but it didn't.

"The Hallisburgs are looking for you," she announced.

"I'm not surprised," Muse said. "But I don't care. You won't tell them?"

"Of course not," Madame responded. "Nevertheless, take precaution. They have hired a bounty hunter."

"A bounty hunter!"

"You must keep *en garde* for the next few weeks, at least until the Hallisburgs return to America at the end of the month. Now tell me," she said, looking around, "what's going on here?"

Madame listened as Muse told of her past: her education, plantation life, the Hallisburgs' plan to sell her once they returned, and how she escaped.

"But the urgency is," Muse said, "the disappearance of my friend Claire Price. That is why I wrote."

She explained how she and Claire met, the schemes they hatched, and their ambition to open a boutique.

"I must find her."

"What is it you think I can do?" Madame asked.

"You know people. You have resources; all I need are leads . . . where to look. I'll find her myself. She may be in trouble or hurt. She has been a blessing; she may need my help."

"Couldn't she have run off with the lover you mentioned?"

"Why wouldn't she tell me? We've been communicating secretly for some weeks. And she put up a lot of money to lease this place; it's paid for six months. Would she walk away from it . . . over a man?"

"*Oh, la la!* Women have done worse things."

Madame gave ear to the dilemma. But her questions to Muse fell along the lines of her own personal goals and her ability to make a success of the shop whether or not Claire turned up.

Madame examined the iris-blue dress on display—the cut, the stitches, the general composition of the garments.

"Not bad. You would benefit from exposure to a master tailor. I can arrange for you to attend a month-long apprenticeship at an exclusive dressmaker's studio. Your work would improve greatly, but it would be without pay. Can you manage?"

Muse understood what accepting an opportunity from Madame meant.

"I thank you for the offer, but I could not pay the fees necessary for the arrangement."

"My fees are not always monetary. Favors are a big part of my wages. Do you understand what I'm saying?"

"I do."

"Then consider it done. And anyway," Madame added, "the training, which is rigorous, will keep you out of sight for a while."

The bell above the entrance door tinkled. Two young women with broad smiles on their faces came in. Muse excused herself to assist them. On their departure, Muse returned to Madame.

"I must leave you now," Madame said. "Muse, you might have something remarkable on your hands. I will make arrangements with the tailor and contact you later. I leave town for a month, but when I return, we will visit again."

Madame took the iris-blue dress and folded it.

"I will take this dress to show Master Barre your talents. It will be returned by messenger."

"*Merci*, Madame."

When Madame reached the door, she turned and said, as an afterthought, "I will find news of your missing friend, but you must be sure to get your identification papers as a free person. You may use my name as a sponsor, if necessary."

Muse nodded.

"See you in a month. *Adieu*."

Muse thought twice before accepting Madame's offer. She was already living from hand to mouth; a month without profits would not be easy. But to pass up an opportunity to study with a master couturier . . . no, she must figure out a way!

And then her mind shifted to a new matter of alarm: a bounty hunter!

PELTIER AT WORK

Peltier lived in Africa for over fifteen years with his father, an experienced slave trader. He had returned to his homeland a few years ago after his father was killed—overpowered by captives in his charge. By then, the Peltiers had amassed a good deal from their dealings in the illicit trade. When he arrived in Paris, he put himself forth as a wealthy man of lawful business, disguising his résumé to show a lucrative marketer of exotic goods. But Louis could not reinvent himself. The French were a shrewd lot; neither legitimate businessmen nor mainstream society bought into his ruse of an accomplished dealer in the foreign trade market. The *demi-monde* took little notice of the interloper, even though he was a native Frenchman. Regardless of ample funds, his limited education and poor social skills proved undesirable traits in Paris. And soon, Louis gravitated toward people with dubious character; with this in addition to his weakness for card playing, drink, and women, by the end of his third year, he faced bankruptcy.

It was near midnight, and Peltier trotted along the cold, damp streets. He got rid of his suit and polished appearance for his normal state of dress so that he blended in with the local rabble. His eyes keenly took in the face of every female who passed him. It felt good to be on the hunt again, narrowing in on the abduction of human flesh for profit. The Hallisburg assignment brought him to the slums of one of the most desperate environs of Paris, an area not unfamiliar to him.

"*Bonsoir*," Peltier said, smiling to an approaching gendarme.

The gendarme perused him but kept his step.

The culture of the neighborhood was a mixed array: the criminal French; prostitutes; an ethnic fusion of Africans, Arabs, Spanish, and a host of others. He paced and prowled the cafés and bars. He drank and observed. At first, he thought the assignment would be easy. To his knowledge, few dark-skinned women lived in Paris. But now, he found more than a meager number present. As he narrowed in on his subjects, he discovered them to be Islanders or Africans; no runaway American slaves. While he studied the various women who crossed his path, he, to his surprise, acknowledged that many appeared attractive. He had only ever inspected women of color as a scout—to be corralled and sold. Even now, he looked around at what he perceived as livestock; on the auction blocks of Africa or in America, he would make a fortune.

He entered a café called Le Bouteille Rouge. It was a smoky, dingy establishment, crowded and brawling. Pierre, the owner, was behind the counter, drying glasses and mugs. They greeted. Peltier ordered a beer.

"I'm looking for a woman, *une négresse*," Peltier said.

Pierre shrugged, as if to say, "What else is new?"

"No, no," Peltier responded. "Not that kind of woman. An American . . . a runaway slave."

Pierre shook his head.

"I've seen no American runaways in my place."

Peltier gulped down his bear.

"*Merci*," Peltier said. He flipped him a coin and left.

Once again out on the street, Peltier hovered around a gas-light lamppost. He pulled his cap down over his ears and shivered; a vapor of mist escaped from his breath. In the dusky corner of the street, he lit a cigarette and lingered. The lights in the cafés soon faded out, and the pedestrians tapered off. One last time, he strode the avenues until they were nearly empty. Another wasted night. Yet it felt good to be working again, exercising his skills as a huntsman. He threw the butt of his cigarette on the ground and pressed it into the pavement with his boot. He readjusted his cap and straightened his waistcoat and, in doing so, stroked, as a habit, the pearl handle of the dagger he kept holstered to his belt. Then he headed for home.

L'ATELIER

A gritty-looking one-story building, near a back alleyway, housed a dressmaking studio. It stood as one unit surrounded by large, noisy factories. The studio was no more than a vessel that accommodated bolts and bolts of fabric. Scraps of brightly colored material and fragments of assorted threads littered the floor like a rainbow of sawdust. Broad windows let in enormous light and gave the illusion of space, but the area, teeming and hot, was meager in size. The windows remained closed, blocking out much of the noise coming from the industrial units outside. But sometimes the closed windows amplified the humidity, and the air reeked of stale odors. Bad circulation also caused breathing difficulties among the young aspiring talent. Wheezing and sneezing resounded across the room.

Groups of young men and women stood or sat in front of long wooden tables, sewing. Almost in unison, as if set to music, their arms extended in and out, plying needles that pulled long fibers of thread, piercing through patches of fabric cut to pattern. The studio was not how Muse imagined. In her mind's eye, she

envisioned elegant premises and chic artistic types skillfully ma-
nipulating fabric and thread, creating stunning gowns. Instead,
she labored with a motley group of needleworkers—she included
herself in this description—of all shapes and sizes, many of whom
appeared to know less about designing quality clothes than her.
But despite the grim setting, Muse knew the endeavor was in-
valuable; she was learning so much. The master, Monsieur Barre,
was one of the best fashion tutors in France. A tall man, rail
thin, very French, and, thought Muse, pale as snow. Stern blue
eyes, lips, and cheeks that shimmered with a faint rose blush, a
blush no student believed to be natural. The suits he wore each
day were impeccable, perfectly fitted, so well cut to his narrow
frame, but made him look skeletal. Yet, she hung on to his every
word, his every instruction. Each morning, he would lecture for
an hour; sometimes he demonstrated a certain kind of stitch, a
complicated bias cut, or an unusual way of draping. He taught
with animation and clarity, keeping his students captivated.

Two trainee tailors worked as a team on one item of clothing.
Because Muse proved quick-minded, she paired with a young
man of advanced talent. He called himself Cheng. They com-
municated effectively, although both struggled with the French
language. He was exotic-looking. Twenty years old, she guessed.
She examined the topaz-yellow hue of his skin and its smooth
texture. He was not much taller than she, slight in build. His eyes
slanted, dark, but kind. A black silk cap with red embroidered
dragons sat on top of his head. She tried not to stare, but with
her side vision, she studied the slick, long, black *queue* that fell
down the middle of his back. At first, she was uncomfortable in
his presence and felt awkward working so close to him, but soon
his humble and pleasant manner appeased her doubts.

She watched Cheng's superior techniques in sewing. The
steady, quick pace of his needlework reminded her of the sewing
machine she admired at L'Exposition. His hands were contoured

like a woman's: long, thin, well-formed fingers that sutured in tiny, straight, and firm stitches.

"Your backstitching is wonderful. How do you do it?"

"I'll show you."

He grabbed a piece of cloth.

"Do you see the difference?" Cheng said. "Your jagged stitches compared to the refined finish of mine? You need but a slight modification. Pierce the needle so as to just touch the back of your last stitch, as straight as possible, like this." He completed three rapid stitches, back to back, so straight it looked like one long one. "All you need is practice."

What Cheng learned from Muse was how to appreciate fabric, style, and texture; what flattered or hindered certain body types and forms. Because her awareness was instinctual, she found it, at first, difficult to explain herself. But in time, she learned how to articulate her understanding—why a certain soft silk would slim a full-busted woman or why a pale satin might or might not complement a fair-haired girl. The intense discussions that took place between Muse, Monsieur Barre, Cheng, and comrades enhanced her knowledge and flowered a deep appreciation for the art of clothing.

A week into the venture, the studio was forced to shut down early due to an accident with the delivery cart transporting the fabric to be used that day. By noon, most of the students had scattered.

"Where do you go?" Cheng asked Muse.

"Home."

"You look thin. When have you eaten last?"

"Breakfast."

"When was the last hot meal?"

She smiled.

"Not for a while."

"My family owns a restaurant. Come."

Cheng took Muse to a district where everyone in the neighborhood looked like him. The restaurant, called Chi's, was tiny, dinky, and crowded. He introduced Muse to his parents, who bowed and smiled and bowed and smiled.

"Have you ever eaten Chinese food?"

"Never."

"You'll like it . . . here," he said, giving her two wooden sticks.

"What are they?"

"Chopsticks."

Cheng showed her how to hold them. She fumbled to control them between her fingers; she struggled to pick up fragments of food, half laughing and half apologizing for her clumsiness. *Why couldn't they just give me a knife and fork?* she wished. Soon, she managed to get morsels into her mouth, albeit awkwardly. She questioned certain servings, ingredients, and cooking procedures. The dumplings filled with pork, and the fried jasmine rice, she loved. She consumed many helpings of new flavors and seasonings, odd-shaped bits and pieces of vegetables, and herbs. Some food was spicy, whereas others were tangy. It didn't matter; she ate it all.

"Take your time," Cheng said, smiling at her obvious hunger.

During dinner, the trainees shared their pasts, their dreams, and their life expectations. She told him about the boutique. He told her about the apprenticeship that awaited him at a men's salon near the rue de la Paix.

"My shop is close by. Will you visit me?"

"I will."

⇥⇤

By the time Muse got home, it was midnight. She let herself in through the back way. The shop was cold and dark. Cheng's parents gave her food to take home. She put the tin box on the table and groped around for a match to light the candle. The back room became visible but only in shadows. Fabric lay piled on the table, material not touched since her apprenticeship started. The plan was to work on her own garments and knickknacks when she got home. But when she returned every night, she simply crawled into bed. She had the energy for nothing else save one ritual: nursing calloused hands with the almond oil given to her by Cheng. Its medicinal use healed and moisturized fingers and hands nicked and punctured by the constant use, sometimes misuse, of needles, pins, and scissors. But she vowed to make more of an effort and promised herself she would wake up an hour earlier to cut out a handkerchief, to embroider, to do something—she needed money coming in.

Many nights as she lay alone on the floor between the crumpled old blankets, panic struck her, fretting over how to survive. What if Claire never turned up? What if the bounty hunter found her? What if she could not pay the rent when the time came? *What if . . . what if?* One night, she was staring at the flickering flame of the candle she had placed on the floor by her side. Her eyelids grew heavy, then suddenly, they widened. She bolted upright, thrust aside the blankets, and grabbed her cloth bag. She foraged around in its interior. Old letters from Claire, papers . . . the book *Uncle Tom's Cabin*. Slid between its pages, a business card with the name and address in bold print: Antonio Clémence, painter, sculptor. She edged back beneath the blankets and stared at the card.

Will he remember me?

LA CELEBRATION

The internship ended. Cheng and Muse celebrated at Chi's. A surprise bottle of wine was opened and poured in their honor. The two new tailors ate vigorously, content, full of joy and hope about the future.

"When do you start your new job?" Muse asked.

"In a week."

"Are you excited?"

"Very much so. It's the new change in men's fashion I want to be a part of, and Paris is the place to be. What about you?"

Muse paused for a moment.

"I want to find temporary work, something to bring in money so that I can buy material and whatnot—work that will not consume all my energy and allow me time to sew."

She reflected.

"What I really want is to make a success of the shop, but for now, if I can keep things going until Claire comes back, that would be good."

"What if your friend never shows?"

"I don't know. I can't run the shop on my own."

Cheng refilled her glass.

"I have an idea. Why don't you make one amazing dress? Wear it around town at cafés and concerts. You are attractive. Don't hide it; flaunt it."

Muse blushed.

"Let people see you wearing your own design. Attract attention to you and your work. That's what Worth does."

"Who's Worth?"

"He is a major up-and-coming designer. I've seen his work. He makes a stunning ensemble for his woman, then takes her about town and shows her off. That's how he is attracting potential clients."

"I can't afford to buy fabric for such a dress . . . not yet, anyway."

Cheng shrugged.

"There is something else . . ."

"What?"

Muse told Cheng about the Hallisburgs and the bounty hunter.

"They should have returned to America by now, but I don't know for sure. And the bounty hunter, well, I still feel I need to be careful."

"*Mon Dieu!* That is different. *Prenez garde!*"

"I will," she said.

He smiled and then reached into his pocket and pulled out a tiny red box.

"For you," he said.

She looked at it in wonder.

"What is it?"

"Open it."

She untied the gold string wound around the box and lifted its minute lid. Her eyes welled up, and she chuckled.

"It's lovely."

She rescued the object from the box and put it on the tip of her middle finger. With her hand stretched out and her fingers spread apart, she modeled the small leather object: a sewing thimble.

"*Merci*, Cheng."

AN ARTIST'S STUDIO

The following day, Muse hurried to dress. Once again, she put on the black uniform—but with an added accessory. A turban: an easy, oval-shaped structure, made from a salvaged piece of black brocade. She created a modish piece à la mode Madame Néville. She walked down the boulevard for several blocks, then along the Seine, where she crossed the Pont Neuf to the boulevard Saint Michel. After a few blocks more, she stopped in front of an old apartment building. She hesitated, pondered the wisdom of her scheme, and mounted the wide stone stairwell to the second floor. Next to the apartment number she sought, a hand-painted sign read, "Antonio Clémence." She knocked.

"*Entrée*," a male voice said.

She entered. The studio was a vast space of natural light. Muse looked around but saw no one.

"*Bonjour*," she said.

"*Oui. Qui est-ce?*"

She followed the voice into another room. And there he was, the man she had danced with at the artist's ball. He was sitting on a sofa, staring at a raw lump of clay jutting from the floor. He looked up at her.

"Who are you? What do you want?"

Muse stood, terrified. *God,* she thought, *what am I doing?* She turned to leave.

"Stop!" he said. "Who are you?"

She gathered her wits and spoke.

"My name is . . . Muse Aggrey."

"*Oui,* Mademoiselle Aggrey. What can I do for you?"

"Uh . . . uh . . . we met at a ball . . . a masquerade ball . . . some months ago."

He looked at her, sizing her up.

"Yes, I remember you."

There was a pause.

"Well, why are you here?"

Twisting the top button of her dress, she stuttered out a few words, but her French failed her. She excused herself, faulting her poor mastery of the language.

"You prefer to speak English?"

"Yes."

"Then we speak English, *d'accord?*" he said.

"Thank you."

He pointed to a chair.

"Please, sit."

Antonio looked much different from when she last saw him. Not tall, average height, forty or so. Swarthy, dark skin, with a mass of gray locks tapering around his shoulders, although thinning along his forehead—and he had shaved off his goatee. His face revealed the clean, chiseled, dark look of a man of Latin descent. Much cleaner without the beard, she thought.

Muse sat down, all the while taking in the sculptures and artwork piled alongside the walls and against the windows. The room was cold, drafty, the fireplace unlit—just as she imagined how an artist's studio would look. Like one of those paintings she saw at the fair.

"You have a wonderful apartment."

"*Merci.* It's my wife's. Sometimes I miss not being closer to the art community in Montmartre, but the light is good, and I work well here, so we stay."

"*Oui.*"

"How have you been?" he asked.

"*Bien.* Uh . . . monsieur . . ."

"Where are my manners?" he said. How about *un café?* Anna!"

A handsome woman appeared, petite, dark eyes, and dark hair pulled back into a thick braid twisted and turned up at the back. She looked about the same age as Antonio; he introduced her as his *femme.*

"Anna, *ma petite,* bring us café."

"*Bien sûr, mon chère.*"

Soon Muse relaxed. They both reminisced about the dance and revisited certain occurrences, types of music, dance, and the art on display.

"May I see your work?" she asked.

"*Bien sûr.*"

He guided her through two large open rooms: one displaying several sculptures; the other, a dozen or more paintings. He showed her different works, talked of his inspirations and the themes he wanted to tackle. Muse was awed but sometimes shocked by his work. He painted graphic scenes of everyday Paris life in the most unflattering way—no glamour, no prettiness, nothing chic or refined, just blatant realism, the local scenes one observes when traveling outside the fashionable neighborhoods. She also noted a fair number of nude portraits of both men and women. She blushed.

They talked for a time about art and its current evolution. Muse could only listen, not knowing anything about art, old or new. Then he asked again,

"Why are you here, Mademoiselle Aggrey?"

She smiled timidly.

"You once asked if I would pose for you."

"*Oui.* It still stands."

"Would I be required to pose nude?"

"*Oui.*"

She went silent.

"One can hardly do a study of *une nue noire* fully clothed, can one?"

Mused chuckled, thinking, *Of course not.*

"Mademoiselle, I am a professional. I pay my models. I am discreet and all the rest of it. Besides, my wife makes sure I behave.

"You said you would pay?"

"*Absolument.* Are you interested?"

"I am."

They walked over to another group of nude paintings, framed but filed on the floor.

"Tell me something about yourself."

Muse spoke openly of her short life, past and present.

"With you, Mademoiselle Aggrey, the nude study is only one aspect of my interest. I want images of your former life in Virginia—that would be inspiring."

He was looking at her smart little black turban with a smirk.

"Do you, by any chance, still have any of your . . . plantation clothing?"

She kept only the tattered headwrap.

"No. But I can duplicate them."

"Then we will begin in two weeks."

"*D'accord?*"

"*D'accord.*"

"It is near lunch. Stay and dine with us."

FURNISHING LA BOUTIQUE

During the apprenticeship, Muse monitored, as did many other students, the alleyway behind the studio. The neglected passage was the dumping ground for not only trash but discarded fabric, either damaged or soiled. The mound grew daily. At the end of the week, street cleaners carted it away. Early one morning, just before the city woke up, Muse found herself alone and knee deep in the pile of cast-off fabric and debris. She searched, looking for cloth that might be usable. She was successful. A bolt of green brocade, stained in spots but usable.

After a while, she learned that living in a large city afforded unorthodox advantages. For one, people threw away all kinds of things. Often after posing for Antonio, she would comb the streets, looking for discarded objects, especially on trash day. She found a cast-off iron bed frame, rusted but functional. An oil lamp, candlestick holders, pots, pans; she even rescued an armoire, a solid-oak piece with only three legs. Little by little, she furnished the shop.

In time, Muse forged a routine. She spent the mornings at Antonio's studio, posing two or three hours depending on the light. In the afternoons, she retreated to the solace of her independence and her own creative pursuits.

Muse worked unwaveringly, but she was running out of fabric. The heap at the back of the studio no longer provided enough suitable cloth to work with, no matter how she tried to cut around stains and snags and rips. Her budget did not allow her to buy material from quality fabric shops in Paris and make a profit. One Saturday, Muse asked Cheng to accompany her to a nearby district where he heard of a troupe of merchants had bonded together to sell quality fabric at low cost. They took an omnibus to the outskirts of the city. For a quarter of a mile, they walked along a nearly impassable path adjacent the swamps until they reach their destination: a muddy-road campground lined with crude stalls and brightly colored drays laden with fabric. The merchants looked like a posse of gypsies milling together.

"This place reminds me of the slums of Morocco," Cheng whispered.

"You've been to Morocco?"

"I've been everywhere, it seems . . . except for America."

Through the marketplace they rambled, observing the assortment of cloth on display. The rareness of the fabric struck them both in awe-inspiring ways. Exotic patterns, elaborate colors, and fine textures influenced by the East kindled their imaginations. The scarves drew Muse in, not only the quality of the silk but the vibrancy of the dyes and tints. She studied the oriental symbols painted on the multicolored handheld fans.

"What does it mean?" she asked the vendor.

"*Peace*, mademoiselle," he answered.

She fingered the dainty-looking charm bracelets that chimed when touched. To test her instincts, she bought a few novel accessories, a bolt of raw silk, and an alluring cotton print she hoped would titillate her small but growing clientele. With the help of Cheng's negotiating skills, her modest few francs stretched.

The excursion also inspired Cheng. The striking prints gave him novel ideas to take back to his new employer. In his budding opinion, the creative efforts of his superior, although classic in technique, seemed rigid, almost dead, compared to what he saw as the current shift in men's style. Men's sense of dress was changing right along with the women's. Where the taut styles of Queen Victoria and her dowdy maids once ruled the mode of the Western world, the queen and her entourage paled compared to the glamorous and vogue consciousness of L'Empresse Eugénie and her beautiful ladies of the court.

By late afternoon, Muse and Cheng, exhausted, with packages in hand and only enough money to get home, hiked back along the waning swamp roads to catch the omnibus for home.

The liaison between model and painter progressed. After finishing the second series of nude sketches, the study of a black female as slave commenced. The interpretations called for more than drawings: an in-depth study in oil. While Antonio worked at a passionate but feverish pace, mental fatigue soon set in, and he needed a break. Late in November, a damp chill permeated the city. He decided to hiatus at his small country cottage not too far from Paris. He fixed on the idea of hosting a *fête*—an evening spotlighting the first sketches of *une femme nue noire*.

"It will be a casual affair, but chic, *ma chérie*; you are my muse, Muse."

She laughed.

"May I bring a friend?"

"Of course, I will send a carriage to fetch you both."

LOUIS'S DILEMMA

The room began to close in on Louis. He sat on the edge of the bed, hunched over a bottle. He felt discouraged. Had he done it again, botched another opportunity? Tomorrow he was to meet with the Hallisburgs to give them an update; they had extended their stay, hoping for information about the slave. To date, nothing. The avenues and boulevards he combed proved futile. Mental and physical fatigue overtook him. No ideas on how to continue the search, no leads, no clues. Where was she? The people he questioned seemed forthcoming and not hesitant to reveal what they knew. Two café acquaintances led him to several other runaway slaves—muscular, fit island men whom Louis wished not to confront.

He imagined the assignment would rejuvenate his former career. He relished going back to work, the hunter once again in search of game, and the money abundant. But how could he once again start up this profession by failing on the first mission? A female slave with no money, no friends, nothing but the clothes on her back, vanishes into thin air; it made no sense.

What to tell the Hallisburgs? A thought rolled over in his head, a scheme, a lie. What if he convinced them that the slave was dead? At least he would receive confirmation for a completed task and maybe still get the bonus; surely he would get a recommendation for his services. He smirked. But they would desire proof. His mind churned deeper. Another notion occurred to him. He had never taken *une femme noire* to bed, but he thought to hire one for the evening at some remote spot and then, with his pearl-handled knife, slash away . . . easily done. And who would miss another whore, a dark one, at that? But he didn't know what the slave called Muse looked like. The Hallisburgs would want to visit the morgue; the corpse would have to be a reasonable facsimile. While darkies all looked alike to him, the Hallisburgs would recognize their own property.

In all honesty, what else could have happened? She must be dead, or else someone snatched her; otherwise, he would have found her. And as he paced the room, his eyes frenzied, he vowed to persuade the Hallisburgs that the slave was dead. Whatever it took, he would do. He needed that bonus.

He stared out the window at the night-cloaked sky, trying to decipher the time; it must be past eight. He took another long swig. The woman he hired to sleep with that night was late. He hated delay and did not want to be alone much longer. He hoped she would hurry. A brunette; he liked brunettes.

PELTIER'S TALE

It was Cassandra who didn't believe him. As soon as Peltier spun his story, she pitched a fit. She interrogated him so vigorously he felt he was on trial.

"I don't believe you. Muse is not dead!" she screamed at him. "Father, he is just saying that to get paid. He's lying. He couldn't find her—that's all. It doesn't mean she's dead."

"Mademoiselle," rebuked Peltier, "I have done everything in my power to find the subject in question. Paris is an international city with many vile and dangerous quarters. If you don't know your way around, if you don't have protection, especially for a woman, Paris will swallow you whole. Trust me! Your Muse, according to you, has no connections, no money, nothing but the ability to read and write; she could have easily been plucked like an exotic piece of fruit and devoured."

"No!" Cassandra said. "Muse knows how to protect herself."

She remembered her brother's assault on Muse and how he came out almost as mangled as she.

"Surely she devised a plan," Cassandra continued. "She wouldn't have run off willy-nilly."

"Ah!" exclaimed Peltier. "It sounds as though mademoiselle has a great affection for her."

"Shut up, you nasty man," she barked. "If she's dead, show us the body."

Peltier stood up as if insulted.

"I will not be spoken to in this way. I'm sorry, but that is my finding. Is there anything else I can do for you?"

Cassandra ran out of the room, shouting, "No, no, no! You're a vile man."

Up the stairs to her chambers she darted, her huge crinoline skirt swaying behind her, disturbing several fine knickknacks. The sound of shattering ornaments brought Mrs. Hallisburg to her feet, and she followed suit. Cassandra slammed the door shut. Mrs. Hallisburg knocked.

"Honey, let me in."

Cassandra opened the door.

"This is Father's fault," Cassandra said. "Had he not planned to sell her in the first place, she would not have run. We got on well together."

Mrs. Hallisburg cupped her daughter's face in her hands and kissed her forehead. "It'll be all right dear. We'll find her."

"If we can't, then I want to go home. Everything has gone wrong."

EMOTIONS

A heartwarming change took place whenever Muse was around Cheng, like having a brother but more. Steadily they grew closer. With both having incomes, together they frequented late-night brasseries, took in poetry readings in dingy cafés, and listened to music in secluded *boits*. Muse soon discerned that when she and Cheng were not together, she missed him, and not like one missed a brother. How was she to interpret these unexpected feelings? She had misread attractions before . . . *the architect*. Now she was free to feel open about whatever she wanted, when she wanted, and with whom she wanted; yet, emotional candor confused her. It seemed so easy for other women to embrace love wholeheartedly, without question, without fore- or afterthought.

Sometimes while sitting alone at a café, she watched young couples and marveled at their lust for *amour*; what was it like? she wondered. When Claire wrote about Gerard, she turned into an almost unrecognizable person. Muse wanted to experience such a stir. But what was she sensing with Cheng? He never touched her in any way other than as a devoted friend, nor suggested anything risqué or improper. She knew the difference in the subtle and not-so-subtle manner of men when it came to love. She recalled the faint hints from Jean-Paul, the malevolent advances made by Jonathan, and the sweetness of the touches and kiss from Joseph—all when she was not free to choose. Nothing of the sort came from Cheng, yet she enjoyed his company immensely.

When he accepted the invitation to Antonio's *fête*, she was excited. She made a dress specifically, designed from the green brocade silk she rescued from the heap behind the studio. The damage to the fabric was substantial: splotched ink stains soaked through the layers, leaving blemishes near the middle of the material. She experimented with cutting around the discoloration and reworking pieces like panels to correspond with a pattern she envisioned. There would be more seams than usual, but with so many folds in the skirt, who would notice? The neck of the décolletage was wide, square, just off the shoulders. A soft flounce of translucent lace, off-white, trimmed the neckline and exposed the sleeves, simple, short, and puffy. With no leisure money to buy a proper hoop undergarment, Muse plodded over making a full layered petticoat with whatever light fabric was lying around. Instead of wearing an expensive evening hat, she wore her hair up and laced the dangling braids with matching ribbons.

They stood before the mirror, arm in arm, she in the green gown and he in a tailored frock coat of gray silk.

"*Parfait*," Cheng said.

ANTONIO'S *FÊTE*

The cottage was unassuming but with character. Large windows opened on a weathered, peach-colored facade. It sat in the middle of a rose garden neighboring a rolling, dense wood. The landscape served as a backdrop in several of Antonio's earlier works—in particular at this time of the year when dying leaves brought on the warm, rustic colors of autumn.

A diverse group of individuals showed up to the *fête*: artists and members of the Paris literati. At first glance, a rough crew, but soon the affair took on an air of modishness. When Muse entered, Antonio embraced his protégé and kissed both her cheeks, but as soon as she finished introducing Cheng, Antonio whisked her away. Cheng was left alone with Anna, groping with the language of introductions. She offered him champagne, insisted he make himself at home, and then excused herself. He sipped the frothy wine, smiling and nodding to those who passed by. Before long, a young man, also smart in look and manner, approached him and struck up a conversation.

⟨—⊹—⟩

Muse was greeted warmly by the guests, with many approaching her to convey compliments and flattery. She felt overwhelmed. So much praise; what remarkable thing had she done but pose naked? Antonio exhibited only the charcoal sketches. She stood before the mounted images, puzzled. In her opinion, the compositions did not resemble her at all. Each looked like a hodgepodge of lines, shades, and light. Anyone could have posed for them. In fact, if not for the subtle female curvature, the dark, steady eyes, would anyone ever suspect the illustrations were of a human form at all?

"Ah!" she heard a spectator remark. "It is this new technique he is trying to develop, poor fool. What a waste of a model."

Some found the representations of a dusky nude provocative and original.

"*Oui, oui*, Antonio is onto something. He's captured a touch of the girl . . . a sense of untamed wildness. See, there, in her eyes, and the arch of her back, there is the sadness of a captive, yet her will is not yet broken."

A violinist played light melodies; the food, drink, and stimulating conversation livened up the cottage. Muse parked herself on a sofa with a glass of champagne and absorbed the repartee of sophisticated and well-developed minds. She sat, listening, taking mental notes on the various debates. Interjected a thought on the issue of America and the growing tension between the North and South. Questions about her past life as a slave arose. She answered freely, as if talking about the experience publicly secured her liberty. Now that the Hallisburgs were gone—she hoped—she felt free to discuss her history.

A man, older, bearded, smelling of cigars and cheap cologne, offered to refresh her drink.

"*Merci.*"

When he returned, he asked, "Might I speak with you?"

"*Bien sûr,*" she said.

"Luc de Nagy from *Le Figaro*," he said and sat down.

"Mademoiselle, you have a story and a history that is fascinating. Readers would be captivated by it, as would I. Would you consider giving me an in-depth interview for the newspaper?"

"*Moi?*"

"*Oui.*" With his index finger, he wrote across thin air, saying, "The former life of a Virginian slave."

Monsieur de Nagy proposed the outline he intended to explore. Muse entertained the proposition for a moment—to tell the truth about the plight of American slaves.

Of late, she had mulled over the idea of attracting attention to the shop. She loved Cheng's notion of designing a dress to wear in public. And a newspaper article would grab attention. But she stopped short. If only she knew for sure the Hallisburgs had returned to America. Even so, who was to say the bounty hunter was not still on the payroll? *No*, she said to herself and declined the offer.

Then suddenly, she remembered her companion. In all the hubbub and attention, she forgot about Cheng. She excused herself and went in search of him. He was neither at the buffet table nor the room that hosted the artwork. She guessed outside for a smoke. Through the cool scented garden, she wandered.

"Cheng! Cheng, are you out here?"

A narrow pathway led from the rose beds to the woods; she followed it. She darted out as far as she thought safe and then withdrew. As she made her way back toward the cottage, she heard a shuffle, then a moan, in the nearby bushes. Clutching the train of her dress, she ducked under branches and followed the murmur of voices, groans, whimpers, and a burst of laughter. In a hollow opening in the woods, she saw two dark figures cuddling. One of them, a man in a red frock coat. His arms folded around another person, but she could not see who. Amid their embrace, they shifted and turned, still holding each other in a long, lingering kiss. It was very dim, but even in the obscurity of the night's darkness, Muse recognized the gray tailored coat and the long, silky, black braid glistening under the mantle of a starry night.

LE PETIT CUL-DE-SAC

The boutique reopened. Customers, still small in numbers, trickled in and out. The patrons referred to the salon as *le petit cul-de-sac*, and it stuck. Muse retired the iris-blue dress and in its place displayed the green brocade, which showed off her now-refined stitching and innovative manipulation of fabric. Subsequently, she attracted her first customer in want of a dressmaker. The family of a young woman visiting from the north of France hired her to make an ensemble for a winter *fête*. Under the coaching of Cheng, Muse sketched out a design, experimented with sample fabrics, and presented it to her young client for approval. Then Muse, along with her client, went down to Fabriques de France on the rue du Pont-Neuf. It was the first time she bought fabric from a legitimate store.

She rose at first light to begin work on the gown, hoping to finish cutting before the store opened. It was nine o'clock when a rough tap sounded at the front door: the post carrier. Muse had received notes from local couriers before but never from the mailman. The handwriting belonged to Madame Néville.

Dear Mademoiselle Aggrey,
I hope this communiqué finds you well. I assume your studies at
the dress studio have ended and your experience there was a good
one. As you know, I am with a new client and find my services
are still needed here in Biarritz. It will be another month before I
return to Paris. I write because I have news.
First, the Hallisburgs have given up their search for you and are
returning to America, as I write. Therefore, my dear, you are truly
a free woman. But, my dear, be aware! The bounty hunter may
still be around.

"Oh, God!" Muse said. "And to think I almost gave an interview."

Secondly, and I am afraid, I've also got news of your friend.
Claire Price is at present serving a one-year prison sentence in
Paris for theft.

"What!"

It seems she and her companion were arrested at the opera with
stolen items found in her evening bag. The objects were taken from
the guests at a nearby hotel. A guest was found unconscious, face-
down, in his hotel room. He suffered a blow to the head. When
he came to some days later, he identified the culprit . . . a one
Monsieur Gerard Diderot. And when the police searched their
apartment, they found several pieces of expensive women's jewelry
and a large stash of hashish.
My dear Muse, who are these people? The man was released on
bail almost immediately. He took a plea bargain, and owing to
the assurances of his family, a prominent clan, he relocated out
of the country. Once the victim found out the affluence of this
family, he did not press charges against Monsieur Diderot—more

than likely, he was paid off. As for your friend, she remains im-
prisoned at Saint-Lazare.
I regret sharing such awful news with you.
Mes plus amicales pensées,
Madame Néville
P.S. I would advise you not to visit her. But if you do, here are
some things you must know when calling on inmates . . .

Muse stared at the letter, not knowing what to do. She ran upstairs to her desk—a large wooden box turned upside down—
and penned a note to Cheng.

SAINT-LAZARE

I t was raining, a soft, steady stream that blanketed the city in tonal glooms of gray. The avenues glistened. A sea of pedestrians filed up and down the streets, balancing huge black umbrellas over their heads. Too tense to wait for the omnibus, Muse coaxed Cheng to walk with her to the Maison d'Arrêt de Saint Lazare.

"Stop trembling," Cheng said as he maneuvered his umbrella through mobs of people.

"I can't help myself," Muse snapped back. She slapped the tip of her umbrella against his.

"Calm down," he said.

They turned off the side street onto the rue Faubourg Saint-Denis. The institution towered over the street. Muse stopped at the sight of it. The façade of the prison complex looked monstrous, like a bleak house of despair.

"Dreadful neoclassical architecture," Cheng said, nudging her on. "Go."

They walked through a massive archway, entering a long, damp corridor that led to a reception area. People settled about the room, talking, while others rested on rows of long wooden benches placed in the middle of the room. Some read, some wrote, but all waited. A woman dressed in a plain black wool dress with a bottleneck collar and long sleeves sat behind a small desk in front of a large, leather-bound book. Severe features—a long, aquiline nose and watery blue eyes that seemed bored. Dozens of people queued before her. Each one took his or her turn, asking for information. And every time they did, she flipped through the pages of the book, in search of an answer.

Muse and Cheng stood at the back of the line. Within an hour, they were facing the woman.

"*Bonjour*, madame," Muse said. "I have an appointment to see Mademoiselle Claire Price."

The receptionist pored over several pages and then looked up at Muse.

"*Oui*. Go across the garden into the building to your left. It is where the convicts are held."

"You may sit," the receptionist said to Cheng. "No men unless related."

Muse blinked, thinking, *Oh God! Must I go in alone?*

The rain ended. Muse marched across the garden as directed. She paused, hoping to subdue her trembling. In doing so, she observed the garden: a beautiful and tranquil patch of ground. A narrow, winding footpath took her past plant life and floral habitation. Even though few flowers were in bloom, she spotted a cluster of winter jasmine where raindrops illuminated its sandy-yellow petals. She noted a handful of trees and a mantle of moist, gleaming foliage sprawled everywhere. *What a paradox!* she thought. *Such natural splendor right in the middle of a prison.*

When Muse entered the building, the pungent odor of disinfectant was so strong it stifled her breathing. Two bedraggled women wearing long, shapeless gray dresses and aprons were on all fours, viciously scrubbing the red tile floors.

She guessed they were inmates; her stomach tightened.

Passing the women, she moved down another gloomy hallway into a solemn, vacant room. She pulled the cord that hung near a closed door; a single bell pealed. She waited. The door opened, and a nun appeared.

She was a robust, sturdy woman donned in full habit: a dark full-length robe, a white apron, and a white *cornette* perched on her head. A long gold crucifix dangled from around her neck. Advanced in years, she sported steady blue eyes, a slit that opened and closed for a mouth, a pale complexion, but a sweet face. Her arms folded between the sleeves of her robe. She introduced herself as Sœur Claudette. She was one of the Sisters of the Order of Marie-Joseph. Muse followed her to the next room, where the sœur gestured for her to sit. The room was freezing and austerely furnished except for two dominant features: a large crucifix on one side of the wall and a framed painting of the Mother Mary on the other.

Muse spoke to Sœur Claudette as a young daughter to an aged mother. She answered with frankness all questions put to her about her association with Claire. Once she approved the visit, Muse asked, "May I meet with Mademoiselle Price in a private room?"

"*Non! C'est impossible,*" Sœur Claudette responded.

"I'm prepared to donate to the Sisters of the Order of Marie-Joseph," Muse said.

Muse slipped the good sœur a few coins, but she frowned. Muse touched her again with a few more coins.

"Ah!" the good sœur said. "There might be an empty cell available."

The good sœur led Muse down another narrow, dank passageway to a wide central compartment. They stopped in front of a large iron door. La Sœur slid a heavy metal key into a rusted keyhole, and the door squeaked opened, like a lamented cry.

"You have thirty minutes, no more!"

"*Merci*," Muse said.

Muse sat alone in the empty cell and waited. A half an hour later, the door opened, and the good sœur ushered in a woman with short, cropped hair. Frail, wearing a drab gray dress and apron, much the same as those worn by the women scrubbing the floors. Muse stood up in shock.

It was Claire. Her red hair shaved almost to the scalp. She was pale and drawn; her green eyes lifeless. A faint malodorous body smell drifted from her. Was she not allowed to bathe? Muse's eyes met Claire's. She saw outrage, hatred. When the sœur left, Claire said, "So, you did emancipate yourself!"

"Yes."

"Then why didn't you come?" Claire asked in a weak and raspy voice.

"Oh, Claire!"

"Aggrey it's been months. Why didn't you come? Why didn't someone help me?"

"I didn't know. I swear to you."

Claire turned her head away.

"I found out two days ago."

Muse flopped back down in the chair.

"I swear to you, dear Claire."

Claire dropped her head and cried, and so did Muse.

After a while, Muse asked, "What happened to your hair?"

"Lice."

"How did you get lice?"

"Probably from the mangy prostitute I sleep next to."

Oh!

"It's been horrible!" Claire cried.

Muse got up to approach her friend.

"No! Stay away. Don't come near me. I'm filthy."

"Never," Muse replied.

"No, Aggrey don't!"

Muse stepped back. No one said anything for a while, and then Muse said, "Claire, I never received a word, not one note from you. I have been at the boutique all of this time."

"Gerard did not contact you?"

"*Non.* Why didn't *you* write?"

"I couldn't remember where the damn shop was. Anyway, I was waiting for Gerard to come. He swore his parents would get me out."

"What about the money? Couldn't it help you find better legal help?"

"I have no more money. It's all in the shop."

"All of it?"

"Well, not all of it. Gerard needed help."

"Oh, Claire. For heaven's sake! What happened?"

"I don't know. I don't . . . they found jewelry in my bag. Gerard stole it, I guess. It was he, I swear. And he beat up a man at a hotel . . . or something. I knew nothing about it. I'm not a thief!"

Muse looked at Claire.

"Of course you're not."

"Where is he? Has he not been freed? Why hasn't he come to see me?"

"Yes, he's free. But his parents sent him away. He's out of the country," Muse said.

"You're lying! How do you know?"

"Madame Néville."

Claire dropped her chin, covered her nearly bald head with her hands, and sobbed.

"Oh, Aggrey, I loved him so much. How could he do this?"

＜＋＋＞

"She's a broken woman," Muse said.

"Well, wouldn't you be?" Cheng countered.

They sat at a café near a window, having lunch. The streets still glistened from the moisture of the rain.

"Now what are you going to do?" he asked.

"I don't know."

THE VISITS

The only thing Muse could do was to make life easier for Claire while she did time. After another small financial donation, an arrangement with the good sœur ensured Claire had a bath once a week. Every Tuesday morning, Muse arrived with a basket crammed with fresh milk, water, bread, and cold chicken or beef. As they were no longer allowed a private room, their meetings took place in the visiting room, along with a dozen other inmates and their families. They sat at a table across from each other with hands folded and in full view of the guards. In the one hour allotted them, they talked.

"Where are you getting the money to help me in this way?" Claire said as she rifled through the basket.

"I've been selling merchandise, doing a little dressmaking, and I pose for an artist, so I've been saving money to pay for the next phase of the rent. It is from that pot I've been pinching."

"Are you posing nude?"

"I am."

"Hmm. Is the pay good?"

"It helps make ends meet . . . that's all."

"When is the rent due?"

"Not for another three months. Good thing you paid in advance."

Muse looked at Claire, hesitant.

"What's it like?"

"What's what like?"

"In here."

Claire rolled her eyes.

"We get up at six; well, *they* do. I get up at five because I work in the kitchen. And we're in bed by eight. I sleep in a crowded dormitory, on a narrow bed with one blanket and a lumpy old bolster for a pillow. Eighty beds lined up in four rows, military style. It's just awful! No privacy whatsoever. Even though the place reeks with disinfectant, it is still infested with vermin . . . everywhere. But hopefully, it will change soon."

"How so?"

"I've been working in the kitchen . . . baking. Apparently, I'm good at it. And as I've been behaving, the nuns are giving me a cell in the *ménagerie*. That means privacy, at last. I'll have a bed, a shelf, a desk, a stool, and a pot to pee in."

"Why did they sentence you for so long? Madame said it should have been but a few months for theft."

"The man Gerard attacked was hurt badly, even though he did not press charges. But as Gerard got off, the blame landed on me, citing a person of bad influence. Plus, my papers were no longer valid because I quit the Grossmonts."

"Didn't you say your mother was French? Doesn't that have weight?"

"I would still need to prove it. I've lost my birth certificate. A copy from the orphanage would take months."

Claire sighed.

"How can Gerard abandon you like this?"

"I don't know."

Claire's recovery progressed. Her strength returned, as did the blush of her cheeks. Her hair grew: strands of red locks soon curled down her neck and reframed her face. With her newly mended self and positive spirit, she required a challenge.

"Aggrey, when you come next time, will you bring me something to read?"

"Of course, what?"

Claire smiled and said, "Anything but *The Count of Monte Cristo.*"

JOYEUSE NOËL

It was two days before Christmas. Le Petit-Cul-de-Sac looked festive. Customers enjoyed mulled wine and *petit pain au lait* while they shopped. Muse put in many long hours, creating small items with holiday flair. Green velvet pincushions, white linen handkerchiefs with embroidered gold bells. The shop welcomed the extra francs. With Claire's guidelines on accounting, they believed they would have the funds necessary to pay the next phase of the lease.

Cheng was celebrating with his new lover, somewhere in the South, and Muse found herself alone during this festive period. Of late, she ruminated over her mother, missing her, loving her. So much so that several weeks ago, she sent her a blue silk scarf. Whether her mother ever received the items she mailed, she did not know, but she shipped them nevertheless.

In Virginia, Muse experienced her fair share of snowy, frigid days and night. She always dreaded that time of the year and its unforgiving low temperatures. Meagerly dressed, forever shivering in her small wooden shack, finding warmth only in the big house. But now, winter was romantic! Out on the streets, wrapped in the new winter-green hooded cape, tailored by Cheng, a Christmas gift, a glorious but rare snow-white evening greeted her. The flurries had stopped, but the city still shimmered in a coverlet of white flakes. The festive window displays of the more established salons, Les Grands Magazines du Louvre, always drew her attention. She listened to the snow crunching beneath her feet and marveled over the winter-bare trees that stood like tall ice figurines. Most of the shops closed early, which made it easier to note the artistic skill of storefront presentations. Stunning windows, elaborate with Christmas themes: porcelain dolls donned in red velvet capes with white-fur-trimmed collars; wooden rocking horses laboring under finely polished leather saddles, bags filled with candy canes. One window, painted a frosty opaque white, displayed a peephole in the middle. Passersby who looked in the opening saw three wise men bearing gifts before a manger, dressed in multicolored silk robes, glistening embroidery along the hems and collars, and fine turbans that seemed to shimmer as they bowed before the Holy Infant, and to Muse's delight, one of the wise men was African.

At one point, Muse caught her reflection in a window. A well-dressed woman stared back at her. The full-length cape, so well made, and just visible beneath it, the green silk brocade dress reaccessorized once again.

She dropped a coin in the cup of a young beggar girl standing on a corner. Pretty: olive skin and dark hair, a poor waif quivering in the cold. And within an instant, Muse's high regard for the city moved from its wealth and beauty to acknowledging its contrast: the disadvantage and destitution of most of its communities.

Antonio and his wife were hosting a Christmas party. She was obliged to attend. An omnibus should have been taken, but the snow, despite the chill, held her spellbound. Muse pulled the hood over her head and dawdled the entire distance to Antonio's apartment.

After making her excuses and wishing all a *Joyeuse Noël*, Muse left Antonio's. A block or two from her home, she descended the bus, wanting to walk the rest of the way. Still having a love affair with the snow, she wandered the avenue, buzzing from the stimulation of cheerful drink. A brasserie filled with merry diners caught her attention. She paused to observe. Seated at the window was a handsome couple immersed in each other's company. Her first instinct: What was the woman wearing? She examined the elegant brunette and decided the red lace cap she wore, plume and all, was *adorable*. Her eyes glided toward the man, but his gaze was already fixated on her. She flinched. A recognition that caused her to lift the train of her skirt and move away.

JEAN-PAUL CHEVREAU

It was he who saw her first: a young African woman peering through the window at his dinner companion. She wore a green cloak. The hood framed her face in such a way . . . she looked familiar. He thought, *What an attractive woman.* He sensed a recollection of her profile: the upturned nose; the full, broad curve of her lips; her silky, dark complexion. But when his eyes locked in on hers, it struck a chord. He knew her! But before he could acknowledge her, she vanished.

Jean-Paul returned his attention to his companion. She was rambling on about a play. She sipped her wine. He sipped his. His eyes struggled to stay focused on her. She said something witty. He smiled. She said something else. He didn't hear her.

"Jean-Paul, are you listening?"

"*Oui, bien sûr.*"

I know that woman! he thought.

"*Excusez-moi, mon chérie,*" Jean-Paul said. "I'll be right back."

"Where are you going?"

"I'll be back," he repeated.

Jean-Paul hurried toward the exit of the restaurant, grabbed his coat, and dashed out. He perused the boulevard until he saw a single figure in a green cloak moving briskly down the street. Even with his vulnerable leg, he trotted after her.

"*Excusez-moi*! Mademoiselle?"

But she did not stop.

"*Excusez-moi*," he repeated. "Mademoiselle!"

He was right upon her.

"Muse! Is that you?"

Muse stopped and turned to face him.

"Monsieur Jean-Paul—how your leg has mended!"

She curtsied. He bowed.

"How are you?" he said. "You look wonderful!"

"*Merci.*"

"And you . . . how are you?"

"*Bien, bien.*"

A short silence ensued. He stared at her, at the fringe of lashes that bordered her dark eyes. He searched for something to say.

"Are you coming or going?" he asked.

"I've just come from *une soirée de Noel* and at the last minute decided to walk the rest of the way home . . . it's such a lovely night!"

He continued to stare at her, taking in all of her.

"How is this possible? Are you the same frightened young woman I knew at La Lumière? What has happened?"

"I ran away months ago."

"*Mon Dieu!* Is everything OK?"

"Yes, very much so."

"You brave soul. May I walk with you a little way?"

He stood there shivering.

"Are you sure?"

"*Oui, bien sûr.*"

"And what about your dinner guest?"

"She'll wait."

"That's not terribly gallant. If you left me stranded in a restaurant, I would never speak to you again."

In jest, Jean-Paul pouted and put his hand over his chest as if wounded.

"*Touché.* But you must tell me where you live, or I will not budge."

She hesitated, then pointed in the distance toward the cul-de-sac and told him the name and the address of the boutique.

"It's cold. I must go," she said.

"I will come to visit you."

"Please do."

"*Alors, adieu,*" he said.

"*Adieu.*"

THINKING OF HIM

Muse spent the night staring out the window. It was snowing again. Small flakes floated down, seeming as light as feathers. The chance encounter with Jean-Paul conjured up more than emotions—gnawing thoughts that had been germinating. The terror she suffered over ever again being owned by another human being morphed into questions of commitment and relationships. Her newfound independence became as vital as breathing. Never would she sacrifice it. Yet, she wanted companionship. She asked herself if a committed relationship canceled out personal freedom or vice versa.

As a spectator of Parisian society, she discerned the behavior of women reliant on their men for support, forced to wear many faces and even more diverse hats than she when she was enslaved. Most of the women were strung along like puppets by husbands or protectors. What woman could she identify as sovereign in her own right? Mrs. Hallisburg? But it was different when born into wealth. The only other woman whole in her own persona and independence was Madame Néville, and she remained unattached.

Her mind fluxed and refluxed on what kind of life she wanted to lead; one question seemed to surface often. Muse pulled at it like a wad of warm taffy, trying to mold it into shape. She wanted to love and be loved but keep her autonomy. Could she do both?

In her fascination with Jean-Paul, her eyes remained open. She knew what he was—a bon vivant, a typical privileged young Frenchmen sallying about town, women in pursuit. Still, there was something about him, the boyish smile that flashed across his face when pleased, the deep tone of his voice, warm and masculine. His intense, gripping eyes grazed the innermost part of her heart and stroked it like the soothing sound of a violin, a vibration caressing her spirit. That night, she searched through the assemblage of old letters and papers and found the two sketches he had drawn for her; she would have them framed.

THINKING OF HER

Jean-Paul squandered the night much the same way as Muse, reliving their encounter. His night differed only in that he was not alone. Jeanine was in his arms, fast asleep. But he held on to the vision of the woman of color he chased down the snow-white streets of Paris. The slave girl from La Lumière. He remembered the way her body moved when she walked toward him, holding a tray. The way she leaned in close to him when pouring his coffee. The smell of her sweet, natural scent lingering long after she left the room. She was always somewhere in the shades of his mind.

He received no communication from La Lumière after Olivier resumed his duties in the war. If Jean-Paul had known of her plight, he would have offered sanctuary. To have witnessed the ruckus following her escape, priceless.

The woman next to him stirred and whimpered a sigh of contentment. She did not, however, deflect him from his reverie—the girl from a distant southern shore. He yawned. In his mind, he turned over what it felt like to stand before her again. But he adjusted his reflection and pulled in the reins of his sentimentality.

His life had changed. He was a different man. He now moved in influential circles, soon able to write his own ticket. A liaison with a former slave would not be an asset. He turned his head toward the window. It was snowing again. With a smile, he recalled her that night in Furet's garden: she in a drab nightgown and an indigo cape; so much an innocent. How meekly she spoke then, but now she met his eyes directly and spoke with a sense of confidence. He could not imagine what happened. How had she freed herself? What about the fine coat and the elegant dress she wore? An outfit of high fashion, was it not? His brow furrowed. She must have a lover or worse. His thoughts grew dim. What did she do for a living? Is she caught up in the darker side of Paris? After all, she was walking the streets late at night, alone.

LA SAINT-SYLVESTRE

Muse hoped he would come, but he didn't. Maybe send a note . . . but nothing, not a word. It was New Year's Eve. If she read him right, he would have surprised her with a visit or perhaps an invitation . . . but no. *Fool!* she thought. He *was* with another woman.

"I'm such an *imbécile.*"

Cheng was still in the South, Madame Néville in Biarritz, Antonio and his wife, also out of the city. Muse knew no one else in this big, wonderful town. The boutique closed the day before Christmas. She spent the week, including Christmas Day, alone, cutting, sewing, and embroidering. At present, she was engrossed in tight stitching of a heavy silk fabric, cream with floral accents, not due for two weeks; no hurry. But still, she kept at it as if obsessed. Soon, she stopped. Anxiety kicked in, and she felt she could not face La Saint-Sylvestre alone. Darkness fell, and the festivities of the coming New Year were under way.

"I've got to get out of here."

She put the garment aside and hastily buttoned up the gray uniform. She snatched the wicker basket from the storage room and packed it with cheese, wine, and pâté, no bread. Wrapped up in the indigo cape, she took a few francs from the cashbox for Sœur Claudette and ventured out into the snow.

⊰┼⊱

"I bet you never imagined spending New Year's Eve in jail," Claire said to Muse.

"Never in a million years."

They took turns drinking wine from the bottle.

"It's way past visiting hours?"

"The good sœur has gotten used to me."

"And the donations, no doubt."

"No doubt."

Claire tore off a piece of bread she'd made that morning and pressed it into a wedge of soft pâté.

"Delicious! Thank you for this."

Muse took another swig of the wine.

"Claire, tell me about Gerard."

"What about him?"

"I want to know—"

"Is there something wrong?"

"No."

Muse did not want to share her encounter with Jean-Paul, not just yet.

"It's just . . ." Muse said. "How do you feel about him after all this . . . his betrayal, his desertion of you?"

"I can tell you how I once felt. But now . . . I'm not sure, other than if I ever get the chance, I will kill him!"

Muse shrugged. Claire smirked.

"Did you love him?"

"Ah! It's strange, Muse. All my life, I've longed to love some-one so completely, so devotedly, so . . . unconditionally. To be with someone who I could turn my essence over to for safekeep-ing; that was my greatest dream."

Then she said, "Be very careful of what you wish for; you might just get it."

"And now?" Muse asked.

"And now, I'm depleted, as fragile and ruptured as if raped."

"Would you do it over again, knowing what you know now?"

"God, I hope I wouldn't, but then again . . ."

Muse looked at Claire as if confused.

"How do you know when you love someone? I mean really love someone?"

"Aggrey. You'll know."

Muse handed the bottle over to Claire.

"Oh, by the way, whatever happened to the bounty hunter tracking you?"

"I'm sure he's long gone by now."

PELTIER'S NEW FRIEND

Peltier waited near a private gentlemen's club off the Champs-Élysées. Out of sight of the entrance, he paced the avenue. The chill of the foggy night nipped at his flesh. Dressed in a black evening frock coat, pressed trousers, polished boots, a clean white silk shirt, and top hat, the only assets he lacked were his gold timepiece, diamond ring, and a heavy evening mantle—all pawned long ago. A contact of his worked evenings at the club, and for a few francs, he promised to get Peltier on the guest list. The tradition of the club allowed for the guest of a member to frequent the club even in his absence—if he was on the list. The contact knew what members were in town and what members were not. With that kind of information, Peltier devised a plot.

The Hallisburgs had declined to give Peltier the bonus. In their opinion, the job was incomplete. He blamed his loss on the bitch of a daughter who kept complaining. A new proposition, however, was proposed. If he found Muse and returned her safely to them by the first of the year, they would reinstate the bonus option. Yesterday, he received a curt letter from America; Mr. Hallisburg wrote:

Monsieur Peltier,
Our slave Mary, Muse's mother, received an anonymous gift from
Paris, a blue silk scarf. It could only mean one thing. Muse is still
alive. You've failed in your efforts. The family no longer requires
your services.
Frederick Hallisburg

Louis grimaced when he read the letter. He cursed the Hallisburgs and acknowledged that the slave was becoming an itch he could not scratch, a blade cut that would not heal. It angered him. No one ever escaped from his clutches, not since his father's death . . . no one.

Once again, Louis faced financial hardship. But he deemed himself good with cards, something of a sharp. The thought occurred to him to get invited to a high-stakes game. He scrounged up enough money to make a decent bid, but he needed an affluent environment and upscale players to entice.

A man dressed in a formal livery approached Peltier on the street; they shook hands.

"You're set. I've put your name on the list. Monsieur Riblon has been a member of the club for over fifteen years. He is in Provence with family, not back for a month. Does that help?"

"*Oui, merci, Jean,*" Peltier said. "It helps a lot." Peltier gave Jean several crisp notes.

"*Bon chance!*" Jean said and left.

Peltier took note of the clock tower at the end of the street. He would wait another twenty minutes before entering the club. While he marked time, he eyed two ladies of the evening loitering under a lamppost. One of them was *une noire*. Without thought, he weighed in on her worth if sold. He wondered if she looked like his escaped slave. *But what does it matter now?*

Peltier entered the exclusive lounge without incident. After a drink or two and several short conversations with various members at the bar, he was invited to sit in on a private game of poker. He played in good form: winning several hands and attracting new acquaintances. One of them was an influential financier in town on business. He was Mr. John Reynolds, an Englishman well known for his advisory skills on foreign commodities. The wealthiest men in the world hired him for his expertise. A few brandies later, a cigar or two, Mr. Reynolds and Louis struck up an acquaintanceship and spent the evening talking about their various travels, the war, and the state of chaos in the world.

"Monsieur Peltier, I tell you this. I detest traveling without my wife, especially when obligated to attend formal social functions."

"Where is Madame Reynolds?"

"She is indisposed . . . with child."

"Congratulations!"

"*Merci.* It will be my sixth."

"Six. *Mon Dieu.*"

Louis was appraising the man who sat across from him. He oozed of wealth. His cufflinks were raw cut diamonds. The chain of his gold pocket watch, a thick and shiny braid, dangled from the inside of his coat, at least eighteen karats. He wore but one ring—his wedding band. Understated but valuable. Peltier's eyes grew ominous. He could overtake this man with little effort, he thought.

"I appreciate you seem able to decipher my poor execution of the French language."

"*Non*, monsieur, you don't speak badly," Peltier lied.

Soon after and under the thick haze of brandy and smoke, Mr. Reynolds said, "I have several business and formal engagements within the next month I must attend. The laborious interviewing process for a secretary is not going well. I need someone who can accompany me on these events . . . someone who can do light translation, answer correspondences as they arise. How's your English?

"Good," Peltier replied.

"You seem like a bright enough fellow; you're French. If you are free, would you consider a short-term stint as my aide-de-camp while I'm in Paris? I'll make it worth your while."

"*Bien sûr*," Louis said without hesitation.

JEAN-PAUL IN MARSEILLE

In his eyes, the Mediterranean was an intense, captivating body of water. The rustling waves, its many shades of blue, ricocheting off each other, seemed to suck him in like a vortex of emotion. At one time, Jean-Paul wanted to devote his life to painting the many moods of her restlessness. He worked on numerous interpretations, but his father refused to let him pursue his passion for art.

"My son," his father remarked more than once to anyone within hearing distance, "may be a bastard, but he will not grow up without a fine education and means to achieve a lucrative career."

Jean-Paul's love for sketching and painting fortuitously converted to the study of engineering and architecture. His father knew best. Jean-Paul was both pleased with his profession and appreciative of his father's stern hand and support.

He moved along the dehydrated, dark corridors of his father's vast estate—a dismal, suffocating parcel of property. The house had settled down. His father was on the mend, thank God! The old man gave them quite a scare.

He put on his overcoat and a floppy felt hat and grabbed the weather-beaten leather sack holding his artist tools. Down toward the old port he wandered, breathing in the grainy, sea-salt air. He strayed along the oceanfront, shaking his head at the deluge of moored boats—so many of them. He noted the fishermen. Tight-fitting black-and-white striped shirts, khaki trousers rolled up to the knee, barefoot; a flock of sun-brown, leathered-skinned men in boats salvaging through piles of *poisson*. He kept afoot, tracking past a long string of fishmongers, and then climbed up a stretch of road leading to his favorite spot as a child. Was it still there—the large flat stone that emerged from the damp soil, where he used to sit for hours, gazing at the sea?

The original plan was to visit his father for the holidays, but spring had sprung, and he was still in the house. He hated the place and seldom returned if he could help it. Even when recuperating from his war injuries, he thanked God when the doctors insisted he remain hospitalized in Paris. But he recovered; he no longer fought in the war or traveled abroad and subsequently ran out of excuses. So he arrived home for *la fête de Noel* at the last possible moment.

The feelings of being an outsider, biracial and illegitimate, resurfaced the moment he stepped foot in his father's house. The dried, brittle walls seemed to hold the essence of his unhappy childhood, even seemed to capture the haunting spirit of his mother, who deserted him for a new life.

He and his mother moved into the estate after his birth. The scandal ruffled feathers within the small elite society of Marseille: his mild-mannered father and the torrid, passionate Algérienne. Had his mother not given his father an ultimatum to marry, they might have continued as they were—something of a family, at least. But his father refused to marry her, citing his family's disapproval. She left and returned to her native land, leaving Jean-Paul behind.

The ancient French blood that ran warmly through his veins would make life difficult for him in Algeria; he was better off with his father—at least he would receive an education.

"I love you, *mon petit*," his mother said to him. "But I go back to my own country, where I am appreciated. Your father loves you also; he will take loving care of you . . . better than I can. Forgive me."

Once she was out of the picture, the family tolerated the illegitimate boy. Jean-Paul was only ten years old when his father married, an arranged liaison reinstating his inheritance.

After celebrating *le fête des Rois*, Monsieur Chevreau senior took ill. As much as Jean-Paul wished to leave Marseille, he was the eldest and could not shirk his duty. His two half brothers were still under the age of fifteen, and Madame Chevreau was at her wit's end with panic; so he took charge.

Fortunately, his last assignment, a small apartment building near l'avenue Gabriel, was finished. The offices of Baron Haussmann gave Jean-Paul permission to remain in Marseille to manage his father's affairs while Chevreau senior recuperated. His new project, still in its initial stages of development, allowed him to work from Marseille, sending sketches and blueprints via messenger.

He pined for Paris: its lights, its cultural diversity . . . its energy. Unlike his friend Olivier, who detested the city, the flames that burned within the urban wonderland kept Jean-Paul's creative juices ignited.

Marseille was an ancient city, although a rough and sordid town. A community port filled with ship owners, sailors, importers, and exporters who relied on the routes and bounty from the sea for their livelihood. The industry attracted a complex society. It housed a sea of inhabitants, black and white, from all parts the world. Jean-Paul grew up in the arms of the old port, entrenched in its nefarious, ambitious, gypsylike reverie; yet its society, its morals, never appealed to him. Once, when he was a child, a few years after his mother left, he told his father he did not want to live in Marseille anymore; he didn't like the seafaring village and wanted to reside somewhere else. His father replied: "Son, Marseille is an exciting city. It is your home. You feel this way only because you miss your mother. Don't worry—I will take care of you. I promise, *mon petit*. And you will one day learn to love this province."

But Jean-Paul never did.

He removed his hat and coat, sat down on the familiar flat, unroughened stone, as in his youth. His body felt better, more flexible and agile than before. The cane served mostly as an accessory, adding elegance to his close-to-normal gait. As he stared at the waves, peace overtook him. The seagulls soaring overhead squawked as if annoyed by his presence. He tried to capture the magnificence of their flight on paper. He struggled to perfect the elongations of their wings and the extension of their feet as they flew. But after several efforts, he gave up. Then he saw a different bird, perched high in a tree, one with coal black feathers, singing as if lamenting. He remembered the sketches he drew of a similar bird at La Lumière, a symbolic bird, a bird of freedom— a bird he'd drawn for her, what seemed like a long time ago.

LE PETIT CUL-DE-SAC GROWS

Because one satisfied customer referred another and another, the commerce of Le Petit Cul-de-Sac gained momentum. It increased to a point whereby Muse needed temporary help, a trainee, until Claire got out of prison. But who?

One afternoon, after leaving Cheng's apartment, she saw again the young beggar girl, the one she saw at Christmas, peddling on the streets. She watched her for a moment, her timid, quiet manner. Muse guessed her to be foreign because of her dark-olive complexion and the thick curls of pitch-black hair escaping from under her cap. She stood in the streets with an outstretched hand holding an empty cup. Average height, gangly, she appeared alert and steadfast, even in her poor circumstances. Muse pictured her presentable, cleaned and dressed in a reserved uniform. After reflecting for a few minutes more, she approached the girl and struck up a conversation.

"It's freezing out here. Would you like a cup of tea?"

"*Oui*, mademoiselle."

"My shop is around the corner. Come with me."

They sat in the back room near the stove.

"What is your name?"

"Maria."

"My name is Muse Aggrey. Nice to meet you."

Maria wrapped her hands around the steaming cup.

"Careful, it's hot."

"Oh, no, mademoiselle, it warms me."

"Tell me about yourself."

Maria told of her parents' relocation to France from Spain three years ago. After a constant struggle, her father took ill and later died, leaving Maria and her mother to fend for themselves. Although her mother worked at various meager jobs, her income was not enough to make ends meet. It was why she begged for *centimes* on the streets, but she did not plan to beg forever.

"My mother is teaching me to read and write and count."

"That's smart of your mother."

"Can you sew?"

"A little."

After Muse met with Maria's mother, she hired Maria to work a few days a week. Maria took to the shop, quick to learn the skills of presentation, greeting customers, and exhibiting merchandise. When the shop slowed, she helped with minor stitching and cleaning. Within a few weeks, Maria managed the storefront running of Le Petit Cul-de-Sac, leaving Muse some free hours to design and tailor dresses.

AN INVITATION

A bleak afternoon as spring struggled to come forth. Muse was working in the back of the shop when Maria brought her an envelope just delivered by a local messenger. Last week, she had paid off the lease for the next six months, so she assumed it was papers from the landlord, but then she recognized Madame Néville's handwriting and the local address. She was back in town. Muse read the note and found an invitation to dine at Madame's private residence. The request was extraordinary! In fact, they never shared a meal or even a drink. In truth, she understood Madame did not receive visitors.

"*Non, non,*" Madame once said. "My home is my sanctuary. I entertain little if at all. It is my place of comfort and solitude; that's all."

Their interaction always centered on either business or study. *What could she want with me?*

An invitation of this type had a purpose. She expected to be examined for whatever the reason. The faithful green brocade was refreshed and reaccessorized. And in her mind, she rolled over every social instruction she could remember when observing Cassandra. Whatever Madame's motives, Muse would be ready.

JEAN-PAUL RETURNS TO PARIS

His father recovered. With life in Marseille back to normal, Jean-Paul was free to go, and he wasted no time reinstating himself in the capital. In his absence from Paris, his workload doubled, leaving him little time for amusement. Two new buildings were proposed: one, an enormous renovation off the rue de Rivoli, the other, a complex, upscale apartment building near Place de Concorde. He welcomed both challenges. Most of the evenings he spent in the company of his colleagues, discussing work and politics, but he soon grew weary of them and wanted diversion.

Twice a week, he ate at Chez Jacques, the brasserie where he last saw her. He tried to re-create the evening, struggling to recall the short walk they took. That evening, he was so flushed with drink and merriment, he could not recollect which way they fared, or where she said she lived, or what avenue she traveled. He sat alone at the same table, staring out the window, watching people parade by, hoping she would too.

After dining, he ventured back into the brisk, cool night air and chanced by an art gallery. Several artists were on display; he knew one or two of them and their work. He engaged himself with several interesting pieces. In front of a collection of drawings, he found himself lingering. The study of a nude *négresse*. The interpretation intrigued him, but at the same time, he found it bizarre. The new artistic movement experimented with the human form or still life as though looking through a shattered glass; he wasn't yet impressed. He noted the artist's name and moved on.

The same artist also created a series of realistic sketches, watercolors, and oils depicting laborers at work. A haunting charcoaled drawing of a man working in the urban sewers stirred him. The subject, an able-bodied, muscular soul, sweat and refuse dripping from his shirtless body while he shoveled the waste of the city. Another illustration encapsulated the image of children engaged in candle making in a ramshackle workhouse. Young boys, dressed in tattered clothes, dirty, harsh faces, some in tears, others working under duress, helplessness imprinted in their eyes. The next picture, a compelling oil of a young American slave, caused him to stop and behold. He knew the face. The artist caught her essential vulnerability, her innocence. Jean-Paul remembered that look—in the garden at La Lumière, the night she pushed him away, the sense of despair shrouding her as she stumbled up to her room.

DINNER WITH MADAME

The hired carriage halted in front of an exclusive apartment building. A footman approached the cab, at first suspicious of the elegantly dressed *femme noire* alone in the cab; nevertheless, he extended his hand, and she dismounted.

Muse climbed the winding rosewood stairs up to the third floor, her hand trailing along the smooth, well-crafted balustrade. When she reached her destination, she paused to pacify her nerves. Erect in front of the door, she took a deep breath and then pulled the long bell cord. A maid answered. Muse stated her name, and she was asked to enter. She followed the maid across the threshold to a small but demure foyer. The maid took her cloak, gloves, and handbag.

"Please, wait here."

A full-size gilded mirror hung in the foyer. Muse took a moment to study her form and the green brocade dress from all angles. She straightened the white lace cap, ornamented with a cluster of white feathers that framed her face. Her hair was styled à la Madame Rolin.

The maid returned and led Muse to a finely carved wooden door and knocked.

"*Entrée.*"

"Mademoiselle Muse Aggrey," the maid said.

Muse entered the salon and gracefully fell into a curtsy. Madame stood near a window, poised and superbly dressed as if she expected royalty; she smiled at her protégé.

"Well done, my dear."

The room was commodious. The walls papered in toile, the color of pale lemons. A jasmine scent permeated the room. Heavy silk curtains dyed in pale shades of summer-straw tints cascaded to the floor, grazing the soft pile of an oriental rug. Muse noted its pastel floral motifs. Upholstered sofas and chairs in creamy satin fabric stood on fluted legs, placed strategically around the room. Madame pointed to a fauteuil, and Muse sat.

"*Merci*, Madame."

Huge potted plants and a large vase filled with fresh flowers adorned the room. An original oil painting of apples, pears, and flowers in a vase hung over the mantel; a fire burned. It was, thought Muse, a woman's room.

"Your hair looks nice . . . Madame Rolin?"

"*Oui*, Madame."

"Did you pay her?"

"An exchange for a hat—I made it for her."

"Good girl! And the cap you're wearing now?"

"I made it as well."

"Chic!"

The two drank aperitifs; they chitchatted and then sat down to dine. The meal was four full courses, each catered according to Madame's instructions. Intimidated by the presentation, Muse at first hesitated.

"Relax," Madame said. "Take a deep breath. If you're not sure, watch me."

She composed herself as the memory of Cassandra's early teachings on dining reemerged. They ate and spoke with easy formality. Muse commented on the touch of cumin in the lentil *potage*. Madame complimented the chef on the leg of lamb with garlic and fava beans. And both decided the accompanying bottles of vintage Bordeaux were a perfect match. Muse played her part as best she could in what seemed like an exam in the art of polite social ceremony. She enjoyed the meal. Good to dine on something other than cheese and bread and Chinese food for a change.

"What have you been reading?" Madame asked.

"I have no time for much reading other than the daily journals."

"You must keep up your reading. Literature: Stendhal, Hugo, Dumas, at least. It's important. I will lend you books."

"Merci."

"What do you find interesting in the daily news?"

"Life at court is always amusing. Empress Eugénie's fashion statements I find interesting. She's not French, is she?"

"Non. L'Empresse was born in Granada. And make no mistake, she is not just a figurehead; she has a strong influence on her husband when it comes to foreign policy. She may be fashionable, but she is also smart."

"I'm glad she gave birth."

"At last!" Madame said. "It's about time. So many miscarriages."

"I also read about the war here and the news from home, of course. Especially the discourse and debates between the North and South. It is all so fascinating, yet alarming."

"Ah! Oui. Do you think there will be war between the states?"

"It sounds like it. The North seems to want to free us slaves, but the South is adamant about keeping slavery alive."

"Watch how you express yourself, *mon chérie*. You're no longer a slave, Muse. You must stop thinking you are."

"*Oui. C'est vrai.* Sometimes I forget."

"Do you miss America?"

"Every so often, because of my mother . . . but mostly no. I love the life I'm building here."

Just then, a boisterous roar exploded from the streets outside the window.

"What's going on?" Madame asked her server.

"I don't know, Madame."

"Please, go and see."

A short time later, the server returned and told Madame that crowds of people were gathering in the streets, celebrating.

"Celebrating! Why? What has happened?"

"The signing of a peace treaty."

"Ah! *Mon Dieu.*"

Madame and Muse rushed out to the terrace to witness the scene below. A chaotic group of people, singing, cheering, raced up and down the boulevards, wielding torches that lit up the streets. Madame called for her maid.

"Go down and get a newspaper."

"*Oui*, Madame."

"Does it mean the war is over?" Muse asked.

"Yes, maybe so."

"France has won?"

"No, not really. It simply means that the French have temporarily found a way to keep the Russians from intimidating the Turks . . . but trust me; it's not over. The Russians will not go away. They still want influence over the Turks. I know they won't go away because I am Russian. And we never go away." She smirked.

"Were you for the war?" Muse asked.

"Absolutely not! I haven't got a political bone in my body. War disrupts my business . . . can't find anything or anybody, for that matter, and therefore I can't make money."

Thoughtfully, but before she could stop herself, Muse asked, "Madame, why is it you never remarried?"

"What has my marriage to do with anything?"

"Nothing. I just wondered."

"Ah! As you are so very good at keeping secrets, *mon chérie*, I will tell you one. Let me refresh our glasses."

She poured.

"Please, Madame, continue."

"The truth of the matter is . . . I am still legally married. My widowhood is a sham of respectability that allows me a career and independence. If I can give you one piece of advice, it is that if you can make a career for yourself, and become a truly independent woman, if you can do that with your store or your sewing, never, ever give it up. Not for love of man, of country, or of religion. Because in the end, they will all, in some way or another, betray you . . . that is to say, us, the supposedly weaker sex. If you are your own woman, you will have power and peace of mind like you can never imagine. It does not mean life will be simple; it will become complicated, lonely, and challenging, but you will be the cabriolet driver of your life and not merely the passenger. Of all the information I may have imparted to you, this is the most vital. Trust me on this one, Mademoiselle Muse."

"I believe you, Madame, and I trust your advice. There is so much to learn. But tell me about your life."

Madame sipped her wine; her eyes wandered toward the window as if she was searching for memories filed away long ago.

"Why not?" she said.

⪥╫⪤

"I was born to an aristocratic family in Saint Petersburg. Bred and educated to marry within the same vein if not higher. My parents orchestrated an arranged marriage when I turned seventeen. To a wealthy young man from a prominent family—well born, same age group, tolerable appearance, but a dimwit. I could not bear to be in his presence. I refused the match. If I could not marry for love, I would not marry at all; it was the beginning of my derailment, however, one I do not regret. A young bon vivant of French nationality appeared out of nowhere and stole my heart. He offered neither station nor fortune, but he loved me, or so I thought. My passion for him was great, uncontrollable. My family rejected the liaison; still, I ran off with him to France."

"You just left?" Muse asked.

"*Oui.* Not much different than your escape from the Hallisburgs. My parents and their culture dominated me to the point of feeling enslaved."

Muse nodded.

"After coming to Paris," Madame continued, "we married at once, in hopes my family would soften. They did not and disowned me outright. When we were sure my family would not help us financially, Alfred's attitude toward me changed. After a few short years, he left me. No word; just went out one morning and never came back. Of course, I thought something happened to him . . . hurt, killed—I do not know what. Then I learned he ran off to the South of France with a well-to-do woman, ten years his senior. I never heard from him again."

"O-o-o-h!" Muse echoed.

"Nearly homeless and desperate, I used the only skills I possessed: social education and a gift for languages. Within a decade, I built a successful career out of nothing. So you see, my dear, how much I relate to you."

"Where is your husband now?" Muse asked.

"I don't know, nor do I care."

Muse looked at Madame, somewhat shocked.

"Why haven't you gotten a divorce?"

"It's not important."

"But suppose he comes back—would he not have access to your financial resources as a lawful husband?"

Madame's eyes widened. She glared at Muse as if struck. *Why hadn't she gotten a divorce?*

The ladies adjourned to the sitting room for coffee. They sipped in silence; all the while, Muse conjectured as to why the lavish entertainment.

Madame, stirring her coffee, said, "Muse, I know you are wondering why I have invited you to my home. I seldom receive guests. But, my dear, this has been a test . . . which, I might add, you've passed."

"What kind of test?"

"To see how much of my previous coaching you've retained. There are a few things in your manner I would like to polish, but all in all, your presentation was more than adequate . . . especially as this was an impromptu evening."

"But why, Madame?"

"I need a favor from you."

Muse did not hesitate.

"Of course, what can I do?"

The server stood in the background, quiet but alert. When he attempted to refill Muse's coffee cup, she shook her head to decline. He promptly retrieved her cup.

"Nothing more for me either," Madame said. "You may clear."

The waiter whisked everything away within minutes and departed. Once alone, Madame continued, "Muse I am getting old and . . . tired. What I have been praying for is one exceptional assignment, one that would allow me to retire and live comfortably until my day's end."

"*Bien sûr*, Madame."

"A family has approached me, a wealthy family from Greece—a rare mixed lineage of an ancient name but new money. They have three children, all daughters, two in adolescence and *un enfant*. The two eldest are at the age to which they must prepare for their coming out and their schooling. The family, Erasmos, is interviewing two instructors for the position, and I am one of them. Countess Kolinsky, a tutor born of a distinguished Polish family, is the other. She is also widowed and has the same training as I, but she is younger, attractive, and her bloodline is bluer . . . if you understand my meaning."

"I do."

"The position would require that one spends at least a year in Paris and two years, maybe more, at their estate in Greece, I believe on an isle. The salary is phenomenal, and if I were to receive such a supplement, I could retreat to anywhere in the world."

Madame got up and went over to the window to rearrange a crease in the curtain that spoiled its drape. She turned to Muse.

"I, of course, never imagined I would ever be a contender for such a position. The countess, you must understand, has a renowned reputation. During my interview, when I was introduced to the children, charming by all accounts, I was asked about former students. In telling them about the Hallisburgs, I mentioned you. Your story captivated them—your emancipation and your occupation as proprietress of a dress salon. And in my narrative, I confess, I may have taken more credit than I deserved for your development. Be that as it may, they are having a formal dinner here in Paris next week; it is to be an intimate but exceptional affair at their leased estate adjacent to the *bois*. There will be people of varied social standing—business acquaintances, personal friends—an international gathering. They have asked if I might invite my premiere student to dine with them. I said yes."

"Madame, of course, I will do whatever you wish."

"You understand, Muse, you will represent me. I need you at your best."

"*Oui* . . . without a doubt."

She paced across the room, heavy in thought.

"What will you wear?"

Muse looked down at the green brocade.

"It is a very lovely ensemble. But it is still spring; you would require an exuberant color representation of the season. Minute details like this are noticed. I have ordered fabric for you, the color of saffron, a stunning contrast to your complexion."

"But, Madame, it is impossible for me to make a complete ensemble by next week. I have three deadlines—three gowns due in the next two weeks. I couldn't manage; there is no time . . . surely I can redesign this green brocade—yet again—and give it a spring flair."

"Who are your clients?"

Muse gave their names.

"*Alors*, I'm acquainted with them. Tell them it is an emergency. Ask for an extension. If they are not in agreement, I will talk to them."

"*Oui*, Madame."

"You must outfit yourself beautifully, and it must be by your own hand. I trust you understand how important this is?"

"I do."

Then she looked at Muse, still reflecting.

"There's something else. I've not mentioned it until now for fear of upsetting you."

"Upsetting me?"

"News from Virginia."

Muse's eyes met hers.

"I received a letter from Monsieur Hallisburg. He wrote to thank me for my services . . . and there was an enclosure, addressed to you."

"What?"

"The strange part is that the Hallisburgs seemed to be under the impression you might be dead. Mademoiselle Cassandra, however, does not believe you are deceased and urged her father to write you a letter just in case. Apparently, a blue silk scarf arrived for your mother from Paris. They found the gift suspicious."

Madame presented the correspondence, to which Muse again gasped.

"Calm down, *ma petite*."

"How does he know where I am?"

"He assumed, and rightly so, as I know everything that goes on in Paris, sooner or later, our paths would cross."

"It's bad news!"

"Read it first, before you upset yourself so."

Muse took the letter, ripped off the seal, and read it, and just as quickly as the tears welled in her eyes, a smile appeared.

"What does it say?"

"He says if this letter finds me, I'm alive, and for that they are grateful. The bounty hunter they hired and subsequently dismissed told them I was dead. My mother is doing well. She is in good health, save for her concern about me; she doesn't believe I'm dead. He also says Mary, my mother, has received several anonymous gifts from France, a blue scarf, presumably from me, which is another reason why she feels I'm alive. She sends her love."

"That's nice. What else?"

Muse read:

I beg you to return to Virginia. We will pay all expenses. By law, you are still the property of the Hallisburgs, but if not for that reason, for the sake of your grieving mother, who longs for her child to, once again, be by her side.

"How dare he!" Muse said. "He was planning to sell me. He doesn't care about my grieving mother."

"*Vache!*" Madame snapped. "Surely you would not consider returning."

"Of course not, but I fear for my mother."

"*Ma petite,* if he is that vicious, there is nothing you can do about it. But he never struck me as that type."

"I wonder if the bounty hunter still looks for me."

"Well, not if he thinks you're dead. Even so, he would be wasting his time and money, now that Hallisburgs are in America. But, my dear, you have an opening here: two choices. If you bridge this opportunity to correspond with the Hallisburgs, you'd be able to keep informed about your mother, as well as the changes taking place in America. I mean, suppose slavery is outlawed one day? It happened here. Or you could go on letting them think you are dead—no more problems."

"I don't know what to do."

"Well, you don't have to decide tonight."

The ride home was tedious. Many of the streets still overflowed with citizens rejoicing over the Paris Peace Treaty. The war would soon be over and many brave young men free to come home. Her mind shuffled back to the memory of Olivier, the only person she knew fighting in the war. He had been polite to her at La Lumière, and she hoped for his safety. Her thoughts turned to Jean-Paul and his iridescent smile; she wondered why she never heard from him. Suddenly, the gloom of constant aloneness covered her like a cloud-flecked cloak. The cabriolet crept along.

The letter from Virginia she held pressed firm to her breast, so firm it crumpled. She smoothed out the creases but then again crushed it to her chest. Tears of relief and gratitude welled up; her mother was safe for now.

"Thank the Lord!" she whispered.

Once back in the arctic stillness of her room, she sat by candle-light, staring out the window. After a while, she orchestrated an imaginary dialog with the Hallisburgs. As a free person, she expressed herself with candor, as was her right. She practiced what she wanted to say, tossing words over and over in her head until she wilted to sleep. The next morning, when she rose, she took out a sheet of paper:

Dear Mr. and Mrs. Hallisburg . . .

LA ROBE

The fabric arrived from Madame Néville: a luxurious weave of silk taffeta, saffron yellow, holding the sheen of sunlight. With it came several yards of cotton-linen lace, off-white, crafted to look like a trail of fine netting. Muse stared at the fabric for hours, hoping for inspiration, but none came. She sent for Cheng. He appeared with a bottle of wine, and they retreated to the back room to study the fabric.

"Where did she find it?" Cheng asked.

"Who knows?"

Muse sketched down a few thoughts and passed them to Cheng, who enhanced her shapes and silhouettes and then passed it back. They went to and fro with ideas for hours until hunger overtook them.

"That's enough for tonight," she said. "Let's go eat."

THE ERASMOSES' DINNER

The Erasmoses rented the estate sight unseen. A massive stone *maison*, constructed hundreds of years ago, bold, pretentious, and built for show. If it enjoyed any charm at all, it was its placement adjacent the *bois*. The house had remained empty for most of the last decade, and upkeep was kept at a minimum. The damp and bitter rooms resonated with a sense of despair. A somewhat dismal atmosphere brought on by its semi-abandoned state still hung in the air.

When Madame Erasmos first laid eyes on the *maison*, she was furious.

"The estate agent who convinced you to sign the lease on this atrocity of a manor should be shot," Madame Erasmos said.

"I'm sorry, *mon chérie*; I should have paid more attention. We've been so pressed for time, so busy. We will not be here long."

"I don't want my children living in this house."

"It'll be less than a year. The house in town is almost ready for occupancy."

"I don't care. I hate this house!"

"It's too late to begin looking again. Please, *mon chérie* . . . eight months tops and we will be in our new home, right in the middle of Paris."

Madame sighed but folded her arms in protest.

On the night of the dinner, Monsieur and Madame Erasmos did what they could to bring life and warmth to the old manor.

The idea to include Muse in their society was Madame Erasmos's. She wanted to see the escaped slave. If Madame Néville could take a former captive with no family, no means, and no station and help transform her into a well-mannered, independent woman, what could she do for her own daughters?

Muse stood next to Madame Néville, waiting to be announced. Wide-eyed and curious, she browsed the interior of the house: big and grotesque, she thought. In her mind, she also recapped Madame's instructions. Posture erect, head held high, and a partial smile gracing the face. But her stomach knotting caused her to take deep breaths to steady herself. She touched the flounce of the cream-colored lace draping around her shoulder; had she overdone the accessory? She readjusted the bodice of the saffron gown and its plunging neckline; was it too low?

"Stop fidgeting," Madame whispered under her breath.

When Muse heard their names announced, she stiffened.

"Madame Sonja Néville and Mademoiselle Muse Aggrey."

They moved through to the reception room. Madame and Monsieur Erasmos greeted them warmly. Presentations followed, introducing two of the children, Alexandria, thirteen, and Anna, twelve, the wards who would study under Madame's tutelage if appointed the post. After the welcoming, the sisters were allowed samplings of appetizers and then ushered away to dine in their rooms.

A burst of commotion followed—a flurry of welcomes, introductions, and a deluge of social interactions. Muse followed Madame's lead, but her perception of the scene seemed mystifying, as if she moved in slow motion.

Every eye gravitated toward her as she and Madame Néville mingled among the guests. Muse was terrified, yet she nodded and smiled. Some guests returned her gestures, but others simply stared.

"*Bonsoir*," she said to a group standing near a large window.

"*Bonsoir*, mademoiselle," the group responded.

She was on display. An acoustic of whispers circled about her, sounding like softly rustling leaves. She caught fragmented remarks.

"Was she a slave? Her skin is as dark as a cinder. Is she an Islander or an African? Lovely dress, though!"

A large fireplace crackled and shimmered with firelight. Its wrought-iron pillars and lower mantel forged with the garish faces of grinning gargoyles sent a chill up her spine. Several large vases arranged with white roses adorned the room. Yet, an exotic, sweet, but strong aroma penetrated the air.

"What scent is it?" she asked Madame Néville.

"Incense."

A footman, dressed in full livery, approached them with a tray of sparkling champagne in tall, slim crystal glasses. A fleeting memory of Jean-Paul tumbled across her mind. She recalled the time she served him champagne at La Lumière. *Whatever happened to him?*

Another footman followed with a tray of Greek delicacies.

"What are they?" Muse asked.

"Saganaki," the footman said.

Muse sampled what looked like small pastry.

"Umm!"

"Goat cheese dredged in flour and seared to a golden brown, with the squeeze of a lemon," the footman responded before she even asked.

⚬⊱⊰⚬

The dining room was ornate. A white lace cloth covered the table, draping to the floor. More flowers, arranged in a crystal vase shaped like a swan with a hollow back, centered the long, elegant table. A cluster of vine leaves and baby's breath scattered around the table, akin to a garden bed. Two candelabras blazed with dozens of illuminated candles. The silverware, each monogrammed with the Greek symbol ∑, shone. Porcelain china, pearly white, appeared as delicate as seashells.

When Muse noticed each place setting for a six-course meal, she turned to Madame Néville with pleading eyes. But Madame shook her head as if to say, "Observe the others; you'll get through it."

More Greek delicacies garnished the dining room's sideboards. Decanted bottles of red and white wine lined the table in a small adjacent room. The staging featured a whole roasted pig perched on a cradle of vegetables. The poor beast, its jaw propped open by an abundance of small red apples and walnuts dripping from its mouth. Glazed cherries replaced its eyes. The entrée appeared to be gazing up at the ceiling. Muse shivered. *Who eats like this?*

Before dinner, Muse learned she would not sit next to Madame Néville but next to Monsieur Dimitris Peloponnese, the youngest son of one of Monsieur Erasmos's largest investors. With an intense and pleading look, Muse implored Madame to request she be seated next to her. Madame shrugged.

"You'll be all right."

Muse took her assigned place. She appraised the table. First the silverware—so many pieces; she counted seven forks alone, varied sizes and shapes. How was she to remember all of Madame's instructions? She then looked up to admire the guests sitting around the table, dressed in splendor. Madame Néville, in a handsome deep-violet gown, was talking to her dinner partner, the host, Monsieur Erasmos. Finally, her eyes met with the young man seated next to her. She smiled.

"I am Dimitris Peloponnese," he said.

"Muse Aggrey . . . *enchanté*, monsieur."

He was not tall, but he was fit and well dressed. A wavy mane of dark locks fell down his neck; his eyes were blue as the sky. Despite the fashion, he paraded no facial hair and sported a smooth, close shave. His good looks increased her discomfort, and she wished, even more, to sit elsewhere.

Sensing her uneasiness, Dimitris unleashed his entire arsenal of charm and congeniality. He had never spoken to anyone of African heritage, yet he found her manner refined. "How the world has begun to intermingle!" he said. "Don't you think?"

"*Oui.*"

Muse soon engaged in polite conversation, tête-à-tête about Paris, the war, the emperor and empress, subjects she could now speak of intelligently, thanks to Madame's encouragement and her own efforts.

"Do you think there will be a confrontation between the North and the South in America?" he asked.

"It's hard to say. The articles and debates I've read are fierce."

"Freeing of the slaves. That's the main issue, *n'est pas?*"

"I believe it is more complex. The freeing of slaves paints the human decency aspects, to be sure, but it is really about leveling the wealth, the economy."

"You know," Dimitris offered, "my country was created around the concept of slavery. In fact, in ancient Greece there was, at one time, a slave populace larger than legal citizens."

Muse reflected.

"You condone slavery?"

"*Mon Dieu,* no! It is just a reality that will probably always exist in some form or another. You're fortunate to have found a way out."

Dimitris's easy, straightforward manner seemed to balance Muse. In time, as they moved from one course to another, she forgot about his intimidating good looks and lost the perception of falling short as a dinner companion. He owned a frankness about him, an uncomplicated way of speaking. His gestures she thought delightful. When he laughed, he brushed his forefinger across her hand without thinking. It warmed her. He seemed not to mind that she was a former slave, a runaway, or *une femme noire.* And his person yielded an aroma of sandalwood and fresh flowers, which made her smile.

While Madame Néville continued her lively discussion with Monsieur Erasmos, Muse noted she was also sizing up the people at the table—especially those who might be her future employers. She grasped a hint of a smile on Madame's face, which Muse read as her belief that the challenge would be an agreeable one.

Another individual caught Muse's eye as she perused the table. A man, French, early thirties, sat at the far end of the table. He had an eye-catching but coarse appearance, as if trying to minimize the rough edges of his persona but not succeeding. He wore formal attire, well tailored but outdated. She sensed apprehension about him, a rehearsed manner of etiquette that appeared mechanical, as if trying to assure a seamless interaction with the social gathering. At first, she brushed him off as a person of no importance even though he sat next to an affluent financier: Mr. Reynolds. What disturbed her was not the desperate expression in his eyes, or his attempt to disguise his lack of eloquence with a half-hearted smirk, but that he occasionally looked at her, a sharp, menacing gaze reminding her of Der Brunnen.

"What would you do if slavery was suddenly abolished in America?" Dimitris asked her.

"I would—"

But before she could reply, the male guest she was studying spoke out: "That, my dear monsieur, will never happen," he said.

"You think not?" Dimitris countered.

"Yes, no doubt in my mind. I know the South, lived in New Orleans for two years. The Southern states would never give up their way of life, their personal property; it is a part of their very being. If the North pushes them too far, there will be a human clash like never seen on American soil, not unlike the revolution here in France."

"Indeed?" Dimitris responded.

As the gentleman's rhetoric surged, Muse again grew conscious of his eyes on her, attacking like daggers.

"Excuse me," the guest said. "I couldn't help overhearing your conversation. The young woman, I take it, is a runaway slave. How smart to flee in France. A successful escape in the South is nearly impossible."

"That's not true," Muse said. "There are reports of many successful escapes."

He glared at her.

"Most are caught. And punishment is severe, as you might well know."

"Possibly," Madame Erasmos interjected. She threw a sharp eye at her husband, and then she turned to her dinner partner, Mr. Reynolds, and said: "Who is that?"

"He is Monsieur Louis Peltier. I fear he came with me."

"Ah! But who is he?"

"Frankly, madame, I don't know. We've only just met. He seemed amiable enough. He has been helping me with business projects and to maneuver around Paris . . . being French and all.

We enjoyed amusing chats at the club . . . things in common. I apologize if he offends."

Madame Erasmos shook her head. "Next time, monsieur, if you come without Madame Reynolds, please tell us. We will find you a proper assistant."

Peltier continued: "I'm surprised the owners did not make more of an effort to recover you," he said, grinning at Muse.

"It would have served no purpose, monsieur," Madame Néville said. "Keep in mind we are now a nation who has taken great pains to liberate ourselves from such barbaric concepts. And besides, her former owners would have no legal recourse in this country."

"True," Peltier replied. "I understand it would be against the law. But there are always ways around such rulings if one is persistent and if one wants their property back bad enough."

The conversation about slavery continued. Muse sat in silence, wanting to interpose. Everyone spoke about her and her plight as if she were not there.

"It sounds to me, monsieur," Dimitris said, speaking to Peltier, "as if you are a supporter the institution."

"I am not committed to the system either way," he lied. "That being said, in the case of the American South, the culture would not survive if the tradition was abandoned."

"Why?" Dimitris asked.

"Because," Mr. Reynolds interceded, "slavery is about money and human domination, power . . . the American South would cease to exist as a profitable wealthy state without those assets."

Peltier's dark eyes rested again on Muse's. She lowered her lashes, flushed with terror.

"Mademoiselle, I do not understand how you accomplished such a feat. You must have had help," Peltier said, wanting to know how she managed.

Muse remained unvoiced, and then with forced deliberation, she met Peltier's eyes and said: "Yes, I had help. But most of all, I had something I never had as a slave . . . an opportunity to exercise my own free will, and I took it."

With that comment, the guests broke into applause.

"On that note," Madame Erasmos said, "we shall adjourn to the salon for dessert."

Madame Erasmos rang the small silver bell placed next to her plate. A servant came forth. She whispered something to him, then rose. "Shall we?" she said. "A violinist awaits us."

A FRIGHTENED MUSE

Madame's carriage made its way through the boulevards. It dropped Muse off in front of the shop.

"*Merci*, Madame," Muse said as she descended.

"*Pas de tout.* You were an asset tonight. I thank you. *Bonsoir.*"

"*Bonsoir*, Madame."

But as soon as Muse entered the shop, all composure dissipated. Agitated without knowing why, she inspected the shop and adjacent rooms as if expecting an intruder. She locked and bolted both doors twice, to be sure, and then secured the windows. Sensitive to every footstep she heard on the street, she felt the calm stream of her peace of mind oozing away. The saffron dress hung in the armoire. A single candle burned. But the flicker of the firelight failed to produce its soothing effect. The grand evening, the unexpected encounter with the young heir, even the possibility of a new client with Madame Erasmos, who adored her gown—none of it mattered! She only remembered the man at the end of the table . . . *Peltier!* Her primitive instincts kicked in at the moment she met his eyes. His sharp, penetrating glare transported her back to Virginia, to the shed attached to the old school storage room. The odious look so common in Virginians who, when she was a child, cursed her or struck her for spilling something or inadvertently walking on the sidewalk for whites only. The same hateful stare still paralyzed her.

Again, the sensation of isolation took hold. She recalled the bleak hours alone in the woods just after her escape. The long-secluded wait to be rescued by someone who did not, and who could not, come. Running from her past down an unknown road, a darkened, barren road, to where? *No man's land.* Her spirit shuddered; a new surge of dread rose. She took stock of her reality. Had she gripped on to a false sense of security? Did she really think she could remain free? Who would protect her? If misfortune befell, where would she turn? Cheng, sweet . . . but no; she doubted if he could defend himself. Antonio and his wife now lived in Provence, and Claire . . . poor Claire. There was only Madame Néville. If she got the job, she would leave as well. Muse trembled, thinking of the Frenchman at the other end of the table, black looming eyes, staring.

Two weeks later, Muse received word from Madame Néville: she got the job. And because Madame Erasmos was unhappy with the house her husband leased:

We leave for Greece within the month.

And in a postscript, Madame added that she filed a petition for a divorce:

Merci, ma petite, for bringing to my attention the folly of remaining legally attached to Monsieur Néville.

A few days after that, Muse took the delivery of a small bouquet of flowers and an invitation to dine with Dimitris. She shared the invitation with Madame Néville, but Madame advised her to decline.

"But why?" Muse asked. "I like him."

"*Oui, ma petite.* But his life is not his own. His father dictates his future, and you will never be a part of it. It is the reality of the world. You would only serve as his mistress, and you are better than that."

Muse lowered her head.

"My frankness is merely to save you from emotional harm."

"He is the first man to ask me out."

"You are still young and innocent despite your past. You've got time."

"Madame, I know I'll never have a traditional life like other women. I accept that, and I don't know if it's a dreadful thing. My path is different, but so are my expectations. I want to know joy, experience diversion . . . but most of all, I'm tired of being alone."

"He will return to Greece in less than six months, and you will never see him again."

Muse looked at Madame and sighed.

"So be it."

"Well, my dear, it's your choice. I will caution you on one thing. Paris is an open-minded city, but it insists on one thing, one thing above all: discretion."

PELTIER'S LOSS

When Peltier entered the private club on the Champs-Élysées, he looked uneasy. He walked across the foyer to the reception area. As he waited for assistance, he glimpsed his image in the grand mirror hanging behind the counter. Although dressed in evening attire, he looked rough around the edges. The clerk on duty eyed him questionably, arching an eyebrow.

"May I help you?"

"My name is Louis Peltier. I'm here to see Monsieur Reynolds."

"Ah!" the clerk said. "Monsieur Reynolds checked out last week. He has returned to England. I could forward a message to him if you wish."

Peltier stared at the clerk.

"Are you all right, monsieur?"

"*Oui*," Peltier responded and excused himself.

Not knowing what to do, he headed for the bar and ordered a beer. Now what? Peltier hadn't seen him in over a month, not since the Erasmoses' dinner. Even though he had paid him well, the money didn't last. He had hoped to renew Mr. Reynolds's acquaintance and offer his services once more . . . or maybe touch him for a loan.

He sipped his beer, watching the bar fill up with members. No one seemed familiar to him. Again, he caught his reflection in the mirror. Tired and withering, he pushed back a lock of unruly hair, then heard the whispering voice of his father: *"You should have found the slave . . . snatched her right off the streets!"*

How had she escaped him when none of the other captives could? If it wasn't for her, he would be sitting pretty instead of scheming for a *centime*. He hated the thought of her . . . the wretched bitch!

He finished his drink and made a move to leave when he heard a voice: "Peltier!"

It was a gentleman he met at an earlier card game with Mr. Reynolds. A polished, well-heeled, thick-mustached Italian named Senior Rizzo, an avid card player. Rizzo waved him over to his table. Peltier greeted him cordially. They fell into good-humored conversation. In time, two other members joined them. Rizzo was in good sorts, picking up the tab for the evening. And then he suggested a game.

Peltier smiled. The last game they played together, Peltier won. Would he chance his last hundred francs?

"Bien sûr," Peltier said as he lit a cigarette. "I'm in."

The game broke up at dawn, just as the city was awakening. Peltier peered through the club's windows; it looked like another gray, wet morning. The gentlemen settled up. Peltier handed over an IOU to Rizzo. He owed hundreds.

"I will be back tomorrow night to tear up that IOU and to win back my losses and then some."

Rizzo patted him on the back.

"Of course you will, Peltier. See you tomorrow, *mon ami.*"

Peltier left but never returned.

330

DESPERATION

Peltier scoured the avenues, looking for work. But he stayed clear of the fashionable boulevards and smart cafés he once frequented, as Rizzo was not the only person to whom he owed money. He ambled around town, not caring what he labored at as long as he earned something. But hours turned into days and days into weeks. Soon, he lost purpose and transitioned into drifting. One night, alone in a dark, narrow strip of an alleyway, he stood fixated on a garbage can nudged into a corner behind a restaurant, a wooden barrel with its lid askew. From the trash protruded the head of a carrot, its long green tentacles limping over the bin. Before he realized it, he had yanked the top from the bin and seized the carrot. He then foraged through the waste to find a discarded apple and a quarter loaf of day-old bread.

He still had a room, yet he roamed the streets, wavering in and out of awareness. Sometimes, he would abruptly come into consciousness, ignorant of where he was or how he got there. It happened that morning. In the middle of a dirt lane, plop, he came to as if released from a daze. Unsure of his location, he stalled, wide-eyed and bewildered, staring at a row of vendor stalls. He then recognized the perimeters of Les Halles. A fruit vendor was feeding scraps of food to a pack of feral dogs. The sight enraged him. He starved while animals ate with gusto. When the seller turned his back and bent to pet a pup, Louis crept up to the fruit cart and snatched two pears. He inched toward a nearby bush, sank to the ground, and bit into the fruit with such voracity, as if afraid they would take it from him.

At that moment, the Saint-Eustache church bells rang, signaling noon. He stood up and by chance glanced across the marketplace. That's when he saw her. The slave. She wore a white dress and a bonnet and carried baskets of food. She was talking to a portly man, a laborer with a mule cart. He sneered. She always seemed on show, smiling as if she owned the world, whereas he descended into stealing food to offset his hunger.

It was at the Erasmoses where he first overheard the conversation between her and the Greek. Stunned to learn she was the runaway. The Hallisburg's escaped slave. No wonder he could not find her. Dressed well, speaking good French, and traveling in elite circles. How does a female slave achieve what he, a Frenchman in his own country, cannot? It made no sense. He remembered watching her at the table, sizing her up, calculating her value on the open market. But at the time, he gave up the reverie. She was no longer an available commodity; she had protectors. But now, as he watched her from a distance, his animal aggressions took hold. She was still worth a price. As his mind unraveled, he thought, *Defeated by a woman, a slave? Never!*

He licked his fingers and slicked back his grisly mane. He smoothed out the wrinkles from his wastrel-looking waistcoat. Closer he moved, darting across the market and resting behind a bush. She and the laborer continued their conversation. His eyes stayed with them until the man drove off. And then he narrowed in on her.

LES HALLES

The Saint-Eustache church bells struck noon. The morning was crisp, the grayness of Paris dispersed, and the sky was clear. Easter passed, summer was approaching, and Les Halles was alive and brimming with quality produce. Muse wore her white uniform dress, and a straw bonnet trimmed with yellow silk flowers shaded her. The baskets she held swelled with fresh food. She ordered chicken and pork. Mulled over recipes— a cassoulet. Her food requirements had increased. Aside from herself, she brought small provisions to Claire every week and offered Maria one meal a day. She hummed as she made her rounds. The commotion and busyness of Les Halles always inspired her. Its orchestra of rattling drays transporting provisions from one end of the avenues to the other. Cries and shouts from the vendors vociferating the superiority of their produce. The multihued tints and assorted fragrances of the fruits and vegetables displayed among the quaint stalls looked, to her, not unlike Antonio's palette. Her eyes drifted along a rainbow canvas of stalls: stacks of pale-yellow corncobs and heaps of bright, fresh lemons merging with piles of onions with reddish to burnt-ochre skins. Tons of *pomme de terre* rich in earth tones, a grazing display of green leafy spinach bundled in bouquets, to the shady, purple cast of *aubergines* and mounds of the long, finger-shaped *haricot verts*—all enraptured her.

She picked up a cluster of bright-red cherries. The vendor encouraged her to taste. She tilted her head back and bit one off. The sweet juice trickled down her chin; she caught the wayward drops with the other hand and laughed.

"I'll take them," she said.

"Mademoiselle Muse!"

Muse dabbed the corner of her mouth with a handkerchief and glanced around.

"Mademoiselle Muse, *c'est vous?*"

To her surprise, sitting in the old cart, pulled by the same old mule, was Serge Laurent from La Lumière. He jumped from the cart.

"How wonderful to see you again. Oh, how the house prayed for you, hoping you survived your ordeal."

"I did. *Merci.*"

They conversed.

"Did you know Monsieur Furet passed away?"

"No! I'm so sorry."

"He has two sons . . . the eldest and his family have returned to live at the estate. Olivier, the youngest, the naval officer, you remember him?"

"*Oui.*"

"He remains at sea, not expected to return soon, even with the Paris Treaty."

"How is Madame Laurent?"

"Oh, as feisty as ever."

She chuckled.

"Whatever happened to Agnès?"

"God knows. She went off to America with the Hallisburgs, and we've never heard from her. But you, mademoiselle, fortune has smiled upon you. You look healthy and, oh, so well!"

"*Merci.*"

"You are free, *n'est pas?*"

Muse didn't know how to answer. Was she really free?

She smiled.

"Are you married?" Serge asked, trying to discern from her fit appearance.

"*Non.* I run a small shop . . . lady's accessories. Le Petit Cul-de-Sac."

"I remember you . . . always sewing."

"You must come see my shop and bring Madame Laurent. I have good merchandise at reasonable prices."

"*Bien sûr.*"

"*Alors* . . ." She hesitated. Do you know what happened to Monsieur Chevreau? He was a friend of Olivier's and a guest at the house when I lived there."

"An architect. *n'est pas?* But no, we never heard from him either."

"Well, please give my respects to your wife."

"I will do so. *Au revoir*, Muse."

"*Au revoir*, Serge."

He mounted his cart and trotted on. She watched him fade away into the crowd like a mirage. Life had changed, she thought.

She returned to her shopping: firm tomatoes with a deep-red blush.

"A half a pound, *s'il vous plaît.*"

The vendor gathered up several tomatoes, wrapped them in a newspaper, and handed it to her. She gave him two *sous*, thanked him, and turned to leave. But a man blocked her way, preventing her from passing. She excused herself and tried to go by again; he remained ridged.

"Forgive me, mademoiselle. Do you remember me?" he said.

She looked up.

"I am Louis Peltier."

Muse met his stark gaze and knew him instantly, but she said nothing. He executed a lazy half bow. She made no effort to curtsy. He cut a ragged figure, and he stank of the streets. She stepped back.

"We dined together some weeks ago at the home of the Erasmoses. Won't you bid me good morning?"

"What do you want?"

"Nothing, Mademoiselle Aggrey. Just to say *bonjour*."

"*Bonjour*," she said.

"Have you heard from the Hallisburgs recently? There is still a pretty price on your head."

Muse gasped, hand over mouth.

"It's you!" she said and backed away from him.

Breathless, heart pounding, she walked on. Les Halles seemed to shrink in size even though hundreds of people swarmed around her. She pushed through the masses, searched for the exit and the safety of the bustling rue Montmartre. Beads of moisture appeared on her brow; she dared not look back. She hurried but thought not to go straight home for fear he would follow. Once she reached the rue de Clery, she dashed along the streets, taking no particular route, then detoured toward the boulevard Bonne Nouvelle. With basket and bags in hand, she climbed the stairs to the second floor of apartment building 307. She paused before number 2A and pulled the bell cord twice. The door opened.

"*Bonjour*, Muse. *Ça va?*" Cheng greeted.

She stood in the hallway, breathing heavily and shaking.

"*Mon Dieu*, you look frightful!"

PELTIER'S PURSUIT

S hunned by a slave—it ignited Louis's fury even more than the wild dogs' feeding. His primal impulses rose higher, transporting him back to the West Coast of Africa where he hunted human beings to sell for profit. Watching her, he felt like a lion sizing up its victim, predicting its every move, its every intention. He followed her as she hurried from the marketplace along the winding streets near Les Halles. At first, he thought she spotted him and was trying to lose him, but soon he sensed her fast pace was anxiety driven. He smiled. She was his now; it was only a matter of time. He kept *en garde*: quick, sprite steps, needling himself through the thick fabric of pedestrians. When she entered the apartment building on the boulevard Bonne Nouvelle, he pulled back. Now he knew where she lived. He would wait.

LE THEATRE

Place de Theatre-Français and its adjacent streets teemed with people. It was a mild evening; the cafés and brasseries spilled over with diners and *buveurs*. The cab stopped. Dimitris descended first and then Muse.

"You're shivering. Are you cold?" he asked.

"*Non*. I'm excited."

The two stood in front of the theater as Dimitris explained his understanding of the classic French façade. Beaming with anticipation, Muse listened but understood hardly a word. They entered the main foyer amid a deluge of theatergoers and steered forward. At one point, Muse halted short, grabbing the train of her dress someone had trampled. Another time, she stopped to unravel her shawl, a sea-green silk that caught the tip of someone's walking cane. With swift, nimble fingers, she set the wrap free as Dimitris gently tugged her on. Finally, they reached the bar.

"Two champagnes, *s'il vous plaît*," he said.

He handed her a glass. She took a deep breath.

"Oh, Dimitris, thank you for this."

"Not at all," he said.

They sipped.

"You will enjoy this play," he said. "It is a revival—Molière. Have you read him?"

"*Non.*"

"He was a fine playwright."

Both grew giddy from the sheer liveliness of the scene surrounding them. The cascade of laughter and conversation, at times so loud, Muse and Dimitris could barely hear each other speak. Her eyes absorbed every detail of a remarkable moment: the fanciful, well-dressed people; the elegant, rich interior of the theater; she felt a part of the city for the first time.

Muse, in her exhilaration and delight, did not recognize the man whose cane got tangled up with her shawl. In the frenzy of trying to free the silk from the walking cane, she glanced at him for a second to apologize but otherwise paid him no attention. He, on the other hand, recognized her at once.

Jean-Paul's eyes followed her to the bar, vigilant as if studying a scene. Her companion, he deduced, good-looking and of means. Again, she wore a breathtaking gown—yellow this time. The only accessory missing from her personage was jewelry. What did it mean? He questioned her profession again but dismissed it, as her innocence was still evident—or was it? If she belonged to the monsieur, tokens or trinkets of some kind would be on display. Ornaments around her neck, cascading down her breast, on her fingers—symbols indicating wife, mistress, or otherwise. Not a single sparkle. He wished he had been bolder when she was in his reach. Even now, he wanted to reintroduce himself, discover who the man was and what she was to him. But he refrained.

He returned his attention back toward his friends. Male companions except for Jeanine. He noticed she looked flushed. She glared at him as she downed her brandy.

"Do you know that woman?" she asked.

"I used to," he replied.

"Well, she seems to have forgotten you."

"It seems so."

The play enacted a young girl held from society and the world to prepare for a loveless match to a much older man. She was allowed no visitors, no exposure to education or life other than the dictates that encouraged docility in women, especially wives; she waited complacently for her day at the altar. The heroine accepted her destiny until a chance encounter with a young man who wrote poetry disturbed her resignation.

Muse related to the sadness and loneliness of the girl and understood surrendering to her fate until she realized the force of her own will and intelligence. Would the heroine have comprehended her potential if not for the love of the young man? Muse asked herself the same thing: Would she have grasped her own aptitude without access to education, friends, and a country that relished liberty for all?

Only within the past several weeks had she fully grasped the gift of her situation. She remembered the words of her shipmate, Martinique: "Freedom is something you must be prepared to die for."

The play's denouement, albeit happy, maneuvered through many thoughtful, yet unpredictable twist and turns. As the curtain closed, Muse dabbed the corners of her eyes with her handkerchief. She thought of Mr. Müller's last words before he left the plantation: "Keep up your education . . . never stop learning."

A LIAISON

After the theater, Muse and Dimitris dined at L'Escargot d'Or. Dimitris spoke about his life and how his future was already mapped out.

"My father owns my life," he said. "He's allowed me to remain in Paris for a few more months."

He touched her hand.

"Bad luck," he said, "that we met so late."

The waiter came to take their order, then left.

"I received word from my family just this week. They've found me a wife. A young girl from a good Greek family. It is loveless, of course."

"Loveless?"

"Yes, but not unexpected. The match is about the merging of both our families . . . family fortunes, that is."

"I see. How do you feel about it?"

"I don't feel anything. It's my duty; that's all."

"When will you marry?"

"Within a year, I'm told."

"Congratulations!"

Dimitris smiled.

"My time as a free man is short."

"Dimitris, you sound as if you're going to be executed."

"In a way, I am."

He paused.

"You are such a singular woman, and I want to spend my last days in Paris with you. Muse, we could have such fun together. Let me take you places, teach you things." He paused. "Let me adore you."

Muse looked around the restaurant at the other diners; almost all were couples. She was afraid to say yes, afraid to say no . . . wanted to run, wanted to stay.

The waiter brought the appetizers and replenished their glasses.

Dimitris took her hand. She did not resist.

"Will you?"

She looked into his eyes and then replied, "*Oui*."

The cab trotted along the avenue. At that late hour, the streets were quiet and empty. Dimitris put his arm around Muse; her head rested on his shoulder. Paris seemed so alive to her, yet so serene. Just as the vehicle pulled into the deserted courtyard of the cul-de-sac, Muse saw a figure lurking in the square, only to disappear into the shadows of the alleyway. She sat up.

"What is it?" Dimitris asked.

"I saw someone."

He looked out.

"Who?"

"Someone."

"No. There's no one."

The cab slowed to a halt. Dimitris helped her down. His hands wrapped softly around her long, smooth neck. She quivered at his touch; her head tilted back. Her mouth parted; her eyes closed. She surrendered, wrapping her arms around him for support. When the passion ended, she rested her head on his shoulder.

"*Alors. Demain soir, ma chérie*," he said.

"*Oui*, tomorrow."

Had he asked to come in that night, to stay with her until the sun rose, Muse would have said yes; but he didn't. She took solace of the agreement made to go away together for a week; she could wait. Once she was inside, Dimitris got into the cab and told the driver to take him home.

As soon as the carriage rode off, she ran up the stairs to the bedroom window facing the courtyard. Not to witness Dimitris's departure but to scan the square for the prowler she was sure she saw. But Dimitris was right; no one was there.

ADVICE FROM CLAIRE

"You should get a pistol," Claire said.

"No! Pistols are dangerous. Someone could get killed."

Claire laughed.

"That's the point. Aggrey, you're so naïve. What am I going to do with you?"

"Stand still," Muse said.

Claire was standing on a small box while Muse took her body measurements.

"You've gotten thin."

"Yes, I know."

Claire, with her arms stretched out, turned around as Muse directed.

"Your hair looks so much better. By the time you get out, it will be a good length."

"Only a few more months," Claire said.

"I'll have finished both dresses by then."

Sometimes they spent hours discussing how ironic their fates.

"It's funny!" Muse said. When I was a captive, you were free. Now I'm free, and you're—"

"A captive," Claire interjected. "The only time we've ever spent together was on a ship or in a prison cell."

Muse shrugged.

"Aggrey, you should think seriously about it."

"About what?"

"A pistol . . . you can't walk around afraid all the time."

"I am afraid of this man. He is so vile; you should see him. But I could never own a gun, let alone shoot one. It's too, too horrible to think about."

Claire sighed.

"Oh, well! You've got Dimitris for a protector."

"For now," Muse said. "He won't be around forever."

"Tell me more about him—he sounds delicious!"

"He is."

"And with money?"

Muse nodded.

"Have you . . . you know?"

Muse blushed.

"Not yet. But he's taking me to Deauville next week."

Muse paused.

"I'm a little anxious. Is there anything I should know?" Muse asked. "I mean . . . I don't want to get pregnant."

"Ha!" Claire laughed. "It is the fear of every unattached woman who engages in intimacy. It's a gamble. Aside from abstinence, there is no other one-hundred-percent-sure prevention. I don't care what they say. But techniques exist, not foolproof, mind you, but they have worked for me. Better still, there is a woman on the rue de Nantes. She educates women about contraceptives. Women on the stage, independent women, and even prostitutes. Go talk to her. Her name is Madame Nadar."

"I will."

DECOY

Peltier shook his head. He gave the slave credit. After following her to the apartment complex on the boulevard Bonne Nouvelle, he monitored the building. For three days, he parked himself on a bench across the way; no person of color entered or exited the building, only a Chinese fellow. How stupid was he? She didn't live there at all. It was a decoy.

"*Quelle vache!* I will find her."

The next morning, Peltier recalled something said at the Erasmoses' dinner. The slave operated a boutique. He cleaned himself up and paid a visit to the Hôtel de Ville de Paris, where a registrar of all local shops and shop owners was kept on file.

Two hours later, he found the information he wanted. He wrote down the names and the address of the proprietresses of Le Petit Cul-de-Sac: Claire Price and Muse Aggrey.

"Now I've got you!"

PELTIER'S SOLITUDE

The long, wretched nights spent alone in the harness of his seamy quarters weighed on Peltier as he continued to drift in and out of the boundaries of reason. Sometimes he imaged the slave in the yellow gown, his hands around her neck, squeezing. The urge to power over her was growing. Without money to hire a woman to pacify his nerves and satisfy his bodily urges, the ghostly voice of his father returned. It spoke to him in low, raspy tones, urging him on toward revenge.

He didn't remember when his father first spoke to him in this manner, but he remembered vividly the day he died. It played out in his mind like a well-orchestrated drama. The reoccurring images, the carnage left behind, seeped deep in the crevasses of his being.

It was a blistering afternoon on the West Coast of Africa, late in July. Louis, his father, Peltier the elder, and their staff were transporting four African male slaves to the local port for boarding. Normally, the captives traveled chained and linked. But as the elder experimented with a vehicle resembling a cage on wheels, pulled by oxen, he saw no need to shackle his charges, saving time. Several hours before reaching the loading dock, the convoy stopped to rest from the intense heat. But just as they were about to resume the journey, a captive escaped.

The party made haste to their horses in pursuit of the fugitive, leaving Louis, Peltier the elder, and one transporter to stand guard over the remaining cargo. One of the wooden staves of the caged vehicle broke in transit, allowing the escapee to maneuver his malnourished body through the opening while the caravan rested. His companions, riddled with fear, remained, but they kept silent.

Once the staff dispersed in hunt of the escapee, Louis, Peltier the elder, and the transporter dragged the three remaining captives from the vehicle and attempted to chain them together. But the captives resisted; they struggled and fought with such ferocity and strength that they overwhelmed their captors. In the brawl, the brute force of human bodies crashing against the frame of the wooden cart damaged the cage further. More of the wooden staves splintered and separated, causing chaos everywhere. In the mayhem, one of the Africans grabbed a long, splintered spoke and, like a spear, thrust it through the neck of Peltier the elder. Louis froze at the sight of his father and the blood gushing from his neck. The other two prisoners followed suit and plunged fragmented spears into the necks and chest of the guard. Louis was stabbed also, but he fought them off and fled on horseback. The slaughter left two slashed-up bodies, a bloody mess for the buzzards to feed on. And the three African prisoners were slaves no more.

⇥⊹⊹⇤

"She's worth a mint, my son. You could start anew."
 "Father."
 Peltier's delirious eyes fixated on the ceiling.
 "You know where she lives . . . do something about it."
 "But Father."
 "Just do it!"

PELTIER FINDS HIS PREY

It took only a few days for Louis to find out everything about the boutique and his prey; he was a hunter, after all. He traced her movements; he learned when the shop opened and when it closed, at what time she rose, when the shop girl arrived and departed, and at what stretch of the night Muse was the most vulnerable. He got in touch with a former acquaintance with connections in Algeria. Several inquiries of transport options were made, but how to get her from Paris to Marseille?

⊨╫╪⊫

By the time Louis arrived at the cul-de-sac, it was quiet. The other shop owners had closed and gone home for the day, all according to schedule. Le Petit Cul-de-Sac was dark. He looked for movement in the shop. There was none. He inched closer to the boutique to get a better look. Through the window he peered; he saw no light, no one stirring. She was not home.

Hours later, in the early morning, the sound of carriage wheels entered the cul-de-sac. Nerves on edge, muscles tight, Louis slipped back into the darkness. From the shadows, he listened and watched. To his surprise, a cab drove up and halted in front of the small shop. Louis witnessed his prey descend in the company of the rich Greek who dined at the Erasmoses. She was wearing the yellow dress, and a green shawl covered her shoulders. She held a program. The theater, he guessed. *So she goes to the theater while I eat from the trash.* He watched them chat, and then the Greek embraced her, kissing her passionately. Peltier, outraged at the spectacle, staggered back into the dim alleyway and fled.

THE BREAK-IN

Maria dawdled that morning. When her mistress was present, she always arrived fifteen minutes before her scheduled time, but Mademoiselle Aggrey was in Deauville with Monsieur Peloponnese. Her mother left for work hours ago. She was alone and wanted to take an unscheduled bath. The bathhouse, in the basement of the tenement, was always free at midmorning after most people had left for the day. It was Mademoiselle Aggrey who insisted she bathe frequently, as her physical presentation was important to the image of the boutique. At first, she resented having to bathe once a week because it cost to have water carried in to fill the tub—only a few coins, but still, it took from her small salary. But soon she learned to appreciate the soothing effect of the hygienic ritual. She even withheld a *centime* or two from the money she gave her mother to buy a bar of fragrant soap.

A warm, clear day, characteristic for Paris in summer. Maria strolled along the avenue, heading toward the shop. But as soon as she turned the corner and stepped into the cul-de-sac, she stopped cold. Something was wrong!

With caution, she approached the boutique. First, she noticed several items in the window were disturbed. She trod closer, gazed through the window, and shuddered. The store was in shambles—merchandise topsy-turvy, scattered over the counter and floor. Frantic, she backed away and took flight, in search for the nearest gendarme.

"Was this window broken before last night?" asked the gendarme, observing the shattered window at the back of the workroom.

"*Non*, monsieur," Maria said.

"And the cashbox, you say it's missing?"

"*Oui*. But there was not much money in it."

Beside herself with angst, Maria sent for Cheng. He rushed over and took charge of the discourses with the police while she cleaned up.

"What else can you tell me, monsieur?" the police asked.

"Mademoiselle Aggrey spoke of a prowler in the courtyard a few weeks ago."

"What time of the day was this?"

"Late at night, past midnight."

"Right. When will she return to Paris?"

"A few days."

The gendarme scribbled down a few more notes and informed Cheng he would post a guard near the cul-de-sac to keep an eye on things.

"When mademoiselle arrives, please have her come to the station at once."

"*Oui*, monsieur."

MUSE TAKES A STAND

"Listen to yourself," Dimitris argued. "You're not making sense."

"I don't care! I won't leave my shop. This is my home," Muse shouted.

She shuffled back and forth, enraged, her eyes blazing and her full skirt whooshing like angry waves.

"It's not forever, just for a short while . . . until the police can sort it out."

"I'm not leaving!"

"I've got so much space. You'll have a room of your own if you want."

"It's not that."

"I would be inattentive as your companion to allow you to live in harm's way," Dimitris said. "*Bon*! If you won't come to me, I will come to you. In the evenings, I will stay with you."

"Dimitris, no. There is no room here, and I certainly cannot offer you the comfort you are accustomed to. I will be all right. Surely the intruder won't return."

"You don't know that. I will send my valet to retrieve a few things from my apartment."

She looked at him; her eyes softened. She broke a half smile. He put his arm around her. And she buried her face in his neck.

"*D'accord*, if you insist," she said.

"I do."

—◄┼┼►—

As soon as Dimitris left, Muse hurried to the back of the store-room. Concealed behind a shelf of a half a dozen large glass jars of buttons and bows and ribbons was a hidden wall cabinet. Another strongbox was kept in the space. After the end of each day, Maria transported the monies from the cashbox under the counter to the strongbox in the cupboard. The strongbox rested, undisturbed.

Muse took the box up to her bedroom. Shards from a Chinese vase and other bric-a-brac speckled the floor. The two drawings by Jean-Paul lay facedown on the desk, frames shattered. Her clothes were strewn about . . . and the saffron dress torn to shreds and its pieces left in a pile on the bed.

Horror swept over her. No less violent than when Jonathan Hallisburg pinned her down on the bed; no different than strip-ping the clothes off her body and boring her legs apart. The break-in and thievery felt equal in offense; twice now, violated.

She removed several wooden planks from the corner of the floor. The opening appeared untampered with. In it, another strongbox rested. No one knew of the private stash except Claire. The modest financial reserves were accumulating, but now the future of the shop, the security of their investment, was compromised.

—◄┼┼►—

With everything in disarray, Muse stared at the luggage on the floor but had no strength to unpack. She gave Maria the day off and closed the shop. Muse examined the inventory, analyzing the slashes in the fabric, thinking she could cut around them; she had done it before. The ripped bolts she would use to make Claire's two dresses. She gazed out the window, watching Dimitris give orders to his coachman and valet. But she was thinking: How could she make her home safe?

PELTIER'S DISAPPOINTMENT

After the theft, Louis, with smugness spread across his face, returned home with Muse's cashbox in hand. He struggled to open the wooden container; then, out of sheer frustration, he hurled the box against the wall. It broke open.

"Christ! Only two francs and some change. Is that all?"

He kicked the pieces of the broken box under the bed. The bitch was making a fool of him.

"I should have burned the place down!"

LE BANQUE

"What do you think, Claire?"
"I don't know. What bank?"
"Le Banque de France," Muse said.
"Will they even let women open accounts?"
Muse shrugged.
"What's the minimum amount required?"
"I have no idea."
"No. We should leave it the way it is. Suppose you need money for an emergency; you'll have faster access to it. The intruder could not be dumb enough to return to the scene of the crime, especially as he only got away with two francs."
"Poor *imbécile*. I bet he was shocked," Muse said.
"What about Dimitris?"
"What about him?"
"Do you love him?"
"Goodness, Claire, you do know how to change the subject."
"Well . . . do you?

"It's not an expression we use toward each other. Yet, his response is always gentle and kind. I still don't quite understand those types of words or those types of feelings . . . not like you do. Your emotions, Claire, seem always to be so open and unconditional. That's real! But I question everything."

"That's because you're clever."

"No cleverer than you."

"Aggrey, I'm the one in prison, not you. I see not where I am so very smart."

"Anyway," Muse said, "he's leaving shortly, and that will be the end of it."

"You should take some of the savings and buy a gun. I mean it."

DIMITRIS MOVES IN

Although she was comforted by Dimitris sharing her bed, the experiment of him moving in, albeit part time, failed. Within three weeks, the living conditions, including the boutique space, fell apart. The bedroom, usually uncluttered, was in disarray. His clothes, her clothes—all tangled together on the floor and left for her to clean up. Muse forbade Dimitris's valet to enter her bedroom. The current circumstances reminded her of when she waited on Cassandra, hand and foot. He arrived in the evening. They might go out or stay in; it depended. Although each morning he left for his office, it seemed to her that he was always there and, much of the time, in the way. She resented it.

Adding to the infringement on the tranquility of her private room, new distractions arose from the comings and goings of Dimitris's entourage: his valet, his driver, his secretary. Gentlemen loitering about the salon, waiting for instructions from their employer, upset the rhythm and pace of the boutique and its female energy. The men disturbed the equilibrium of women coming in for fittings or browsing among the accessories in the shop. It violated the unspoken ambiance that surrounded women when shopping to enhance their physical appearance. The only time women wished for the company of men to intrude on their sport of shopping is if they intended to pay the bill. The customers complained. Muse had had enough.

"Go home, Dimitris," she said. "It's not working."

"You are still in a vulnerable situation," he insisted.

"I'll be fine."

"Come stay with me."

"No, no, no."

"I don't understand. Why not?"

"Because . . ." She hesitated.

"Because of what?"

"I'm fond of you . . . more so than ever," she said. "You . . . and your lifestyle."

"Is that bad?"

"It's not good. You will leave soon . . . start a new life, and I'll go back as before. When you go, there will no longer be grand restaurants, trips to Deauville, and all the rest of it. I will be alone again with a very simple life. It might as well start now."

"It was our pact; I promised you an enjoyable time."

"And I've had one."

He paused. His eyes held hers.

"Why won't you let me give you gifts?"

"I don't want gifts. This was about you and me . . . being in your company, committed, yet free. I don't need trinkets to comfort me. I will have memories. I don't need to be bought."

Dimitris was stunned by her comment.

"Do you think that if I want to give you a gift, it's a payoff? Is that warped residue left over from when you were a slave?"

Muse folded her arms across her chest and glared at him. He said the wrong thing.

"Never mind, then," he said. "Let's not pursue the subject. I have no right. It is true I will be leaving. But remember this: it will be the same for me. I will not forget you. *La belle noire* I adored in Paris. Has the making of a poem, don't you think?"

He held out his hand.

"Come stay with me until I leave, until the end. I beg you."

A NEW PROFESSION

Louis had the dream again: the slave in the billowing yellow gown. But he destroyed the dress; why was she still wearing it? Why was she smiling? He sat up in bed, sweating. The room turned. He was suffocating—he must find something to do . . . something, until he could get his hands on her.

Peltier senior often told him to dwell on his strengths. Breaking into Le Petit Cul-de-Sac, despite no great profit, was in many ways a success. He committed a crime, and no one suspected him. If he planned better, picked his victims and venues carefully, he might scratch out a living.

He remembered a wine shop he frequented when prosperous. The sommelier often escorted him down to the cellar to view and taste exclusive vintages. While the owner rummaged through his desk searching for a list of special reserves, Louis noticed an open strongbox in the lower left-hand drawer. It must have secured over fifty francs; at the time, he thought nothing of it. But now, he recalled the scene, the cellar, in detail. But his ragged, ne'er-do-well appearance made gaining entrance to the shop unlikely. Instead, he spent the afternoon staking out the exterior of the store until he spotted a small window at the base of the building. If memory served him right, it led to the basement.

The wooden drawer cracked apart as soon as he booted it. The metal cashbox was in its place but locked. Also, it was too heavy for him to negotiate by way of the window he wormed through. He found an iron rod behind a shelf lined with bottles of wine. He inserted the rod into the lock and twisted, but the device held fast. Continuously, he finagled it, stepped on it, jerked it, and even threw it against the wall. Nothing. With his foot, he pressed down hard on the lid while driving the shaft into its seams. He rammed the lever in farther until the lid popped open. A grin crept across his face as coins and bills sprawled to the floor.

After the deed, Louis rediscovered his former swagger. He took on his new profession with all the discipline and zest of past years under his father's rule. He adopted the habit of reading the society pages, circling excerpts that revealed when an affluent family, a couple, or business elite left or returned to town. Higher society almost always secured their homes and valuables; he strategized accordingly. His inflated sense of self drove him to believe keenly in his skills of agility and ingenuity. Two break-ins later, Louis bought himself a presentable set of clothes and moved out of his rat-infested room to a modest apartment.

THE SOCIETY PAGES

Louis paid off the woman he had hired for the night. He woke refreshed, not dreaming of the slave at all; a sense of relief prevailed.

"Do you want me to come tonight?" she asked.

"*Oui*," he replied. "And don't be late."

Another observation occurred to him: when in the company of a woman, he no longer heard the rambling, dictating voice of his father. The silence was liberating.

As soon as she left, he hastened to dress and hurried down to the avenue for his coffee, *du pain*, and the daily journal. He had no set routine when unemployed. Life was better when he worked, a job to do, something to plan, to occupy his mind, to execute. He continued to search for venues and shops to rob. Scanning through the paper, deciphering the daily news, he folded the sheets back to the society pages. The first two announcements caught his attention. But his face lit up after reading the third notice:

Monsieur Dimitris Peloponnese, son and heir of the eminent Milos Peloponnese, left Paris yesterday to return to his home in Athens, Greece. He is soon to wed the youngest daughter of an equally distinguished Corinthian family.

"She's alone again."

THE PROWLER

No sooner had Dimitris left the country than Muse missed him. She moved back into her tiny accommodations and her own modest surroundings. The bed seemed enormous without him, and attempts to sleep proved frustrating. As much as his presence sometimes annoyed her, his absence left a great void. She got up and fumbled in the dark to light a candle, then changed her mind. In the dead of the night, a haze of light beamed through the partially closed drapes. The unusual glow told her of a full moon. She went to the window and pushed the curtains apart; her eyes gravitated up to the skies and rested on a shimmering moon. But a movement in the court caused her to recoil. Concealed behind the curtain, she peered into the street. A tall figure of a man was leaning against the wall. She made out the silhouette of a top hat, the lit end of a cigarette, and a thin cloud of smoke oozing in the mist. He stood smoking. She watched him until the sound of footsteps nearing the entrance of the cul-de-sac caused him to duck into the alleyway and disappear. A minute later, the gendarme, on his nightly patrol, came into view.

PROTECTION

Even with extra locks and window fasteners installed, Muse's survival instincts still whispered, *It's not enough!* This time, she paid heed. During one of her visits to the prison, Claire gave her the name and address of an individual, an acquaintance of Gerard's: a weapons dealer.

"Will you come with me?" Muse asked Cheng.

"No!" he replied. "I want nothing to do with firearms."

"Please. I can't go by myself."

"Think about what you're doing. If you buy a weapon, you'll have to learn to use it. And suppose you shoot somebody or even kill them?"

"It's awful. But I have to do something."

They were in the back room of the shop, analyzing a heavy piece of brocade. Cheng refilled her wine glass.

"Good wine!"

"Yes, and expensive," he said. "Compliments of a client."

He sipped.

"Muse, you need to consider a few things before you decide. True, you are a free woman, allowed to make up your own mind and exercise your own will. But even within that framework, your situation is still limited, as is mine. Under no circumstances do you want to get on the wrong side of the law in this country. You and I are guests. They don't mind we are here, as long as we cause no trouble. If you harmed someone, especially a French citizen, the tables would turn—the balance of justice would tip, and not in your favor."

"Even if it's self-defense?" she asked.

"You've got a lot working against you from the start, as do I. You are a woman, you are foreign, and of color. I'm Chinese, also not white, and I have unorthodox sexual appetites . . . although I'm discreet, still—"

"What's your point?"

"Let me put it this way. Do you think Claire would have gotten so severe a sentence if she were French? Never. She is a foreigner, a woman of low-class status . . . and mind you, she's white. What do you think they would do to us?"

Muse rolled her eyes.

"I've got to do something," she reiterated.

"There is another possibility, without the use of arms."

"Like what?"

"If you've got time tomorrow, let me introduce you to someone who might give you other options. He has helped me very much."

"In what way?"

"All I will tell you is . . . I may not look like much, but I can handle myself."

"What does that mean?"

THE INTRODUCTION

The following morning, Cheng took Muse to the neighborhood of his parents' restaurant. She trailed him down a tapered, stone road that curved into an even narrower street. The odor of the community changed from the sour smell of poor sanitation to the fragrance of sweet incense. Red fabric curtains with prints of fire-breathing gold dragons flapped in the wind, concealing a stone archway entrance. Muse touched the curtains.

"Pretty," she said.

The entrance was alight with tapers and incense exuding a fragrant aroma that infused the air. A Chinese elder entered the foyer. Cheng bowed to him, and he returned the gesture.

"This is Mademoiselle Muse Aggrey," Cheng announced.

The elder smiled and bowed, as did Muse.

"Muse this is Wan Fu. He is my instructor."

Muse smiled at the old man.

"Instructor in what?" she asked.

"He will explain. I will leave the two of you alone. I'll wait at the restaurant."

Cheng bowed and departed.

Muse stood in front of the elder, bemused as to what to say or what to do. After a few moments of silence, the elder said, "Tea?"

L'ANNIVERSAIRE

Muse awakened to a hazy late morning. She yawned, stretched, wishing to remain longer in bed. But today was special—her eighteenth birthday. She sat up and began practicing the breathing exercise administered to her by Wan Fu. Not totally understanding the purpose of the procedure, she kept at it, as she promised, because the lessons were a birthday gift from Cheng.

In meditation, she monitored her mind, its rapid fluctuation in and out of reflections, until she found a place within herself where all thought ceased, and calm governed. At first, it was difficult to remain still, silent. But the more she practiced, the longer she stayed within, escaping all reality, fear, and concerns. It felt good, she acknowledged. But what it had to do with self-defense made no sense.

"Soon, my child," Wan Fu said. "Be patient."

Muse looked forward to a glorious day. She expected only the congenial company of two close friends. Cheng and his partner, Stephan, invited her to dine later that evening. She gave Maria the day off, proposing to close the shop early and prepare for the evening. A few customers strolled in, bought scarves, handbags, whatnots. One woman wanted an appointment for a fitting and singled out a bolt of linen she admired. By noon the traffic in the boutique grew slow. Just as Muse posted the closed sign in the window, the mail carrier appeared. He gave her a letter. It was from America and by the hand of Cassandra Hallisburg. Muse locked the door and rushed up to her room to read it.

A BIRTHDAY LETTER

Dear Muse,

By the time you receive this letter, you should be about to celebrate your eighteenth birthday as I will be celebrating my nineteenth . . . I did not forget. I miss you! You were a good companion. If I was ever abusive to you, and I know I was, I apologize. Mother and Father, however, are still seething over your escape, but I am not. I have come to see things differently. I have been able to imagine what it must have been like to walk in your shoes. Please forgive me; I knew no better.

I have news: I've met someone, and I'm engaged to be married. It was a chance encounter in New York, at a ball of no consequence. He asked me to dance, a waltz—and I knew the moment his eyes met mine, and he placed his hands around my waist, this was the man I wanted. He is a Southerner but was educated in England. His name is Ashley Bar, and I love him. Father pitched a fit, of course, as you know he can do. He protested because Ashley has not the financial wealth or connections the family hoped for. But I don't care! He is presentable, personable, financially stable, and has a distinguished career ahead of him. He is a lawyer. It is he, dear Muse, who spoke to me in a different and honest manner; he opened my eyes to a different point of view, made me realize that while we are all different, we are the same.

One night, Ashley asked me, "What if there were a war, and foreigners confiscated Der Brunnen and all your family's property? What if your father was killed or taken away, and you and your mother were forced to serve and obey those who conquered you and your culture? Suppose you were forced to live in a world where your person, your body, was no longer your own, where you were treated no different than animals . . . bought, sold, beaten, mutilated, or even exterminated on the whim of your master. You were giving neither spiritual freedom nor education . . . imagine, Cassandra," he kept saying, "imagine if it were you." I challenged his observation as absurd. Such a thing could never happen. I didn't understand what he was trying to make me see. "Envision the scenario in your mind's eye, Cassandra. What would you do?" Suddenly the horrors of being owned by another person came forth. Still, he asked, "What would you do, dear Cassandra?" I would kill myself—that was my reply. "Ah!" he responded, "Then Muse is a much stronger woman than you, for she has chosen to live."

After the wedding ceremonies in September, we will live in New York where his family and office are located. I'm excited, can't wait! So many things to see and do in that northern city. I'll be closer to Jonathan, as well . . . he behaves so much better when he is in New York than when in Virginia.

Your mother is doing well; healthy, strong, and she still runs the kitchen with efficiency. Mary sends her love, hugs, and a bunch of kisses and is relieved to know you are doing well in health and your lady's shop. She is proud of you and simply laughs out loud at the thought of you managing your own boutique, contrary, of course, to Mother and Father. They still believe you will return.

Your mother asked me if there were any churches in Paris. I said, of course, and she told me to tell you to go pray if you can. Mothers are all the same, aren't they?

Do you remember Agnès, the French maid we brought back with us from Paris? She was employed with us for only six months, and then she and Bailey ran off together, to God knows where. They left the plantation without a foreman and me without a personal maid . . . how difficult it has been!

The slaves are becoming restless, lackadaisical, and sometimes subordinate. No wonder, with the talks and debates bouncing back and forth between the North and South. Anger and discontent saturate both sides of the tobacco fields. Without Bailey, Father has lost much of his stamina and has a grim time staying on top of the financial affairs of the estate; I fear we may have lost a lot of money. The year has been difficult for everyone. Once the dowry is paid, I will be out of my father's hair. I hope it will make life easier for him.

Jonathan got into trouble last summer while visiting New Orleans; he was arrested and jailed. Father bailed him out and sent him back to New York. Jonathan seems to have calmed down and is back on track with his studies. Father feels he should not return to the South as it tends to disrupt his mind . . . whatever that means.

Please write me.

Happy Birthday!

Your former mistress and, hopefully, new friend,

Cassandra Hallisburg

Soon to be Mrs. Ashley Bar, address as of October will be . . .

The letter brought Muse to tears; she sobbed for hours.

CHEZ JACQUE

M use wanted to dine at Chez Jacque. When passing the brasserie, it appeared small, intimate, and lively—a young clientele. The chef was a new breed of chef de cuisine, reinterpreting traditional cuisine. He presented a different menu each day—never the same thing twice, his admirers boasted. Not a restaurant to eat in alone, so Muse refrained. She once mentioned the brasserie to Dimitris, but he thought it bohemian, not sufficiently grand enough for his tastes.

The waiter escorted Muse, Cheng, and Stephan, Cheng's love interest, to a reserved table. A group of men sat at a circular table in the middle of the room, vigorously confabulating. Their exchange halted when Muse passed. She wore a soft white cotton dress with a taut décolleté bodice covered with black silk embroidery and small puffed sleeves. As she and her entourage moved through, a split-second stray gaze toward the table of men caused her to catch the eye of one of them. They clung to each other for a moment. She smiled, and he smiled back. Muse acknowledged Jean-Paul.

⇥⇤

Jean-Paul watched as the waiter seated her: radiant, yet again. He eyed her two companions, his mind wondering, *Who are they?* The entourage settled. The waiter brought menus. His concentration so focused, he heard nothing of his colleagues' conversation; his eyes were mesmerized by her. She and her friends pored over the carte du jour, discussing entrees, but now and then, she glanced in his direction. How to proceed, what to do? Of all the women he had known, this one continued to befuddle him like an awkward adolescent. He summoned the waiter and ordered a bottle of champagne for the mademoiselle. When the bottle arrived, the table roared with joy at the surprise. Muse summoned Jean-Paul to the table. He excused himself from his colleagues.

"*Bonsoir.*"

"*Bonsoir,*" responded Muse, Cheng, and Stephan.

"I wasn't sure if it was you," Jean-Paul said.

"*Oui, c'est moi,*" she responded.

"You look grand."

"*Merci.*"

She made introductions.

"Champagne. How delightful!" she said.

"Not at all. It looked as if you were celebrating something special, so I thought—"

"We are," Cheng said. "Mademoiselle celebrates her eighteenth birthday today."

Jean-Paul met her eyes.

"*Bon anniversaire!*"

She smiled and lifted her glass, as did all.

"*Salut.*"

"Will you join us?" she asked.

"No. I must get back to my colleagues . . . business," he said with a frown.

"*Oui, bien sûr,*" she responded.

Again, he stalled, wanting to say more. Jean-Paul searched for words, but not knowing whether she was attached to one of the gentlemen, he struggled with small talk. Still, she wore no jewels, no trinkets of any kind, nothing to enlighten.

To break the awkwardness of the reunion, Muse said, "I ran into Serge Laurent a while ago. You remember him. He was the caretaker at La Lumière. Did you know Monsieur Furet was dead?"

"No, no, I've not heard anything, not a word from La Lumière or from Olivier. We must have coffee sometime and catch up."

"I'd like that," she responded.

"How about Sunday?"

"Perfect. Come to the shop."

"The shop?"

"Le Petit Cul-de-Sac." She gave him a card. "I also live there."

"Shall we say, Sunday . . . ten o'clock?" he asked.

"*D'accord.*"

Jean-Paul bowed and returned to his table.

"Who was that?" Cheng asked.

"It's a long story."

A LETTER FOR CLAIRE

The heat in the kitchen seemed unusually intense for so early in the morning. Claire leaned over an open oven, shuffling in loaves of unbaked bread. The headwrap she wore caught most of the beads of perspiration trickling down her brow. She had been up since five o'clock and needed a break. Finally, one of the other prison bakers relieved her. The freshest of the bread had already been picked over by the nuns and the staff. The inmates received the leftovers. But when no one was looking, Claire cut a warm slice from a loaf right out of the oven and layered it with butter. She slipped out the back. Within the confines of the courtyard, she sat, looking up at tepid, late-summer skies. She ate heartily, enjoying the fruits of her labor. She could open a bakery, she pondered.

"Claire!"

"*Oui*, Sœur Charlotte. I'm here."

"There's a letter for you. To my recollection, you've never received mail."

"*Non*, Sœur."

"You must be close to your release."

"*Oui*, Sœur."

Claire accepted the mail. She stared at the envelope, post-marked Rome, Italy.

DIMANCHE

Often, Muse worked on Sundays even though the shop was closed. The cul-de-sac was quiet, and if you listened, you could hear the tolling bells of *la cathédrale*. She visited the house of worship only once; her curiosity and growing love for architecture led her to explore the Gothic structure and embrace its historical authenticity. But also, before then, she had never been inside a church. Ironic her first experience would be in one of the most renowned sanctuaries in the world. At the time of her visit, a small noon mass was in progress. She entered through the Portal to the Virgin and tiptoed down the nave until she spotted an empty seat in the wooden pews. She knelt, mimicking the others as they crossed themselves and clasped both hands together in prayer. But she was not praying; she was absorbing everything around her. A choir of monks filled the chancel; they stood regimentally in several rows, draped in dark robes, their cowls covering most of their faces. They chanted with angelic voices, emitting glorious tones that reverberated throughout the cathedral. She knelt near the transepts, her head turned up, her eyes, in awe, staring toward the south rose window: a circular array of stained-glass panes depicting colorful figures, virgins and apostles, telling stories from the Old Testament. Muse had not yet read the Bible in full; she only remembered excerpts of the spiritual narratives told by the elders in the slave community at Der Brunnen. The priest, dressed in a rich, satin, cream-colored robe, lectured with a steady, solemn tenor voice in Latin; she did not understand a word, but the language sounded ethereal, sacred in quality; she felt a connection. But she asked herself, Was it not easy to feel the presence of God in such a prosperous, saintly environment? Was it a true awareness? Could the experience be only that of spectacle and grandeur? Odd questions to ask oneself, she reflected. Not that she denounced religion; it was that she never thought of an Almighty in the same way as fundamental religions or in the simplistic doctrines told on the grounds of Der Brunnen. Wan Fu helped her to identify and construe what she believed in her heart. What occurred as an outcome of her meditation and search for spiritual identity was that she embraced a different conclusion. A simple life force that always seemed to be within her—that was how she now understood God.

She stood in front of the shop, on this hushed Sunday morning, examining its façade, the window display, and the overall appearance of the shop. Many ideas took form as to how to keep the premises appealing. Of the three-storied standing, she occupied only two of the floors. With Claire returning, they needed more space . . . that is, if Claire was returning. She was acting strange of late, Muse noted.

After talking with the owner of the premises, Muse learned the third floor could be let. And it stored only a few personal things.

"Of course," the owner added, "there would be an adjustment in the lease."

"Naturellement."

The sound of carriage wheels reverberating near the cul-de-sac triggered Muse to rush inside, her billowing petticoats squeezing through the door. She ran upstairs, checked herself in the mirror, and then peered out of the bedroom window and smiled . . . it was he.

TOGETHER

Coffee led to lunch, and lunch led to a lingering walk about the city. They passed l'Arc de Triomphe de l'Etoile, l'Place de la Concorde, and trailed alongside the Seine. Muse behaved like a tourist in the town she now called home, realizing how much of Paris she had yet to see. Jean-Paul knew the history of the city, aware of every important nook and cranny; he also knew about the changes taking place. They strode passed Le Louvre and saw much of the palace under renovation.

"What are they doing?" she asked.

"They're adding a wing, clearing the area around the Arc du Carrousel, finishing the North Gallery and some other work . . . monuments, gates, and such."

"The entire city is being restructured."

"It is. When Baron Haussmann is finished, Paris will be the most beautiful city in the world and the greatest of walking pleasures. Come this way."

They detoured across the road, walked down the rue de Rivoli, then down a few narrow streets to a section of town near the boulevard des Capucines. It looked abandoned.

"This entire neighborhood will be torn down," Jean-Paul said. "In its place, a magnificent opera house. I've seen the drawings. The architect, Garnier, is a genius."

"It must be wonderful to be part of such innovation," she said.

"*Oui.* But surely you understand such feelings. You make incredible clothes . . . I mean, I saw you one evening at a play. You looked like a dream; you wore a yellow dress. I'll never forget it."

"You saw me at a play?"

"*Oui.*"

"Why didn't you say hello?"

"I almost did, but you were with a man, so I decided not to disturb you."

Jean-Paul looked at his companion, pointing her toward another boulevard.

"I want to show you my first design project, an apartment building."

"Oh!"

They walked in silence.

"Paris is a different city when on foot, moving along aimlessly with a knowledgeable guide to point out its subtle treasures," she commented.

"*Oui,* it can be quite different. Do you recognize this building?" Jean-Paul asked.

"*Bien sûr.* L'Exposition Universelle."

"It is where we first met."

"*Oui.* It looks abandoned."

"Not always. But, it's to be torn down too."

"Pity."

They walked on.

"And here is my building."

Jean-Paul pointed to a four-level structure shaped like a crescent. It faced the street as if smiling. Its dominant feature was a handsomely framed archway entrance crowned by a red awning embracing modernity.

"You designed this building?

"Oui."

"Please," Muse begged. "Explain to me what I'm looking at."

The evening shadows moved in. They crossed the Pont Neuf and strolled along the boulevards of the Latin Quarter. At a small outdoor café, they ordered aperitifs. "What are you looking at?" he said.

"You," she responded.

"Well, do you like what you see?"

"You are of mixed blood?"

"Oui. My mother is Algerian; she is dark like you."

The wound on his face had healed well, leaving a slight, crescent-shaped scar.

"Did you use the salve I gave you?"

"I did."

"Your face looks good."

Muse fastened in on his attractiveness. For the first time, she saw in his tanned complexion dominant traces of his Algerian ancestry. But his real beauty, she thought as she examined him, came from within him. He possessed a calm, clear aura . . . *aura,* a novel word she learned from Wan Fu. There was something more to him than just a bon vivant.

"I'm illegitimate," he blurted out.

"As am I, I suppose," responded Muse. "I've never really thought about it."

"Few people know of my heritage and social status. My father . . ." he started, then hesitated.

"Go on," Muse said.

"My father loved my mother, or so he says, but refused to go against his family's wishes for fear of disinheritance. So, I became an outcast."

"Much like me."

"In some way, I did relate to you on that level . . . it is true."

"Your father has taken loving care of you, *n'est pas?*"

"He has."

"He loves you?"

"He does."

"Well, you are blessed. I never knew my father."

They babbled on for another hour, and then his eyebrows grew taut, as if something puzzled him.

"Who was he?"

"Who was who?"

"Your escort at the play."

Muse smiled.

"Dimitris."

"I mean, who was he to you?"

With ease and no wavering, she said, "He was my lover."

Jean-Paul set back in his chair.

"You look disappointed," she commented.

"In a way, I am."

"Why?"

"I don't know."

He asked a shower of questions—how they met, the duration of their liaison, all kinds of inquiries that Muse answered forthwith. She felt uninhibited about her life and her sexuality, as if it were a way of respecting her liberation, her right as a free person to do and say what she pleased. But then she, good-humoredly, turned the tables on him.

"A rumor floated around La Lumière," she said, "of you and Agnès having an affair. Was that true?"

Jean-Paul looked at her, at first annoyed and then resigned with a smile.

"It's true. She was available . . . so was I. But how I wished it had been you."

"It could never have been me, not at that time, anyway, not unless by force. I was then not free . . . not free to make a choice, to say yes or to say no. Dimitris was the first man who had the right to ask, as I the right to refuse, but I didn't . . . no regrets."

She paused.

"I feel as though I don't have the luxury of counting on a future like other people. I can only live for today."

"I would never have forced you."

Muse looked at him.

"I know. But that's not the point."

"Did you love him?"

"I was fond of him."

"Did he lavish expensive gifts on you?"

"No. I wouldn't accept gifts."

"When he left, how did you feel?"

"At first, sadness . . . and then . . . pleasure to have known him, to have had the freedom to enjoy his company outright. But I always knew our time together would be short. It was made clear in the beginning."

"I see," Jean-Paul said, looking away.

"Do you know where Agnès is now?" she asked in a teasing manner.

"*Non.*"

"Do you care?"

"*Non.*"

Muse giggled.

"She's in America and has just run off with the Hallisburgs' foreman."

"The foreman! What a shock. If you said the heir, I would not be surprised . . . but the foreman!"

They both laughed.

He took her hand. She let him.

THE THIRD FLOOR

"At times, I fear I will wake up to find this life is a dream. That I am still once again that scrawny, captive little girl living in the shack next to the old schoolhouse storage room," Muse said to Jean-Paul.

Two weeks gone since their first day together. She showed him the various rooms of the shop. She referenced her intentions for expansion, needing more room for Claire, who would soon join her. Because she needed a second seamstress or tailor to help, she required more space.

As they rambled through the shop, Jean-Paul offered suggestions for designing a good space. She marveled at what he could imagine from an empty room: putting up a divider at one end and taking down a wall at the other to create a cohesive working quarter. But then he changed the subject.

"Earlier you mentioned nightmares. What did you mean?"

They were now on the third floor. The owner of the building removed most of his possessions save for a few pieces of furniture and odds and ends that Muse wanted. It was a musty space. She pushed aside small crates with her foot and made a pathway for them to pass.

"No, not exactly nightmares . . . but a terror it is going to end."

"What's going to end?"

"I will be snatched from this life and back to the old . . . sounds silly. I am happier than I have ever been . . . ever. Then I think, why me? Many people are suffering. Why should I be happy?"

"Why not you? Why not any of us? Is it not our right to be happy and content?"

Jean-Paul stopped in front of a broad door.

"What's in here?"

"I don't know."

He rattled and pushed the door until it flew open, revealing a spacious storage room. At first look, the room appeared to have no windows, but upon inspection, Jean-Paul found the windows were boarded up.

"This would make a wonderful bedroom. You would have the view of the city and catch the morning sun. Remove the boards. Partition off the other end of the room for your friend and make the entire third floor living quarters and the first and second floors devoted to the salon."

"Aaaah!"

"You're not sleeping well. Is it because of the break-in?"

"No. It started before that happened. For a while I thought I was being watched, anxious all the time, nervous, hearing things."

"Well, maybe you were being watched. A robbery took place as soon as you were out of town."

"That's true."

He brushed his hand softly across her cheek.

"Dinner with me tonight?"

"Bien sûr."

"At my place. I have something to show you."

"What is it?"

"I'll show you when you come."

A PARTNER FOR PELTIER

L ouis had become too sure of himself. His cockiness, his arrogance led to a series of ill-planned and bumbled heists. On a job a week ago, did he not drop the loot trying to escape out of the house? And last night, did not the owners, in residence and not out of town, get a glimpse of him? He bungled it. And was convinced he would be identified. But thieving was his only source of income. In his aggravated mental state, his increasing distress, he continued to believe absolutely that if he had received the bonus and the reference he was due from the Hallisburgs, he would not have sunk so low. The thought of the slave still burned him, like cancer dormant one day and spreading wild the next. They would meet again, he swore.

For a weekend, he stayed boarded up in his apartment, anxious to go out for fear of recognition. But the walls soon closed in, and the deafening voice of his father resurfaced.

By midnight, Peltier took to the streets with his burlap sack in search of a target. An obscure tobacco shop stood nudged near an isolated alleyway. It was dark and vacant. Through the window, he saw goods he could easily dispose of for a quick profit. Entrance into the shop was not complicated; he broke the side window closest to the back door's inside latch and unlocked it. He seized smoking pipes, cigarettes, candles, snuffboxes, enough smoking accessories to fill his sack. It was good plunder.

One evening, dining in a seedy café, he met up with Pierre, an old acquaintance who also knew better days. They shared a bottle and reminisced about their past.

"Where are you staying, my friend?" Louis asked Pierre.

"I'm living near the *bois* in an old flatbed cart . . . just me and my mule; that's all that's left."

"Well, you are welcome to stay the night at my place. I have an apartment."

JEAN-PAUL'S APARTMENT

Muse had not expected Jean-Paul to occupy such handsome living quarters. The entire top floor was at his disposal. The commodious rooms possessed lofty ceilings, two enormous fireplaces, and long, narrow windows where sunlight poured in; the French doors leading to an outside balcony offered a scene of a small public garden.

"You seem surprised," he said.

"I am," Muse responded. "It's so . . . so well designed, true, but I didn't expect finery."

"As an architect, I can barter and trade every now and again. Many times, I get something for almost nothing, for example . . ."

He walked into an adjacent room and pointed to the carpet.

"This is an authentic Persian rug—a gift. I noticed a construction flaw in an architectural design that would have been detrimental to the balance of the building in question. A former university mate, also an architect, made the error. We sorted it out together; he was grateful, as it was his first professional project. The situation could have derailed his budding career.

As a result, in appreciation, he gave me the carpet, a family heirloom."

He paused.

"Sorry, am I rambling?"

"No, not at all."

She brushed her fingers across the drapes hanging over the windows, stroked the texture of the upholstery, and touched the smooth grain of the wood-paneled walls and the finely carved marble framing the main fireplace.

"Your home is lovely."

"How does it compare with Dimitris's?"

"Oh, Dimitris. He showed a distinctive style altogether. Only the best for him, the most modern . . . and hang the cost. It was like visiting a museum or a fine furniture salon. It held little warmth, little of his true personality, and absolutely none of his spirit. On the other hand, I feel your presence here; it is a residence lived in and not for display."

Muse shared with Jean-Paul the anecdote of the dinner and the estate of the Erasmoses where she met Dimitris.

"It was the most depressing home imaginable. A shame because of its brilliant space and location, so marvelously near the *bois*."

"Do you ever hear from him?"

"Who? Oh, Dimitris. No."

Jean-Paul opened a bottle of champagne and brought a glass to Muse, who was sitting on a cushioned settee.

"I thought this was to be a casual evening."

"It is."

"Why the champagne?"

"You like champagne, *n'est-ce pas?*"

"I do."

They toasted.

"Come, I want to show you something," he said.

"What is it?"

Jean-Paul pulled her up from the settee.

"Come, I want to show you my library."

"Oh yes, please."

He took her by hand and led her to the next room. Shelves filled with books lined three of the four walls. Lured in by the volumes, she cocked her head to one side, examining the many titles. A long table, a master writing desk, covered with various books, papers, and sketches, governed the room.

"What do you think of the fireplace?"

She turned and was about to praise the hearth when her eyes floated up to a framed portrait. It centered the mantel. She looked at the work, speechless.

"Where did you get it?"

"I bought it."

"When?"

"In the spring."

Muse stared at the portrait; her own image by Antoine stared back: *Study of an American Slave.*

She sat down at his desk, her eyes transfixed on the painting.

"I remember her so well . . . yet, in a fog, as if she was someone else, someone I was watching through a small window and could only see a mist of her."

Jean-Paul motioned toward her. He slipped his hand beneath her tapering braids and stroked the back of her neck.

"May I ask you something?"

"Anything," he replied.

"That night . . . that night during Christmas when we met outside of the restaurant . . . you said you would come visit me, but you never did. Why?"

Jean-Paul explained about his obligation to return home for the holidays and his father's illness that kept him there for months.

"And when I returned to Paris, I simply could not remember where you said you lived. But I swear to you, I looked, I waited . . . in that restaurant, hoping you would walk by."

Muse looked up at him. He kissed her lips; their bodies quivered.

"Will you stay with me tonight?"

She smiled.

━┼┼━

Making love to Jean-Paul was as different from her experience with Dimitris as red wine is from white. Jean-Paul's embraces seemed to quench the sears of her thirst; a wild, fragrant, bold taste. Less sweet and less delicate than Dimitris's. The sheer natural smell of him, hypnotic; the musky, aromatic scent void of contrived exotic odors or the perfume of the day; his scent melted her. A true red vintage. A spiritual encounter that rose beyond the simple pleasures of the body; an emotional affection that caught her off guard. Jean-Paul's touch, so gentle, yet his caresses firm, as if she had been rescued. He was neither hesitant nor awkward with his moves. She seemed to sink right into him, opened every portion of her body like a blossoming flower and accepted him. He kissed her in such an overpowering way, as though she thought to escape, but he knew his kisses would bind her. Two humid bodies, black and white, twisted and turned beneath cool, pale sheets. Fast and furiously they intertwined, trading places, positions, he on top, then she, then he; they rolled about, excitedly laughing and loving, wholeheartedly. No regrets, no fears . . . unadulterated submission the entire night long. Only the first rays of sunlight broke the spell that overtook them. Exhausted, they collapsed into a mound of tired, shimmering flesh. It was he who drifted off first. Then Muse fell asleep, but not before she smiled with pleasure that he was not her first. She found comfort in her ability to meet him on equal terms, able to answer with her body the questions he asked with his.

ODD BEHAVIOR

Claire's behavior changed, as if out of sync with everything around her. She seemed restless and confused. It was the last week of her internment. Muse brought over the usual provisions, including the two dresses she made.

They sat across from each other in the visiting room.

"Aggrey, will you leave both dresses? I'm not sure which one I'll want to wear."

"Yes, of course. What time shall I pick you up?"

Claire hesitated.

"Is something wrong?" Muse asked.

"No. I'm to be released Monday at about eight o'clock in the morning."

"Good. I'll leave the dresses and the spare keys to the shop with Sœur Claudette, just in case."

"Don't worry," Claire said.

"I'm not worried. But you seem tense."

"Do I?"

"I promise all will be well. Everything is arranged for you. You will love the shop. And we will have so much fun building it up."

"Yes, we will. I love you, Aggrey. You are a loyal friend . . . no matter what happens."

"You're sure you are all right?"

"Stop asking me that! I'm fine," Claire snapped.

"OK!"

Claire leaned forward and took Muse's hands firmly.

"For heaven's sake, Claire . . . it's only a few days."

"It's just that I will be so glad to get out of this place, Muse. I need a fresh start with someone who cares about me."

"Of course. And I care about you. Tell you what . . . I will reserve a table for Monday evening. At what restaurant shall we dine?" Muse asked.

"I'd love to go to the brasserie where you and Jean-Paul met. I like the sound of it and of him . . . can't wait to meet him."

"And he you."

"Oh! Are you going to see him this weekend?" Claire asked.

"Yes, I will be with Jean-Paul the entire weekend. But I promise to be prompt when you are set free."

CLAIRE'S RELEASE

Claire moved through mist-infested boulevards. Paris veiled in fog—she hardly recognized it. She wore one of the dresses Muse made and a bonnet that covered her hair, not yet at full length. Under her arms, she carried a small bundle of belongings. Gerard's landlord sold off their things to pay the back rent. She owned nothing. Uncertain and hesitant, she marched through the streets, a stranger in her hometown. A few blocks more, she contemplated, just past the cathedral; finally, Les Halles came into view. She took refuge in the café she used to frequent.

"Mademoiselle Claire, we've missed you. Where have you been?" the proprietor said.

"I was in America visiting relatives," she lied.

"Well, we are glad to see you back. Your usual?"

"*Oui, merci.*"

She sat peering out the window, thinking about what had transpired in the past two years. A sneer crossed her face as she remembered the man in the yellow trousers and the theft she committed. The deed was the start of her downfall. How ironic of fate to punish her for an act she did not commit to pay for the one she did. *We're even; the slate is clean.* From her bag, she pulled out a bunch of letters postmarked Italy, all from Gerard. She read and reread them many times. One letter begged for her to come to him. But how could she? She had no money, and neither did he; his parents kept him on a strict allowance. But his last letter reminded her of her investment.

Rome, she thought. She knew nothing about it. It was ancient, historic, infamous like Paris, but not Paris. Paris was her city . . . the city she loved. A forgiving town, it would let her start anew. The stage was set; Muse made sure of it. All she had to do was to show up. The lifelong dream of becoming an independent woman was unfolding before her eyes . . . what she always wanted, but the dream had the undercurrent of loneliness. But no, with her newfound energy and focus she would thrive and in time find love again—of course she would. If she went to him, if she met his eyes, if he touched her, she knew, another stage lay on the horizon. A different play, a life of passion, love, and companionship but also instability, intrigue, poverty, even crime. Gerard would never change.

The bells of Saint Eustache rang: 10:00 a.m. Flocks of parishioners, veiled by the fog, made their pilgrimage to the cathedral for mass. Claire drank her coffee slowly as if to fortify her for what she must do. She sat for a while longer and then paid the tab with the little money she earned from baking.

The avenues filled up as the fog dissipated. From the café to the boulevards, she retraced the steps she made more than a year ago. She stalled twice, trying to remember which way to go, then regrouped and persevered as she recalled the street signage—a certain kiosk, a boulangerie on a corner—until she stood before the cul-de-sac. Now she remembered the shop. She let herself in through the back way with the spare key Muse left with Sœur Claudette.

"Muse? Muse, are you here?" There was no reply.

She closed the door behind her. When she last saw the shop, it was an empty space of dusty shelves. Muse had done wonders. While still modest, it possessed charm. The shop exuded feminine mystique. Claire sighed.

From the ground floor, she climbed the stairs to Muse's room but thought to first check the third floor, where she would live. Only a bed and wardrobe, yet cozy. Her eyes welled. She returned to Muse's room. It was quaint and bohemian, not unlike her friend. She glanced at her image in the mirror on the armoire. The dress Muse made complemented her; the colors brought out the greenness in her eyes and reddish hues of her too-short hair. But Claire was thin, wastrel, and she looked years older. Her youthful beauty had not survived the time in jail. No one would buy dresses and accouterments from such a hard-looking woman.

She turned away, and her attention gravitated to the floor. She pulled back the carpet and pressed each floor panel with her foot until she detected a loose board. Using the tip of the door key to penetrate the seam of the floorboard, she popped the panel out. Below, wrapped in cloth, were the strongbox and Muse's savings. Their savings. She stooped down to open it and counted the francs; she calculated correctly. Gerard advised her to take it all and not to worry about Muse.

"She has the store; she'll manage."

They needed every *centime* to start life anew. She folded the bills and stuffed them in her pocket. What was she doing? She stalled and then recounted the money and only took her initial investment of six months' rent and put the rest back into the strongbox. It was enough for Muse to meet the rent obligations for the next few months. The box she replaced, then restored the wood floor and then the carpet. After securing and relocking the back door, she retreated. With quick steps, she moved toward the exit of the cul-de-sac but stopped short when she saw the proprietor of the furniture shop across the courtyard. He was watering his plants. Claire approached him.

"*Bonjour,* monsieur. Do you know mademoiselle?" She pointed to the shop.

"*Oui.*"

"Would you see she gets these keys? *Merci.*"

WAITING FOR CLAIRE

It was nine o'clock Monday morning. Only a few people occupied the waiting room. Muse paced the holding area with a bouquet in her hands. Within the last half hour, three inmates were released. What was keeping Claire? By ten o'clock, Muse asked to speak with Sœur Claudette.

"Thank you, Sœur Claudette, for seeing me."

"How can I help?"

"I'm concerned. Claire is to be released this morning, and . . ."

"Oh, my dear! Claire received her release papers yesterday, Sunday. Didn't she tell you?"

"She told me Monday. My goodness!"

Muse hesitated.

"Then, where is she?"

"I don't know. I thought she would be with you, as you were her only visitor."

"That's odd."

"Oh, wait!" Sœur Claudette said.

She called for her assistant.

"Sœur Jeanine, wasn't there a letter for Mademoiselle Aggrey?"

"*Oui.* I'll get it."

Sœur Jeanine returned with a sealed envelope.

"*Pour vous,* mademoiselle. It's from Claire."

Muse looked at the envelope.

"*Merci, ma Sœur Claudette, ma Sœur Jeanine.*"

SCRAMBLED

The letter from Claire, two pages, lay crumpled on the bed. Muse sat on the floor, holding the strongbox. She fingered through the remaining francs.

I'm not stealing, the letter said. *You'll manage. Forgive me!*

She was not stealing? In principle, perhaps not, but it seemed so much worse. Muse could not breathe.

The back door of the shop rattled, then opened.

"*Bonjour*, mademoiselle," Maria said.

Muse got up and went to the banister, wiping tears from her eyes.

"*Bonjour*, Maria. I won't be down today. Please reschedule any appointments set for this afternoon. Tell Monsieur Chevreau I must cancel tonight. And close the shop at noon; take the rest of the day off."

"*Oui*, mademoiselle. Is there something wrong?"

"*Non.*"

Muse returned to her room, her thoughts swarming. "Now what?" She paced, fuming. She glared at the strongbox. What a fool! And what of the new space she just leased—what would she do with it all?

Again, Muse sank to the floor, crossed her legs, and tried to slow her breathing to rhythmic inhalations to calm down, but she could not.

"It is good, mademoiselle, you've come," Wan Fu said. "I have not seen you for a while. Your anxiety is great. I can feel it from here. It must be released. How will you execute movements if your mind is riddled with tension? Let's begin."

She missed several classes with Wan Fu. It was not just for lack of time but also the frustration she endured learning to master defense techniques. The rigorous exercises to increase strength, endurance, and flexibility were exhausting in and of themselves. The repetitive movements and the intense elongation of body limbs required such concentration and focus that by the end of the session, she could barely walk home. If she found the strength to conquer one technique of the disciplines, she performed poorly in the other two. In vain, Muse tried to assert balance, structure, and stance cohesively. But too often, she tensed up, reducing punching speed and power.

"Relax. Use your whole body when you punch."

She tried again. He stopped her.

"Today is no good. Your energy is scrambled. You've missed every mark and made many errors; it won't do."

She limped home, plodding through the wet streets of Paris. With every step, she pondered whether ever to return. By the time she reached the shop, she found Jean-Paul pacing in front of the boutique as if *en garde*.

"What are you doing here?"

"Waiting for you."

"Didn't you get my message?"

"I did."

She smiled.

"You're impossible."

"Yes, well . . . what happened with Claire?"

"Come in, and I'll tell you about it." Muse unlocked the door. "Are you hungry?"

"*Oui.*"

"I've got wine and a leftover cassoulet."

"*Parfait.*"

CLAIRE'S APOLOGY

A blue cotton cloth blanketed the worktable in the rear of the salon. Muse placed a candelabrum with burning tapers in the center. Various plates of bread and pâté, a large tureen of warmed-over cassoulet, bowls, and wine glasses crowded a portion of the table where the two dined. She poured wine. He fed her fragments of bread; she offered him a spoonful of the stew. He sipped from her glass and she from his. Wrapped in each other's arms, they nibbled between gales of mirth and passion.

Then he whispered, "Let's have coffee on the third floor—the view."

"*Oui*, you go up. I'll make coffee."

The boards no longer covered the windows on the third floor. The panoramic rooftop view of the city was mystical. One window did not close all the way, causing a chill to pierce the room.

When Muse entered with a tray of coffee and an assortment of biscuits, Jean-Paul was standing on a box, trying to adjust the clasp on its casement. "What are you doing?" Muse asked.

"This window won't close. Make sure you get it fixed."

"Forget about the window. Come drink your coffee while it's hot."

She placed the tray on the small table next to Claire's bed.

As soon as she put the tray down, Jean-Paul entangled her and wrestled her to the bed. Again, they laughed.

She offered him his coffee. He sipped.

"So," he said. "I don't understand the dilemma."

"What do you mean, you don't understand? I can't run this shop on my own."

"Of course you can. You've been doing it for more than a year."

"It's hard!"

"Then hire help."

She offered him biscuits.

"*Merci*. What did the letter say?"

"The letter apologizes, but at the same time, she tries to justify what she's doing. It said she had no intentions of deceiving me the last few weeks. But she did not know what would happen. She wasn't sure if she was making a fool of herself again, or what. If so, she didn't want me to know."

"What is she talking about?"

"She's talking about Gerard."

"The runaway boyfriend?"

"*Exactement.*"

"So, he must be serious about her."

"How can he be? She spent a year in prison because of him. He never came forth, left the country like a coward, didn't even hire a lawyer for her. His behavior was outrageous!"

"What else did the letter say?"

"For me not to worry. That she loved him more than life and had to be with him . . . that I didn't need her at the shop; it would probably run smoother without her."

"It's true."

"The shop only exists because of her. I could never have done it on my own. But more than that, she's my friend."

"After this?"

Muse nodded.

"How much money did she take?"

"I think she changed her mind. In the letter, she said she was taking it all. But she only took what she put in."

"You should map out a plan," Jean-Paul said. "More space to expand? It's a good idea."

AN ARMS DEALER

Muse made a decision. One she did not share with Jean-Paul or Cheng. Of course she would keep the shop—what else would she do for a living? But if so, it would not be without personal protection. She ceased going to Wan Fu's defense training. A dozen reasons not to continue his studies conjured up in her mind. But what was the underlying reason? Was it the aggressiveness of the sport, the up-close, hands-on combat, or were the brutality and violence too extreme, even if she was in danger? She wanted distance between her and her foe.

Instead, she paid a visit to the district Claire once suggested and spoke to an arms dealer named Desmond.

"You see, mademoiselle, it is small enough to fit in your purse, even your pocket."

"Can you show me how to use it?"

"Mais, oui."

The dealer led Muse down to the basement of his home. He showed her how to load the pistol, to hold it, to aim, and to fire. He lined up a dozen empty beer bottles, picked off the first three, and then handed her the gun, handle first. When she touched it, she trembled; a chilling instrument that could take a life. She held the gun with both hands.

"Don't grip so hard," Desmond said. "Relax. Take a deep breath."

Muse aimed, closed one eye, and shot. Of the nine bottles that remained, she hit none.

"Practice, mademoiselle, practice."

During the next few weeks, Muse spent whatever spare time she could steal practicing in the woods. Until one day, out of six lined up bottles, she struck one.

PUBLICITY

With no resolution as to what to do with Le Petit Cul-de-Sac, Muse left things as they stood. She lost the vision and the will to develop the boutique. Until one afternoon, near closing time, a shiny black carriage pulled by a fine dark horse stopped in front of the boutique. A woman descended. She wore a full-length black cape with a hood concealing most of her face. Her footman opened the door of the shop, and she entered.

Maria was stooped behind the counter, but Muse, from the back room, saw the woman enter the shop. When Maria realized a customer was before her, she quickly stood up and greeted the hooded woman. They politely conversed for a moment when Maria's face lit up. For the first time, Muse heard her employee speak her native tongue, Spanish. Moments later, Maria fetched Muse, saying the customer wanted to speak with her. Muse took off her apron, checked herself in the mirror, and welcomed the madame.

"*Bonjour*, madame," Muse greeted.

"*Bonjour*, mademoiselle," the woman responded.

"This is an amusing shop. You have interesting things."

"*Merci.*"

Muse sought to identify the patron, but she was well hidden beneath the hood, and it seemed intentionally done. She noted the fabric of the cape: exceptional, thick raw silk, expensive and crafted by a master tailor. Her skin tone was olive in hue; this she observed by the pallor of her gloveless hands, a complexion shade like Maria's—hence, perhaps, the language compatibility. She wore no jewelry or frills of any kind but sported a well-finished manicure.

"A friend of mine," the woman said, "spoke of a woman fitting your description who dined at a restaurant months ago, wearing a white ensemble needled with black embroidery work on the bodice. Was that you?"

"Why, yes, it was."

"May I see the dress . . . do you mind?"

"Of course not," replied Muse. "If you will excuse me, I'll fetch it."

Muse ran up to her bedroom and retrieved the dress.

"*Voila*, madame."

She held the dress up for the woman to inspect.

"*Oui, c'est merveilleuse!* I love the embroidery. Thank you for showing it to me."

The woman browsed among other items on display. Muse and Maria watched her as she shifted through the shop.

"What fabric is this?" asked the woman, holding up a small evening bag.

Muse approached her.

"It's a tapestry."

"Really?"

"I cut pattern forms from a tapestry to make the purses."

"How clever!"

She held one depicting the image of a unicorn.

"Are they all unicorns?"

"No, some are centaurs, monkeys, and birds," Muse answered.

"How many do you have on hand now?"

"Four, I believe."

Maria hurried to retrieve the items.

"Yes, I will take them," she said in Spanish to Maria. In French, she said to Muse: "I would like to order three more, for my ladies."

"Your ladies?"

The woman corrected herself.

"*Excusez-moi*, my French is not perfect; I meant my nieces."

"*Oui, bien sûr.*"

"I will send a servant around to pick them up . . . next week?"

"They will be ready by Wednesday."

"*Merci.* I have a dress—it's already made, but it needs something extra. May I send it around for you to examine? Perhaps you could create a design in black embroidery to enhance it."

"I would love to see it," Muse replied.

The woman paid for all seven of the bags, a few knickknacks, mirrors, scarves, handheld fans and so on. The footman collected all the parcels, and they departed.

Some weeks later, Muse and Maria detected an increase in clientele, not only for the front of the shop but an increase in appointments for fittings and tailoring. But it was Cheng who spotted the small article in the fashion section of the paper.

The ladies-in-waiting to L'Empresse Eugénie were gifted lovely little tapestry handbags featuring figures of centaurs and unicorns. The bags, purchased from Le Petit-Cul-de-Sac, are the perfect accessory to liven up an evening dress.

Just like that, Muse's interest in the shop sprang back to life. The article, the influx of new clientele, the endorsement by such a prominent member of society, all of it prompted Muse to rethink her options for expansion and research ways to develop the shop. In a city such as Paris, anything was possible.

A LIKELY PARTNER

A month passed. For a while, Muse basked in a glorious peace of mind. She embraced the precious sensations and rhythms of life, as one does when watching the beauty of a butterfly flutter around, all the while knowing it will soar away. The relationship between her and Jean-Paul flourished. She spent many evenings at his apartments and he at hers. They never spoke of the future or the past. The present was their world. The pulse of life they created vibrated like music personified, poetry expressed, a story well told. She trusted him on so many levels. What endeared him to her, even more, was the freedom he allowed her to continue to discover who she was. Also, a surprising opportunity presented itself, one that promised to take her career to the next level. It came from a surprising, albeit not unlikely, source.

Cheng was so excited by the write-up of Le Petit-Cul-de-Sac, he could scarcely contain himself. So ecstatic about it, he proposed to Muse a business proposition. He had suffered under the tutelage of a master tailor for almost two years. He was bored stiff from making the same style of suit again and again. His superiors accepted none of his designs or suggestions. He wanted to move on but found no other prospects until now.

"Muse, we not only get on well, but we work together well. We have complementary taste and vision on how to dress *le monde*, don't you think?"

"That's true," she agreed.

"I have saved some money. If need be, I can borrow more from my parents. I want to invest in the shop as a partner . . . the two of us in a joint venture."

"You forget, Cheng," she interrupted. "You forget about Claire."

"Claire's gone."

"She'll be back."

"No, she won't."

"If it were not for Claire, I would not be sitting on this piece of property. It was her funds that got the whole thing started."

"But it was you who did all the work."

"Do you think I would have ever been able to lease this place without her? Would you have been able to? I think not. If I can do anything at all, I want her investment to remain intact."

"What investment? She took it back when she left."

Muse flinched. It was a harsh statement, but true.

"Well, let me think about it."

"You need help now, Muse. Why wait?"

"Well, if she does return, it will be the three of us. *D'accord?*"

"*D'accord*," Cheng said.

PARTNERS IN CRIME

Even with a partner, Louis's station in life improved little. Together, he and Pierre pulled off many minor pilferages, but with slim pickings.

"We need one huge plunder," Louis said to Pierre.

"*Oui*, but what?"

"I have an idea," Louis said.

He shuffled through the morning paper.

"Listen to this. Monsieur Erasmos, the renowned steamship magnate, left Paris yesterday to join his family in Greece. The Erasmoses will return to France at the end of the year when their newly built residence, off the Champs-Élysées, is ready for occupancy."

The Erasmoses. He remembered them well: the dinner, the luscious surroundings, and the silver.

"I know them," he said. "I've been in their house. I've seen the wealth."

Then Louis stopped; his eyes glazed, staring straight ahead. The image of the slave, dressed in the yellow gown, resurfaced. He sat as if frozen.

Louis, are you, OK?" Pierre asked.

"*Oui* . . . where was I . . . the silver. They have silver that is worth a fortune."

"Silver," Pierre repeated.

"If we could score a prize as valuable as fine silver, it would be as good as gold!"

"And easy to get rid of," Pierre offered. "But how would we go about it?"

"The estate is surrounded by woods. We'd camouflage well. I recall two long, narrow windows in the dining area. What is in our favor? The house is huge. The servants' quarters are on the third floor at the rear of the structure, whereas the china and silver are kept in an unsecured area near the dining room. I remember the servants going back and forth, fetching silver trays and dishes while we dined."

"We would need the cart for this caprice, *n'est-ce pas?*" Pierre said.

"*Oui*, but not your cart—it rattles . . . would bring attention to us, and the mule is god-awfully slow."

"We should do it on foot," Pierre said.

"No, the silver would be too heavy to carry for a long distance, especially at night."

"Why not bury the loot and pick it up later . . . when everything has calmed down?"

"Good thinking," Peltier said.

They spent the afternoon strategizing. Early the next morning, they drove to the woods bordering the Erasmoses' home. In observing the estate, they noticed little security other than the servants—no dogs, no guards. After a week of surveillance, Louis and Pierre executed the break-in.

Filthy as gravediggers, they wound their way through the dark streets of the city. By the time they got back to the apartment, day had broken. The deed was done. They buried the goods in a shallow grave in the *bois* adjacent the estate. For two weeks, they stayed clear of the bundle and made no reference to the theft or the merchandise. And on the third week, Louis arranged to meet with a man who could take the loot off their hands.

The Erasmoses' burglary received much attention. Every journal exploited the caprice. Louis was overjoyed by the notoriety. And the gendarmes discovered no clues as to who committed the crime.

Finally, Louis and Pierre ventured forth to retrieve their prize. It was early, market day, and they, in their mule cart, blended with the crowd. No one paid them any mind as the streets of Paris choked with carts driving to and from Les Halles. The vehicle crawled down the back roads of the town, turning and twisting through the bushy woods until they reached the chosen spot. They shoveled and dug for hours until they recovered the hidden spoils. It was late afternoon and growing dark.

They tracked through the narrow dirt roads at the edge of the city, ambling past the swamps, down a wide, murky road. It led to a neighborhood of caravans, wood-planked domiciles that looked like huge crates with doors. An armed guard met them at the entrance.

"I'm called Peltier. I have a shipment for Monsieur Elonge."

The guard admitted them.

Monsieur Elonge, a short, stout man with a grisly-looking beard, stood by an open fire, conversing with comrades, when the cart rolled up.

"Ah! Louis Peltier, welcome."

Elonge, a specialist, operated an unlawful business of transporting ill-gotten goods out of the country, items with high profiles like the Erasmoses' silver. Notably, the wealthy engraved or initialed their valued pieces, making it difficult to resell at home. But the foreign market proved lucrative for prominent pilfered items.

The men never met before, yet they embraced like old friends. They sat around the fire. A peasant woman poured wine and then brought out food. After full bellies, the men talked about a job well done, the publicity that circulated, and the quality of the merchandise. The negotiations progressed well. Monsieur Elonge haggled little, hoping to engage in further activity with Louis and Pierre, who looked to know what they were about.

"Who owns the cart?" Monsieur Elonge asked.

"I do," Pierre said.

"I need another vehicle tonight. It's urgent. I'll take it off your hands. How much do you want for it?"

Pierre rambled off a price.

"If one of you is up for it, I have a small job needing attention tonight. It's just a pickup. I'll be willing to pay handsomely."

"I don't mind doing it," Louis said. "But with the mule, it will take forever."

"No problem; hook up one of my horses."

"D'accord."

Louis got his instructions, hitched up the horse, and took to the road. Just as he turned off the side trail onto the main fairway, he heard a sudden, thunderous sound of hooves. He stopped the cart to listen. The next moment, a half a dozen gendarmes astride horses dashed passed him and turned onto the side road leading toward the district below. Panicked, Louis pulled over the cart, jumped from the wagon, and snarled through the bushes, where he watched in shock as the police raided the encampment. He heard gunshots and men shouting and yelling. Terrified, he mounted again, cracked his whip, and took off at full gallop.

Smart enough not to go anywhere near the pickup site for fear gendarmes waited, Louis's first thought was to drive back to the apartment and gather up his things. He figured the goods were lost, meaning no money forthwith, and Pierre, if caught, would certainly give him up.

Forget about the apartment. I must leave Paris, now.

THE NIGHTMARE

Muse sensed the heady scent of the raw earth of Der Brunnen. She lay in bed in the old cotton nightshirt with the ragged hem. With every twist and turn, the familiar squeaking sound of the wrought-iron cot penetrated the shack. Her eyes half opened, half closed; she felt exhausted—was it another laborious day in the big house? Suddenly, she discerned a presence in the bedimmed, isolated room . . . a low, heavy breathing echoed. She opened her eyes fully; a faint glow of candlelight moved about the room.

"Mama!" Muse said.

At the sound of her voice, the movement of the candlelight stopped dead.

"Mama, is that you?"

She sat up. The candlelight once again swayed, and Master Jonathan came into view. He approached the bed.

"You've been drinking," she said.

His hand reached out to stroke her face.

"No!"

But before she could move, he leaped forward and wrestled her to the dirt floor. They fought. To her horror, his face grew dark and deadly. She squirmed free. He grabbed her, tumbled her back to the ground. Muse faced her attacker with courage unfamiliar to her. Head to head, eye to eye, they struggled. But in combat, the face towering over her morphed and changed into another being. No longer was she wrangling with Jonathan; she fought an unknown, a phantom whose features transformed into the face of Louis Peltier. She screamed.

"*Ma chérie*, wake up," Jean-Paul whispered.

"What is it?"

"You're having a bad dream. Wake up."

"What?"

"You were screaming."

Jean-Paul held her tight as she struggled to control her breathing.

"Shh! *Ma petite?*"

"Oh!"

"Come closer."

He fluffed up her pillow and straightened out the coverlet.

"Now, now, go back to sleep. You are safe. I am here."

Jean-Paul was adamant.

"What are you in fear of?" he demanded.

"I don't know."

"Move in with me."

"No. You forget I'm renovating the third floor for living quarters."

"Forget about the third floor."

"No! I can't forget about it. I've paid money up front."

"Then tell me what is upsetting you so. I will not leave off until you do."

She looked at him, lowered her eyes, and then sighed.

"Something happened months ago."

"What?"

"Remember the dinner I told you about . . . that large, sad mansion near the park . . . the Erasmoses?"

"Oui."

"There was a man at the table . . . a terrifying person. I knew instinctively what he was but not who he was."

"What do you mean?"

"It was how he looked at me. Such hatred. I've seen it before, many times, on the plantation. Men who hunt down slaves like animals and return them to their owners for a fee. I didn't know it then, but I learned later he was the bounty hunter the Hallisburgs hired to bring me back. Since the Hallisburgs had returned to America, I thought I was safe. A month after the dinner, I saw him again at the market. He looked dreadful. He tried to speak to me, and that's when he said who he was. I fled. Ever since, I've lived in dread."

"Why didn't you tell me?"

"There's nothing you can do."

"What do you mean? I can protect you."

Muse looked at Jean-Paul, smiled, and nodded as if appeased. But she knew what kind of people bounty hunters were: ruthless and relentless. Jean-Paul, his gentleness, his grace, his integrity; he would be no match for such a degenerate being.

"Have you seen him since?" Jean-Paul asked.

"No. But every now and again, I sense him . . . like a foul creature, yet I've never seen him other than that one time."

Jean-Paul reached for the daily journal.

"There is something in the paper about that Greek family."

"What?"

"Their home, it was burglarized . . . fine silver and china stolen."

"They owned beautiful silver."

"Do you remember the name of the man?"

"Pel . . . Pelter . . . something like that."

Jean-Paul kissed her on the forehead.

"What are we going to do? You can't live like this."

She paused, meeting his eyes.

"You win. I'll move in, at least until the renovation is done."

"*Bon*," replied Jean-Paul.

NOWHERE TO HIDE

In the dead of night, Louis sat huddled under a tree, his head buried between his knees. His mind muddled. What happened? Monsieur Elonge profited as an elusive criminal for years. How is it the law caught up with him just when he was about to score big? *Incroyable!*

He shivered. The rustling trees agitated him even more. A full moon glared down at him. The woods seemed ablaze with light. No place to hide. The horse snorted. A sturdy animal, he thought. The cart was strong but rattled and thumped. How far would it take him? The whispered voice once again ricocheted through his mind—a single phrase.

"Snatch the girl and flee."

PACKING

A lone in the shop for the last time, Muse busied herself with packing. She was still apprehensive about giving up her independence, yet again, but pressed on.

"It's the right thing to do!" she told herself.

The stillness of the cul-de-sac told Muse her neighbors had closed for the evening. Maria left an hour ago. She sat at her desk, making a list of things to do. What to take to Jean-Paul's, what to leave behind. Day and evening dresses would go with her, but uniforms would stay at the shop. She pondered whether to relocate her bedroom to the third floor and turn the second floor into a proper office where she and Cheng could work.

There was a separate list of things to discuss with Cheng. He wanted to travel to Lyon, the center of the weaving industry in France. It attracted master weavers and fabric merchants from all over the world. He explained how important it was to expose themselves to what the future of textiles held as well as negotiation opportunities.

What else . . . ?

The pistol. Did she need a weapon now? What if Jean-Paul found it? She didn't want to explain why she owned one. A small, plain wooden box sat on the desk. In it were keys. One of them unlocked the bottom drawer where the pistol rested. Her hands fumbled through loose papers, thread, and fabric swatches until withdrawing the black gun case. She held the loaded pistol; it handled well. *How light!* She aimed at a dress hanging from the armoire, pretending to shoot. Then she shook her head; what was she thinking, buying this piece of iron? She would leave it.

THE ABDUCTION

The horse cart drove up and down the back alleyway of Le Petit Cul-de-Sac until the dead-end street shut down for the night. Louis parked the vehicle out of sight. On foot, he closed in on the side of the boutique. He checked for the gendarme; he was not in sight. He slipped around to the front of the boutique, across the court, where he could screen the shop, unnoticed. Light beamed from the second floor, third window. The bedroom. Through closed curtains, the silhouette of a female figure strode back and forth. She was alone.

The building was better secured than when he last prowled. At first, he saw no way to gain entrance until noticing the third floor, which had been boarded up. Peltier orbited the structure again, focusing only on that floor. A window, slightly ajar, held together by a strip of wire, caught his eye. The neighboring fence steadied him as he hoisted himself up and climbed to the third-floor ledge. He scaled the side of the building, gripping the fringe of the structure, until he reached the window. With one hand, he clung to the building; the other hand stretched out to the window casement and unraveled the wire securing the window. He pulled at it, and then it opened.

⤚⇤+⇥⤙

Muse stopped. *What was that?* She went to the window and looked out to the courtyard. Nothing. She returned to her desk, took up her pen, and continued to work, then paused again, on alert.

"Did you lock the doors?" she whispered to herself.

Downstairs, she hurried to recheck the back and front doors, even the windows . . . all in order. *Silly woman.* She lifted the folds of her skirt and mounted the stairs. And as soon as she entered the room, the door slammed shut behind her. She spun around and gasped. Louis Peltier stood before her. She tried to scream, but he was upon her, his hand pressing hard over her mouth.

"Not one word if you value your life."

He slowly removed his hand from her mouth.

"Not a word, I say."

"What do you want?"

He held her by the neck and appraised her body. Touching her hair, her skin, her breasts, but the full skirt would not let him go farther. She struggled.

"Be still!"

"What do you want?" she repeated.

"You owe me."

He released her and said: "Take off that petticoat, and put on your boots."

Louis rummaged through the armoire, pulled out the indigo cape, and threw it at her.

"Take off the petticoat," he repeated.

Muse could not move.

"Take it off . . . and hurry," he yelled.

Muse raised her skirt and unlaced the undergarment; it slid to the floor.

"Put on the boots!"

"Please," Muse begged.

"Now!"

With hands shaking, she slipped on the boots and laced them.

"Please don't hurt me. I can give you money."

"Money? Show me."

She went to the desk, opened the top drawer, and pulled out a wade of francs.

"Please take it and go."

Louis grabbed the money and put it in his coat pocket.

"You're coming with me."

"*Non.*"

"I don't want to hurt you, but I will."

"*Non.*" And with lightning speed, she grabbed the small box on the desk, tore it open, and snatched out the keys.

Louis rushed her. She dodged behind the desk, holding the key tight in her fist. The maneuver tripped him up, and he plunged into the curtains, ripping them from their attachments. He wobbled, lost balance, and crashed against the windowpane, breaking it. She labored to open the bottom drawer, but he recovered fast enough to grab hold of her skirt. It ripped, taking her down. They thrashed about. Again, she tried to force her way to the desk, to open the drawer, to get to the gun. But in the battle, a leg of the desk gave way, and it crashed to the floor; papers flew everywhere, but the bottom drawer did not open. He got to his feet first and yanked her up. When she sliced the nape of his neck with the key, he yelled, "Ow!"

Writhing in pain, his left hand felt the blood seep from his neck, while his right hand slapped Muse so violently she collapsed against the wall, hitting the back of her head; the key sailed across the room. Dizzy and petrified, she slid to the floor.

He reached into his waistcoat and pulled out the pearl-handled knife.

"If you don't behave, I will slit your throat. Come!"

"Where are we going?" she mumbled.

He laughed.

"I've finally got you."

She shrank with fear.

"Get up! I said get up—move it!"

He pushed her through the door and half dragged her down the stairs. Once on the ground floor, Louis bound Muse's arms behind her back, gagged her, and covered her head with the hood of the cape. They filed out of the back entrance and walked down the dark, misty alleyway to where the horse cart waited. He forced Muse to lie down in the back of the wagon; he bound her feet and covered her body with a blanket.

"Not one word," he warned.

Bundled up in a fetal position, benumbed, her body contorted as if stuffed into the belly of an abyss. The only perception was in the activity of her mind, bouncing from image to image, pictures of her life fleeting by like rapidly turning pages of a short-story ending. He muttered something about Algeria. She knew what that meant and what was about to happen.

The cart gyrated as if out of alignment. The sound of the horse's hooves clopped along the streets, clattering offbeat. She lay quiet, made no sound, no attempt to move or extricate herself. Her body swayed along with the tempo of the old vehicle. She remained so until her senses weakened and she lost consciousness.

TOO LATE

Jean-Paul asked one of his contractors to help move a few of Muse's things and a large trunk to his apartment. After giving street directions to Maxim, he fell silent. How beautiful Paris looked, showered by the moon's light. The energy of the city, the vivaciousness of its inhabitants, never ceased to amaze him. The dampness of the night unsettled his chronic leg wound, but he didn't mind; he felt rejuvenated. He warmed at the thought of her being with him all the time. So many women, yet she was the one who affected him the most. He wanted only to love her and protect her. If he could do that . . . if he could appease her fears, make her forget her past, he would have done his duty.

They drove into the cul-de-sac and parked in front of the shop. Jean-Paul got out and knocked on the front door. No answer. He stepped back and looked up. Light spilled from her bedroom window, the glass pane shattered.

"Wait here," he said to Maxim.

He hastened around to the rear. The back door flared wide open. He ran in.

"*Cherie!* Where are you?"

He started up the stairs.

"Muse!"

When he reached her room, he stalled in terror.

"*Oh! Mon Dieu!*"

He faced a demolished room: a fragmented desk, shards of glass from the mirror, broken vases. He limped up to the third floor. No disturbance other than the faulty window he had fastened closed with a wire; it was also open. He hobbled back down to her room and yelled out the window, "Maxim! Find a gendarme. Hurry!"

He combed through the chaos, looking for hints of what had happened. The clothes in her armoire were tossed and mangled. She owned a limited wardrobe, and he knew every piece. The indigo cape was gone. He examined the desk and its splintered leg, he tried to set it upright, but it crashed sideways again. This time, the bottom drawer shot open. The gun case dropped to the floor and popped opened.

"A gun! *Merde!*"

Jean-Paul sat staring at the smashed window. There was blood on the sill—was it hers or his? The gendarme swarmed the place, taking notes, writing reports.

"What do you imagine happened?" a gendarme asked.

"I don't know," Jean-Paul snapped.

"Was she involved in any criminal activities?"

"Of course not!"

"She complained of a prowler . . . and there was a break-in about a year ago," Cheng interjected.

So much commotion, such a ruse, thought Jean-Paul. His eyes followed each gendarme. The whole scene was a farce, a pretense. He saw it in their faces, their demeanor, their body language. The gendarme would not spare precious resources to investigate the disappearance of a woman of color, *une vendeuse*, and a foreigner, at that. A search party would form in the morning, they said. But what was the point? They would be long gone, out of the jurisdiction of the Paris gendarmerie. Notifying neighboring territories would take time.

As the gendarme left, Jean-Paul thanked them for their help and insisted on being part of the search party.

"You should go home and get some sleep," Cheng said.

"No, no, I'm staying here . . . she may return."

He walked Cheng to the door.

"What are you going to do?" Cheng asked.

"I don't know."

A feeble effort to put Muse's room back in order was attempted. Jean-Paul wound a rope around the wobbly leg of the desk, and once again it stood upright and somewhat stable. In a frenzy, as if mad, he rummaged through the drawers, pulling out paper, sketches, cloth samples, looking for . . . he knew not what. Then he noticed a small newspaper clipping embedded in the corner of a drawer. It was the article about the Erasmoses' burglary—and written in its margins, in Muse's own handwriting, the name *Peltier* and words *bounty hunter.*

Until that moment, he hadn't put it together. Now it made sense.

"It was Peltier who took her."

He went downstairs, searching for brandy . . . anything to calm his nerves. He settled at the worktable, his thoughts swirling. Would Peltier take her back to America to claim his fees? If so, that means they would travel to Le Havre. He grabbed the daily paper to check out international passenger ships bound for America, but there was nothing scheduled for at least a month. Then he noticed a ship called the *Poseidon* leaving from Marseille to Algeria in a few weeks.

"Algeria," he said. *Algeria and Turkey held the two largest slave-trading markets in Europe.* He knew the *Poseidon*; it was the ship his mother sailed on when she returned to Algeria.

◄─╫─►

A half an hour later, Jean-Paul was banging on the door of a local blacksmith who leased horses.

"It's an emergency! I'll pay well."

By dawn, Jean-Paul was riding out of town on the main road, heading south. The blacksmith gave him specific instructions as to where he could change or refresh the horse en route.

As he rode, he thought he might overtake them, as he imagined them traveling at a slower pace. But it was all speculation, a wild guess; he knew nothing for certain . . . where she was going, if she was hurt, or even alive. Yet, he must try . . . make the effort . . . he loved her! He didn't realize it until now. And the thought of never seeing her again was unendurable. His leg throbbed more; the knife strapped to his waist added to his discomfort, but he galloped on.

A JOURNEY BACK TO THE PAST

How many hours had they traveled? Muse did not know. She remained still under the thick blanket, listening for the usual street noises, but heard little, just an occasional passing of a carriage. After a while, the horse's hooves changed to thudding sounds instead of the normal high-pitched clip-clop. No longer within the city limits, she surmised, but probably trotting down a country road. If he planned to journey to Algeria, they were going south to Marseille or west to Le Havre. She guessed south. That meant days of traveling.

Soon the horse and four-wheeler slowed to a heavy walk; it turned onto a gravelly path and pulled to a halt. She listened as Louis jumped out of the wagon, unhitched the horse, and tied it to a nearby shrub. The blanket was yanked away. He stripped the hood from her head, unbound her feet, and removed the rag covering her mouth. He pulled her out of the wagon.

"You've been good," Louis said. "If you remain so, our journey will go without difficulty. Do you understand?"

Muse nodded.

The brightness of daylight blurred her vision, but once it adjusted, she deciphered that it was near sundown.

"I'll make a fire, and we'll eat."

He tethered her to a nearby tree.

"I will free you when it is time."

Louis threw an assortment of vegetables and beans into a pot and produced a greasy, poor man's version of a cassoulet.

"Ah!" he said. "This will get us through the night.

He untied her hands and put a bowl and a utensil in front of her.

"Eat!" he said. "Or I will feed you by force. I will not have you malnourished; it will devalue your price."

She picked up the spoon, gleaming of quality silver . . . an engraved design she recognized. The Erasmoses. She shoved a spoonful of the stew into her mouth and grimaced as she swallowed. But he was right, she thought; she must keep up her strength.

Just before she had passed out, she prayed to God to show her the way out, to help her find the fortitude. But when she came to, her heart sank. It was not one of her nightmares; it was real. A daunting question mulled over in her mind: Did she have the wherewithal to will death like Perche? Poor Perche! His memory flashed like a flicker of light. Had he felt like this the night he slept, never to wake up? Did he know such despair, such wretchedness, hopelessness that drenched the soul? She understood him now and how he could not go on living. To follow in his footsteps, to close her eyes and sink away, was what she wanted—or did she?

After a while, an awareness of her plight grew clearer. She slipped into a meditative state as she ate the cassoulet, conscious of the flame burning within, the glow of life she wished to extinguish. It seemed to have a will of its own and was not yet ready to let go of its existence, not without a fight. She thought of her mother, of Cheng, even of the Hallisburgs . . . people she might never see again. But most of all, Jean-Paul . . . he would be missing her by now, knowing something terrible had happened. Surely, he would find her, rescue her . . . but no. By the time he figured it out, she would be on a ship to Algeria or some such place. She was on her own.

PELTIER WATCHES HER SLEEP

He never touched her sexually. Spoiled by the rich Greek was enough damage. Further activities along those lines would limit negotiation. That's what he told himself. But at night when she slept, he watched her and listened to her slow, rhythmic breathing. She was pretty for a dark-skinned woman, well in form and shape; he *would* like a taste. He never touched a woman of color before, not in that way. To force her could go unnoticed by potential buyers if he took her from other angles. He fantasized about the diverse ways to violate her. But he controlled his urges for fear of making a fool of himself again. The embarrassing memory of his last encounter remained fresh. The previous woman he had hired to keep his bed had lain in wait, ready, impatient for him to come; but he faltered so many times. The lingering smirk on her face, her sideways glance of pity, left its imprint. He threw her out and no longer took a woman to his bed. Would he chance another humiliation, another possible limp performance? No . . . not in front of an inferior. Suppose she laughed as well.

Something else annoyed him. She refused to speak, save for *oui* or *non*. He remembered her at the Erasmoses. How inviting she looked in the yellow dress, how well she spoke, her gay smile, yet she showed him none of that sparkle. The silence and her sense of indignation wore on him, like the dawdling squeak of a lopsided wheel.

"Why won't you speak?" he complained. "This is business, nothing personal."

The second the words spilled from his mouth, he wished to take them back. Cold, irate eyes stared at him as if to say, "*Imbécile!*"

Still, hovering by the fire, he prattled. Never mind her lack of response. For him, his loquacious behavior broke the silence of the night and blocked out the dogged paternal voice. And after a few drinks, Louis became even more gregarious. He ranted about his life in Africa, his father, the crime sprees, the Erasmos escapade. He told of the *Poseidon*, the ship bound for Algeria in a short time.

"Because of your good looks, style, mastery of French, you will fetch a considerable sum. Your servitude would be a commodity for pleasure, not labor. And a beginning career for me!"

Muse listened but never said a word. Oddly, the revelation abated much of her fear. A lucid but shrewd feeling took over; now she understood the challenge she faced. She deciphered it was not yet the moment to make a move. Wait until closer to Marseille.

THE CHASE

Muse awoke to an indescribable morning. No words in English or in French could illustrate the strange mind-set engulfing her. Still fettered to a tree, her consciousness soared. An almost pristine sky medicated her sense of despair as she focused on a single cloud floating across the heavens like a soothing aria. She smiled because it was a phrase Jean-Paul once used after they attended an opera. The autumn landscape resonated with color and images, none of which looked real, more dream-like in vision, something similar to Antonio's paintings. Energy churned within her. Her perceptions acute. Rabbits ran wild, yet moved as if in slow motion. Birds flew overhead, soaring lazily, not unlike butterflies. A strong breeze brought forth the perfume of the sea. Marseille!

The effect of a meditative awareness raised her sensitivity to a level she did not know existed. A feeling of self-control emerged where mind, body, and spirit seemed to align. Where trust in her untapped ability took a huge leap forward. At last, she understood what Wan Fu tried to instill in her. His wise, soft-spoken voice lecturing and instructing, so many times, yet she could not see or feel it then. Movement relates to thought; they were inseparable. She lay on the moist, soft ground, bent on one very precise truth: Louis would never get her on that ship alive!

Her eyes turned in his direction. Wrapped in a blanket, cuddled near the smoldering fire, he snored, loud and coarse, reminding her of Matilda, the old black-and-white sow at Der Brunnen. She waited for him to stir. He moved. Eyes opened. He looked around and yawned. As soon as he stood up, she said: "You are binding me too tight. My wrists are scarring."

He jumped back. The sound of her voice startled him.

"What?"

She repeated herself. He looked at her wrists. The flesh was chafing. He leered but untied her.

⚔

That morning, they stayed put.

"Are we near Marseille?" she asked.

He glanced at her.

"Never you mind."

"Why are we not traveling?" she asked. "Are we waiting for someone?"

"My, aren't we chatty this morning? You've said only two words during the whole trip, and now you're just full of questions. Shut up!"

Muse fell silent.

He got up, rummaged around the site for a few minutes, and then hitched up the horse.

"I've got to go into the village for provisions. Give me your hands."

She submitted. He tied her hands behind her back and then hogtied her again to the tree, but this time with less intensity.

He was so close to her. She could hardly breathe from his malodorous smell. But when she noticed the back of his neck and the wound she inflicted crusted over with blood, she smiled. And she felt adrenaline percolating.

"Stay quiet," he said. "I'll be back shortly."

He mounted the cart and left. When he was out of sight, she searched the surrounding ground, looking for something—anything—to help her get loose. She had little wiggle room, but more than before. With exploring fingers, she found a jagged surface on the tree trunk. She fingered an indent in the tree and the sharp, firm edge of an embedded fibrous bark. With her body twisted at an angle, she grated the rope against the bark. A laborious process, yet she worked it, cautious not to cut herself. The sun allowed her to keep track of time. She hurried, slicing at the threads of the rope until they unraveled.

But no sooner were her hands free than she heard the dawdling rattle of cartwheels. She rushed to untie her ankles and disengaged from the web of rope. She jetted up and darted across the heart of the landscape. But Louis saw her. He whipped the horse, and the cart lurched forward in a chase. Muse took flight toward the thick of the woods, too dense for the horse cart. Louis dismounted the vehicle and pursued her on foot.

The hunter and the hunted dashed through the woods. Muse sprinted like a gazelle, weaving through narrow, intricate trails in the disheveled forest, but the hunter kept pace. At one point, she climbed a branchy tree as she had done many times on the plantation. She pinpointed his whereabouts. High in the tree, holding her breath, she witnessed him beneath her, tipping around, trying to engage her scent. Again, she thought, *Imbécile!* While hidden in the close-knit branches of the tree, Muse distinguished the outline of a road, noting she must backtrack through the forest to gain access to it.

She waited until Louis ventured deeper into the bush and then climbed down. With her cape wrapped securely, she loped through the thicket toward what she hoped was the main road. But minutes later, she again lost her bearings.

Panting, she sank to her knees. She recessed, then heard the faint sound of crushing twigs and dead leaves. Alert and still, she listened. Was it animal or human? She rose to her feet; her eyes scanned back and forth across the woodland. Streams of sunlight trickled through dense vegetation. The direction in which the light fell suggested midafternoon. They had been gallivanting since late morning. She took another educated guess as to the way out.

En route, she jogged, focused, determined, when suddenly snatched by the tail of her cape so hard, she flew up in the air and landed flat on the ground. She scurried to her feet, heart pounding, adrenaline running. Face to face with Louis. She had never sized him up. Yet, it was the one thing Wan Fu said often: size up your opponent. When her eyes fastened in on Peltier, the outside world ceased to exist. Everything she needed to know reflected in his eyes. In his licentious glare, she saw not just arrogance but a vacuous spirit, desperate, entrenched with as much fear as she.

Wan Fu was adamant about her hitting her mark, absolutely, but not one moment before she believed she could. Until she embraced her strength, her courage, she would flounder. Something clicked as she stood toe to toe with Louis; everything Wan Fu had taught her now made sense.

Louis was blocking her path, yet she did not attempt to flee. In position, she stared him down as if possessed.

"This is my fault," he said. "I knew you were a clever one. I should never have been so lenient. But the game is over. We have a ship to catch. The *Poseidon* awaits us."

He took a step toward her; she stepped back.

"Enough!" he said. "Come."

He drew nearer. Then he leaped, but she shifted aside. He wavered, faltered forward, but held ground. She was *en garde.* Center stance, her arms and hands bent and extended, one in front of other. She glared at him.

"I have warned you," he said.

He dove forth. She parried out of his line of attack. Louis lost balance and tumbled to the ground, but he hastened up again. She turned to run, managed only a few steps before he grabbed her from the back, his arm around her neck. Her elbow jabbed into his rib, causing him to loosen his grip. She scratched his face, his eyes, and then, in the heat of the brawl, her hand worked its way to the back of his head, where she clutched and pulled. With her body bending forth, in a quick, sharp move, she caused Louis's entire torso to flip across her back, landing him flat on the ground. He lay on spongy soil, disoriented. She stood her ground.

His wits shattered. Fear in his eyes. He rallied up and whipped out the knife. It shimmered. She took off her cape and flung it aside. With swift movements, she raised her skirt to knee level and tied the hem into a knot between her legs for better movement. She returned to her center stance; her gaze absorbed him. She waited.

He advanced, brandishing the weapon. Even with quick, fleeting sidesteps, a sharp pain pierced her upper arm. She shrieked and scuttled back, holding her arm. He swaggered forth, yelling obscenities. Again, she braced resolute, and by means of a swift, thrusting motion, she kicked the knife out of his hand. It flew into the bramble. He stood dazed—mouth open. She held steadfast, watched his mind calculate. He rushed her. As soon as he got within an inch, she kicked him between the legs; he doubled over, and her knee thrust up against his chin. He surged backward and collapsed. She rummaged through shrubbery and thorns.

"There it is," she said. "The knife."

With little thought, she grabbed the knife, the cape, and ran in search of the road. Her only compass was the light. Not much of the daylight seeped through. But parts of the forest radiated more than others. It was toward that glow she sprinted. Within minutes, she was in the daylight of a late afternoon.

Not until she reached the road did she stop running. Bent over, heaving, both hands bracing her knees for support, her mind spinning, what to do next? The pain in her arm throbbed. He stabbed her twice, but there was not much blood. *I'll be all right,* she thought. She turned to look back at the distance of her run. The forest appeared serene, a placid mass of green. Swathed under the cape and hood, she took to the road. Every few feet, she turned to ensure no one followed. In the near distance, she heard the neigh of a horse. Parked on the side of the road was Louis's cart. She delved through its belly, looking for something to wrap up her arm, and found an old rag. The wagon was loaded with provisions, and the canteens were filled with water. She drank.

She knew nothing about horses, having never driven a cart or rode, neither on the plantation nor in the city. Mimicking every driver she had ever seen, she first made eye contact and assured the animal of her friendship. She gave it water and mounted the cart. The reins: What did Perche do with the reins? He gathered them in one hand and, with the crop in the other, gave the animal a firm smack.

"Walk on."

Within minutes, she was on the main road leading to Marseille.

Mile after mile they rode, woman and horse, silent, each in their own world. The sun was setting, but she drove on. And then the animal ceased, in distress, breathing hard and erratic. She pulled off the road into a little field. She did not unhitch the animal for fear of the difficulties of hitching it up again. But it would neither feed nor drink.

"Aren't you well?"

She secured him to a tree and left him to rest. Soon afterward, she climbed in the back of the cart and fell asleep, unshackled and once again free. At dawn, while breaking camp, she noticed the horse lying on the ground, still. She nudged the animal with the tip of her boot, but it did not move.

"*Bonjour,* monsieur horse," she said, prodding the animal with a stick.

The horse was dead. The pitiable creature had walked, trotted, all the way from Paris. Louis had not changed horses once or allowed the animal to rest properly.

"*Pauvre bête.*"

She took what food and water she could carry and ventured on foot. Not too much farther, she determined. The definite scent of brine was evident. By noon, she faced the Mediterranean.

THE FOREST CLOSES IN

Louis regained consciousness but was confused about what happened. Then he realized *la négresse* had thrashed him. It was not possible! Aware she was nearby, searching for the knife she kicked out of his hand, he hurried to his feet and took off. He would leave her to die alone in the cold, godforsaken woods. Deeper into the forest he ran, moving fast but without direction. Forget catching the *Poseidon*, he thought, or the money. She, he swore, would find death right here and now and wind up food for the wild.

He, in his aimless, reckless trot, soon observed that the woods appeared to grow darker and less penetrable. He panicked. Had he been traveling in circles? Within the thick maze of foliage, he no longer discerned the sunlight. Moments turned into minutes, minutes to hours, and still, he roamed, trying to distinguish one tree from another.

The dimness of the forest grew sinister. Now and then, he glimpsed the image of an animal flitting by. His fear grew. He begged for light. Even when morning came, he thought, he would still be deprived of it if he found no exit. The resurgence of his father's voice echoed in his head. And to his astonishment, he heard himself call out for Muse.

"I won't hurt you anymore. I promise."

He tracked the forest, his hands holding his ears, trying to silence his father. Exhausted, he fell to his knees, rocking back and forth. On the ground, he lay curled up in a fetal position, sobbing for *la négresse* to come back.

"Don't leave me, *s'il vous plaît!*"

SEARCHING

Jean-Paul changed horses, breakfasted, and was back on the road. Frustrated and bemused, he thought he was making decent time, yet he found nothing—no trace, no leads of the woman he loved. Was he just spinning his wheels, making no progress? But he had to do something . . . he couldn't stay in Paris, sitting around, waiting for the gendarme to do their work if they did anything at all. *Non*, he would find her himself.

While traveling, he met a local villager who shared information he took to heart.

"The main road leading south may make for an easy journey, but it is not the fastest way to get to Marseille," the villager said. "There are many who know of shortcuts to the south if they want to travel unseen."

The villager sketched a map on the back of a deer hide, giving covert directions that would quicken his journey.

Reluctantly, Jean-Paul trotted along the recommended route, a winding, rough patch of road through thick, overgrown territory. It felt hopeless. But a few hours into the journey, he drew his horse to a full stop. A horrid smell of decay caused him to pause. Then he spotted an abandoned wagon. He dismounted, tied up his horse, and approached it. He inspected the wagon with curiosity but startled at the sight of a dead horse, devoured by vultures. In the back of the vehicle, he found traces of provisions picked over by birds, squirrels, and who knew what else. But there was a small barrel of water. As he replenished his canteens, he noticed a torn piece of fabric caught in the seams of the wagon's wooden bed. He recognized it: a strip of fabric torn from Muse's indigo cape.

He surveyed the ground around the wagon and discovered only one trail of footprints—that of woman's leading to the main road. *She's alive!*

MARSEILLE

The warm waters of the Mediterranean caused Muse to wince. Saltwater on open wounds stung. She tore off pieces of her dress to rebandage her injuries. The village was within sight; she limped toward it. A crowded port: a cauldron of nationalities, mostly poverty-stricken and shabbily dressed. She blended right in.

Once in the center of the town, she asked a local vendor to direct her to the offices of the gendarme. He pointed at a large terracotta building. She followed his aim. Five minutes later, she stood in front of the official office of the police.

An immixture of men and women competing for attention packed the rooms of the reception. When she crossed the lobby, several policemen glanced her way; she read their looks: *What tramp is this?* Although weak, she pushed through the mob to an officer to ask for help. He ignored her. She approached another gendarme, tried to speak, but the room swirled, and she swooned. The officer caught her and carried her to the nearest bench.

"Give her room! Someone bring water."

When she came to, he asked what the problem was.

"I have been abducted. I need to get word to Paris where I live."

The officer eyed her suspiciously.

"What is your name?"

"Muse Aggrey . . . I live in Paris."

She told him her tale. He questioned her; she answered. She recounted the kidnapping, the journey, the passenger ship, the *Poseidon*. She described Louis Peltier and reiterated his part in thefts in Paris, specifically the Erasmos burglary.

"Ah! The Erasmos burglary. It was reported in the local journal. How do you know these things?"

"He told me."

"And where is this Monsieur Peltier?"

"In the forest, I guess."

After taking sufficient notes, the gendarme concluded Muse's ordeal genuine.

"Whom do you need to contact in Paris?"

"Monsieur Jean-Paul Chevreau . . ." And she rambled off his address, but her voice grew faint.

"Chevreau the architect, the son of Monsieur Rafael Chevreau?"

But she did not hear the question. She went limp and passed out.

Only then did the officer notice her bloodstained clothes.

The room was dismal but a goodly size. Worn silk panels, olive green, entrenched the walls. The furniture was dark, rustic, but old—no doubt fashionable in its day. Flanked by sheer, breezy, white curtains, a pair of glass door windows opened out onto a terrace. A marble fireplace, unlit, overlooked the chamber. The sound of waves charged in and out while the shrill of seagulls saturated the air. Daylight poured into the room, making for a mild temperature. She slept until the strong fragrance of freshly brewed coffee seeped into the chamber, followed by a light knock at the door.

She attempted to sit up but flinched—her arm. Gradually, she realized she lay in a large bed under soft coverlets. A white cotton nightgown enveloped her body, and clean cloth bandages were wrapped tightly around her left arm. Little by little, remnants of her ordeal returned.

The knock at the door repeated.

"*Entrée.*"

An elderly woman, in a maid's uniform, entered the room, toting a breakfast tray of porridge and a large cup of coffee.

"*Bonjour,* mademoiselle," she greeted.

"*Bonjour,*" Muse said, looking at the woman with wonderment.

The woman sat the tray down and helped Muse to sit up.

"*Merci.*"

The woman put the four-legged tray of food on the bed over Muse's lap, took a chair, and placed it next to the bed. The woman helped her to drink. As soon as the warm coffee surged through her body, her vitality returned.

"*Merci,* madame. May I ask where I am? Is this a hospital?"

"No. You are in the home of Monsieur and Madame Rafael Chevreau."

"Chevreau . . . Chevreau? Jean-Paul's family?"

"*Exactement,*" the woman replied.

God! thought Muse. Of course, Jean-Paul was born in Marseille. It never occurred to her to contact his family. *Oh! Mon Dieu.*

"How long have I been here?"

"Two days."

"But how, how is it . . . is Jean-Paul here?"

"*Non*, mademoiselle, he is not."

"How am I here?"

"Calm yourself and drink. Monsieur Chevreau senior will come to explain."

Propped up in bed so she might gaze out at the ocean, Muse awaited his presence. Apprehension set in, much like when summoned by Mrs. Hallisburg or by her mother for one misdeed or another. She held the view of the sea, contemplating what to say to the father of her lover.

Monsieur Chevreau arrived in a wheelchair pushed by the maid. Muse was reminded of Monsieur Furet. But Monsieur Chevreau had clear eyes and a healthy pallor. He greeted her with a smile.

"*Bonsoir*, mademoiselle," he said.

"*Bonsoir*, Monsieur Chevreau."

She faltered for words.

"*Merci* for your kindness in allowing me a haven."

He shrugged. After a lengthy appraisal of her, he said, "You're pretty. Even in rags, you have flair. I understand my son's attraction to you."

As he spoke, Muse grew self-conscious about her looks, trying to smooth down her wayward hair, knowing she must look a fright.

"I'm sorry we had to burn your clothes."

"Oh! Not the cape," she said.

"We'll get you another. I know with your arm you won't be able to sew, but we'll have something made up."

Muse held his eyes.

"Also, we found this in the pocket of your dress."

He presented the pearl-handled knife and placed it on a side table.

She smiled.

"You know about me, monsieur?"

"*Mon Dieu, oui.* You have been a subject of heated conversation in this household. Mind you . . . driving my wife to despair."

Muse raised her eyebrows as if to say, "Oh Lord!"

"You see, my wife is not as tolerant of different races as I am. You know, of course, Jean-Paul's mother is Algerian."

She nodded.

"Dark-skinned like you. She was beautiful! I loved her but had not the courage to go against my family's wishes. It was a question of inheritance. Jean-Paul is a different kind of fish . . . making his own way. Doesn't need me to dictate or interfere."

"How is it you've heard of me?"

"My son has always loved the ladies. Even after his injuries in the war, he was still popular. But the family never met any of his conquests. Which is as it should be if he is not serious. Then, without warning, and only within the last few months, every letter I received made mention of a young *femme noire*. A former slave, an ambitious tailor . . . he described you in such detail . . . something about a white dress with black embroidered flowers. Oh! He went on, so much so I could picture you. So when the police came to the door rattling on about *une femme noire* who passed out at the station from wounds and was trying to get a message to my son, I thought it must be you. But it made no sense because as far as I understood, the woman—you, that is—lived in Paris. What drama!" Monsieur Chevreau said. "What theater!"

"Oh!" Muse moaned.

"I've asked dinner be served in your room. May I join you if you are up to it?"

"*Oui, bien sûr.*"

"Now, tell the entire story of your abduction from beginning to end. I won't believe a word of it, of course. I mean, how could such a thing happen?"

Muse smiled.

"But it *did* happen."

She scanned the room.

"Whose room is this?"

"Jean-Paul's."

"Madame Chevreau . . . will she mind I'm here?"

"Probably. But she and my two younger sons are in Nice, visiting relatives. We have the whole house to ourselves."

"I must write to Jean-Paul."

"I've already written to him. No doubt he's at his wit's end looking for you. You can write to him when you are stronger. In the meantime, tell me what happened. Start from the beginning."

She was sitting at Jean-Paul's desk, writing. Her left arm pulsated, but her right hand remained steady enough to pen letters. First, she wrote to Cheng, giving facets of the kidnapping, telling him she was well, and asking him not to worry, for she would be home soon. While she recovered, she suggested he research and plan the trip to Lyon, perhaps during the end of the year, as discussed.

The second letter she scripted to Maria, urging her to keep the shop open and help Monsieur Cheng settle in.

Tell our customers I'm temporarily indisposed but will return to Paris in a month.

The third letter focused on Jean-Paul. Again, she explained her ordeal, assuring him of her full recovery and of his father's diligent care of her.

You are in the middle of two important projects; please don't come down on my account. I'll be back in Paris soon.

She added that she would count the days until they were to-gether again. But then she stopped. There was a commotion in the courtyard. Monsieur Chevreau was shouting. She could not understand what was said. Still weak, she got up and walked out-side to the terrace to view the cause of the uproar. When she peered down, she saw Jean-Paul embracing his father, who ram-bled on, speaking so fast Jean-Paul cautioned him, "Father! Calm down. You'll give yourself another attack. What is wrong? What has happened?"

Monsieur Chevreau pointed up to the terrace where Muse stood smiling.

⚒

Jean-Paul embraced her so passionately, it caused Muse to gasp from the pain.

"Careful, *chérie* . . . you're hurting me," she said, her eyes well-ing with joy.

"I thought I'd lost you," he said. "I tried to find you, my love. I wasn't sure of the path. Then I found the wagon . . . the dead horse. When I got to Marseille, I took to the docks. The *Poseidon* hadn't sailed, and your name wasn't on the passenger list. Then to the police, who told me a woman fitting your description had been wounded and taken to Father's house to recover . . . I didn't know what to think."

"Shh!" Muse said. "Relax, take a deep breath. I'm here. I'm safe."

"Muse, I love you. There, I've said it. The thought of not being with you was too much to bear. I never want to leave your side. I love you, do you hear?"

She looked into his eyes and hesitated. Was she sure of her feelings? She pushed back a lock of hair veiling his eyes; his in-tense, loving eyes. She gazed into them and knew.

"I love you, too, Jean-Paul . . . I do."

⊷⊶

But that night they slept in separate rooms . . . Father's house, Father's rules.

Muse woke at dawn. The sounds and rumblings of the seashore seemed to encourage her. One last letter to write. Of the three, it proved the most difficult to originate. How to start, how to convey her deepest appreciation for sharing his expertise, imparting knowledge that saved her life? She glanced at the pearl-handled knife. What to say to the man who showed her how to access the depths of her being . . . what words?

The rhythmic dance of the sea, hypnotic as it was, helped her to unravel her tangled thoughts. A blackbird rested on the rail of the balustrade, also finding comfort gazing out. Then it extended its small wings and flew. Watching the bird soar, she felt a sensation, a vast expansion taking place within her, a profound knowing; she was free at last.

Muse returned to the blank page. Would the words come to her now, potent and honest enough to reveal her heartfelt appreciation? She dipped the pin into the jar of ink, paused, and wrote:

Cher Monsieur Wan Fu,
Merci . . .

AFTERWORD

One winter's morning, a year later, a young hunter and his hound went in search of the evening's meal. The rabbits in that part of the wood ran rampant, so they expected to make quick work of it. No sooner had the two ventured forth when the hound got scent of prey. He barked and took chase. The hunter, having his own good speed and agility, kept pace with the animal. Soon he grew concerned, as the animal was tracking too deep into the forest. He yelled for the dog to cease.

"*Arête!*" the hunter shouted. "Come, César."

But the hound kept pursuit despite the forest having a renowned reputation for swallowing men up whole. Only the most skilled huntsman dared tackle the bowels of the infamous wood. He was not one of them, especially not for a prize so small as a rabbit. In the distance, he heard his dog howl.

"Ah! He's found something."

The seeker ran toward his hound's cry. When he arrived, the animal held no prey. Instead, he circled a flat area near a tree. The hunter approached and stood back in horror. Lying on the ground in the fetal position were the skeletal remains of a man.

"Poor soul," the hunter said as he grabbed his hound by the collar.

"Come here, César." He petted his dog.

"See how his hands are pressed together . . . as though he was praying. Poor devil! We should bury him."

ACKNOWLEDGEMENTS

Much thanks to the late Ted Poyser who was the President of the Friends of the Library at the John C. Fremont Library in Los Angeles. He was such an inspiration, urging and guiding me to put my first drafts of storytelling on paper. Also, to TV Writers Fund for the Future's Novel Writing Workshop with Lisa Doctor. To all the fellow writers in our group, thoughtful, experience, and constructive. A shout out to Lola Martin for her intuitiveness in finding and creating amazing images. Beate McDermott for her knowledge of 19th century fashion and great springboard for chatting about Paris in the 19th century.

67700495R00261

Made in the USA
Columbia, SC
30 July 2019